MADDY DUNE AND THE BALEFUL LANTERN

MADDY DUNE AND THE BALEFUL LANTERN

FREEMAN UNIVERSE
BOOK 2

PATRICK O'SULLIVAN

dunkerron press

A Dunkerron Press™ Book.

Copyright © 2012, 2023 by Patrick O'Sullivan

PatrickOSullivan.com

Cover design by Deranged Doctor Design

www.derangeddoctordesign.com

ISBN-13: 978-1-62560-037-0

ISBN-10: 1-62560-037-2

This is a work of fiction. Names, characters, dialogue, places and incidents are either the product of the author's imagination or are used fictitiously, and any resemblance to actual persons, living or dead, business establishments, events or locales is entirely coincidental.

Dunkerron Press and the Dunkerron colophon are trademarks of Dunkerron, LLC.

BOOKS IN THIS SERIES

Novels:

Beneath the Hidden Gyre

Maddy Dune and the Baleful Lantern

Maddy Dune and the Martyr's Crown (Early 2023)

Maddy Dune and the Huntress of Souls (Late 2023)

Novellas, Novelettes, and Short Stories:

Maddy Dune's First and Only Spelling Bee

The Fogbound Realm Series Book 2

Maddy Dune
and the
Baleful Lantern

PATRICK O'SULLIVAN

1

——————

Maddy leaned her weight into the massive door of St. Anselm's Orphanage and shoved. It shoved back.

"Isn't anyone going to help me with this?"

Her ridiculous family shuffled their collective feet.

"I don't like the smell of this place," Uncle Leo said. He mounted the stairs with a rolling gait, as if he were still parading the quarterdeck of a ship.

"I don't like the looks of it." Emma mounted the stairs as well, basket in hand. Maddy's sister ran a gloved fingertip across the door latch. "Rather shabby." She pursed her lips and studied the resulting grime.

"Kill them all," her brother Rookhaven croaked. He hopped once on Maddy's shoulder before he hammered his grey-black beak thrice against the door.

"Do you have anything to add, Madame Aubergine?" Maddy said. Her father's familiar sprawled languorously in the basket Emma carried. The blue-black cat knotted a paw. Steel claws gleamed in the dim lamplight. Madame Aubergine began to clean the fur between her toes.

A key scratched in the lock and hinges grated in the damp evening. The gas lamp above the doorway gave body to the shadows as the door moved inward a handsbreadth.

A rusty voice called out. "State your name and purpose."

"Maddy Dune, here for the Spelling Bee."

There was the sound of rustling papers, of labored breathing, of a pen scratching on parchment.

"No Maddy Dune listed."

"Madeleine Dune," Maddy said. "Of Mundane House."

"We have a Madeleine Oortsgarten-Quille."

"That's me," Maddy said. Adopted daughter of Eusebius Quille and Nadine Oortsgarten, both away on business. That Quille was away seemed bearable; when he was home he was never fully there. But Nadine. She had promised to be here for the Spelling Bee. She had given her word.

"Very well." The door crept open with a squeal. "You may enter this way if you wish, but the human entrance is... Oh. How... extraordinary. Of course, you must come this way."

Maddy swallowed the lump in her throat and clutched her purse tight in her fist.

Uncle Leo caught her sleeve. "You don't have to go in there."

Emma brushed a tear from Maddy's cheek. "You're as human as the rest of us."

"I'll look for you in the audience," Maddy said. She squeezed her uncle's hand. She stood on her tiptoes and kissed her sister's cheek. She ran her fingers through Madame Aubergine's luxurious fur.

Rookhaven caught her earlobe and pulled her close. "Kill them all."

"I'll settle for out-spelling them," Maddy said. She didn't have to listen to that little voice inside of her that whispered loud enough for her brother to hear. She didn't have to kill them all.

"Very few half-castes enter the contest," Sister Kale said. She was seated behind a table, processing Maddy's entry form.

"I see." Maddy shifted in her seat. Half-caste. She hadn't heard that one before. "I'm—"

"Don't tell me," Sister Kale said. "Let me guess." She studied Maddy as if she were viewing a beast in a menagerie.

Maddy stared back, examining a point on the wall behind the Sister. From a distance Maddy could be taken for a thirteen-year-old girl. Up close, people could see the truth. That's when they stepped back. All except Nadine. This would be so much easier if her mother was here. But she wasn't. Even though she promised.

"Red eyes... that glow," the Sister said. "They don't belong in such a pretty face. Show us your teeth, girl."

Absolutely not. "My birth-mother was a Spectral Hound," Maddy said. "Captain Leonides Farrago and... My new family... They rescued me from crypto-naturalist pirates off the coast of Ghula."

"I asked you not to tell."

"You'd already guessed." Maddy chewed her lip and tried to imagine being elsewhere. Anywhere else.

"Yes, well. Near enough, I suppose." Sister Kale leaned forward. "Now show us those teeth like a good little beast-girl."

Maddy crossed her arms and glanced at Sister Kale. "I fail to see what this has to do with my entry in the Spelling Bee."

"Your eyes burn with an inner fire. I can see the flames," Sister Kale said. "How extraordinary!" She waved her hand. "Sister Blue, you really must see this. Sister Agnes—"

"Please," Maddy said. "The announcement said the contest is open to any student in Arduvulin City in the seventh through ninth books and—"

"Yes, of course," Sister Kale said. "But we so rarely get to examine such a... It's—"

"Outlandish," Sister Blue said. She examined Maddy's ears. "Though these seem nearly normal, Sister Kale."

"Uncanny," Sister Agnes said. She coiled a lock of Maddy's black hair around her fingers. "It is very fine. Not at all like fur. Get undressed, girl."

Maddy brushed the woman's hands away. "I will not."

"We need to know if you've dugs like a hound, or—"

Maddy growled, and the Sisters jerked back. She could kill them all. Except she had promised her mother. And Maddy kept her promises. Even if no one else did. "I'd like to go now, and take my place," Maddy said. "For the Spelling Bee."

An officious-looking Sister passed in the hallway outside, shouting. "Five minutes, Sisters! We need all the contestants on the stage now!"

The three Sisters kept their distance. That always happened with people. Eventually. Maybe if she won the Spelling Bee people would start treating her like a human. Maybe Nadine would forgive her, whatever it was she had done. She must have done something, otherwise Nadine would be here.

She wasn't going to win anything sitting in this chair. Maddy stood. "Right, which way is the stage?"

MADDY HADN'T EXPECTED THERE to be so many contestants. There were at least three dozen seated on the stage. Maddy took a seat near the back, next to a large cabinet of extravagantly carved mahogany. It was really quite an odd bit of furniture, taller than a tall man, wide as a parlor sofa in all directions, and carved in a lattice so fine it was hard to see what was inside. Maddy was pressing her forehead to the cabinet, trying to see in, when the referee called out,

"All rise for Its Royal Highness, Emperor of the Fogbound Realm, Sovereign of Arduvulin. Long may It reign."

There was a great deal of noise from the audience, some of it clapping. Maddy tried to find her family, but her view was blocked by a carved cabinet very much like the one next to her, but considerably larger, being carried on the bent backs of a dozen liveried men. As the cabinet passed, the noise of the audience grew louder until the cabinet was placed on a dais near the stage.

"My esteemed progenitor," the cabinet next to her said. "Doesn't It cut an imposing figure?"

"What?"

"Its Royal Highness," the cabinet said. "Clearly you've not met It before."

"No," Maddy said. "I don't—"

"Very few do," the cabinet said. "I am Its Royal Tanist. Its... progeny. You may call me Tan, Miss—"

"I, um," Maddy said. "I thought Its Royal Highness was so loathsome in visage that—"

"It needs to spend Its days locked in the Nonesuch Palace," the cabinet next to her said. "Or in a box."

Maddy's cheeks burned. "I beg your pardon, I didn't—"

"Very few do," Tan said.

Maddy's tongue felt a dozen feet thick. "Your Royal—"

"Shhhh," Tan said. "It begins."

"But—"

"Quiet, please," Tan said. "If I'm to win I need to know the rules."

If Maddy was to win, she needed to know the rules as well. She was going to win. Then Nadine would have to forgive her for whatever she had done.

"Attention," a man in the yellow and black costume of the Spelling Bee said. "We shall begin. The rules are simple. One must work one's spells unaided. One must complete one's spell correctly. One must not raise the dead or engage in sorcery of any kind. Bonus points will be awarded for originality, flair, and emotional congruence."

"That's it?" Tan said. "This should be cake."

"Right," Maddy said. She surveyed the contestants. With the exception of two or three, they were all eighth or ninth book. She was just beginning seventh. And they were all fully human. All except the creature in the cabinet next to her. Maddy shivered. "Cake."

"Algernon Adovado," the referee called, and a slope-shouldered boy of fifteen or sixteen marched to stand on an *X* marked near the center-front of the stage. He swallowed once and bobbed his head when asked if he was ready.

The first-round spells were trivial: make Greek Fire, shatter a wall of stone with sound, compose music from the murmuring of the audience. Tan had to do that one, and it was a strange and haunting song he produced, full of feelings that Maddy didn't like to think about: a single heart beating in a dusty corridor; the steps of a lone pilgrim across rainy cobbles; the creak of an empty chair, in an empty room, in an empty house. Now that she had thought about them, that was, it was hard to concentrate. She looked for her family in the audience and found them. Rookhaven was perched on Uncle Leo's tricorne hat, peering to and fro. Madame Aubergine curled in Emma's lap. Leo waved when Maddy caught his eye. Emma cheered when Maddy was called to work her spell.

"Create the illusion of galloping horses."

Maddy repeated the challenge, stalling for time. "Create the illusion of galloping horses."

"That is correct."

Great. Quille had horses; they pulled a vast carriage and walked a stately mile. Uncle Leo had dray-horses to haul the great wagons that trundled trade goods from warehouse to ship-side. Maddy had never seen nor heard horses galloping.

Except she had. When she was with her birth mother, before she was stolen away. Maddy tried to recall the experience, but she had been a child. A very young child. She could either rely on the flawed recollection of a toddler or be eliminated in the first round.

Maddy began. From the crowd she drew the sounds of hammering hooves, the scent of harness and lathered flesh. She had some loose change in her pocket; it provided the essence of harness jingling. There was a draft in the great hall; Maddy channeled it to her purposes, amplifying it, bending it in on itself and converging it. The crowd grew louder as they felt the horses stream by. She added the sound of the hounds, her birth mother's cries, her uncles and aunts of the pack. Maddy closed her eyes and refined; accenting and augmenting the vibrations in the air. She compressed the moisture of spent breath, building misty shapes of cloud. The crowd noise rose; she added the half-heard cries of the Huntsman and his Pack. She amplified the scent of fear, the rush of unharvested grain against the thighs of the prey, the welling tears of terror, the whimper of despair. Maddy twisted and bent sound, and scent, and touch; the grasping fingers of wind, the stumbling gait of the man, the twist of the backward glance, the leap, jaws open for the throat.

There. That was galloping horses. She opened her eyes.

The hall was empty, or so it seemed at first. Uncle Leo stood in the aisle, cutlass drawn. Rookhaven flapped overhead, crying, "Kill them all, kill them all." Emma sat in her seat and smiled at Maddy, Madame Aubergine curled in her lap. A ring of men blocked her view of Its Majesty; their muskets were aimed at Maddy. The remaining audience crowded the exits, struggling to escape the hall. The stage was empty except for Tan's ornately carved cabinet, the curtain behind the stage torn down. A dozen Sisters of St. Anselm poured forth, burnished helms on their brows. Sister Kale held them back with a slash of her broadsword.

"The illusion of galloping horses," Maddy said. She pressed her palms against her face. She bit her lip. A tear ran down her cheek.

"There will be a short intermission," the referee said.

MADDY PACED BACK and forth while the chaos she wrought was put to right. Where was Nadine? She'd promised. Maddy didn't know what to do. She needed supervision. Now.

"That was fantastic," Tan said. "They ask for galloping horses and you give them the Wild Hunt."

Maddy slapped the cabinet before she remembered it held the heir to the throne. "Oh, no, sorry, Your Royal—"

"Tan," the cabinet said. "And that was truly spectacular, Maddy Oortsgarten-Quille. I see now why you didn't want to tell me your name."

"It's Maddy Dune," Maddy said. "Professor Quille and Detective Inspector Oortsgarten had no hand in the mess I've made."

"Oh, I wouldn't be so sure," Tan said. "They say Quille is the greatest enchanter who ever lived. Surely he taught you a thing or two."

Maddy laughed. "I can't understand half of what he says."

"The Detective Inspector—"

"Promised she'd be here for me," Maddy said. "I don't know what I did to anger her. I'm trying my best." They nearly had the audience settled back into their seats and the stage backdrop re-erected.

"Perhaps her duty called her away," Tan said.

"Not without saying something," Maddy said. "She's not that way."

"What way?" Tan said.

"Undependable," Maddy said. "That's my department." Maddy bit her nails as a Sister herded a half dozen of the audience back to their seats. "I need her."

"Perhaps you only think you do," Tan said.

"Look around, man," Maddy said. She tried to peer into the cabinet.

"Please don't," Tan said. "Look, that is. Name me man anytime you wish. Few do, you know."

"Your... um, Tan—"

"Shush. As for the rest, you were asked to complete a task. You did. Better than anyone could have imagined."

"I scared the hell out of them," Maddy said.

"We do that just by being," Tan said. "Trust me. I know."

"That song you made. It was beautiful," Maddy said. It looked like the judges were taking their seats.

"I'm glad you liked it," Tan said. "I made it for you."

AT THE END of the second round, there were only six left: two boys from the Cosmopolitan Day School, two Acolytes of the Sisters of St. Anselm, Tan, and Maddy. The challenges were more difficult, focused on the enchantment of objects: make a chair dance, cause a clock to run backwards, that sort of thing. Maddy was weakest here. Such enchantments used up the enchanter's life-force, aging them in the process. Her adoptive father, Eusebius Quille, refused her access to his library on permanent spells, and only the most trivial were covered in the seventh book. Maddy could make a broom sweep on its own accord; that was the limit of her skill.

Tan was challenged to ring the bells of St. Anselm's. He did, playing the same song he had played earlier. That tune of loneliness rang out across the city, and when Maddy dried her eyes she found she wasn't the only one weeping. A single bell toned on, in time with her beating heart.

When her turn came, the audience was already headed for the exits. The referee looked at her and shook his head. He smiled when he read the challenge.

"Make a broom sweep on its own accord." A grim-faced Sister darted out and handed Maddy a willow broom before she dashed away stage left.

"Make a broom sweep on its own accord," Maddy said. She held the broom at arm's length. It was far from the best broom she had ever seen. It didn't look up to the task.

"That is correct."

Maddy watched the broom move back and forth like the clapper in a bell. She would make it to the third round, but it would be a hollow victory. The judges were afraid of her. They'd given her child's play to assuage their own fear. She was so tired, so very tired of being feared. That was the root of her loneliness. Only Nadine didn't fear her. That was why she needed her. Where was Nadine? The sound of the broom scratching across the stage tore at her. Surely there was something... Maddy stretched her consciousness out. She reached up, and up, and there, she found them, the bells of St. Anselm's, still vibrating to Tan's song. She knew that song now, every note. She had been born with it playing in her heart. She tolled the bells slowly, in time with her sweeping broom. The sound resonated in her, stirring up memories she'd rather not think about. Somewhere there had to be an answer to that song, an antidote to the feeling that poured through her.

Maddy closed her eyes. She needed Nadine. If her mother were here, Maddy wouldn't have to be afraid. Maddy imagined that, and slowly the music changed. Tan's song was still there, but another tune entwined it, danced around it, holding it, not fighting it, but redirecting it, answering it, an answer that negated the very question itself. There was no need for Tan's song, not really. It didn't have to be. Tan's song existed, there was no denying it. But it didn't need to linger there alone. Maddy knew that in her heart. Knew it now. She willed the bells to silence. She willed the broom to still. When she opened her eyes, she wasn't standing on the X. She was very far stage right, the broom in her arms. She felt her face flush an instant before the crowd burst into applause. She'd been dancing with a broom.

"You dance quite well," Tan said.

Maddy felt her face burn. "I had no intention of dancing."

"So much of what we do is without intent," Tan said. "I've been thinking of your mother."

"So have I," Maddy said. "She's never lied to me before."

"What makes you think she has in this case?" Tan said.

"She promised to be here, and she isn't." Maddy leaned her back against Tan's cabinet.

"I watched you dance," Tan said. "Did you learn those steps on your own?"

"Yes," Maddy said. "No. I don't know."

"Maddy," Tan said. "May I tell you a secret?"

"Must I keep it?" Maddy pressed her palms against the cabinet.

"I hope not," Tan said.

"What is it?" Maddy leaned her cheek against the finely carved wood.

"That song I wrote for you?" Tan said. "It was the only song I knew. Until today."

Maddy pressed her forehead against the cabinet and closed one eye. Perhaps then she might see.

"Don't," Tan said. "I beg you."

Maddy jerked away as if the cabinet were on fire. "Very well,

Your Highness." She stalked away to find a drink of water. By the time she had found a Sister, they were calling for third round. Only an Acolyte of the Sisters of St. Anselm, Tan, and Maddy had made it through.

"Project your happiest memory," the referee said. This was the same challenge the Acolyte had received. That girl's memory was of playing with a clowder of kittens in the straw, only the image of a Sister with a sack and the dunking pond in the distance marring the final moments.

Maddy studied the audience. They leaned forward in their seats. Uncle Leo sat back, his arms crossed, his face dark. Emma shook her head *no*. Madame Aubergine was awake. She stared intently at Maddy. Rookhaven hopped from foot to foot. Maddy didn't need to hear him to know his words. She searched the crowd for Nadine. Her mother had broken her word.

"Project my happiest memory," Maddy said.

"That is correct."

She studied the crowd. So easily swayed. They crawl before the Wild Hunt. They swoon before the dancing broom-girl. She glanced toward Tam's cabinet. She couldn't see inside. Tan wouldn't allow it. How bad could it be? Her prince had no idea what ugliness was.

"Very well."

Maddy was in her cage on the deck of the *Polyphemus*. It reeked of fear and waste. The sails were burning. Another ship was drawn alongside, grappling hooks holding the two together while men clambered aboard. The sorcerer who had bound her threw spells like rays of black sunfire about as a sure-footed woman leapt to the deck. Nadine Oortsgarten drew her sidearm. Around her, men shriveled and burned.

A clumsy man followed her aboard, but when his feet struck wood, it was as if he were rooted to the spot. Eusebius Quille slammed his ashplant to the deck and the *Polyphemus* shuddered. Maddy howled and beat herself against the bars of the cage. The sorcerer turned his attention to Quille. Black fire burned in the sky, arcing upward, falling in sheets toward Quille only to pour around him and fall away in dark, searing waves.

Maddy was distracted; another man was boarding, a golden man with cutlass flashing, and a young woman, parasol in hand, carrying a blue-black cat. Maddy bashed herself against the bars of her cage. A dark bird fluttered overhead. Maddy licked her lips and waited.

Captain Leonides Farrago carved a path through the crew with his cutlass. The smell of blood was past bearing. Maddy pounded again and again against her cage, and then Emma, the girl with the parasol, had her hand on the latch. Emma didn't see him, Maddy's guard, the one who had promised to do things to Maddy after she had her first blood, who whispered to her in the night, who petted her, laughing deep in his throat. Now he crept toward the girl, his steps behind her drowned in the cries of dying men. Madame Aubergine was a blue-black whirlwind, razor-claws shredding the guard's face as he raised the boarding ax above his head. Emma turned at the sound, a fluid motion that terminated with a discharged pistol and a fountain of gore. Maddy licked her lips and howled. The bird Rookhaven alighted on the bars overhead. Maddy watched him and waited as Emma unlatched the door to her cage.

"Kill them all," Rookhaven crowed. Maddy's heart soared as her feet hit the deck.

Nadine pressed the muzzle of her handgun against the forehead of the sorcerer and fired. The undead thing blinked once before he shook his head and laughed. He was still laughing when Quille slammed him to the deck with a transfixion spell.

Nadine worked the Undeath Hood over the sorcerer's head before he had a chance to stand. He was standing again by the time she actuated the plunger that sucked the hood tight about his skull and kept on shrinking.

Maddy paused long enough to bark out a cry of joy before she barreled down the companionway to the crew's quarters. He was here, somewhere, hiding amongst the other creatures too weak or insufficiently willful to earn a cage. A cage where the men could prod and tease her every moment of the day. Maddy could smell him. Maddy could see him, hiding between two packing crates. He discharged a pistol as Maddy advanced. The ball whizzed past her ear. She could taste his fear. Maddy smiled at the man who had stolen her away from the Hunt. Maddy longed for the feel of his throat between her teeth. She burned for the taste of his pain.

That was where they found her, her new family. Even then, no one had the nerve to come near. Except Nadine. The Detective Inspector clapped the man in irons. Captain Farrago inched forward and dragged him away.

Maddy licked Nadine's blood-soaked hand and arched her back in contentment. She was safe. Safe and free.

Maddy faced the crowd, and for once she didn't stifle the growl that swelled inside her.

"My happiest memory," Maddy said. Maddy bared her teeth. She imagined her fangs shone like ivory in the stage light.

No sound was to be heard but a young girl's soft sobbing.

TAN'S CABINET was pulled carefully forward and positioned on the X.

"Project your happiest memory," the referee said.

"Certainly," Tan said.

A ruby-eyed girl danced with a broom. She moved as if she knew his every thought, as if together they shared that dark knowledge of the cage he was born to wear.

WHEN THE REFEREE called the Acolyte of the Sisters of St. Anselm's for the fourth round, she ignored him. She sat, back to the audience, rocking side to side and whispering.

The referee placed his hand on the young woman's shoulder. "Really, miss—"

She turned, tears streaming down her face. "I brought them back." She stood. A moist and rotted sack dripped murky water onto the stage. "See?"

"You brought what back?" the referee said.

"The kittens," the Acolyte said. "From my happy day."

The bag had begun to writhe as if something large and powerful were trying to break loose. The referee stepped back. He jerked his head toward the opposite side of the stage. "We'll just put that over here." A half dozen Sisters picked up their helms.

The sack twisted and made a tearing sound. The scent of corruption poured forth. A claw pushed out, then another. If those were kitten claws—

"Kill them all, kill them all," Rookhaven croaked. He swooped overhead just as the bag parted and its contents flopped out onto the stage. Not kittens. Grimfoxes. A half dozen of them. They swarmed the Acolyte and the sack fell from her hand to transform, melding into the stage, shifting to open a black pool of emptiness. A withered hand gripped the edge of that black portal, then another. Someone was coming through. Something. The Acolyte had worked sorcery and raised the dead.

"Maddy, step back," Nadine said.

"Mom?" Maddy twisted around. Nadine's voice was coming from Tan's cabinet.

"I'm coming out," Nadine said. A crack appeared in the cabinet; it grew in size, a door, then the sound of the crowd made Maddy look away. The sorcerer was free of the portal-sack. He rained black fire on the audience almost casually as he made his way toward the cabinet of Its Royal Highness. A musket volley tore across the stage, several balls struck the sorcerer, and one might have struck Maddy if Nadine hadn't tackled her and pulled her down.

"What are you doing here?" Maddy said.

"I promised you," Nadine said. "And someone needed to guard Its Royal Tanist. A last-minute assignment." Nadine unholstered her handgun and unclipped the Undeath Hood from her belt. "Your father is with Its Royal Highness."

"Mom—"

"Stay back, Maddy." Nadine clambered to her feet. She cocked her firearm.

The sorcerer rained death down on the musketeers. They shriveled and burned in his dark fire.

"Mom—"

"Wait here, Maddy," Nadine said. "I'll be back in a moment."

More creatures were coming through the portal now, Grey Men, and Uncle Leo and Emma had their hands full.

There was nothing but a pile of well-picked bones where the Acolyte had been. The grimfoxes disappeared, one by one, through the cracked door of Its Royal Tanist's cabinet.

Maddy darted into the cabinet and kicked the door shut with her heel. She didn't need anything else sneaking up on her.

Tan was surrounded by grimfoxes. They shied away, unwilling to approach Tan closer. Yet. Maddy couldn't blame them. Tan burned from head to toe with a crimson flame that flickered and danced.

"Maddy, stay back," Tan said. "I told you not to look."

"You're beautiful," Maddy said.

"They can't hurt me," Tan said.

"They can hurt anyone," Maddy said. Grimfoxes were pure, cunning evil, shades of vile men too weak for sorcery but too strong to die.

One of the grimfoxes noticed her. Then another.

"Maddy, go now," Tan said. "Leave. Hurry."

"No," Maddy said. Three of the grimfoxes were trying to get behind her. "Not without you."

"I can't go out there," Tan said.

"I can see that," Maddy said. One look at Tan and everyone in the crowd would feel as dirty and half-made as she did when they looked at her.

"Maddy—"

"There's only one thing to do." Maddy swallowed. "You may not want to watch."

"Kill them all," Rookhaven cried. He'd landed on Tan's cabinet. Tan's cage. "Kill them all."

"I'm sorry," she said. "It's what I was made for."

"No, it's not," Tan said. "Trust me. I know."

Rookhaven flapped away when Maddy growled. It wasn't just Maddy in the cage this time. This wasn't just another sick game. Someone needed her. Tan needed her. Needed her to kill them all.

THERE WAS NO FIFTH ROUND.

MADDY TRIED TO SIT UP, but her uncle Leo's strong arms stopped her. "You need to rest."

Eusebius Quille leaned on his ashplant and smiled. "Well done, daughter."

"A professional job, Sis." Emma patted Maddy's bandaged hand. Only Maddy's fingertips stood proud of the bandages.

Madame Aubergine padded on Maddy's pillow before she circled twice and settled in for a nap. Maddy felt at home in her room at Mundane House for the first time ever.

"Shoo, all of you," Nadine said. "I need to speak with my daughter."

They all left, except Madame Aubergine, who cracked an eye and settled in, purring loudly.

"Maddy—"

"You were there for me," Maddy said. "That's all that matters. I'm sorry I doubted your word."

"I couldn't speak," Nadine said. "Anyone...anything, might have heard."

"I know that," Maddy said. "Now."

"Maddy—"

"I don't see how you can do it," Maddy said. "I can't think of anything else."

"Do what?"

"Guard Tan," Maddy said. "And then come back to the world."

"Its Tanist has...a winning personality. He's quite witty, and..."

"He burns like fire, Mother."

"Does he?" Nadine swallowed. "Quille does much the same, you know. For me."

"What does Tan look like to you?"

"Well," Nadine said. "I try not to look."

"Nadine—"

"Shush, dear heart, and listen." Nadine took Maddy's

bandaged hand in hers. "Its Royal Highness and Its Tanist are cursed. When we look into their eyes, we see our souls reflected."

"But he burns!" Maddy closed her eyes and remembered. "He burns with a magnificent fire."

Nadine's lips touch Maddy's forehead. "I have no doubt, daughter." She squeezed Maddy's fingers gently and touched her hair. "Who could help but love such a one?"

The door to Maddy's room opened and closed quietly when Nadine left. It opened and closed again shortly thereafter.

"Maddy?" Tan's voice was tentative and soft. Gentle fingers of fire touched her hand. Soft lips of flame brushed one fingertip, then another.

Maddy opened her eyes. Her room was lit with an endless, burning light.

Rookhaven landed on Tan's shoulder. He tugged on Its Tanist's blazing earlobe thrice and croaked out Maddy's inner thoughts, the ones she didn't dare voice. "Kiss them all! Kiss them all!"

"I will, bird," Tan said. "In time." Tan's lips brushed Maddy's fingertips and she felt an answering flame in her heart. "For now, two will have to do. Your well-armed relatives insist that Maddy needs her rest."

"I really don't," Maddy said.

"You do if you wish to join me for breakfast tomorrow. There's a small ceremony, where I'm to pass the Spelling Bee trophy to this year's champion. Apparently spelling grimfoxes back to Hell earns a tremendous bonus in flair points."

"I could have killed them all," Maddy said. "But I didn't want to ruin my gown."

"A plausible story, Maddy Dune," Tan said. "We'll come up with a better one tomorrow."

"Or the next day," Maddy said.

"Or the day after that," Tan said.

"This could take forever," Maddy said.

Tan blazed with a brighter flame when the pounding on the door began. "All right, I'm coming out! Avert your eyes."

"See you tomorrow, Tan," Maddy said.

"Right," Tan said. "I like the sound of that."

"Me, too," Maddy said. "So get used to it."

2

A evil of Grey Rock tossed the report onto her desk. She massaged her temples and peered into the fire. It was nearly midnight by the celestial clock. Music drifted in her open window from the courtyard below, blending with the whispers of murmuring voices, the bright echoes of a tittering laugh, the crystal clink of countless glasses. She should be at the nightly revel, mingling with her kin, touched and touching, seeing and being seen.

As Chief Deemster of the Night Court, she had other duties. Unpleasant duties. Aevil's spies laced the city above; human spies, largely, though with sympathies toward the Folk. Pliable enough to treat with, useful enough to tolerate, and every now and then, bearers of actionable intelligence.

Its Royal Highness and Its heir were nearly slaughtered this day. Nearly. Quille and Oortsgarten saving the Royal It, the Royal Get daringly rescued by one of the Unseelie Folk. The spawn of the Moddey Dhoo, so Aevil was to believe, entwining its fate with that of the oppressors.

Aevil paced, the hem of her gown whispering across crescent-patterned carpet. All the warmth seemed sucked from her chambers. She rubbed her arms briskly, the embroidered cuffs of her hanging sleeves brushing gently against the silk velvet of her moonstone-studded gown. Twice she nearly tossed the report into the blazing fire. Twice she nearly strode across the rich carpets, and down the broad marble stairs of Castle Aon, and into the sunless court garlanded and candlelit beneath an artful moon. But the dance had begun, and Aevil led this dance. Aevil could not afford to be diverted. Not at this late date. She had come too far. Had risked too much.

Aevil withdrew her pouch of augury bones. She gathered the hem of her gown and settled to the carpet, curling her legs beneath her. She leaned forward, holding her long plait of pale hair back with one hand, while with the other she cast the bones.

Always her father and her mother disagreed. Tonight, his knucklebones spoke of prophesy, of terror from beyond the Dead Gate, of a nightmare promised, of a shadow across the moon. Her mother's bones whispered of history, of alliances broken, of Grey Rock shattered, her courts dispersed, her people scattered to the four corners. The Black Gate. The Yellow Gate. The Arduvulin Gate. Even unto the White Gate.

Aevil's fingers shook as she cast the bones again. A host of nightmares, beasts riding beasts, those ever dead and those never alive allied in blood. Scouring the earth, scourging the living, clotting the sky. Dragon bone cracking. Adamantine crumbling. The sundering of the Aos Sí.

Aevil shivered and gathered the bones. The Hag of Barna was now Deemster of the Unseelie Court, as dangerous a creature as was ever born, and tied by blood to the Moddey Dhoo. Aevil did not wish to set herself against that thing. Nor did she wish to set herself against Quille. Eusebius Quille was no friend, and he was no enemy. That he remained so was essential to Aevil's plans.

It would be work enough seeing Its Vile Travesty over-

thrown, and this endless, caustic fog lifted. Closing the Arduvulin Gate for all time was Aevil's first priority. Anything
diverting her from this task diminished the odds of success.
The time to act drew near. She did not need enemies on three
fronts.

Aevil cast the bones again. Death stalking the Aos Sí.
Stalking all the worlds beyond the Aos Sí. The Yellow Gate
sundered, the eternal beauty of Moinmoy razed, the Seelie Folk
broken, fallen, forgotten. The heart of the Aos Sí butchered.
Charred to ash. Devoured.

Aevil gathered the bones, dropping them one by one into
the cracked and brittle leather of the ancient pouch. Auguries
were vague and open to countless interpretations. Aevil's
mother and father never agreed. Not in life and not in death.
Even on the simplest of matters they battled endlessly. But the
bones never lied. And they never spoke with one voice.
Until now.

Murdering innocents solely upon the advice of prophets
was never wise. All who once served in the Army of Return
recalled that painful and humiliating lesson. But some tasks
could not be avoided. Aevil's labors were a calling, not a willful
exercise in ambition, as some fools whispered, but of responsibility shouldered, of duty to all her kin, Vulinish and Archipel-
agic alike.

She would sleep and reconsider in the morning. Decisions
of life and death were best made with eyes wide open and heart
nailed shut. Perhaps simply sending this daughter of shadow
packing would be enough. In the morning, she would decide.
In the morning, after Queen Aevil of the Seelie Folk cast an eye
upon this Maddy Dune.

Madeleine Oortsgarten-Quille stood in the perfect heart of the crater. Madeleine's brother Rookhaven walked slightly uphill, slightly outward. A vast ruin of hardwood forest stretched flattened and smoldering all about her. Great trunks of oak, ash, and hawthorn lay tossed to the ground with shattering force, laid out without proper care or rites, endless rank upon rank uprooted in the blast radiating outward from Madeleine's bare feet. Lightning coursed across a leaden sky. Plumes of smoke rose from leaf and limb ignited in the firestorm that raged upon their arrival, only to be snuffed out by the whirlwind rising in the aftermath.

"Where are we?" Madeleine said.

"Night." Rookhaven's voice creaked with age, a sound at odds with his young man's body. Rookhaven dressed archaically with his black tailcoat and trousers. His shirtfront and necktie were coal black as well. His outfit matched the glossy black feathers he kept combed off his forehead and neatly parted down his neck. The plumage of his burnsides framed the notched hook of his nose with a schoolmaster's severity, the chalky dust he wiped from his fingers adding to this impression. Rookhaven peered at Madeleine through spectacles, perfectly round hoops of silver wire holding bottle-thick lenses tinted a murky grey green.

There was no wind to speak of, no sound save Madeleine's and Rookhaven's voices and the whispering ghosts of murdered trees. The air reeked of spent fire and fresh ashes. Madeleine detected no life, no motion at all save the little wisps of smoke rising here and there in quavering skyward plumes. The clouds parted for an instant. Madeleine caught a glimpse of the moon, gibbous and silver bright.

Madeleine shivered in the cold night air. Around her all was death and ruin. "I'm dreaming."

"I wish." Rookhaven began hiking toward the rim of the crater. "We'd best get to work." His boots crushed coals beneath their heels in a steady, ground-eating gait.

"Wait."

Rookhaven ignored her. She had to run to keep up. Each step her bare feet took kicked up a cloud of dust. Not a single flame or coal touched her. She might have been walking on velvet from the feel of the world. She clutched her nightgown tightly about her.

"Where are we going?" Madeleine struggled to keep pace with Rookhaven's tireless strides.

"I'm following Maddy."

"That makes no sense."

Rookhaven quickened his relentless pace. He pointed. "She's getting away. We'll have to hurry."

A shape paced in the moonlight, a black shape, moving ahead of them, silently striding forward on all fours. Madeleine couldn't tell how big it was, how far away it was, but it was far too close for comfort.

"Let it go." Madeleine slowed. She stopped.

"I won't give up," Rookhaven said. "Not when it's my sister in danger. We need to catch her. Come on now, Madeleine."

"No." Madeleine conjured a stone, one that had been, or would be, in just this spot sometime in the past or the future. She adjusted its age until it was weathered and worn to the size of a chair. She took a seat. A dead covering of ancient moss adhered to the stone, but only at the base. It was clean enough for sitting. She called out to Rookhaven. "Let it go!"

He spun about to face her, walking backward at breakneck speed. "You wait there and catch your breath. I'd be a poor brother if I lost sight of Maddy." He waved a chalky hand before turning back to his task. "Rookhaven is on the job!"

Madeleine kicked a glowing coal downslope and watched it disappear into the distance.

Night. There were different rules in Night. She was probably in her bed, sleeping. Rookhaven was probably on her windowsill, head tucked under his wing. Madame Aubergine was probably curled on the pillow next to Maddy Dune, purring.

Probably.

"Move the foot," Madame Aubergine said.

"What?" The ground below Madeleine's left foot vibrated. A straight black line appeared in the ashes, then two more lines at opposite ends of that line and at right angles to it.

"I hoped to make the entrance grand. Now I settle for the entrance. Move your foot, my dear heart. This ladder is, um... rickety. Metaphorically speaking, of course."

Madeleine moved her foot. Madame Aubergine thrust the trapdoor open. She climbed out into Night, somehow managing to squeeze her ample bulk through the minuscule portal. She smoothed her perfectly white apron and gloves. She shook ashes from her crisp, blue-black matron's gown. She silently brushed grit from the long, stiff cat whiskers framing her nearly human features. Madame Aubergine was dignity personified if not for the white gum boots she wore beneath her severe and proper outfit. The boots were absurd.

"I heard that," Madame Aubergine said.

"Heard what?" Madeleine said. Madame Aubergine was a clockwork cat. She wasn't even alive. She shouldn't be able to shift shape. Or do anything she wasn't programmed for.

"My boots are not absurd." Madame Aubergine smoothed her cat whiskers with her left hand. "They are essential to your education. Now where is Maddy's bird-brained brother?"

Madeleine studied the ashes beneath her feet. The trapdoor had disappeared, leaving behind nothing but remnants of ruin. "Gone," Maddy said.

"He comes now," Madame Aubergine said. "Prepare yourself, Madeleine. Soon we begin."

"I don't want to begin," Madeleine said. She wanted to sleep. To be left alone. In the morning, something good would happen. Something magical.

"In the morning, Maddy's heart will soar and break," Madame Aubergine said. "And in time you will cause this." Madame Aubergine swept her arm about, taking in the shattered stone beneath the crater, the dead and charred forest, the dusty, windless silence where no life could exist for long.

"I won't," Madeleine said.

"We shall see, dear heart." Madame Aubergine flexed her claws. Slivers of steel jutted through the thin fabric of her gloves. Even in Night Madame Aubergine remained a clockwork cat. Although she looked less like an enchanter's familiar and more like an actual person, clockwork or otherwise. "It is for the prevention of such an eventuality that we labor."

Rookhaven brought a monstrous, shaggy hound with him, a night-black beast the size of a donkey. Its eyes burned with the fires of hell. Madeleine tore her gaze away. That wasn't her. She wasn't an animal. She could smell it from here, the sulfurous stench of a fumarole. A spectral hound. A living, breathing nightmare.

Madame Aubergine touched Madeleine's hand. "Quille made me from wires and gears, my sweetness. Do you image I am a machine?"

"That's different," Madeleine said. "Quille's an enchanter. He just created your... shell. He just made it possible for you to become you."

"Oh, well, yes, of course, Madeleine. That is very different. You were born fully made. Now one needs only to stand back and watch in terror until you wind down."

"I don't," Madeleine said. "I didn't—"

Rookhaven strode toward Madeleine. The spectral hound paced at his side, smoldering and reeking of sulfur and red-hot iron. Madeleine refused to meet its gaze.

"I'm sorry I strayed," the creature said. "I just wanted to see over the edge."

It spoke in Madeleine's voice. But it wasn't her. Not really.

"And now that you have, my sweetness, what will you do?" Madame Aubergine gripped Madeleine by the chin and forced her to face the spectral hound.

It paced toward Madeleine. Every step it took crushed ash to stone, melted stone to lava. It was tall as Madeleine seated on her stone so that they saw eye to eye. The creature's eyes weren't eyes at all, but windows on a dreadful forge. Madeleine tried to turn away, but Madame Aubergine had a grip of steel.

The monstrous hound snarled and bared its fangs. "I'm going to stop them." The fur on its back rucked into a stiff and spiky ridge down its spine.

Madeleine jerked her chin free of Madame Aubergine's grasp. She lurched to her feet and took two steps back, puffing ash into the air with each step.

"You?" Madeleine said. "Stop pretending to be me! That's what you have to stop!"

Madeleine turned to Rookhaven. He craned his neck, his head thrust forward, his black eyes gleaming and cold over the rims of his spectacles. He shook his head side to side; small, slow motions only, not a full gesture of negation. Certainly not.

Madame Aubergine touched her fingers to the spectral hound's back. "You do not—"

"No," the hideous creature said. "I'm fine. Really. I can't afford to flinch." It took a step toward Madeleine. "Look at the stone."

Madeleine took another step back. "Madame Aubergine couldn't care less about a stone."

"Not her. You. Me." The hellhound had somehow managed to herd Madeleine back to her starting point. "Look at the stone you conjured up."

"I have," Madeleine said. "It's just a stone. It doesn't—"

"Turn it over." The hound took a step toward her.

Madeleine glanced at the stone. She licked her lips. "I can't."

The hound's iron-hard claws gouged pale channels in the stone. "I can."

Madeleine took another step back. "Don't."

"I have to." The hound opened its jaws wide, great ivory fangs gleaming, steaming breath swirling. Acid saliva dripped from its lips, boiling solid rock. It gripped the stone in its crushing jaws.

Madeleine ran for her life. Her legs worked, devouring ground, uphill, away, as far away as her feet would carry her. If she had wings, she might soar away into Night, untouched, untouchable. Even Rookhaven didn't have wings in Night. Madeleine conjured as she ran, planning a work in flesh, forbidden sorcery elsewhere. In Night, the rules were different. In Night, she could—

Madeleine's chest slammed into the ground, ashes billowing from under her, pulverized stone grinding into her cheek, charcoal grit on her tongue. A massive paw pressed her into the debris.

"Look!" The hellhound spoke with Madeleine's voice, mocked her. "Look at what we've done!"

The hellhound reduced its pressure on her back so that she might worm her way up to the edge of the crater to see. When she paused, it threatened to grip her neck in its fangs and toss her over the edge. Madeleine squirmed one more time and felt the slope drop away below her.

"Open your eyes!"

She pressed her eyelids together more tightly. There was sand in her lashes, and the grit cut in. If she rubbed her eyes, she might blind herself.

The hellhound howled. "Open them!"

Rookhaven stroked Madeleine's earlobe gently before he tugged thrice and pulled her fingers away from her eyes. "Fighting won't change anything, Madeleine."

"Open them!"

Madeleine dug around in the coarse rubble at the crater's edge. If she could find a stone, a sharp-edged bit of flint or obsidian, she might gouge her eyes out. Her fingers found an edge at last.

Madame Aubergine's soft touch tickled the back of Madeleine's hand. "That is not the way, dear heart."

"Open your eyes," the hellhound whispered in her ears. "Don't leave me here alone."

Madeleine opened her eyes. She screamed.

4

Emma Sunbury's face was inches from Maddy's own.
Maddy screamed again.

Emma blinked. "That was uncalled for, Sis."
Emma shifted forward in the bedside chair. She smelled of
damp, and fog, and hours spent beneath cold stone. Maddy's
sister was always so impeccably dressed and incredibly golden,
from the perfectly coiffed tresses that fell to her elegant shoulders in bright curls, to the subtle hue suffusing her flawless skin
with the barest hint of morning sunlight. Tall and slender and
perfectly fitted out in the latest fashion of the day. Everything a
girl might aspire to.

Maddy's brain was still more than halfway in Night. She
rubbed her eyes and blinked. "What?"

"I only asked you to open your eyes." Emma straightened
her back and adjusted her dress. "Now you've disturbed our
mother."

Nadine Oortsgarten slipped into Maddy's bedroom in her
dressing gown. Nadine kept her independently minded hair
tightly bound in a chignon during the day. Tonight, her hair
was free, framing her face in dark softness and spilling about

her shoulders in silken waves. The huge pistol she carried seemed absurdly out of place in Maddy's bedroom.

When Maddy was first brought to Mundane House, she hadn't cared for her bedroom at all. It was enormous with a towering four-poster bed, a fine dresser for clothes, an armoire of satinwood, and an ancient chest, larger than a seaman's locker, at the foot of her bed. Not to mention the attached bathroom where Maddy was expected to purposely soak her body in water no less than three times a week.

Maddy thought at first, this might be some new cruel and unusual cage, one designed to make her let her guard down. But it wasn't a cage. And she had let her guard down. But that was acceptable in Mundane House. Her family had her back. That was why her dream had been so terrifying. In Night, she was expected to be in charge. In Night, she was expected to know what to do.

Nadine kept her voice low. "What is wrong?"

"I looked in on Maddy and found her twitching. Her bedclothes are soaked with sweat. I couldn't rouse her at first. When I did, she chose to bellow in my ear. Twice."

"I'm sorry," Maddy said.

"You should be," Emma said. "It was quite upsetting. I thought you'd—"

"You thought what?" Nadine shooed Emma out of the bedside chair. "And why are you dressed in street clothes at three o'clock in the morning?"

"I thought she might have died," Emma said. "She was barely breathing."

Nadine took Maddy's hand in hers. She checked Maddy's pulse.

Emma hugged herself and paced. "The doctors feared there might still be grimfox venom in her system. They said not to worry, that they'd almost certainly extracted it all."

Maddy adjusted her pillow and sat up. "Wait a minute. Grimfoxes have venom?"

"Certainly," Emma said. "It is common knowledge."

"Apparently not," Nadine said. She patted Maddy's hand and released it. She lay her cool fingers across Maddy's forehead. "This is the sort of ignorance that can get a girl killed."

"Young woman killed." Emma winked at Maddy. "We are, neither of us, girls, mother."

"You're my girls," Nadine said. "And if you intend to distract me from the question of your apparel, you are mistaken. Young women or not, Oortsgarten-Quilles do not traipse about Arduvulin City at night unescorted."

"You do," Maddy said. "All the time."

"Detective Inspectors in the Department of Criminal Magic are expected to do so. Pretty, young, unmarried girls are not."

"You're pretty and young," Maddy said.

"I am neither," Nadine said. "And this is not about me."

"One's own opinion has little bearing on the common perception," Emma said. "Perhaps we should find husbands, Maddy. The other two situations are beyond our control."

"If you believe marriage frees you from a mother's interrogations, you are mistaken," Nadine said. "This is a lie perpetuated by feckless storytellers."

"Quille could let me use his library on permanent enchantments," Maddy said. "I wouldn't be young for long. No one's likely to marry me anyway. I do a very convincing ugly."

"No you don't," Emma said. "Oortsgarten-Quille women are cursed with spectacularly fine figures and unforgettable features. Not to mention our unimpeachable characters and quickness of wit."

Maddy had almost forgotten about Night until then. She had unforgettable features, no doubt. "I—"

"Try to distract me from your sister's unanswered question," Nadine said.

"I'm an adult," Emma said.

"And your father is embroiled in another of his disputes," Nadine said. "I don't question your right to do as you wish. Your judgment in doing so is under examination. We can't afford a scandal at this moment."

"I've done nothing scandalous, Mother." Emma stared at Nadine.

"See that you do not." Nadine adjusted Maddy's comforter before she stood. "Now we should leave your sister to rest."

"I'm fine," Maddy said. "You can stay."

"Better get some sleep, Sis." Emma kissed Maddy's forehead. "Breakfast with Its Royal Highness. Tomorrow is a big day."

"Today," Nadine said. "It is already past yesterday, and my daughter just returned from who knows where."

Maddy's stomach churned.

Emma touched Nadine's sleeve. "Mother—"

"I know," Nadine said. She held the door for Emma. "I worry for both of you."

"About us," Emma said. "You worry about both of us."

Maddy's bedroom door slowly closed.

"That is what I said."

"No, you said..."

Madame Aubergine shifted on the pillow next to Maddy. She flexed her paws and purred.

Rookhaven fluttered over to land on Maddy's headboard. "Back to Night, back to Night."

Maddy touched the bandages on her hands. Her fingers were smothered with salves and ointments, all but her fingertips. She'd thought the bandages were purely medicinal, but now that she examined them closely, she could feel the magic there. She should have looked closer earlier. Ignorance could get a girl killed.

Grimfoxes had venom. If she'd known, it wouldn't have

stopped her from saving Its Royal Tanist, no matter what the cost. It might have saved her some pain, though. And saved her sister a bedside vigil. Of course Emma wouldn't tell Nadine the truth. Nadine was a worrier, and she had enough to worry about. Her daughters could look after one another. If they weren't blindly ignorant or so terrified of their own nightmares that they couldn't dare face them.

Rookhaven hopped from foot to foot on Maddy's headboard. "Open your eyes, open your eyes."

Maddy lay her head down and tried to get comfortable. She would open her eyes. She had to be strong. "I will," she said. "I promise." She'd open her eyes just as soon as she got back to sleep. If she ever got back to sleep.

5

M addy covered her cough with her fingers just as
Emma had taught her. Breakfast at Mundane
House was always very nice. There was plenty
that was safe to eat, something that wasn't at all the case when
Maddy had been a prisoner of crypto-natural pirates. And
Maddy always learned something interesting or funny at break-
fast. Usually both.

Emma had any number of young men chasing after her.
She often recounted their antics in a cold and aloof voice that
was so perfectly Emma. Maddy glanced outside, past the
ornately carved sideboard and spare dining chairs straightened
and squared away. It always looked like winter in Arduvulin
City. Today was forecast to be unseasonably warm. The
constant fog pressing against the bow window of Quille's breakfast room only gave the impression of short days, and frozen
ratlines, and ice on the slop bucket.

Emma and the fog might as well have been related. Both
hid things for certain, but that was just the way they were
made. Cold to look at, but warm to the touch, and mysterious,
and everywhere. Emma knew all the gossip in Arduvulin City

and recounted it as if she'd been there. At least, she did on those mornings when she could remain awake after her nightly rambles. This morning Emma dozed in her seat.

Professor of Enchantment Eusebius Quille folded the morning newspaper and placed it next to his breakfast plate. He toyed with it for a moment before sliding it into his lap. He sipped his coffee in silence.

Maddy pushed a piece of toast around her plate. It was charred, as usual. Quille's cook burned everything. Everything that wouldn't boil. "I don't see why we're having breakfast here if we're going to breakfast at the Nonesuch Palace."

Quille peered off into space. Emma's chin rested on her breastbone, her eyes closed. Nadine's gaze was glued to the paper Quille attempted to squirrel away.

Nadine's arched eyebrow spoke volumes. *Don't interrupt, Maddy, I'm detecting.* Nadine was always at work, regardless of where she was.

"Mom," Maddy said.

Nadine plucked the newspaper from Quille's lap. "What is it, Maddy?" She peered at the front page.

Quille rested his elbow on the mahogany table and cupped his chin in his palm. He stared at the tarnished tea set on the sideboard behind Maddy, not seeing it, as usual. Quille was lightly connected to the world. Maddy wondered if, when she was a powerful enchanter, she'd see things that weren't there and overlook all the things that were. She hoped not. Quille's housekeeper robbed him blind.

Besides the tarnish on the neglected silver, there were cobwebs on the filigreed picture moldings, and the silk and woolen carpets needed a beating a decade ago. Everything about Mundane House spoke of quality and neglect, from the warped ebony of the floor-to-ceiling pocket doors that stubbornly refused to close to the gold and crystal gas chandelier overhead that hissed and sputtered in complaint. Shadows danced on the unpolished marquetry of the tabletop, slaves to the flickering lamplight. Delicate satinwood and pear deserved better care, and even normally reticent mahogany seemed to mutter just a little.

Madame Aubergine sharpened her claws on the verdure border of the carpet and dared Maddy to say a word. She hopped into Quille's lap and circled before settling.

Maddy repeated her question. "Why are we eating at home if we're to—"

Nadine's nostrils flared as she sucked in a great breath. "Of all the..." She nudged Quille. "Have you seen this?"

Quille blinked and stared blankly at his wife. "Eh?"

Quille's impersonation of Quille was not very convincing.

Nadine slapped Quille on the arm with the paper. "You have. What are you going to do about it?"

Emma's chin dropped another inch before she jerked upright with a gasp.

Quille smiled at his eldest daughter. "Late night?"

Emma cupped her hand to her mouth and stage whispered. "Early morning." She swirled her coffee cup, sending spirals of steam spinning toward Maddy. Even the coffee smelled burned.

"Is it standard operating procedure in this household to change the subject?" Nadine snapped the paper against the tabletop. "Quille, I asked you a question. What are you—"

Quille swallowed and looked sideways at Maddy. "I don't know why we bother having the blasted thing delivered. It's not as if we have a parakeet. That rag isn't fit for a fish wrapper, and—"

"People read it," Nadine said. "Fools believe it. We live cheek by jowl with them. That is why."

"What would you have me do?" Quille said. "Burn Broadsheet House down and melt their presses?"

"I could do that," Maddy said. "I learned how to make Greek Fire in the Seventh Book."

Quille chuckled. "You could, except you're a good girl, and wise enough to know right from wrong. These newspaper people don't, but it's not our business to be responding to their lies, or even acknowledging their existence."

Emma toyed with her toast. "What did they say that is so bad?"

"Nothing out of the ordinary," Quille said. "I'm a sorcerer, and your mother's using her position with the Department of Criminal Magic to protect me."

"Well, isn't she?" Emma said.

"I am not," Nadine said. "Quille is not a sorcerer, and—"

"Of course Quille's not," Emma said. "But that doesn't mean you're not using your position to protect him."

Nadine shifted her chair back and placed the folded paper on the table. She was dressed in her finest night-blue uniform, though it wasn't really an official uniform. Detective Inspectors didn't wear uniforms, but Nadine said she liked the freedom of movement. If she chose to wear trousers and a short jacket instead of broad skirts, it was her own business. She'd worn a uniform in the Department most of her adult life, and making Detective, and then Detective Inspector, didn't change a thing. No one would mistake Nadine Oortsgarten for a civilian. Even if they missed the massive sidearm holster and the Undeath Hood clipped to her belt.

Nadine stiffened her spine and peered down her nose at Emma. "I do not abuse my authority."

"You're the one who said 'abuse'," Emma said. "Not me."

"This accusation is clear in every word of these scandalous lies," Nadine said. "These...worms...lack the spine to make a public declaration, preferring to insinuate and imply."

"Worms don't need a spine," Emma said. "The host supplies the backbone."

"Though these worms have no shortage of neck," Quille said. "No more letters to the editor, Nadine."

"What kind of worms are we talking about?" Maddy said.

Emma turned to Maddy. "Tapeworms. They're a type of parasite that attaches to a host's digestive tract. Very nasty. You'll want to see a surgeon if you—"

Nadine's brows narrowed. She sucked in a great breath with a gasp. "Have you seen this picture of our daughter?" Nadine's accent always sharpened when she grew angry. "No one, Quille! No one shall dare to look at our children so much as sideways. I swear to you, I shall go to this place of filth so naming itself *The Times of Arduvulin* and find this serpent and we will speak. I will hound this miscreant to the ends of the earth." Nadine shook the paper in her fist. "I will make him eat this foul collection of lies. Every single copy I lay my hands upon will scour its way through his convoluted and verminous intestines. So help, me Quille." Nadine rocked back in her chair and rolled the paper tightly. She kept rolling it, twisting it until it crinkled in protest. Nadine stood. Took a step. Glared out the window into the fog. Dropped back into her seat. "After breakfast with Its Royal Highness." Nadine's hands shook. The paper moaned.

Maddy swallowed. The two slices of toast she'd had for breakfast tried to claw back out. "What picture?"

Emma clasped her hands in her lap and studied the wilted centerpiece. Quille winced and pretended to appraise the largest wine stain on the carpet.

Nadine stuffed the newspaper into her jacket pocket. "It is nothing." She smiled at Maddy. It was a good smile. Very convincing. Good, but not great.

"You didn't seem to think it was nothing a minute ago," Maddy said.

"We should get our coats," Nadine said. "Leo will be here in a moment, and we don't wish to—"

"Mom." Maddy held out her hand. "Can I see?"

"She's not a child," Emma said. "And she doesn't have your temper."

Quille rested his elbows on the table and his chin on his fists. He seemed a caricature of a man pretending to be a parent, wisely considering his child. Then Maddy realized he wasn't really looking at her, but at something behind her.

Rookhaven hopped on the sideboard. He plucked the cherry from a tart on the pastry tray, crushed it in his beak, tossed his head skyward, and swallowed. He moved on to the next tart, and the one after that.

Quille smiled. "I love my family." He held out his hand for the paper. "Every child a blessing."

Nadine considered Quille's palm for a moment before she handed him the paper. Quille held the paper for Maddy. When she tried to pull it free, Quille held on. Maddy tugged again, but Quille held fast.

"Now, Maddy, these people at the paper are trying to get under our skins." His gaze met hers. "Do you know why that is?"

"Sure," Maddy said. "Now let go. I want to see."

"Tell your mother why," Quille said, "so she'll have one less thing to worry over."

Nadine glared at Quille. "I don't worry over nothing, I—"

Emma rolled her eyes. "Oh, please."

Maddy pulled again, but Quille was strong. He used enchantment to reinforce the paper's grip on his fingers. It had to be.

"Tell your mother, so she can stop fretting."

Maddy sighed. "They do it to make us predictable. Now let go!"

Quille blinked. "That's a new one. I hadn't thought of that."

"They poke and poke and poke," Maddy said. "In a thousand different ways. To make sure they know what you'll do. Or to train you to do it."

"I see." Quille's eyes focused on something a yard over Maddy's head. "Interesting." His fingers never relented.

"I want to see!"

"Oh," Quille said. He let go.

Maddy plopped back into her seat.

"By 'they,' you mean pirates," Quille said.

"Crypto-naturalist pirates," Maddy said. "I don't know any regular pirates."

"Of course," Quille said. He scratched his chin. "Why do your crypto-naturalist pirates do such a thing?"

Maddy's hands shook as she flipped the pages. "So they can find the right cage." There it was, an article about the Spelling Bee. "One that will hold." She flipped to the next page. It was illustrated.

Maddy jerked her head away from the page. A tear rolled down her cheek.

Nadine held out her hand. "Sweetheart—"

"I'm fine," Maddy said. She chewed her lips till it hurt. The illustrator had drawn a picture of Maddy. Huge ivory fangs jutting out of her face, and flames burning behind her pupils, and they even drew her with the muzzle of a dog. It would have been funny if it weren't so cruel. Instead of making it look as though Maddy was saving Tan from the grimfoxes, they'd made it look as if she was leading Grey Men and grimfoxes forth from Hell. It looked like she was ready to murder everyone in the world for the pure enjoyment of it.

Emma took Maddy's hand and squeezed.

Rookhaven hopped onto the table and dropped a cherry on Maddy's plate. "Kill them all."

Maddy wiped her nose. "Not going to happen, brother."

Maddy read the article. The news people made it sound like she was some sort of half-feral beast masquerading as a girl, and that it was really her father who worked the magic, and it was probably sorcery because Quille was of questionable character, and Nadine was using her position with the Department of Criminal Magic to protect him and their weird menagerie of "children" and Quille's shady foreign friend Leonides Farrago from the just hand of the law. The paper said a lot more, interviews with terrified people who were at the Spelling Bee, scientific experts commenting on the unpredictability of chimeral life forms, pious sisters of St. Anselm opining on the theological implications of transhumanism. Maddy just glanced through those. She would read them later, though. Ignorance was danger. She needed to be armed against it.

When Maddy looked up from the paper, the room was very silent, all but for the gurgling of the radiator Quille had promised to have repaired three months ago. Mundane House was warm where it counted, though.

"My fangs do not jut," she said. "The newspaper illustrator needs glasses."

"There were many witnesses, and not all of them fools," Quille said. "He needs his head examined."

"He needs it broken," Nadine said. "Maddy, did you read the nice words Its Royal Highness wrote in the sidebar?"

"No," Maddy said. "I—"

The hall door swung open. A yellow-bearded lion of a man had to duck in order to step through.

Maddy sprung out of her seat. "Uncle Leo!"

Leonides Farrago was a big man with a big smile. It was hard to tell when he was dressed in his finery, but he was a strong man, too. When he was working the deck or loading cargo, it was pretty clear Uncle Leo was all muscle. Captain Leonides Farrago commanded the vessel that had freed Maddy from the crypto-naturalist pirates and their sorcerer. Emma claimed that the heart was a muscle.

Uncle Leo grinned at his favorite niece. That's what Uncle Leo called her, anyway. "Maddy Dune, the hero of the day!"

Leo placed his tricorne hat on the sideboard and unbuttoned his street coat. Beneath he wore his best uniform, brilliant gold-trimmed, crimson wool.

"You're late," Nadine said. "Don't bother removing your coat."

"Why on earth are you having breakfast?" Leo said. "We're to have breakfast with Its Royal Highness."

"What rubbish they cook there," Nadine said. "Here I know my children do not go hungry."

"Of course," Uncle Leo said. "I imagine the Sovereign of Arduvulin and Emperor of the Fogbound Realm sets out a nasty table full of poisonous and repulsive pustules and globs. Food poisoning really is the best way to thank the young woman who saved your only progeny from certain annihilation."

"Jape if you wish," Nadine said. "You have not dined there."

"And you have?" Leo asked.

"Many times." Nadine began passing out coats. "They do not cook their vegetables."

"You mean they don't boil them to mush," Leo said. "Here, let me hold that for you, Emma."

Emma slid into her coat gracefully. Maddy had her coat half on. She circled, trying to catch the loose arm.

Uncle Leo placed his hands on Maddy's shoulders and held her still. "Allow me."

Maddy slid the rest of the way into her coat.

Uncle Leo turned Maddy around and squared her shoulders. "You've grown into quite the lady."

"That's not what the papers say."

Uncle Leo's golden eyes blazed copper for an instant. "They wouldn't know a lady if one hopped up and bit them."

"I doubt a lady would do such a thing," Emma said. She pulled on her gloves.

Uncle Leo scratched his temple. "Which, the hopping or the biting? Because I've known ladies to—"

"This is not a sailing vessel, and these are not your rowdies," Nadine said. "Pretend to be a gentleman."

Quille tapped his ashplant on the floor. The breakfast dishes began to move toward the kitchen. The cutlery followed along as well, handles first, the tablecloth trailing behind.

"Assembled and ready?" Quille said.

Madame Aubergine hopped into the cat basket. Emma scooped it up elegantly. Madame Aubergine liked Emma best, and that was fine with Maddy. Rookhaven liked Maddy best.

"Ready," Emma said.

Rookhaven perched on Maddy's shoulder and tugged her earlobe. "Not ready."

"Wait!" Maddy snagged the cherry as her breakfast plate sailed by. Her brother knew what she liked, and maybe Nadine was right. Maddy's stomach was already fretting over breakfast at the Nonesuch Palace.

"Now I'm ready," Maddy said.

"Are you certain?" Quille asked.

"Not really." Maddy took her dad's hand.

"Then you're a wise young woman, Maddy mine." Quille fished out his pocket watch and fiddled with it. "You'll go far." He tightened his grip on Maddy's hand. "Hold on now." He pressed the watch stem.

The air crackled with energy. Maddy felt the power of enchantment seep into her bones. Quille never expended power like this. It didn't seem possible that one man could harness so much raw energy.

Quille's face glistened pale and clammy when he glanced over at Maddy. He smiled a half-smile. "In five, four, three, two, one—"

The world collapsed and kept on collapsing.

6

And expanded. The world kept on expanding. Maddy was the size of a flea, a fly, a pheasant. She was her own size for an instant, but she kept growing. She was the size of a hellhound, a phynodderree, a buganne, and then she was shrinking again, oscillating about her natural size until finally, mercifully, the ringing in her ears stopped and the world stood still.

"I do not like this mode of travel," Nadine said. Her sidearm gleamed in her fist. She took a step away from her family and turned slowly about. "This is not the Nonesuch Palace."

"Bloody Nora." Uncle Leo overturned a smoldering ember with the tip of his cutlass. His feet kicked up dusty clouds of ash. "What is this place?"

"I rather like the symmetry of it," Emma said. "All these charred deadfalls are aligned as if we were lodestones and they metal shavings. I imagine from the air, it looks as if we're in the bottom of a bowl." Emma opened her parasol and walked a bit away. "I wonder what lurks over the edge of our vessel?"

Rookhaven hopped up and down on Maddy's shoulder and tugged on her earlobe. "Night! Night!"

Quille consulted his pocket watch. "Link hands, all of you. Quickly."

"Quille, what is wrong?" Nadine said. "Emma, get back here and do as your father asks." She held onto her weapon, holstering it at the last moment.

Quille rested his ashplant against his leg and held out his hand for Maddy's. He glanced at her when she placed her shaking fingers in his. "I will try again, but I warn you, you must hold hands firmly."

"Will we be late for breakfast?" Emma said.

"Definitely," Quille said. "Now hold on."

Quille checked that they were all holding hands. Emma gripped Madame Aubergine's paw and Uncle Leo pinched Rookhaven's leg between his fingers. Quille pressed the stem of his watch.

The world melted and ran like lava. It kept on melting, heating, expanding. Maddy was liquid, she was gas, she was the emptiness within gas. Then she was condensing, she was every-where, seeping under windowsills, gathering in dips and hollows, carried high and blown to foreign lands. Then the rain came, and she was a droplet, a rivulet, a torrent. She closed her eyes as she plummeted over a high falls.

"MUCH BETTER," Nadine said.

Maddy opened her eyes. They were in a vast cavern, dimly lit and roughly carved. Maddy could not see the ceiling over-head nor the walls to the left or right. A thick river of dank fog flowed past her and down a massive tunnel in front of her. The air smelled of wet stone, that just-rained smell that coaxed earthworms out to writhe on the paving stones. The cavern resonated with distilled magic, with enchantment, with powerful magic pouring toward her from every direction. A jumble of silent voices shouted in accents ancient and strange and only marginally familiar.

Maddy scrubbed her shoe across the rough cavern floor. Limestone. The echo of dripping water sounded from everywhere, droplets collecting the dim, bluish light and reflecting it back like crystal. Stalagmites towered in weeping dragon's teeth every few feet for as far as Maddy could see, their pale, mineral-streaked surfaces moist and glistening. Next to the tunnel of endless fog stood a massive doorway of ironbound oak, taller than ten men, barred with tree trunks and girded with chains, each link the size of a carriage wheel. A dozen locks larger than boulders festooned the chains.

Maddy's stomach still ached from their stop in Night. She'd thought it was just a place she'd dreamed up. That it wasn't real. She glanced over at her sister. Emma's face glowed a pale blue in the queer cavern light. But it couldn't have been Night. Otherwise Rookhaven would have seemed more man than bird, and Madame Aubergine would have been wearing white gumboots. But if it hadn't been Night, then what was it?

Maddy shivered. She didn't want to know. It looked like Night. Maybe Rookhaven and Madame Aubergine had purposely stayed in their familiar forms. For some unknown reason.

Emma's gaze never rested, scanning one dark corner after another. Maddy's sister knew all about the dangers that could lurk in the smallest sliver of shadow. Her gaze met Maddy's. "Impressive."

"I'll say." Maddy had never seen anything like that doorway.

"Quille." Nadine holstered her weapon. "Why did you bring us here?"

"Because I knew we'd arrive." Quille wiped his handkerchief across his forehead before returning it to his pocket. "That alone is no small feat."

"We shall walk home," Nadine said. "Like ordinary people."

"We'll ride," Uncle Leo said. "I've a carriage meeting us at the Palace at ten." Leo pushed his tricorne hat back. He scratched his forehead and gazed over Maddy's head. "I take it we are at the Palace this time, Quilley?"

"Beneath it," Quille said.

"Then we must be at—"

"The Arduvulin Gate," Nadine said. "You must tell no one, and forget you were ever here."

"Where did they get oak trees tall enough to make the doors?" Maddy said. "They're both carved from a single slab!"

"The door valves are solid adamantine," Quille said. "The frame is dragon bone."

"That's oak," Maddy said. No question. Oak spoke slowly and pronounced carefully. Oak was patient and sure of itself. Dependable. Maddy would never be oak, but she could admire it. No axe had touched the wood of those doors. A tree had heard the heart of an enchanter, and judged the worthiness of the enchanter's task, and volunteered to serve. There wasn't a pencil in Mundane House that didn't choose to be there. Surely Quille knew oak when he saw it.

Uncle Leo gripped Maddy by the shoulders. He turned her about.

A massive portal, large enough to swallow the moon, towered above her. It was round and so broad and tall that Maddy couldn't see the stone it was set in. The door valves were warped and nearly closed. A thick sheet of fog spewed from between the valves to congeal into a massive rope of greyness plunging into the tunnel behind her. The fabric of the portal whispered and screamed. It was a magical device, like Quille's teleportation watch, or the magic bullets he made for the Department of Criminal Magic, or the Undeath Hood that forever dangled from Nadine's belt. Permanent magic. Maddy couldn't begin to measure the life bound up in a single hinge, let alone the device as a whole. "Oh."

"Oh indeed," Leo said.

"It's not really large enough to swallow the moon," Maddy said.

Quille tapped Maddy's sleeve with his ashplant. "It could swallow the world." He studied Maddy with his Professor's gaze. Quille only wore that look when he was at work. "Do you know what would be left then?"

"I didn't know such a thing existed," Maddy said. "I haven't given it any thought."

"Do so," Quille said. "I'm not asking as your father, but as one enchanter to another. Give it as much thought as anything in the world. Then give it more."

"Right now?" Crypto-naturalist pirates were always looking for dragons. The crew of the *Polyphemus* didn't sight a dragon in all the time Maddy was their captive. Here was a giant ring of dragon bones. They spoke a language Maddy didn't understand, but they spoke it in an accent identical to Its Royal Tanist's. Maddy wanted to study the gate, but Quille kept stepping in front of her.

Quille placed two fingers under Maddy's chin. He pressed gently until she looked him in the eye. "What do you suppose would be left of the world should such a power break free?"

"I—"

"We must go," Nadine said. "We will be late as it is."

"In a moment," Quille said. He searched Maddy's eyes. After a moment, he smiled. He patted Maddy's hand. "You don't have to answer me now. In the morning will be soon enough."

"I doubt I'll know more then than I do now," Maddy said.

"You might not," Quille said. "But you'll be able to answer my question." Quille pulled out his pocket watch and flicked it open. He ran his thumb across the crystal. He seemed to have lost the thread of their conversation. That happened all the time with Quille. Maddy started to walk away. Quille fixed Maddy with his gaze.

"Sleep on it." Quille checked the time. He pocketed his teleportation device. "Such questions often make the most sense in darkest night."

Maddy swallowed. "I will." *Quille knew.* Maddy had pulled her family off course and into Night. Into her own private hell. Except it wasn't private. It existed. It was real.

"Good girl." Quille patted Maddy's hand. "I will ask you in the morning, Maddy. Don't assume I'll forget our conversation. Not this one."

"Yes, father."

Quille tilted his head and craned his neck. He peered at Maddy. Maybe Rookhaven really was Quille's son. Quille's eyes gleamed in the strange cavern light, a flickering blue that seemed to dance. Maybe Maddy really was Quille's daughter, even though there wasn't a drop of his blood in her veins.

"I will, Dad. Really."

Quille smiled. "That's my girl. Come on now, before your mother bursts a vein."

⌖

NADINE STOOD before a narrow door set in the left-hand valve of the massive oak doorway. She unbuttoned the top button of her blouse and reached within. "Don't look."

"Of course not." Uncle Leo turned his back and glanced over his shoulder.

Nadine undid another button and delved deeper.

Quille tapped his ashplant against the stone. "That's my wife you're leering at, Leonides."

"Sorry, Quilley," Uncle Leo said. "Curse of the sailor, I'm afraid. The all-seeing eye, any port in a storm, that sort of thing. Nothing I can do to stop it. You understand."

Emma shifted Madame Aubergine's basket. Madame

Aubergine seemed not to notice. "I would turn him into a toad for that, Dad."

"Ahah!" Nadine gripped a key on a silver chain, one of more than a dozen she wore around her neck. Each chain held a single key. Nadine never took them off, but until now Maddy had never seen her use a single one.

"Leonides hops around the world seeking a princess to kiss," Nadine said. "Additional toadness would not inconvenience him too much, I think." Nadine placed the key in the inset door's lock.

Quille cleared his throat. "That would be sorcery. To turn a man into a toad."

"It's a fairy tale," Maddy said. "A...literary allusion."

"It's sorcery," Quille said. "Working in flesh. The Folk do no such thing. Not living flesh."

"Perhaps you could crush me between the gear-operated mitts of some enormous clockwork golem, Quilley." Uncle Leo smiled. "You know, turn me into a paste instead of a toad. That wouldn't be sorcery."

"That would be a great deal of work," Quille said. "But I'll consider it."

Nadine stepped away from the lock. Quille did something then, a power-consuming and complicated enchantment. Maddy couldn't follow even a tenth of it, but she could tell it had nothing to do with locks and keys and doors. The parts of the spell she understood made her think of Nadine.

Quille stepped back. The door opened silently on well-oiled hinges.

"One at a time, and sideways," Nadine said. "We will all fit through."

Emma went through first, then Maddy. It wasn't a room at all behind the door, but a landing, a small space at the bottom of a rough-hewn stone stairway leading up into blackness.

Quille took off his street coat, his frock coat, and his waistcoat. He passed them to Nadine. Leo rested his massive palm on Quille's shoulder. "That's a sorcerous belt you're wearing. It's working into your flesh."

Quille sucked in his gut and squeezed through the narrow doorway. Uncle Leo was fast behind him. Leo had to wriggle to force his muscled body through.

Quille tapped his ashplant. "Leo, this isn't a joking matter. When I die I will—"

"When you die, Eusebius Quille," Uncle Leo said, "your family will be there to save your soul and the world. And to finish your work if it's worthy. You need have no fear other than to see that your work is worthy."

"There is no guarantee of that," Quille said. "Already they're saying I'm a sorcerer. You have no idea how much damage I could do if that were true."

"It won't be true." Leo patted Quille on the back and gazed up the stairway. "So, how many steps, Detective Inspector?"

"Two thousand three hundred and forty-six."

Nadine ignited the fairy light Quille handed her. Fairy lights really didn't have anything to do with the Folk. That's just what people called them. They were enchanted candles, ones that remained cool to the touch and never burned down. Maddy often made fairy lights under Quille's direction. They were simple affairs, magic right out of the Sixth Book. Maddy's fairy lights were long lasting, reasonably priced, and sold well. The ones Quille handed out were made with permanent magic, their handles scarred from repeated use. Priceless to the right buyers: tomb robbers, sailors in fear of shipboard fire, the Department of Criminal Magic.

Leo gazed up and past the tiny circle of light. "That's a fair hike. Any landings?"

"None."

"All right," Uncle Leo said. "Quilley, I suggest you lead the way."

"Is it that dangerous?" Maddy said. "I thought we were in the Nonesuch Palace."

"Your Uncle Leo expects I'll slip and break my neck," Quille said. "He wants to be behind to stop me tumbling all the way down."

"I want us all behind you to prevent that," Uncle Leo said.

"I will take the rear," Nadine said. "Maddy, you and Emma behind Leo."

Three steps up Nadine cocked her handgun. Maddy turned at the sound.

"We are beneath the Nonesuch Palace," Nadine whispered. "That means we are most definitely not safe."

"But why doesn't Quille just spell us to the—"

"We'd just end up back here," Emma said. "Up close, the Gate acts as a supremely powerful magnet for magic."

"For enchantment and common magic," Quille said. "It has no effect on sorcery or true magic. And I wouldn't say it was a magnet, more like a—"

"So it was the Gate that brought us here," Maddy said. "Because you couldn't."

"I used the Gate," Quille said. "For navigation." Quille's forehead wrinkled. "It's... complicated. A matter of affinity. You see—"

"We can discuss this later," Nadine said. "We're late as it is. Now get on, all of you."

A dozen steps up, Maddy stumbled. In the steps, in the walls, everywhere, there were fossils, skeletal shapes caught in dark stone. Creatures captured and frozen forever. So they seemed when viewed straight on. Seen out of the corner of the eye, they writhed and moved toward the Gate.

"Maddy, look where you're going." Nadine pressed her palm against the small of Maddy's back. "That means go." She gripped a belt loop on Maddy's coat and tugged. "That means stop. Should you feel either one, they both mean

silence. You will pass whatever signal I make forward immediately."

Maddy twisted so that she could look back at her mother.
"Should I tell Emma?"

"She already knows how to work as part of a family."
Nadine grimaced. "We should have had this talk before. When
we get home, we will speak."

Rookhaven landed on Maddy's shoulder. He gripped her
ear and tugged. "If we get home. If we get home." The dim light
flickered.

Nadine shook her fairy light. "Blast it!" Quille's fairy lights
never burned down. Except this one was. And so was Maddy's.
Burning down. A trilobite dashed out from under Maddy's toes
in the flickering half-light.

"Extinguish your lights," Nadine called out. "We may need
them later."

Stars danced in the blackness. When Maddy closed her
eyes, the stars were still there. A chill wind whistled down the
stairwell, carrying the odor of wet stone. All Maddy could hear
was Quille's labored breath and dripping water somewhere up
ahead. Nadine's palm pressed against Maddy's back. Maddy
started forward.

"Ouch," Emma said.

"Sorry," Maddy whispered. Maddy pressed her palm
against Emma's back and left it there. She started forward when
Emma began to move.

Nadine's hair tickled Maddy's neck when she whispered in
Maddy's ear. "Shaky at first, but a nice recovery, daughter. Now
keep your head, and carry on."

"I will," Maddy whispered.

"I know it," Nadine whispered. "Silence now. And mind
your footing. Ignore anything you see."

"It might help if you closed your eyes," Emma said.

"Do you?" Maddy whispered.

Emma chuckled. "And miss the show?"

The fossils glowed a sickening whitish green. And they did move, proceeding down the stairway at a pace no faster than Maddy proceeded up. Up ahead, Quille's breath rasped in and out, his ashplant tapping steadily in time with his steps. Maddy closed her eyes and began to count.

"Two thousand three hundred and forty-five," Maddy said. They stood on a shallow landing behind a door that was twin to the one below. Quille leaned on his ashplant.

"Forty-two," Emma said.

"Forty-six, I said. Do not doubt me." Nadine unbuttoned her blouse and fished for her keys.

Uncle Leo lit his fairy light. "First time carrying a torch has ever done me any good." The light flickered but held as he grinned and craned his neck.

Quille tapped his cane and sparks flew. "It wouldn't be sorcery to push you down these stairs, Leonides."

"Out of character, Quilley," Uncle Leo said. Nadine undid another button and thrust her arm deeper in.

"There's not a man alive would blame me," Quille said.

Uncle Leo pulled his gaze away from Nadine's bodice and smiled at Quille. "You would."

Quille blinked.

The lock clicked.

"There are three women who would," Nadine said. She straightened her uniform that wasn't a uniform. She unholstered her weapon. "And all of them watching the two of you acting fools."

"Leonides Farrago is all roving eyes and empty talk," Emma said.

Quille let his breath out slowly. "Is he now?" Quille said. "And how would you know, daughter?"

The corners of Emma's lips curled up. "I read it in the letters to the editor."

"Stop baiting your father," Nadine said. "The newspaper said Leo and I are lovers. Am I expected to let that stand?"

"They imply," Emma said, "that Quille is a cuckold."

"What's a cuckold?" Maddy said.

Emma turned to Maddy. "A cuckold is a man whose wife is unfaithful, usually without his knowledge. It refers to the cuckoo bird that places its eggs in another bird's nest in order to—"

Maddy's face heated. "I get it."

"There was an illustration in last Friday's edition," Emma said. "Quille with the horns of a buck, and Nadine—"

Quille laughed. "I saw it." He stared at his hands.

"As did I," Uncle Leo said. His face was flush. "Eusebius, there's not a word of—"

Quille placed his hand on Leo's sleeve. "I know, my friend. I'm afraid I'm a bit on edge. Our little detour—"

"We're late," Nadine said. "Girls, get behind these two fools and shove. Now."

Once through the door, Quille caught Maddy's sleeve. "I'd like you to start reading the paper every morning."

"I will." Maddy swallowed. If Quille wanted her to do it, she would. She couldn't imagine a more unpleasant task, though. "Am I looking for anything in particular?"

"Anything that smells like a cage," Quille said. "One that might fit your old da."

"It would hurt you more if it fit Nadine," Maddy said. "I'll look for that first."

Quille placed his palm atop Maddy's head. His fingers lingered for a moment. "Did I tell you how much I love you, Maddy mine?"

Maddy took Quille's hand and tugged. "Every day, Dad. Now come on, or Nadine will shoot us both."

————

7

M addy spun around, taking it all in, stifling her disappointment. She'd expected better of Tan's palace.

Bare grey walls, devoid of any ornamentation. Wide, empty corridors of work-polished flagstones, stair steps rutted from eons of trudging feet. Dust in every corner but a few. Cobwebs in those. The yellowing ceiling high above, marked with mold and red-rimmed water stains. Rippled glass set in wide blackened mullions. The endless fog pressing against the panes like a shroud. The Nonesuch Palace made Mundane House seem a well-kept mansion of splendor.

Its Royal Highness's home was big, but so was the empty breadth of the ocean. Both were equally repelling. Though the ocean had one advantage. No one had tried to improve it. The ocean didn't reek of resentment. The Nonesuch Palace's dim hallways were wrong, horribly wrong, every stone grumbling of its placement, every pane of glass longing for the strand, lapping waves, and sunlight. Quille said the Nonesuch Palace had once been a mountain, carved and hollowed out over the ages. Whoever had done the carving hadn't considered the mountain's feelings at all. Maddy shivered with each step. The farther they moved from the Arduvulin Gate, the worse she felt. The Gate's powerful magic masked the underlying feelings of the Nonesuch Palace. But those feelings were there. The Nonesuch Palace wished no one well. Maddy's feet dragged. She found herself gazing longingly into the fog. The fog had no feelings. None that Maddy could sense, anyway.

Maddy had to run to catch up with her family. They passed three abreast through a pointed arch of finely carved stone, one with all the detail below shoulder-height chipped away. "This is a palace?"

"It is the Nonesuch Palace," Nadine said. "Its Royal Highness has...special needs."

"It looks like a tomb," Emma said. She shifted Madame Aubergine's basket on her arm.

"I've never seen a tomb," Maddy said.

"Now you have," Uncle Leo said. He tugged on the lapels of his coat as they approached a great bronze doorway, verdigris-tinted with age. Gold and alabaster statues flanked the doorway, figures of giant men. Taller than Uncle Leo, with pikes in their pale hands, finely carved and incredibly lifelike.

"Let me do the talking," Nadine said.

Quille chuckled.

Nadine glared at him. "What?"

"Nothing," Quille said.

Up close, the statues seemed to sleep, their eyes closed. Their pikes were braced against the wall and half as tall as the enormous doorway. One statue's breastplate was beaten and gilded into the shape of a many-rayed sunrise. The other's was gilded as well, inset with bright silver in the sharp-pointed shape of a crescent moon. The sunrise statue opened its eyes. Maddy stared into pink-rimmed red. The other opened its eyes as well. It glared at Uncle Leo.

"The Oortsgarten-Quilles to see Its Royal Highness," Nadine said.

The left-most statue sounded as if it needed a drink of water. "And the man with the cutlass?"

"Captain Leonides Farrago," Nadine said. "Madeleine Oortsgarten-Quille's uncle. Family."

The door guard sniffed the air. It spoke again in its rusty voice. Maddy tried not to stare at the garnet eyes set in its bloodless and immobile face. "Not a blood relative. From the Archipelago."

Nadine's nostrils flared. "He—"

"Long ago," Leo said. He took a step toward the door guards. The one on the right shifted. The tip of its pike nearly touched the bridge of Leo's nose.

Uncle Leo grinned. "No need for alarm, chaps." He stuffed his hands into his pockets.

"Captain Farrago is known to Its Royal Highness through his work as alchemical supplier to the Crown," Nadine said. "He is no stranger."

"He is from the Archipelago," the one holding the pike toward Leo's nose said. "Recently."

"Impossible," Nadine said. "He—"

"That's true." Leo shifted his feet and the pike followed him. "I deal in hard to find and difficult to obtain goods. One goes where the cargo is, my friend."

"One does not go to the Archipelago," the one on the right said. "Under any circumstances."

One of the valves of the door cracked open with a groan. Another alabaster-skinned creature stepped through. It was dressed in black, gold, and silver robes sweeping so low they dusted the floor, the fabric of the robe patterned again and again with bright suns and palest moons. Its hair was whiter than bone and would have been shoulder length had it not been pulled back severely from its pale forehead and secured by a ruby band at the nape of its neck. It turned its head side to side and scented the air. It paused, facing Maddy. Its eyes were red as blood. When Maddy looked into them, no one looked back. It was blind. All three of the pale statue-men were.

"Good," Nadine said. "Sir Silas—"

Silas's voice was little more than a whisper. "You're late."

"This one has lied to us." The sun guard touched Leo's nose with the tip of his pike. He flicked the blade up. A single droplet of blood swelled on the bridge of Leo's nose. "He first claimed to have been to the Archipelago long ago. Later he claimed to have recently come from there."

"He was born there," Sir Silas said. "And very likely he will die there." Sir Silas smiled. That smile made Emma's cold grin seem summer soft. "Is that not so, Captain?"

Uncle Leo shrugged. "I go where the cargo is. It's a living until it's not."

"Indeed," Sir Silas said. He held out his arm. "May I escort the guest of honor?"

Maddy looked to Nadine. Her mother nodded. Maddy swallowed once. Her breakfast wanted to leap out her throat. Maddy swallowed again and moistened her lips. She placed her hand on Sir Silas's sleeve just as Emma had taught her.

"Follow us," Sir Silas said. The great doors opened onto a splendid, musty hall. The walls were hung with rich tapestries. Between them stood suits of armor, some gold-chased and ornately engraved steel, others battered and bloodstained iron. All were neglected, rusty and age blackened, and terribly fierce with slit-eyed, beaked visors bent into scowling masks mimicking the faces of demons. The floors were parquet of oak overlaid with cartload after cartload of rich and water-stained carpets. High above, the carved and coffered ceiling caught the fog-shrouded light from cracked stained-glass windows, tinting it in fractured shades at war with the uniform greyness above.

"Albinism," Sir Silas said. "And hereditary blindness."

"Sir?" Maddy kept her eyes on the floor in front of her. The carpets were thick, and it would be easy to trip. The room reeked of moldy dampness and discontent, the floorboards beneath the carpets bent but not buckled.

"Those of us who serve in the Nonesuch Palace," Sir Silas said. "You do understand the curse on Its Royal Highness and Its Tanist?"

"That we see our souls reflected when we look at them?"

"Just so," Sir Silas said. He led Maddy slowly down the great hall toward another set of bronze doors matching the first. "All those who serve here are blind. Are born blind."

"Oh."

Sir Silas chuckled. "You imagine this a handicap."

"I—"

Sir Silas touched Maddy's lips with his fingers. There was no fumbling, merely a delicate touch, warm and gentle. "Speak your heart, girl."

The memory of Tan burned in her mind. To live without that memory would be unbearable. "That must be dreadful."

"In the olden days, the poorest of the poor would gouge their children's eyes out and bring them to the Palace," Sir Silas said. "Hoping they might be rid of a mouth to feed. Its Royal Highness is always in need of servants."

"That's horrible."

"Doubly so, since it did no one good. Only those born without sight are immune to the curse."

In Ghula, Maddy had seen many blind and crippled beggar children working the docks, accosting sailors for handouts. There was nothing like that in Arduvulin City. "What became of the children?"

"Its Royal Highness ate them."

Maddy's feet refused to move. She pulled her arm free. "What?"

"Come along. Its Royal Highness is not to be trifled with. You are expected for breakfast." Sir Silas smiled his cold smile.

"I will not." Maddy looked about for her family. They lagged behind, the guards preceding them and holding them to a stately walk.

"It won't eat you," Sir Silas said. "You saved Its Royal Tanist's life. It wishes to reward you richly. Most richly. You need only dine with It."

Maddy peeled her fingers free. She began walking back the way she came.

Sir Silas marched at her side. "It can give you what you want most in the world." His fingers dug into Maddy's arm. She tried to pull away, to no avail. Sir Silas was set like stone.

"Let go," Maddy said. She gazed up at Sir Silas's blind eyes, so red and so like her own. No wonder people drew back when they saw her up close.

"It can make you human," Sir Silas said.

"I am human," Maddy said. "Almost. Now let go."

"Fully human," Sir Silas said. He leaned in close. "No one would look at you and see a monster."

"I would," Maddy said. She stamped her heel down on Sir Silas's boot. His fingers faltered and she pulled free. Maddy ran. Sir Silas paced behind her, a walk just short of a run. Maddy skidded to a stop in front of her family.

"Let's go home," Maddy said.

Sir Silas clapped his hand on Maddy's shoulder.

Maddy twisted free. She took a step back and growled. No one touched her unless she let them. Not twice.

"Sir Silas," Uncle Leo said, "if you lay another hand on my niece, I doubt you'll get it back."

Quille slammed his ashplant against oak. The flooring rippled. He lobbed a matchstick onto the floor. Great slats of parquet tore free, thrusting the carpets aside. The flooring shifted and clacked together, tumbling, rising, piling one on the other, taking the shape of a man made of swirling, spinning timber. More of the wood tore free, linking, joining, stretching upward in a towering giant of animated oak. The oaken giant lumbered between Maddy and Sir Silas, arms pinwheeling, spread wide. Sheltering Maddy from Sir Silas.

Sir Silas smiled his wintery smile. "Overreacting, aren't we, Quille?"

"I take it you have no daughters." Quille's face glistened with sweat.

"Only sons," Sir Silas said. "Your wife has a hand musket pressed to the spine of one. Your Emma has a folding blade beneath the chin of the other."

"Then I suggest you do not so much as move toward my child," Quille said. "Maddy, come here."

"It eats children," Maddy said.

Quille's brow wrinkled. "Sir Silas eats children?"

"No," Maddy said. "Its Royal Highness. Let's go. Don't hurt them. Let's just go home."

"Its Royal Highness does not eat meat," Nadine said.

"And It doesn't cook Its vegetables." Uncle Leo's cutlass gleamed. "According to some."

"I told the girl one of the tales about Its Royal Highness," Sir Silas said. "The blind beggar story."

"Whatever for?" Uncle Leo said. "Everyone knows that's a lie."

Maddy's face burned. "I didn't." Her arms shook. Her whole body shook.

"There are so many who wish to curry favor with Its Royal Highness," Sir Silas said. "One needs be certain of motives."

"So you terrorize my daughter with these lies!" Quille's ashplant shifted and the oak golem swung a mighty fist.

"I tempt her with her deepest desire," Sir Silas said. "If she were only to dine with a monster. In this way, truth is revealed."

"When we found her, she was skin and bones," Uncle Leo

said. "And locked in a filthy cage on the deck of a ship crewed by monsters." Leo waved his hand. "Come here, Maddy." Leo put his arm around Maddy. "There was a full bucket of... dinner... in that cage." Leo cleared his throat. "Untouched."

"I've lost my appetite," Quille said. The oak golem collapsed in a clattering heap. Sir Silas leapt backward to avoid the falling mass of timbers. Quille flicked his pocket watch open. "Come here, all of you." Nadine and Uncle Leo held the guards at bay until the last moment. The world began to swirl as Quille counted down and his spell took hold.

"Oh." Maddy had forgotten. She'd promised Tan. Maddy whispered to her sister and let her fingers slip from Emma's at the last moment. Her family disappeared in a swirl of shifting fog and odorous steam. The last she saw of them was Nadine's outraged glare. This wasn't going to turn out well. But she'd promised Tan, and Maddy kept her promises.

Sir Silas toed a splinter of oak. "Well, lads, I don't know how I'm going to explain this to Its Royal Highness."

"Explain what?" Maddy said.

Sir Silas took a step back. "You—"

"I don't dine with monsters," Maddy said. "I can eat with Tan. I mean, Its Royal Tanist."

"But your family—"

"Thinks I'm as fragile as when they rescued me," Maddy said. "But I'm not." And she'd promised Tan she'd be there. To receive the trophy.

"That doesn't explain why you stayed."

"I should have known it was a lie when I heard the whole offer," Maddy said. "If Its Royal Highness could make me fully human, then it could surely cure blindness. I overreacted."

Sir Silas didn't know how to deal with the rucked-up flooring. Neither did his sons. Maddy helped the guards back to their posts before she picked up Quille's enchanted matchstick and pocketed it. The floor began to shuffle back in place.

Maddy took Sir Silas's hand and began to lead him toward the far end of the room.

"People aren't loyal to monsters," Maddy said. "Unless they're monsters, too. And even then, it's not really loyalty."

"What makes you think I'm loyal to Its Royal Highness?"

"Because you decided to test me without telling It."

"It might have doubted you and asked me to test you."

"No," Maddy said. "It was there. At the Spelling Bee. It knows the truth."

"And what of your family?" Sir Silas said. He wrapped his fingers around the gilded door handle.

Maddy swallowed. "She's going to be really mad," Maddy said. "But I told Emma I was staying." Uncle Leo had arranged for a carriage home. Maddy would commandeer it. "They'll understand." Understand and worry. Either way, Maddy had promised Tan she'd be there today, and Maddy kept her word.

Maddy smoothed her skirt. She stood up straight and tried to remember all the rules of etiquette Emma had drilled into her. Maddy knew how to act in polite company now. Even Nadine said so. All she had to do was get through this without getting frightened or angry. Maddy fixed the image of Tan in her mind. She touched Sir Silas's sleeve. "I'm ready."

Sir Silas tilted his head and nodded. "I believe you are." He twisted the door handles and pushed.

Maddy stood up straight and tried to keep from shaking.

8

A great wooden table ran the length of a long, narrow room. The floor was bare of carpets, being simple flagstones only, all a dull grey. The walls were stone as well, cleverly set, their color matching the fog struggling against the floor-to ceiling windows lining both of the longest walls. Maddy felt as though she stood surrounded by the fog on all sides, though a fog that grumbled. A poor relation to the silent, emotionless fog that slithered and slid along the streets and lanes of Arduvulin City, blanketing windows and doorways, creeping through cracks and mouse holes when it could.

The Nonesuch Palace seemed unplumbed for gas. Overhead, two massive wheel-shaped chandeliers studded with fairy lights burned without a sound. Their warm glow reflected from water glasses and hand-polished silverware. A long woven runner stretched the length of the table, worked in a complicated geometric pattern of rust red and iron black.

More than a dozen people sat at the table in tall, straight-backed wooden chairs, the chairs ornately carved, the wood so age blackened as to be unknowable. Farthest from her, just before the table plunged through a filigreed floor-to-ceiling screen of mahogany, were empty places for Maddy and her family. Hard, empty seats at the head of the enormous table. Every eyeball turned on Maddy when Sir Silas cleared his throat. Maddy stood up straighter just as Emma had taught her. Maddy squared her shoulders. Marching into battle, Emma called it. Finally, Maddy understood.

"Madeleine Oortsgarten-Quille," Sir Silas announced. His words were nearly drowned out by a commotion behind Maddy, the sound of a thousand birds taking flight. The air swirled in a whirlwind thick with the odor of rain-soaked leaves. A bolt of lightning danced from floor to ceiling before it arced off, struck a suit of armor, and sent a great helm clattering.

"And family," Nadine said. She sounded out of breath. Those seated at the table gaped and chattered. Someone laughed a high-pitched laugh that threatened to escalate into a scream. A pair of pale children dashed out through a hidden door in the mahogany lattice and began to put the armor to rights. Another pair raced to claim Maddy's street coat and those of her family.

Maddy had no sooner turned her head than Nadine's fingers slipped into hers and Nadine was at her side. "Eyes forward," Nadine whispered through barely cracked lips. She smiled a thin smile at the gathered throng. "We will discuss your behavior at home."

Sir Silas cleared his throat again. "And family."

Nadine escorted Maddy past all the people seated at the table to a chair just next to the filigreed screen, steering Maddy up one side of the table. Rookhaven, Uncle Leo, and Quille made the long walk up the other. When Maddy began to sit, the slightest pressure from Nadine's fingers held her standing. Maddy's neck heated. Her face felt as if it glowed cherry red. She couldn't do anything right.

Quille grimaced and flicked his pocket watch closed. His

face was slick with sweat. He had to lean on Leo in order to make it to his seat. Rookhaven perched on Leo's shoulder, peering side to side, as if sizing up the other guests. Last of all, Emma walked firmly behind, following Maddy, cat-basket looped over her forearm. Madame Aubergine cracked one eyelid, then another. When Maddy turned and met Madame Aubergine's gaze, she could feel the disappointment there. Quille wiped his handkerchief across his face and smiled at Maddy. His jacket sleeve bunched up beneath Leo's firm fingers. It seemed for an instant that the only thing holding Quille upright was the strength of his friend's grip. Uncle Leo did not smile. That sealed it. Maddy had really done something wrong this time.

Crying about it would only make it worse.

"All rise for Its Royal Highness, Sovereign of Arduvulin and Emperor of the Fogbound Realm."

Maddy tried to study the other guests as they rose. There were the three Sisters from the Spelling Bee; Sister Agnes, Sister Blue, and the iron-hard Sister Kale. The Spelling Bee himself was in attendance dressed in his yellow and black livery. Maddy noted those she didn't recognize. A bushy-haired man with a thick, drooping mustache, whose gaze kept darting toward Nadine. A thin man in a black suit, his head shaved bald, including his eyebrows. He grunted and mumbled, "Farrago."

Uncle Leo frowned and kept his gaze fixed on the man for the longest time.

In addition, there were two of the Folk, both women, probably. One was wrapped in a glamour so tight nothing of his or her true nature slipped past. It had chosen to wear the disguise of a beautiful fae woman, a woman only slightly more beautiful than the other representative of the Folk. That little contest meant they were both women, almost certainly.

A threadbare man and a woman in a wrinkled gown were

seated closest to Maddy's family, one on either side of the table. She had a sketchpad in her hands. He had a pen and tablet. Maddy's gaze brushed across and rebounded from the rest of the spectators, all of them human seeming, and all of them surely waiting for Maddy to do something horrid or embarrassing. Or both. Something more horrid and embarrassing.

"Be seated," a rumbling voice said from behind the screen. Its Royal Highness. Tan's...something. Nadine said it wasn't right to think about Its Royal Highness in terms of father or mother. Forebear. Predecessor. Nadine searched for a dozen more words before settling upon progenitor.

Maddy didn't dare try to peer through the screen with so many watching. It wouldn't be long until she could see Tan again. When Tan presented her with the trophy.

Servants began to circulate about the table, pale boys and girls, all of them with the same strange garnet eyes as Sir Silas and his sons. Their blindness didn't seem to hinder their efficiency. Soon the table was laid out with bowl after heaping bowl of fresh vegetables. Uncle Leo studied a forkload of cauliflower before his gaze met Nadine's. He winked as he plunged the mouthful of uncooked crispness between his lips. Nadine did not smile. She hadn't touched a thing on her plate. She kept glancing across the table at Quille, who sat hunched and pale in his chair. He leaned forward, left hand gripping the table edge, his shoulders rocking back and forth with each labored breath.

"We had a rather uneventful return," Emma said to Maddy. "Straight here, no detours."

"Oh." No being pulled off course into Night, no having to climb thousands of stairs. "I'm sorry," Maddy said. "I'd forgotten I'd promised Tan, and—"

"We shall discuss this later," Nadine said. "Emma, take your sister in hand."

Maddy's mouth was very dry. Her eyes felt as if they might burst into tears at any moment.

"Note who attends," Emma said, as if Maddy hadn't heard their mother at all. "You know the Sisters of St. Alselm's. Agnes, Blue, and Kale."

Maddy nodded. "And I know the Spelling Bee."

"I doubt it," Emma said. "Pierre Reynard. That is his given name. He trades under the registered trademark *Reynardine*."

"Quille hates Reynardine," Maddy whispered. "He says their products are rubbish."

"Reynard isn't half the enchanter Quille is. And he is a factor."

"Oh." Maddy studied the Spelling Bee. He had curiously orange eyebrows and smelled of cutting oil. "That's why Quille hates him."

"You have no idea what a factor is," Emma said.

"A factor buys the work of other enchanters at a discount. He sells that work at a profit. Without attribution."

"With his name on their work," Emma said. "Did you ever wonder what happens to the losers at the Spelling Bee, those who almost made the cut?"

"No," Maddy said. She had mostly thought of Tan since the Spelling Bee.

"Reynard has a room, a workshop, on Merlin Street."

"That makes sense," Maddy said. "A posh address could help sales."

"Well, at that posh address are scores of young enchanters; half-trained, working like slaves, and poorly compensated. And Pierre Reynard, our good and benevolent Spelling Bee, lording over them all. Giving the unfortunate losers a second chance to prove their worth. Working permanent spells, Maddy. And he keeps the profits."

"I'll bet no one forces them to work for him," Maddy said. "It doesn't sound all that bad."

"They grow old and die. He does not," Emma said.

"Then they should quit," Maddy said. "And start their own businesses."

"They're half-trained," Emma said. "How can they?"

"Emma." Nadine glared at Maddy's sister. "Keep your voice down. And your politics to yourself."

"The Professor is not looking well," the threadbare man seated next to Nadine said. He placed his pen and tablet on the table. He smiled.

Nadine never took her eyes off Quille. "It's been a busy day."

"I imagine," the man said. "A busy two days for the old devil."

Quille heard that. His eyes swiveled to peer at the man. He coughed into his handkerchief.

"Who are those Folk?" Maddy said. Both of them stared at her.

"On the right, Queen Aevil," Emma said. "Chief Deemster of the Silly Court. On the left, the Hag of Barna, the sole Deemster of the Serious Court." Emma frowned.

"She's in a glamour," Maddy said. "How do you know that's who it is?"

"Who else could it be?" Emma leaned in close. "No one has seen the Hag in a thousand years. She is recently returned to Arduvulin. Rumor has it she is hideous, vengeful, and unseemly haughty and proud. Look at the way she vies with Aevil."

"Trounces her, if you ask me," Maddy said. The Hag of Barna's glamour was impeccable. "Doesn't Queen Aevil have any magic?"

"Not that sort," Emma said. "They say the Hag is an enchanter."

"Folk can't be enchanters," Maddy said.

"You are," Emma said.

"I'm not Folk," Maddy said. "My birth-mother was from Hell."

"There is no such thing as Hell," Emma said.

"We've had this argument," Maddy said. Emma didn't know what she was talking about.

Uncle Leo leaned forward in his seat. He addressed the threadbare man. "I haven't had the pleasure of your acquaintance Mr.—"

"Call me Goodfellow," the man said. "Justice Goodfellow."

"Leonides Farrago," Uncle Leo said. "Is that handle your real name?"

"Bolive Defarish," the woman across from Goodfellow said. "That's the name he was born with." She stopped sketching on her pad and grinned.

Nadine's eyebrows angled down. Her brow wrinkled. She gazed at her plate in thought. "I know that name."

Maddy tapped Emma on the shoulder. "Who is the man with the big mustache?"

"Detective Nightingale."

Maddy sucked in her breath. "No."

"Yes. Quille's one-time rival for Nadine's hand. At least according to Nightingale."

Maddy frowned at Nightingale. "It's like Its Royal Highness gathered all our family's enemies together."

"Gather ten people and eight would hate Quille," Emma said. "If two of them had never heard of him. See that bald-headed man?"

"Yes." Maddy had noticed him right away.

"His name is Esmond Larque. He gets along with Quille. Quille sometimes buys things from him."

"Bolive. Like the berry or the fruit prepended with a plosive?" Leo glanced at Quille. "What of the olive? Berry or fruit?"

"Fruit." Quille pushed his handkerchief into his pocket.

"Though berries are a class of fruit as well." Maddy's dad looked a little less winded, a little more himself. "Nadine, perhaps you might like to exchange seats with me." Quille leaned on his ashplant and stood.

Nadine stood. "He said his name was Goodfellow."

"He didn't say that was his name," Emma said. "He implied it. Then the woman with the sketchpad claimed that he pretends his name is Goodfellow. One would imagine that to be the sort of information best kept to oneself."

The woman next to Goodfellow snorted. "I told him as much. What's the point of writing under a pseudonym if you run around declaring yourself to be that person?"

"I stand by every word," Goodfellow said.

Nadine and Quille were forced to exchange places by passing the long way around the table.

"Esmond Larque is Leonides Farrago's fiercest competitor," Emma whispered.

"So he hates Uncle Leo," Maddy said.

"With a passion," Emma said. "Larque is alchemist to the Enclave of St. Anne."

"Oh." Uncle Leo was alchemist to Its Royal Highness. Uncle Leo would have nothing to do with St. Anne's or St. Anselm's. Persuading him to attend the Spelling Bee had been a chore.

When Quille and Nadine were farthest away Uncle Leo leaned across the table. "I don't suppose you're related to a certain Goodfellow who writes for the *Times*."

The man bowed and swirled his hand in a flourish. "Unmasked." When he looked up, the smile retreated from his face.

Nadine settled into the seat next to Leo. Quille leaned heavily on Goodfellow's shoulder. He dropped into the seat next to the newspaperman.

Nadine had her business face on. She leaned across the

table. "You are the worm who spreads corruption. Is this not so?"

"You've a rather unusual accent, Madame." Goodfellow's lips peeled back from his teeth. His grin had ceased to be a smile. "Beatrice, perhaps you would like to sketch the happy couple as they sit side by side and chit chat."

Nadine's gaze turned to the woman. "And you are the artist who illustrates these disgusting fantasies?"

"Beatrice Cannon," the woman said. She shrugged before she picked up her pen and pad. She began sketching, glancing up now and then at Nadine and Leo. "It's a living."

"Cannons are made to be fired," Uncle Leo said.

"Oh, I have been, Captain." Beatrice laughed. "Don't think I haven't heard that one before. Cannons are forged of stern metal. Could you maybe lower your chin a little? You've a little too much neck showing."

"You are all public figures," Goodfellow said. "Fair game. It's all about circulation. Nothing personal."

"Our children aren't," Quille said. "Public figures."

"Oh, this one is," Goodfellow said. He hooked his thumb toward Maddy. "From now on."

"Circulation can be cut off." Emma smiled her perfectly cold, perfectly deadly smile. "It will be, if you don't leave Maddy alone."

"*The Times of Arduvulin* doesn't respond to threats," Goodfellow said.

"I don't see Emma Sunbury smiling at *The Times of Arduvulin*," Leo said.

"Personal threats don't frighten me, either," Goodfellow said.

Quilled drummed his fingers on the tabletop for a moment before he turned to face Goodfellow. "Don't they?"

Goodfellow lurched back in his seat. The blood drained from his face.

Beatrice Cannon stiffened and stifled a scream before she began sketching wildly.

Quille was normally the most mild of men. When he was angry, though, he had a look that could peel paint. Maddy was pretty sure he had a look that could flay skin off bones, too. If Quille was a sorcerer. But he wasn't. Not yet. It wasn't a cage they were trying to fit Quille for. It was a hood, and a coffin.

Quille's voice was low with a bloodless character that made Maddy shiver. "My girls are—"

Emma nearly shouted, drowning Quille out. "Pleased to be so prominently featured." Emma glanced at Maddy and gestured toward Quille. Maddy's dad was about to do something irreversible. In public. "The attention really does so much for our prospects."

"This morning's illustration was particularly striking," Maddy said, aping Emma's tone. "You have an eye for the fantastic, Madame Cannon. Such big teeth I have." Maddy smiled a totally false, totally toothless grin at Beatrice Cannon.

Quille leaned back in his seat, his gaze never leaving Goodfellow's terrified eyes.

The color began to return to Beatrice Cannon's face. She cleared her throat. Twice. "So many fail to appreciate the nuance of caricature. I thought the blazing pupils were a nice touch, personally." Cannon wiggled her ringless fingers. "But it's Mademoiselle."

"There's a shocker." Leo leaned back in his seat and munched a carrot.

Nadine gasped. "There is no need to be cruel, Leonides. Do not stoop."

Quille's gaze shifted and softened at Nadine's words. Goodfellow used the lull to shove his seat further away from Quille's.

"No," Quille said. "There is not. Thank you, my dear."

"Look," Cannon said. "I like it this way. I have a career, and I don't need any man to—"

"You are to be admired," Emma said. "I imagine you have overcome many obstacles. It must be a great accomplishment, this independence."

"Now you're making fun," Cannon said. "But it's true."

"I am not making fun," Emma said. "I imagine it must be difficult, being mocked and derided at every turn. Having lies concocted to explain your unconventional lifestyle. Having to suffer. For your perfectly harmless though atypical behavior."

"I see what you're trying to do." Cannon shifted in her seat. "But it won't work. I'm not a..."

"A what?" Emma said. "A Sapphic?"

Cannon bobbed her head as she gazed at Maddy's family, one at a time. "A public figure." Cannon scribbled out something on her pad. She flipped to a new page and began to sketch.

"We'll see," Emma said, though Maddy doubted Beatrice Cannon heard.

"You are rather tongue-tied, scrivener," Leo said.

Goodfellow's voice shook. "I don't see any point in—"

Sir Silas struck a crystal gong with a leather beater. "Come to order. Its Royal Highness will speak."

Maddy glanced down the table. There were many people seated, some she recognized now and some she didn't. All were hanging on her family's words and behavior. When she glanced at Goodfellow he leaned back. He crossed his arms and smiled. He had surveyed the audience as well. He seemed well satisfied. Maddy felt a chill pass through her, a chill that had nothing to do with the way Its Royal Highness's voice resonated in the chamber with the grumbling tone of dragon bones.

9

"We are honored to preside over the one thousand and fifteenth presentation of the All-Arduvulin Spelling Bee trophy to this year's champion."

Its Royal Highness spoke on, but Maddy found it impossible to listen to Its words. Its voice was not unusual in any way, other than its similarity to Tan's voice, and the similarity to the voices of the dragon bones whispering in the cavern of the Arduvulin Gate.

Quille said that not everyone could hear the dead, could understand the captured voices of the essences trapped in objects. Maddy found that odd. She always had—heard the voices, that is. And worse, she felt the disposition of their deaths. That was why Mundane House was so peaceful and such a fine place to live. Even the stuffed dragonlet in Quille's study was honored to be there.

In the Nonesuch Palace that was not the case. The mahogany screen between her and Its Royal Highness was satisfied with its purpose. The table was not. It was carved from a single great tree of a sort Maddy didn't recognize. It dreamed of mountains, and mist, and cool nights and sunny days. It had not chosen this use. Likewise, the silverware, and the place settings, even the flowers that decorated the centerpieces were reluctant participants to this event. The silverware was ancient, mismatched, and even the most quiescent of the enormous set longed for a past where hard rock embraced it. No effort, no effort at all had been expended to make these objects feel at home. And, most importantly, needed and cherished. Its Royal Highness was no enchanter. To live in a home populated with such grumbling and reluctance would drive a sensitive person mad.

Nadine tugged on Maddy's sleeve. "You're to rise and receive the trophy from Its Royal Highness."

"Oh." Maddy jerked out of her seat. "Tan is to present the trophy."

Nadine frowned. "Weren't you listening? Its Royal Tanist regrets It cannot attend."

"Oh." But Tan promised. Maddy didn't know what to do. She hadn't been listening.

"Its Royal Highness wishes you to approach the screen." Nadine pointed. "There is a doorway. To the left of the armor."

"Oh." Maddy saw the faint outline of the doorway.

"It is waiting," Nadine said. "It lacks patience."

Maddy licked her lips. She took the six steps to the doorway. Six was a very unlucky number. She took one more tiny step. Seven was lucky. She stood before the doorway and it looked no different than the rest of the screen. Where was Tan? Tan had promised to be here, to present her with the trophy. To see Tan again was the only reason she was here.

After a moment, the doorway cracked open a handsbreadth. It cracked open the width of a forearm. A very small forearm. A scratching sound issued from near the floor. Maddy looked down just as the door gap widened and a dark stick pushed a repulsive amber object across the threshold. The stick retreated and the doorway snicked closed with certainty.

The Spelling Bee trophy was a massive lump of amber carved in the shape of a beehive. Maddy wanted to step away from it. There were insects trapped inside, frozen in amber. Some were confused, but others, the majority of the trapped creatures, were furious. Maddy took another step back.

"Pick it up," Its Royal Highness said. "It is yours, for a year and a day."

"I don't want it." The words were past Maddy's lips before she could stop them. She wanted Tan. This whole day was nothing, was worse than nothing without Tan.

"Nevertheless, you have earned it," Its Royal Highness said. "It is your duty to care for. For a year and a day."

"No." That wasn't her duty. Her duty was to her family, and to Tan, and to no one else. Maddy was as certain of this as anything in the world. "Where is Tan?"

"Indisposed," Its Royal Highness said. "Do you refuse this honor?"

Maddy heard the whispering behind her, many voices, not just of outraged serving plates and salt shakers, but of the others, the living witnesses assembled here to participate in this foul travesty. Maddy glanced again at the hideous thing she had won. There was something utterly wrong with the world if saving a life earned her that.

"That's no honor." Maddy's feet had a mind of their own. When she turned, she felt the outraged gaze of Its Royal Highness's guests as a physical wave. There wasn't an eye fixed on her that didn't cast repulsion and anger toward her. Not an eye save Quille's bright gaze. Nadine stared at the flagstones. Maddy didn't have to bear up under her mother's mortified gaze. Uncle Leo seemed puzzled. Rookhaven hopped from foot to foot, his dark eyes shifting from the trophy to Maddy's face. Madame Aubergine slept. Emma's face was the same placid mask she always wore. But the others. They didn't understand. They couldn't feel the rage the trophy spit out in burning beams. If she closed her eyes, Maddy was certain that she would still see it, a baleful lantern of anger and hate.

"It is yours," Its Royal Highness said. "For a year and a day. Take it away when you leave."

Maddy couldn't bring herself to touch the trophy. Uncle Leo stood slowly and crossed to Maddy's side, a long, silent walk around the table and past the spiteful eyes of the Sisters and the Spelling Bee himself and all the rest, one by one, until he knelt slowly and picked up the trophy. He cradled it in his arms.

"It can't hurt you, Maddy."

Uncle Leo was a good man, a great man, but he didn't understand. It already had.

"I think we should go."

He held his arm out for Maddy but she jerked away. She had saved that touch for Tan.

The disgusting little newspaper reporter laughed out loud. "Now that's good copy." He picked up his pen and began scribbling lies, a crooked smirk on his face. He stuffed a peppered cracker into his petty little mouth and chewed, speaking with his mouth full. "Brilliant copy."

Maddy had had enough. There was more than one kind of magic. Maddy wasn't much of an enchanter. Not yet. She hadn't been studying human ways for long. But she was born a magical creature—a half-magic creature, anyway—and people like Maddy had their own magic. *Like finds like.* That was old magic. What Quille called true magic. It was why humans burned their hair and fingernail clippings, lest someone magical find them and use them. The pepper pot grumbled as Maddy passed. There was pepper on Goodfellow's tongue. It was easy enough to spell the contents of the pepper pot into the man's filthy lying gob. Maddy melted the pepper pot into the shape it chose for itself as she passed. One good deed deserved another.

Justice Goodfellow clasped his throat and bellowed. He spewed a black cloud when Uncle Leo clapped him on the back.

"Pimiento, Quilley." Uncle Leo clapped hands with Maddy's Dad and pulled him from his seat. "Now is that a vegetable or a fruit?"

"Vegetable," Quille said. "Your peppers are a class of vegetable." Quille tapped his bony finger on Goodfellow's writing pad. "Make sure you get your facts straight for the late edition, Bolive."

Quille pulled out his pocket watch. "Come here now, family mine."

"I think we'll ride this time, Quilley." Uncle Leo gestured toward the distant doors before he smiled at Maddy. "Your carriage awaits, my princess."

"I'm not anyone's anything," Maddy said, but she knew that was a lie as soon as the words were past her lips. She watched the faces of Its Royal Highness's guests as their gazes followed her.

"You're your father's daughter," Uncle Leo said. "That's pretty plain."

Right. And now she was a whole host of people's enemy. She felt their anger and disgust following her out the door. She couldn't wait to read this evening's paper.

Nadine's face was set in stone as she marched in front of Maddy and Uncle Leo. The man with the wild hair and droopy mustache, Detective Nightingale, tried to catch Nadine's attention as she passed. Maddy's mother ignored him, just as she ignored her embarrassing daughter as Maddy trailed behind her. The man with the shaved head, Esmond Larque, followed Maddy with his gaze, and there wasn't anything nice about the look on his face as Maddy passed nearby. One of the Folk, Queen Aevil, touched Emma's fingers as Emma passed.

The Hag of Barna slept. Maddy could hear her soft snoring.

Maybe the Hag was related to Madame Aubergine. Or maybe, after she'd lived to be a thousand years old, she had witnessed every possible way a girl could make a fool of herself. And disgrace the people who cared for her. Whose love she'd failed to be worthy of.

This fiasco was all Maddy's fault. Again. She paced at Leo's side, even forgetting to hold her spine straight. Emma's whispered words jerked Maddy upright. She'd been perilously close to loping out the doors on all fours. Maddy's face burned all the way to the carriage. It blazed and roasted a thousand times brighter under the force of Nadine's blistering tongue-lashing. Not that Maddy hadn't deserved every word.

Quille retired early, exhausted. Uncle Leo departed for the Docklands. Maddy stayed up a little later, but eventually she crawled into bed, Spelling Bee trophy beaming rage from the small bookcase beneath her windowsill. It should have been impossible to sleep under such an assault, but Maddy was beat, and in time she faded into a restless and heaving slumber. She was certain that she would wake in moments, to pace another darkness through the hideous and dusty ruin of Night.

10

The next morning, Maddy climbed the stairs to Quille's workroom. She could have taken the lift, but she needed time to think. Putting one foot in front of the other again and again gave her that. The day began with a cold rain, the wind whipping it sideways. Maddy dashed across the muddy yard where a normal home's gardens would be. She caught her shattered reflection in rippled puddles again and again, her tangled hair flying wild across a slate-grey background, a fitting setting given her feelings. Nothing, absolutely nothing, was working out as she planned.

She had expected to see Tan yesterday. But Its Royal Tanist was "indisposed." That could mean anything at all, from a lack of desire to see Maddy ever again, to an illness that caused Tan to reluctantly miss the ceremony, to physical confinement against Tan's will. Maddy needed to discover which it was, because she'd promised Tan that she would be there. If Tan didn't want her as a friend, she would have to live with that. She just couldn't imagine Tan felt that way, so he must be hurt or in trouble.

The Spelling Bee trophy was an abomination. It was discontent incarnate, and it didn't matter if no one besides Quille and Maddy could tell. There was no getting away from it, either. It had followed her into Night, where it glowed so hideously that it physically hurt to view it. That was why she was heading to Quille's workroom this morning. To talk over the subject with him. To come up with a plan of action. It was always foolish to think too long about a topic before discussing it with Quille. Inevitably, Quille knew some detail, some trivial fact Maddy had overlooked that changed everything. It was better to not even think about the trophy until she'd talked to Quille. Still, the object was so balefully malevolent, and it was in her bedroom. Perhaps sheathing it with lead would shutter its hideous emanations. Quille would know.

Maddy had made a total hash of the trophy presentation and, as a result, made enemies. When Nadine's anger cooled, she said that was an overstatement, that most of those in attendance were already Quille's enemies. But Maddy had made things worse, and not in anywise better with a single person. She had insulted the Spelling Bee and the Sisters of St. Anselm's, she had insulted Its Royal Highness, and she had made a spectacle of herself and her family in front of the very people who wanted nothing better.

She'd even looked a fool in front of the Folk, and they were dangerous people. The Folk weren't forgiving like humans. They never forgot a slight. If Maddy had offended the Folk, then she was in a world of fresh trouble.

She had just been shocked, truly shocked, when Its Royal Highness shoved the trophy at her. He might as well have buried her in offal. It was that bad. But she was supposed to be an adult now, and beyond such shocks.

Emma wouldn't have flinched. Emma would have been cool under pressure and taken whatever Its Royal Highness dished out, all the while planning how she might even the score in private, without witnesses and without any incriminating trail of evidence. Maddy had been so stupid and so juvenile, and that was the worst part. She'd acted just as one might expect a beast-child to. With no consideration for the feelings of others.

It was a long way up the shot tower to Quille's chambers. It had to be, in order to drop the molten lead, silver, or magic-imbued alloy and have it form into a perfect sphere before it struck the cold liquid of the cooling vat far below. Quille might have put in a handrail, but the idea wouldn't have occurred to him. He'd constructed an enchanted lift instead. The stairs were for emergencies only. Maddy looked down. Way, way down. This was an emergency. Maddy was more than halfway up, but she wasn't even breathing hard until she'd looked down and remembered yesterday's ugly detour.

There was no denying that there was something strange about Quille's pocket-watch transporter when Maddy was part of the party. She'd sucked her entire family into Night, and that shouldn't have been possible. Then Quille had to navigate back to the real world by using the Arduvulin Gate as a magical beacon. And he was expecting her to have an answer for his question. *What would happen if all the power in the Arduvulin Gate broke free?*

Maddy had thought about that over breakfast, but really there were other things to think about then. The picture of an angry Quille in the paper was terrifying, not because it was a caricature, but because it wasn't. The sketch of Maddy turning her back on Its Royal Highness and turning her nose up at the most celebrated trophy in all Arduvulin was better than the last drawing of Maddy at the Spelling Bee. Her fangs didn't jut, and she didn't have a dog's muzzle in this picture, but her eyes still blazed with a hellfire flame, and she looked like just the sort of girl she didn't want to be. One who thought she was something special.

No one was surprised at the pictures, or the accompanying story, except Emma couldn't shut up about how big Uncle Leo's feet appeared in Beatrice Cannon's illustrations. Uncle Leo protested, saying that they appeared proportionally correct to him. He would consult his boot maker to settle the dispute. Nadine shushed the pair of them. She thought Quille looked quite fierce and handsome in his illustration, very protective of his children and exceedingly trim. She suggested that Quille might like to begin taking a morning constitutional. Just to settle breakfast. Maddy liked that idea, and she volunteered to go with Quille. Quille agreed that they could start tomorrow or the next day. Or next month.

There was something Maddy was forgetting, but she could think about that later. She'd made it to Quille's workroom door. She hammered the knocker against its anvil. She glanced down. That was a long way to fall. Maddy shivered. The cooling pool looked very wet. Maddy hated getting wet.

Quille's pince-nez perched on the tip of his nose. His eyebrows rose when he saw it was Maddy knocking. "I didn't hear the lift."

"I walked." Maddy shoved past her dad and into his parlor. She flopped down on the divan, a bouncy horsehair-stuffed affair that was her favorite piece of furniture in the whole world. She'd spent many hours curled up, book in hand, with Quille at his worktable and Nadine napping in the lounging chair after a hard day's work. Quille's workrooms were the best rooms in all Mundane House. Perched atop the shot tower, they were private and cozy and above the perpetual fog that blanketed most of Arduvulin.

They were also adjacent to Quille's library. Even though Quille kept his books on permanent magic under lock and key, there was so much to learn, so many words and ideas Maddy would one day be permitted to explore. Maddy could spend eternity in these rooms and never feel like she'd missed a thing going on outside. Quille said that was a sure sign Maddy was an enchanter at heart. Maddy liked that idea very much. That she was more than what she saw reflected in other people's eyes.

Quille scooted his desk chair over to face Maddy. Madame Aubergine hopped up onto the divan and circled before settling in, nose to tail. She closed her eyes and purred as Maddy stroked her luxurious fur.

"You've remembered my question," Quille said. "Good girl." He tented his fingers over his ample waistcoat and waited.

"I really wanted to talk about the lantern." Maddy scrubbed the toe of her shoe across the extravagantly patterned carpet. "I can't get comfortable with it in my room."

Quille chuckled. "I thought I was the opaque one in the family." He inched his chair closer. "Whatever are you talking about?"

"The lantern of rage." Maddy thought for certain that Quille could feel it. "The device Its Royal Highness foisted on me yesterday."

Quille tilted his head as if remembering. "You mean the Spelling Bee trophy?"

Maddy crossed her arms and sucked in her breath. She leaned back against the cushions. She was so certain Quille could feel the wrongness. "That's what they call it. And maybe it is, but that's not all it is. I was hoping you could make a cover of lead for it. Or something."

"Back up," Quille said. "You mean to say yesterday's theatrics weren't simply a response to Its Royal Tanist's absence?"

"What?" Maddy gripped the arm of her seat. "That's what you thought?"

Quille glanced away. "Well—"

"How could you think so little of me?" Maddy found she was standing. "I would never embarrass you like that over something so... trivial."

"I wouldn't call such a thing trivial," Quille said. "Not when it involves your deepest feelings, and—"

"Those are private, Dad. Not something I would trot out for others to gape at." No matter how much it hurt that Tan had lied to her. Had broken a promise. Maddy paced back and forth. "Anyway, Tan might have been ill, or some emergency may have demanded Tan's attention, or any number of circumstances might explain Tan's absence, important circumstances that I'm not yet privy to." Maddy had made that mistake once with Nadine and she had no intention of repeating that embarrassment.

Quille studied his boots.

"What do you know, Dad?" Maddy knelt before her father. "Tell me."

"Your mother is best at this sort of thing."

"She'll try to sugarcoat it." Maddy held her father's hand. "Is it something I did?"

"No," Quille said. His gaze met Maddy's. "It is rather something that Its Royal Highness fears you will do."

"And it involves Tan?"

"Intimately."

Maddy's cheeks burned. She pulled her hand free. "How dare It? I would never—"

"It is not concerned with matters of virtue, Maddy." Quille waved for Maddy to come to him. "You're a good girl, and Its Royal Highness knows that. You may rest assured. It's rather the matter of the Gate, and its care, that troubles Its Royal Highness."

"What do I have to do with the Arduvulin Gate?"

"Not a thing," Quille said. "And that's the problem."

"I don't see how that can be a—"

"Its Royal Tanist speaks of nothing but you. Thinks of nothing but you. It neglects its duties."

Maddy felt a warmth spread from her solar plexus out to suffuse her limbs with fire. "That's—"

"You are a distraction, Madeleine Quille." Quille smiled. "You are too much of a good thing."

Maddy knew the feeling. There were hours when she thought of nothing but seeing Tan again, of hearing Tan's voice. It was painful, thinking of Tan so much, but she couldn't stop it. She didn't want to stop it.

"But—"

"I've argued in favor of infatuation. That by separating the pair of you, Its Royal Highness does nothing but prolong this state. Given time together, you would both find enthusiasm flag. Order would be restored. Novelty would fade."

"Like I'm a spanking-new puppy and Tan a fickle child."

"I believe those were my exact words," Quille said. "Give or take an adjective."

"You're wrong."

"So Its Royal Highness argued. It claimed superior knowledge gained through hard experience."

"Its Royal Highness doesn't want me to see Tan."

"Its Royal Highness commands that Tan not see you." Quille leaned on his ashplant. "This has the same effect, but quite different consequences. For Its Royal Tanist."

"I don't understand."

"That is plain." Quille shoved to his feet. "Its Royal Tanist cannot see you. Its Royal Highness is thorough. Its Royal Tanist cannot hear, smell, or touch you, either. Am I missing any senses? Let's see..."

"Taste," Maddy said. This was horrible. It was wrong.

Quille's face colored. "Just so. How foolish. Five human senses. You know that gives me an idea. We so rarely use the sense of taste in enchantment." Quille lapsed into silence. He touched his tongue.

Maddy stomped her foot. "Dad!"

Quille looked up. "Eh?"

"Don't you dare." Maddy was tired of being manipulated or ignored. "How was this done?" Maddy's chin quivered. "This erasing of me from Tan's perceptions?"

"It's quite rudimentary," Quille said. "One would construct a filter—think of it as a very fine lace—and upon it suspend a synthetic inversion of those attributes of you that could be perceived. Any of these attributes passing through the filter would be cancelled by its sinister inverse. Then it is simply a matter of draping this construct about the subject."

"Is that what Its Royal Highness did?"

"That's one possibility," Quille said. He was silent for a good long time. "However it was done, it would have the same effect." Quille wouldn't meet Maddy's gaze.

"You did this," Maddy said. "You did this to me and to Tan."

"Well—"

"How could you?" Maddy stamped her foot. "How *could* you?"

"Reluctantly," Quille said. He rubbed the handle of his ashplant absently. "Very reluctantly."

"But you did it anyway." Maddy had thought she could trust her dad. She'd thought he was on her side.

"Maddy," Quille said. "I serve Its Royal Highness. I—"

"Can't think for yourself," Maddy said.

Quille's words were very precise when he spoke. His gaze met Maddy's and held. "You'll wish to reconsider this line of attack."

Of course he could think for himself. He was Eusebius Quille. The greatest enchanter in the world. And Eusebius Quille had done Its Royal Highness's bidding. Because Its Royal Highness's arguments made sense. To Quille. Who knew a lot more than Maddy. So much more that Maddy could study her whole life and maybe, just maybe, she'd be able to hold a conversation with Quille and follow his soaring thoughts for the length of an hour. Even ten minutes was beyond her now. That was a fact. An ugly, indisputable fact. But it was still wrong. He was supposed to be on her side.

Maddy crossed her arms. "This is just great."

"Great sometimes isn't an option," Quille said. "Sometimes good isn't an option, either. Your mother is much better at explaining these things than I am."

"So all I need to do is rip this lace off Tan and Tan would be able to see me?"

"No," Quille said. "That was a metaphor. It's more likely that Its Royal Tanist has been ordered dipped in the filtering material, head to toe. Or whatever."

"So I wash it off."

"Unlikely," Quille said. "Once it's dry, it's there. In time it should wear away."

"How much time?"

"That depends," Quille said. "In this case..." His hands jerked, palms up, while he considered. "Decades, at least. Until the danger has passed."

"What danger?"

Quille swallowed. "You."

"Perhaps It means to kill me with this baleful lantern," Maddy said. "That would solve the problem for It as well." This was so screwed up. It wasn't just Maddy being jerked around. It was Tan as well. "Tan will search for me," Maddy said.

"No doubt," Quille said. "But Its Royal Tanist will perceive only shadows and absence. Let's go see this lantern."

"Dad." Maddy placed her palm above her father's heart. She gazed up into his eyes. "It would destroy the world. If the power behind the Gate were to break free." Nothing less would cause Its Royal Highness to be so selfish and cruel. Nothing less would cause her father to hurt her so. To think otherwise would be treason. But it was still wrong. Its Royal Highness was wrong. And both her parents worked for It.

Quille nodded. "It would indeed. And not just our world. So you can understand Its Royal Highness's concern. Its duty, and Its Royal Tanist's soon enough, is to guard the Gate. Nothing is more important in all the world to our dear It."

"Not even love."

Quille shook his head slowly. "I often forget how young you are, Maddy mine." Quille squeezed Maddy's hand. "We'll take the lift, if it's all the same to you."

11

Quille poked the hateful lantern with his ashplant. "This is almost certainly what it appears to be. The Spelling Bee trophy."

"How do you know?" Nadine said. She peered over Quille's shoulder.

"It was in my possession for a year and a day. Some years ago."

"It rages," Maddy said.

"Does it, Eusebius?" Nadine's fingers strayed toward her sidearm.

"It might," Quille said. He adjusted his optics. "There is no small number of creatures captured in its matrix."

"That one," Maddy tapped the amber over the dragonfly imbedded nearest the surface. "And those three." She tapped again. "And that pair, and this one, and—"

"Can you tell what it is that disturbs them so?" Quille removed his pince-nez and polished them.

"Being trapped for all time in a tasteless and gaudy bauble," Nadine said. "It should be obvious."

"No," Maddy said. "That's not it." Not just that. "They repine."

"Of course one might fret, being trapped forever in a tasteless and—"

"I believe Maddy means they yearn," Quille said. He took a step back and scratched his chin.

"Right."

Nadine peered to the right before her eyebrows arrowed down. "Maddy, how many times have I told you—"

"Sorry. I mean correct Maddy's use of crypto-naturalist slang was distracting, according to her mother. Certain words were off limits unless they were used precisely.

"If it is harmful, we should destroy it." Nadine glanced at Quille. "At the very least, we should remove it from our home."

"I'm not certain," Quille said. "Its Royal Highness rarely does anything without reason."

Nadine huffed. "It is not omniscient. If Madeleine perceives a danger, then—"

"The trophy is unhappy," Maddy said. "It's not supposed to be here."

"Then it is dangerous." Nadine shoved past Quille. "We must destroy it."

"I'm not certain that's prescribed," Quille said. "Or safe."

"We can't leave it in our daughter's bedroom."

"If you say so," Quille said. "Maddy, you called it a lantern."

Maddy couldn't stand looking at the trophy anymore. She flopped down on her bed and buried her face in her pillow. "It is."

"What does it illuminate?"

Nadine touched Maddy's wrist. "Madeleine?"

She couldn't tell them. She couldn't tell anyone. She'd sucked her family into Night by accident once. They didn't belong there. No one did. No one but those pitiful creatures bound into the lantern. And her. Both parts of her. She thought Quille could feel it. He couldn't. It wasn't his problem. It was hers. Hers alone, now that she couldn't count on Quille to see it. Or on Tan to see her.

Maddy pushed her face into her pillow, drying her eyes, smothering her tears. She rolled over. She couldn't afford to act like a child anymore. She sniffed. "Maybe I'm imagining things. Maybe I'm just so disappointed about Tan. Its Royal Tanist. I'm probably overwrought." Maddy sat up.

Quille studied Maddy's face, searching for the lie.

Maybe she really was imagining things. "If Dad had it for a year and a day and it didn't hurt him, and all the other winners going back thousands of years—"

"One thousand and fifteen," Quille said.

"Ri—I mean correct," Maddy said. "Then I doubt it could hurt me. I'm being stupid."

"It is quite ugly," Nadine said.

"But it's probably not evil," Maddy said. She was glad she couldn't see the lantern. "Leave it be. I'll just have to grow up."

Quille didn't say a word.

Nadine didn't seem inclined to speak, either.

"Seriously," Maddy said. "Leave it. I won it fair and square. I guess I deserve it. I'm just being silly."

"You are many things, Madeleine." Nadine holstered her sidearm. "Silly you are not."

Quille seemed to make his mind up. "Quite the opposite, in fact. We will leave it. For now."

"It disturbs our daughter," Nadine said. "We should—"

"No," Maddy said. "I have to learn to live with it. Sooner or later."

Quille's mouth quirked into a grin. "Maddy, we will begin our morning constitutionals tomorrow." He seemed to find that idea immensely humorous. "I hope you can keep up."

Maddy sat up straighter. "Can Rookhaven come with us?"

"I doubt we'll be able to keep him away." Quille consulted

his pocket watch. "I believe Madame Aubergine may choose to join us as well."

"That would be great," Maddy said. Her dad wasn't as clueless as he let on. He had something to say. He just didn't want Nadine to hear it.

"Missing a breakfast or two won't hurt you," Nadine said.

"Oh, that won't happen," Quille said. "We shall depart at dawn."

Nadine snorted. "I'll believe it when I see it."

"That's what I love about my family," Quille said. "The skepticism."

"I prefer to think of it as honesty," Nadine said.

Quille kissed Nadine on the cheek. "And that, my dear, is why I cherish you."

             —————

12

There was really no good way to judge the moment of dawn in the Fogbound Realm. Maddy and Rookhaven waited in her bedroom until she heard the quiet rap of Quille's knuckles on her doorframe. She lurched out of bed, full dressed. Madame Aubergine pranced about, twining her way between Quille's ankles—and Maddy's.

Mundane House dominated a rather dilapidated part of Arduvulin City. Perhaps that was because of Mundane House itself, which, behind its high brick walls, resembled an industrial estate more than the manicured, grand home it once was. Quille's work demanded that he have a shot tower and a forge and a foundry and a vast roofed structure for assembly, and, according to Quille, great mounds of scrap. Nadine thought that a little much, but Quille was adamant. Besides his family, Quille's work was his life, and his work created a great deal of scrap. Quille's neighbors shared this affectation. Or perhaps they simply collected rubbish.

Rookhaven took flight, stretching his wings. Madame Aubergine paced ahead into the gloom. Quille walked incredibly slowly, ashplant tapping. Maddy could have crawled along and kept up.

"So," Quille said. "I don't doubt there's a problem with the Spelling Bee trophy."

"Then why did you pretend that you couldn't feel its anger?"

"I wasn't pretending," Quille said. "And that brings us to our little walk."

"But I thought—"

"Your mother sees evil behind every conflict," Quille said. "And there is only one way to deal with evil."

"I know," Maddy said. "Root it out and blast it to pieces."

"It's a very difficult job she has, and there is no more dangerous one."

"But we're not here to talk about Mom."

"In a way," Quille said, "we are. Enchantment is somewhat greyer than black and white. Like the fog, we feel our way along. Edges aren't so crisp."

"And Mom doesn't understand that."

"She understands it far too well," Quille said. "Our senses and our judgment, those are an enchanter's tools, save one. Should our tools fail, we fail. And the results all too often become the responsibility of the Department of Criminal Magic."

"I'm not certain it's evil," Maddy said. "The trophy."

"You don't know much about it, though." Quille glanced over at his daughter. "And I can't help. My senses tell me it is an unexceptionally ugly lump. Nothing magical about it at all. But my judgment tells me that my senses are wrong. Whom to believe?"

"Your judgment," Maddy said. That was pretty obvious. She thought about Tan, and what Its Royal Highness had done to Tan. And to her. Senses could be tricked.

"Well," Quille said. "There I find myself divided as well. My head says that my senses work perfectly fine, that the trophy is just as it appears. My heart wants to believe my daughter speaks the truth, and it soars at the thought that she may have discovered a hidden mystery that has eluded enchanters for over a thousand years. My head finds that fact hardest to rationalize. Particularly since the mystery eluded the great Eusebius Quille when the trophy was in his youthful and proud hands."

"Oh." Maddy had to stretch to step across a puddle. Maddy thought about Quille's problem. "Maybe something has changed between the time you had the trophy and I received it," Maddy said. "Maybe when you had it there was nothing to sense."

"Maybe."

"Or maybe, since I'm half magical, I have different senses, ones that you don't have."

"Possibly."

When Maddy thought about it there were dozens of possibilities. Only one of which was that she was imagining things.

"Someone ought to investigate," Maddy said.

"That is just the sort of thinking that gets enchanters into trouble," Quille said. "It's the sort of thinking that gets the world in trouble if we're talking about evil here."

"Oh," Maddy said. "What do you think I ought to do?"

"I think you ought to ponder your options, and use your senses and your judgment, and then decide for yourself." Quille grasped Maddy's arm. "Keeping in mind that you have resources, including your old da, and his judgment, honed by a vast amount of experience you've not had the misfortune to endure."

"What if it is evil?"

"It's always best to assume that it isn't," Quille said.

"Mom always assumes the opposite," Maddy said.

"And that is why we make such a powerful team," Quille

said. "Our null hypoteses overlap. You'll need your mother, or someone like her, if you decide to proceed."

"I don't know anyone else like her," Maddy said.

Quille turned back toward Mundane House. "Neither do I. So at the faintest whiff of evil, you go running to her."

"I haven't decided what I'm going to do yet."

"You're a Quille."

"I'm also an Oortsgarten."

"I see your problem."

Her dad didn't, though. See her problem. He was letting his judgment overrule his senses. It was very kind of him, and of Nadine, but she wasn't really either an Oortsgarten or a Quille. She was Maddy Dune, and there wasn't any way of changing that, and there wasn't any way of hiding it. All one had to do was look at her and it was plain. Now she'd discovered another difference that set her apart. She could sense things no one else could. No one fully human.

But that didn't mean no one else. Tan might be able to sense it.

"I may need access to your library," Maddy said. "If I decide to investigate."

Quille paused just outside the door to Mundane House. "You have it."

"All of your library, Dad."

Quille tilted his head and considered Maddy. She could almost feel the intensity of his consideration as a wave of heat or a beam of light focused on her and her alone. He dipped his hand into his pocket. He withdrew it and tossed her a key. "No permanent spells," Quille said. "I will have your promise, Maddy."

"No permanent spells," Maddy said. Permanent spells were a necessary part of enchantment. But they weren't healthy for the enchanter. Permanent spells changed the spellcaster. "I promise, Dad."

"And you'll keep that promise," Quille said. "I know it. I don't have to worry about Maddy mine on that account."

"You don't," Maddy said.

Breakfast was already on the table by the time Quille had his street coat off.

Nadine stopped Quille in the entry hall. "There's been a murder. Our services are required." She shoved Quille's street coat back into his hands.

"The murder method?"

"Sorcerous inversion."

"You don't need me then," Quille said. "I'll have my breakfast and—"

"You're coming." Nadine shook Quille's coat at him. Nadine glanced at Maddy before she pulled Quille away by the elbow. She leaned her forehead close to Quille's and whispered, "To the Nonesuch Palace."

Maddy's heart raced. "Not Tan!"

"No, sweetness," Nadine said. "Not Its Royal Tanist. Come, Quille, we must go."

"Who was it?"

Emma sauntered out of the breakfast room, toasted muffin in her hand. "Beatrice Cannon. The illustrator. The paper is already saying it was the work of The Fifteen."

"But the body was just discovered."

"It appears Miss Cannon was a public figure since before press time last night."

Nadine shook her finger. "Emma!"

"Don't expect me to feel sorry for someone profiting at the expense of others."

Maddy felt sick. "I thought she was rather nice. In person."

"Nice or not," Nadine said, "she is my responsibility now. Come along, Quille."

"Is there a need to hurry?" Quille eyed the breakfast room doorway. "If she has been dead since—"

"This is not how we work." Nadine shoved the street door open. "Quille, I do not wish to go alone."

"All right." Quille plucked the half-eaten muffin from Emma's hand. "Look after your sister, and try to get some sleep. You look as if you've been out all night."

"Yes, father."

Quille pulled an opened letter from his pocket and handed it to Maddy. "Run that up to my desk when you go."

"Can I read it?"

"Go on." Quille pulled his coat close. "Maybe you can make some sense of it."

The great doors of Mundane House slammed against their stops with a bang.

Emma leaned against the breakfast room doorframe. "You'll want to see the morning paper, Maddy. It has all the gory details."

"I need to wash up first," Maddy said. And she had seen enough gory details to last a lifetime with the crypto-naturalist pirates. She had no need to seek more out.

13

M addy had to hurry. She rushed up Quille's tower and placed the letter on his desk. She checked the time on Quille's noiseless repeater. She had time to peek. She plopped down into Quille's desk chair and thumbed through the letter. It wasn't that long if she ignored the illustrations and equations.

Dear Professor Quille,

I'll get right to it. As I thought I made clear, I do not know nor care who your mathematician friend is; magic is not a function of geometric and alchemical formulae. Or rather, not merely a function of geometry and alchemy. I will stipulate those facts on which we agree:

1) That, fundamentally, magical potential ebbs and flows in time. If you care to describe these ebbs and flows as cone-shaped gyres, you may do so. I do not see the point. You might as well say that magical potential resembles the tides, or the rising and setting of the sun, or the cycle of birth and redeath. I will further stipulate, though you could state this more clearly, that self-similar magical forces ebb and flow in those beings resident in the world. I am of the mind that these forces exist in beings only, and that any forces attributed to the world per se are simply the aggregate of forces seated in beings. For practical purposes there is no meaningful difference. To quote your own words, "There exist no acts without actors."

2) That there is more than one class of magic, and that these classes of magic oppose one another. Your classifying magic as dexter or sinister seems both too weak and too strong. Too weak, because it implies that one might, through nurture, change one's natural-born handedness; and too strong, because it burdens these opposing forces with values they do not possess. If you wish to say that magic may be classified as good or evil, then say so directly; do not hint at it through overloaded euphemisms. In any case, you are mistaken. Is the gas lamp evil because it shortens the peaceful hours of the night? Is the bonfire good because it roasts a meddlesome saint? Surely a rational man would not judge the properties of flame solely by its fuel, or hold the flame to account for the results of its application.

3) That the classes of magic practiced by the living and the dead are related. On this we agree fully, though I believe you are deluded by the common perception that there are but four classes of magic, and those evenly divided into good, or dexter magic, and evil, or sinister magic, and those distributed amongst the living and the dead in the order of goodness to the living, or ascendant, and evilness to the dead, or descendant (to use your own terms). How one explains the nature of the Folk in this system I fail to understand, but this is not my taxonomy, nor is it one I would choose to defend before my peers.

Here is where we disagree, and you must pay careful attention to detail. There is a fifth class of magic, and a sixth, those classes being allocated to those beings never alive and not dead and those beings never dead and not alive. I have consulted with a mathematically minded colleague, who assures me that I can best communicate the origin of these elusive powers to you in your own geometric terms:

Consider the living as on the surface of a gyre that spirals clockwise, flowing and ebbing in regular cycles. Consider the dead as on a surface of a proportionally equivalent gyre that spirals counterclockwise, also flowing and ebbing in regular cycles. Undisturbed, these *gyres share a perfect axial alignment for all time, synchronously interlocked and out of phase by one-half cycle.*

My colleague assures me that an enchanter of your intellect would prefer to contemplate this structure in peace, and that any of my own conclusions and commentary, though based solely on the irrefutable evidence of history, would merely muddy the waters for you.

I look forward to your further thoughts on this subject. In particular, I would know your thoughts on those classes of magic you have heretofore overlooked, and if my colleague's description is sufficient for you to fit these facts into your unified theory of magic. Such a theory is consonant with my own thoughts. If this theory is to be useful, however, it must be complete.

As usual, you may post to me care of Adrigole's.

Your friend and colleague,

Sir Hugh Munninson, PhD.

P.S. I have enclosed a number of illustrations and formulae that my colleague assures me will be of use to you.

"Huh." Maddy looked at the drawings. They looked like cones and hourglasses overlapping. The formulae were what Quille called equations, ones with equal signs or arrows in the middle. Maddy didn't have the math skills to understand them. Yet. She stuffed the whole mess back into the envelope. She placed it in the center of Quille's desk. She glanced at the locked library doors. She almost paused to try her new key, but Emma was waiting, and Maddy's sister was terribly impatient when she wanted to go shopping.

14

"This isn't working out." Maddy and Emma were in their fifth stationer's shop. The clerk was very nice, but the merchandise grumbled and wept.

"I don't see why you can't borrow some of Quille's supplies."

"I just can't." Every enchanter needed her own things. Borrowing a journal and pen from Quille would make her his apprentice, and he hadn't offered that. She was to investigate the trophy herself, and that meant having her own tools. "None of these will do."

"What else is on your list?"

"Sheet lead."

"Quille has a great heap of that in the back garden. Next to the mound of cruciform extrusions."

"I need my own."

"How are you going to pay for these supplies?"

"With my savings."

"With your allowance. From Quille."

"No." Her allowance was for things a daughter might need. She couldn't use that money for enchanting supplies. "I did copy work for Quille. When I was first... You know. Rescued. He paid by the page."

"That was to teach you to read and write."

"It might have been," Maddy said. "But he also used the work I did." Maddy copied out page after page of the same spell, the one that Quille used to imbue his magic bullets with sorcerer-penetrating properties. He needed a written copy for every carton of ammunition he created. Demand was high. Maddy wrote that spell so many times she could do it in her sleep now. She still helped Quille from time to time.

"Let's go look at gowns," Emma said. "Then we'll have lunch and try for your precious plumbum later."

"I don't need any more gowns," Maddy said.

"That is a matter of opinion," Emma said. "But in any case, you aren't the only one on a mission."

"Oh." Maddy thanked the clerk and followed her sister out into the fog. "What sort of mission are you on?"

"One of requital." Emma grasped Maddy's hand and together they plunged into the overwhelming midday throng.

Arduvulin City was the most prosperous city in the world, and Greanling Street its heart. The storefronts blazed with gaslights, each one designed to penetrate the everlasting gloom of the fog. Brightly colored signs reflected the glow. Everything in the world was available in Arduvulin City. For a price. Everything but those items Its Royal Highness declared contraband. Anything from the Archipelago. Anything undead or created by sorcery. Magical creatures, no matter how small or how big. Humans, and half-humans, living or dead, in whole, or in part. Emma said that such wares were offered in alleyways and silent meetings behind closed doors. Maddy doubted that. The Department of Criminal Magic was exceedingly thorough.

Emma navigated the city with ease. Maddy still needed to ask directions. That always turned out badly. It wasn't that Maddy's memory was poor, merely that the city was so vast and so organically constructed and convoluted and the obvious fact that young women Maddy's age did not wander the city alone. Certainly not if a young woman's eyes blazed with the fires of Hell and her fangs flashed ivory in the dim gaslight.

With Emma as a guide, and with Emma's perfect knowledge of the city, it was easy to take a follower's disinterest in her surroundings. Maddy, even though she had traipsed across great swaths of Arduvulin City, recalled the plan of very little of it. Maddy vowed to pay attention in the future. Though it was pleasant to be towed along in Emma's wake.

Well-dressed gentlemen inevitably smiled and tipped their hats to Emma. Some crossed the street to converse with her. Emma brushed past with a word or two spoken. Or the gentlemen took a step back and dashed away when they smiled at Maddy and Maddy stupidly smiled back.

"It is so tedious," Emma said as they entered the modiste's.

"Being admired and sought after?" Maddy said. "You are so put upon."

"Maddy, those young men would not want me if they knew me," Emma said. "They want what they see, and what they have heard, or read. They chase illusion."

Maddy had never heard her sister speak this way.

"You know," Emma said, "our dear, dead Beatrice Cannon imagined I mocked her. Nothing could be further from the truth."

Maddy hadn't forgotten about Mademoiselle Cannon. She hadn't been thinking about her on purpose. Emma entered the shop and Maddy followed.

"Mademoiselle Sunbury," the modiste said. "And you have brought your lovely sister." The shopkeeper took a step back and grimaced.

Maddy's sister smiled coldly at the modiste. "I'm looking for something suitable for a funeral."

Maddy wandered the shop, just to be alone for a few

moments. Emma enjoyed shocking people. Maddy did not. There were many things Emma did that Maddy chose not to, but Emma was without a doubt the finest sister a girl could desire. Emma was patient when Maddy was slow to learn, and protective, and so knowledgeable in all those skills Maddy lacked. Were it not for Emma's tutoring, Maddy would barely pass for human. Certainly she would not be able to walk the streets of Arduvulin City without attracting a torch-wielding mob. Maddy wished there was something she could do for Emma in return. There simply wasn't. Emma Sunbury was a puzzle and a cipher. And perfectly self-contained.

The modiste's shop stocked goods from throughout the world, from all of Arduvulin and from Ghula, and, Emma whispered, even from the Archipelago, though no one would be so bold as to put those goods on display. Maddy wandered and touched, linen, wool, silk. It was amazing what a skilled seamstress could do. Bolts of cloth were so flat and unappealingly similar. It took imagination to produce the lovely and varied clothing so popular in Arduvulin City. Imagination and skill. Maddy wondered if tailors stocked different goods. There was nothing in this shop to rival the brilliance of Uncle Leo's dress uniform. There were rubies, and crimsons, and vermilions, but all the shop's cloth was finer in weave, less firm and definitely less wonderfully scratchy. Maddy decided she liked this shop. All the merchandise seemed satisfied, even happy to be there. Nearly joyous.

"What are you looking at?" Emma said.

"This cloth," Maddy said.

"Well you've been standing there for five minutes, not moving."

"It's very nice, don't you think?" Maddy had never felt anything like it. The cloth liked her.

"Maddy, these are remnants," Emma said. "Not for us.

There's some portly matron running around draped in hectares of this stuff."

"Not that," the modiste said. She carried the bolt of cloth to a cutting table. She unrolled a yard and ran her fingers across the weave. Seen up close, there was a very fine pattern, but from a distance, it merely seemed iridescent, the color of a midnight scarab's carapace.

"You like this, Mademoiselle?" the modiste said.

"Very much so," Maddy said.

"And you do not like any of the others?"

"None of the others like me," Maddy said.

"Hah," the modiste said. "You are not so frightening. I see this now."

"Could you make that into a waistcoat?" It would look brilliant on Quille."

"I could make it into a dirigible," the modiste said. "But I will not. This cloth wishes to be a gown."

"Maddy, I think we should go now." Emma gripped Maddy's hand and tugged.

"Your sister does not understand," the modiste said. "She has fine taste, and a discerning eye. But her heart is cold."

"And she is standing right here," Emma said.

"You know this is true," the modiste said. She smiled at Emma. "Such a heart is required in your profession."

"Maddy, let's go," Emma said.

"How much is it?" Maddy said.

The modiste named a price equivalent to a year's allowance.

"It's a remnant," Maddy said.

"Mislabeled."

"Your mistake," Maddy said. "Not mine." Maddy offered one month's allowance. She had that in her pocket.

The modiste laughed. "Absurd. I am not a charity."

Maddy had spent forever with crypto-naturalist pirates. Tough negotiations were an everyday occurrence. After much back and forth, it occurred to Maddy that they were an everyday occurrence in the modiste's shop as well. In the end, Maddy agreed to pay four month's allowance for the cloth and another four month's allowance for the making of it into a gown. A gown she didn't need.

"When will you be back for the measurements?" the modiste said.

Maddy frowned and jangled the change in her pocket. "In seven months."

"In one month," the modiste said.

"I won't have saved enough by then."

"In one month," the modiste said. "I need time to think about the design. And to lay out the pattern."

"Madame Peria," Emma said. "When one purchases a gown, one expects to choose the pattern oneself."

"This is of course true," the modiste said, "were one merely purchasing a gown. But the mademoiselle is not purchasing. She is ransoming."

"I am?" Maddy said.

"Indeed," Madame Peria said. "Or recruiting. It is impossible to say for certain until gown and girl are united."

"And my funeral dress?" Emma said.

"It will be ready tomorrow," Madame Peria said. "And thank you for your custom."

IT WAS at lunch that Emma suggested that they might find sheet lead in the Docklands. Maddy was glad for the suggestion. She was tired of being questioned about why she would spend three quarters of a year's allowance on a gown that she only moments earlier declared she did not need. Emma doubted the gown would flatter Maddy's complexion. Or that Madame Peria would do the cloth justice. She was the best in her profession on Greanling Street, but perhaps they should look further afield in the future. That reminded Maddy of something.

"The modiste said something about your profession," Maddy said.

"If we leave now, we could stop at Leo's and ask if he knows of a suitable stationer." Emma grasped her parasol and stood.

"You do have a profession," Maddy said.

"I would expect Scronton's to have sheet lead," Emma said. "They certainly have sheet copper."

"What is it?"

"Thin plates. For hull sheathing. Copper is repellant to wood borers and—"

"No, I mean your profession," Maddy said. "Does Quille know? Oh, does Nadine?"

"Maddy, we really must hurry if we're to finish your shopping."

"We can hurry," Maddy said. "And you can tell me all about your profession. Or I could guess."

"You can't guess," Emma said.

"Well, you're out all night," Maddy said. "And you're very tired when you drag in."

"Can we just leave this?"

"And all the gentlemen in the city seem to know you by name. And greet you with great affection."

"Not all," Emma said.

"All the wealthy, attractive ones," Maddy said. "Maybe I don't have to guess. Maybe I'll just use our mother's deductive powers." Maddy tried to sound like Nadine. "The evidence, I will consider it dispassionately."

"Maddy, don't," Emma said.

"I conclude that your profession, Emma Sunbury, is..." Maddy thought about all the facts as Nadine would see them. *Oh no.* "Never mind." That couldn't be Emma's profession.

This was not a topic for the lunch table. Or the breakfast table.

"You see the problem," Emma said. "Quille hates barristers nearly as much as Nadine does."

"What does that have to do with your profession?"

"That is my profession," Emma said. "Well, I'd like it to be. It will be. Once my studies are complete."

"There are no women barristers," Maddy said.

"There are female Deemsters of the Night Court," Emma said.

"Oh." Maddy didn't think that would sit well with anyone. The Night Court was an underground vigilante organization. "I think it's better if Nadine just concludes you're a prostitute." Maddy's hand jerked to her lips as her face heated. "I mean a... um... courtesan." Maddy followed Emma into the street.

"I don't believe that would work," Emma said. "You can't breathe a word of this."

"Sooner or later, they'll find out," Maddy said. "You ought to stop. The Folk are untrustworthy." The Night Court was composed completely of Folk. It didn't make sense that Emma would have anything to do with them.

"I won't stop," Emma said.

"Then you ought to tell. Quille, at least. You ought to explain."

"What is there to explain?"

"Well, you might begin with why. It's not like you don't have everything you could ever want, and—"

Emma laughed. "Even my own sister doesn't understand."

"I'd like to," Maddy said. "But you never talk about anything of consequence. Not with me."

They were just passing through Eeling Park. Emma pulled Maddy onto a bench near the spawning pond. "Maddy, I have no recollection of who I was before being captured by a sorcerer. And used."

"By Ilse January," Maddy said. Nadine's sister turned sorcerer. "I know all that."

"No, you don't," Emma said. "You've heard all that. You don't know it. Knowing it is wandering a strange, fogbound city where you don't recognize anyone and no one recognizes you."

"They recognize you—"

"Now they do. Not at first." Emma studied the blankness of the sky. "Knowing it is lying awake at night feeling certain there is something you were meant to do, something important. But the knowledge of that has been ripped from you against your will. That you will fail before you've begun, because you will never begin. You are merely occupying the space where something greater than you was meant to be."

"Emma—"

"Its Royal Highness doesn't know. Quille doesn't know. Nadine doesn't know. No one knows."

"Know what?"

Emma looked at Maddy. For the first time in her life, Maddy saw something behind Emma's eyes other than a calm blackness.

"Who I am. What I am. What I was made for."

"I'll help you find out," Maddy said.

Emma squeezed Maddy's fingers. "That's a kind offer, but I have a plan. If no humans in Arduvulin recognized me, perhaps someone amongst the Folk will."

"So you joined the Night Court."

"I attended at first," Emma said, "but now I've joined, yes. And I'm training to be a Deemster. A judge. Expanding my circle of contacts. Someone must eventually recognize me."

"Nadine will hate this," Maddy said.

"That's why we can't tell her."

"I don't know," Maddy said. "It doesn't feel right."

"It feels better than living in ignorance," Emma said. "Of

doing nothing to change it. Or marrying and... ugh... spawning."

"Isn't there any other way?"

"I'm open to suggestions."

"I'll think about it."

"But you won't tell?"

"Tell what?"

Emma squeezed Maddy's hand. "Thanks, Sis."

It still felt wrong, but Maddy wouldn't tell. She had her own secrets. Emma was simply meeting with the old inhabitants of Arduvulin, the Folk, against Its Royal Highness's wishes. It's wishes, but not against the law. Not technically.

Maddy plunged nightly into Hell. Surely Emma's transgressions paled in comparison. But Maddy was certain Nadine would be outraged at Emma's behavior. Nadine wouldn't even begin to fathom Maddy's behavior or, for that matter, believe that it was real. Bad dreams, that was all. The thought of keeping secrets from Nadine made Maddy's stomach churn.

"Let's go see Uncle Leo," Maddy said.

"You can't tell him, either," Emma said.

"It would go in one ear and out the other," Maddy said. "He doesn't find you all that interesting."

"That suits me," Emma said. "He's too flamboyant for my taste."

"That's obvious," Maddy said. "That you think he is."

"Is it?" Emma said.

"Definitely."

"And you think that's wrong."

"It's cruel," Maddy said. "Plus, Uncle Leo travels all over the world." Maddy pulled Emma along towards Uncle Leo's. "Places even the Folk have never been."

"I suppose he might," Emma said. Her steps slowed.

"I know he does," Maddy said. "But no one consulted me."

"Point taken, Sis."

It took most of the afternoon to find the sheet lead, but Uncle Leo was able to direct Maddy and Emma to a stationer's where the merchandise practically purred with joy. Maddy found an etching pen very much to her liking, and a philosopher's notebook like Quille used, fat with stamped and numbered sheets of lovely pearl. She purchased a number of temporary notepads as well, and a graphite pen, one that she could spell to be self-sharpening for hours at a time. Not a permanent spell, but definitely a spell that exercised the same muscles.

On the way home, Maddy purchased a hammer, a small anvil, some rivets, and a bucking bar. Emma suggested that the shop man send the anvil around in the morning. Maddy insisted that she was stronger than she looked, and she was not spending another night without at least trying to shroud the hideous lantern in her bedroom. The shop man said that he would send a boy with the packages, and much to his credit, he did. The gratuity took the last of her savings, but Maddy liked the smile on the boy's face as he doffed his cap. There was something strange about his eyes, but Maddy wasn't one to complain. She'd thought they'd glinted violet for an instant, but when she looked closely, they seemed perfectly normal. Perfectly normal and focused on her, without flinching.

"Ask for Geoff if you need anything else brought up, Miss."

Maddy said she would. He'd said that even after Maddy had smiled. So all in all, the day hadn't been as horrible as it might have been.

15

Maddy spent the evening hammering and bending lead into a shroud for the Spelling Bee trophy. In the end, it did not look very pretty at all, but when she plunged the trophy into it, it felt as if the sun had come out. She slid a sheet of lead beneath it and surveyed her work. Quille and Nadine were still not home, so Maddy, Rookhaven, and Emma made do with cold cuts. Madame Aubergine paced back and forth until she heard the street door open.

Nadine shrugged out of her coat and tossed it to Quille. He hung it with his own in the entry hallway.

"Well?" Emma said.

"It appears to be the work of The Fifteen," Nadine said. She slumped into a dining chair and picked at the cold roast beef.

Quille was noticeably silent. He looked pale and drawn, and not at all his usual pale and undrawn self. He took his seat and studied the gas lamp overhead. It hissed on and on.

"What would The Fifteen have against Beatrice Cannon?" Emma said.

"Apparently she was a young woman in love. And truly loved in return."

"That seems unlikely," Emma said.

"Unlikely as it seems, we now need only ascertain the identity of this lover."

"I doubt we have long to wait," Quille said. "I expect this to turn unpleasant."

"Will you arrest him?" Maddy said.

"It doesn't work that way," Emma said. "The unknown lover was innocent. Whoever he was is already dead. It's just his body that lives on, and whatever filthy old soul The Fifteen have transferred into it."

"Then you arrest that," Maddy said. "How horrible."

"We have no evidence," Nadine said. "The reprehensible young woman had no friends or family."

"Search her lodgings," Maddy said. "Maybe there are love letters."

"Burned," Nadine said. "An entire block of flats."

"Her associates," Emma said. "Confront that loathsome pepper-man."

Quille smiled at that. "I doubt that will be necessary."

There was something no one was saying. "What was Beatrice Cannon doing at the Nonesuch Palace?"

"That is unclear," Nadine said. "Perhaps the greater question is how The Fifteen smuggled a sorcerer into the Nonesuch Palace."

"Perhaps," Quille said.

Someone hammered on the street door. Quille shoved out of his chair and scooped up his ashplant. "I'll get it," Quille said. "I feel certain it is for me."

A pistol discharged in the hallway. Nadine was out of her seat, handgun in her fist. Maddy heard the thud of a body striking the flagstones. Emma shouldered past Maddy and disappeared into the hall.

Justice Goodfellow stood, backlit in the doorway, smoking pistol in hand. He dropped the weapon. Quille lay on his back on the floor. Goodfellow pulled a second pistol from his waistband.

"Drop that!" Nadine shouted. A second pistol discharged. Goodfellow's pistol shattered in his hand. He stared at the ruin for a moment before he clutched his mangled fingers to his breast. He cupped them in his left hand.

Emma calmly reloaded.

"At least I got him," Goodfellow said. He stared numbly at his ruined fingers.

"Quille, are you all right?" Nadine's pistol never wavered from Goodfellow.

"I've been better," Quille said. He rolled over on his stomach and clawed for his cane.

"Maddy, help your father." Nadine gestured with her left hand.

"I shot him!" Goodfellow shouted. "Point blank!" Blood splattered on the flagstones, reflecting the dim light in shattered rays.

"A confession is hardly necessary." Nadine holstered her weapon. She grabbed Goodfellow by the lapels and kicked his feet out from under him. He landed on his ruined hand and screamed. She produced a pair of Department shackles from her belt and twisted the man's hands behind him. He screamed loud enough that Nadine had to raise her voice. "Emma, see if you can find a patrolman. Be careful. This fool may have allies."

"Him?"

"Be careful, in any event."

Maddy helped Quille stand. He handed Maddy the ball of lead in his palm. "For your collection."

"I don't have a collection," Maddy said.

"You will," Quille said. "That's a given around here."

"But I shot him!" Goodfellow wriggled. Nadine held him down with her heel.

"Son, you're in Mundane House," Quille said. "I'd be long

dead if someone could just march in and gun me down. Don't you read the rubbish your own paper prints?"

"He spouts lies," Nadine said. "He concludes that everything he reads is also a lie."

Maddy knew about Mundane House's wards, but she thought they were to keep Quille in when he died and became a sorcerer. Her dad looked pretty shaken up but otherwise alive and unharmed. "Why did he do it?"

"He believes I murdered Beatrice Cannon," Quille said.

"You did, but it didn't work!" Goodfellow shouted. "I'm still me!"

"More's the pity," Quille said. "Though in any case, I had nothing to do with it."

"What other sorcerer could get inside the Nonesuch Palace?" Goodfellow wriggled.

Quille bent down and tapped the man on the crown of his head with his ashplant. "Son, if I were a sorcerer, you'd be dead. And we wouldn't be having this conversation. But as I'm not, I have a word of advice for you."

"I don't want your advice!"

"That's pretty clear," Quille said. "But as you're in my house, mucking up my flooring, you'll have it." Quille groaned and held his hand out. "Maddy, help your old da straighten up, will you now?"

Quille limped toward the hall doors. "Don't believe everything you read, Mr. Bolive Defarish. And don't not believe it, either, Mr. Justice Goodfellow." Quille turned and fished in his pockets. He tossed a carton of the magical bullets he manufactured for the Department onto the floor. Goodfellow could read the label if he crossed his eyes. "If you go hunting sorcerers, you'll need those. Those and a clear, dispassionate head."

"I couldn't find one," Emma said. "A patrolman."

"Let him go," Quille said. "The man's been through enough."

"He attempted to murder you," Nadine said.

"Nadine, if something had happened to you, I'd more than attempt. He's not in his right mind, and locking him in a cell won't make him any wiser."

"Neither will letting him go."

"Maybe not. But it'll let me get to my dinner sooner. So just do it, and let's argue about it later. In private." Quille hobbled off toward the dining room.

"Are you going to let him order you around?" Emma said.

"Yes," Nadine said. "When he's right. Now help me get this horrid man upright and out into the street."

Quille hunched over the dining table. He did not look well. "It seems to me, back in the day they aimed for the heart. Now it's always the noggin." Quille waved his hand. "Maddy, see if we have any willow tea, will you?"

When Maddy returned with the tea, Nadine stood, arms crossed, glaring at Quille.

"Don't," Quille said. He sipped his tea loudly.

Nadine tapped her foot. "How could an inversion be worked and the lover not be transformed?"

"You're the one said it was an inversion," Quille said.

"You inspected the evidence yourself."

"Aye," Quille said. "And a good thing."

"What was done to Beatrice Cannon was—"

"That wasn't Beatrice Cannon," Quille said. "That was something grown from her hair and fingernails."

"Then it wasn't The Fifteen," Emma said.

"It might still have been," Quille said. "Though if it was, they have new help. From the most unlikely of all sources."

Maddy bounced on the edge of her seat. "Does this mean Beatrice Cannon is still alive?"

"Possibly."

Nadine placed her hand on Quille's shoulder. "What new help, Quille?"

Quille winced and pulled away. "I fell badly."

"I'm sorry," Nadine said. "What new help?"

Emma frowned. "I've just purchased a new dress for Cannon's funeral."

"You may still get to use it," Quille said. He sipped his tea and studied the dining room table.

"Quille?"

"Eh?"

"The hair and fingernails," Maddy said. "You'd need that to build a changeling. Old magic is involved."

"Enchanters call it true magic," Quille said. "The magic of naturally magical creatures."

"Like my birth mother," Maddy said.

"And you," Quille said. "Don't think I didn't understand that trick you pulled with the pepper."

"We are seeking what here, Quille?" Nadine had her business face on. Her eyes gleamed.

"A sorcerer or a kyloch. And someone able to work true magic," Quille said. "Two people, most likely. If it is one person, it would have to be—"

"Half-human," Maddy said. "Like me."

"Not like you, Maddy," Quille said. "A local. But I doubt many would make the distinction."

"What, then?" Nadine slapped her hand against her trouser leg. "Tell me, Quille."

"I'm afraid you'll overreact," Quille said. "This isn't your problem."

"Oh," Maddy said. She chewed her knuckles. It was a problem for the Night Court.

"Maddy?"

"He means the Folk," Emma said. "And that this crime is outside your jurisdiction."

"It involves sorcery and it occurred in the Nonesuch Palace. That makes it my jurisdiction."

"The Folk won't agree," Emma said. "Not if it involves a changeling. And The Fifteen. You've mucked up the Night Court's crime scene."

Nadine's eyebrows narrowed. She stared at Emma. "As if I care."

"It wasn't a murder," Quille said. "It might not even be an abduction. We have no evidence that Beatrice Cannon was involved at all. Only her hair and skin. Technically, it's not even a human crime."

"But why?" Maddy didn't understand. "What was the point? Why make a changeling and then destroy it?"

"I'd say it was a warning," Quille said. "Or some sort of lure or distraction. Changelings lack the life-force to power a soul transfer. It's all very strange."

"It got Justice Goodfellow to shoot you," Maddy said. "It made you seem guilty of sorcery. I'll bet it's in the papers tomorrow."

Quille massaged his temples. "No doubt."

Nadine pointed her finger at Maddy, then at Emma. "You two, to bed."

Emma glanced toward the street door. "I'd planned to—"

Quille slammed his fist against the dining room table. Cups and saucers rattled and danced. "Emma Quille, for once in your life will you listen to your mother?"

"That's not my name," Emma said.

"It is to me," Quille said. "And I beg you, do not go out tonight. There is much broken in the world and I need time to make sense of it. I can't do that if I'm worried about you."

"You don't have to worry about me."

"I choose to, daughter."

"Now you sound like Nadine."

"If that doesn't send you running for the covers, then nothing will." Quille rubbed his palm over his face. "Make up your own mind, but if you leave this house, don't do it skulking. See me first. I'll be in my chambers."

Quille levered himself out of his chair. Maddy had never seen him so beaten.

"Mom?" Maddy said.

"What, Maddy?" Nadine wasn't paying attention. She was watching Quille limp away.

"Can I sleep in Emma's room tonight?"

Nadine rubbed her eyes. "That would be fine."

MADDY NESTLED BENEATH THE COVERS. Emma scooted over to make room.

"I have something I need to tell you," Maddy said.

"I have something I need to tell you, too," Emma said.

"You first," Maddy said.

"All right." Emma started to speak, but stopped. She didn't make a sound for nearly a minute. "I'm scared. All the time."

Emma wasn't telling Maddy what she intended to say. Only what she trusted Maddy to know. That thought should have hurt, but it didn't. At least Emma was telling Maddy something. For once.

"You hide it very well," Maddy said.

"I've had a lot of practice." Emma rolled over so she could see Maddy. "What did you want to tell me?"

"Never mind."

"No, say."

"I don't want to scare you."

"You couldn't."

Maddy licked her lips and just said it. "Since the grimfoxes bit me, I don't think I really sleep."

"I know," Emma said.

"I think I die. Every night."

Emma ran her fingers through Maddy's hair. "I think you do, too. Almost die, anyway."

"Don't tell Nadine." Maddy rolled over and studied the ceiling. "I don't want her to worry."

"I won't, Maddy." Emma tucked the covers under Maddy's chin. "So long as you promise to wake in the morning."

"I promise," Maddy said. She would. If she could.

16

Madeleine found the baleful lantern in her hands even though it was sheathed in lead in the waking world. Its light slashed out in sickly green spears to disappear into the monochrome gloom of Night. The false Maddy paced back and forth at the edge of the crater, its muzzle puffing superheated steam. Rookhaven stood at the creature's side, his fingers carelessly scratching the stiff fur behind the hellhound's ears.

"You're here," Rookhaven said. His ancient voice was still shocking. If Madeleine closed her eyes and just listened, she would never in a million years conjure the image of her young and rail-thin brother.

"Now, dearest heart," Madame Aubergine said, "you must go to the edge and look down. Leave your lantern here. In no way should its light be seen from afar." She paced ahead in her white gumboots.

Madeleine detested Night in every way. It smelled of charcoal and ashes, and each footfall puffed a little cloud that seemed to hang in the breezeless air. The light was not good; there were no colors to speak of save black, and grey. The taste of sulfur was ever on her tongue. The constant moan of dead and dying trees and the scritch of her feet against the charred and crumbling ruin grated on her ears. Her own breath, her own heartbeat made no sound. That was how she knew she was dead.

The hound that pretended to be her huffed out a great puff of superheated breath. "So nice of you to join us." That the hound spoke with Maddy's voice was both loathsome and insulting. Madeleine hated Night.

From the edge of the crater, it was possible to see very far into Night. The forest around the crater had been knocked down for miles and burned. In the distance, the only sight of color in all the world wept out of a great gash in the earth's crust, a jagged tear that slashed and widened to rip through the heart of a blasted and ruined city. A dead city.

Madeleine feared at first that she was seeing the future. That the city was Arduvulin City. But the topography was wrong. This city was much smaller, and perched on the edge of an evaporated bay, a dried and cracking semicircle through which the gash in the world roared and gaped, oozing lava the color of blood.

"All right," Madeleine said. "What do I need to do?" She stood next to Rookhaven but as far away as she could from the filthy beast that bumped against his right leg.

"We need to stop them," the hound said.

Madeleine scanned the view from foot to horizon. "I don't see anyone."

"Of course not," the hound said. "They are pure cunning and evil. Too weak for sorcery, too—"

"Strong to die," Madeleine said. "We're hunting grimfoxes."

"Not just any grimfoxes, dear heart," Madame Aubergine said.

"Our grimfoxes," the hound said. "The ones we sent here."

"Why?" Madeleine turned to Madame Aubergine. "Hell is full of grimfoxes."

"You are such a stupid girl," the hound said. It turned and paced toward the bottom of the crater.

Rookhaven patted Madeleine on the shoulder as he followed the hound. "Come along."

"This isn't Hell," Madeleine said.

"Close to Hell," Madame Aubergine said. "But not quite. It was a good effort, Madeleine. Your spelling was nearly perfect."

"If this isn't Hell, what is it?"

"Night," Madame Aubergine said. "I thought that was clear." She began to traipse toward the center of the crater where the hound and Rookhaven grubbed in the rubble. Madeleine followed along.

The hound dug madly with both front paws, trying to unearth Madeleine's stone. Madeleine's stomach roiled and she turned away. She was halfway up the slope of the crater before Rookhaven caught her. "Please don't be afraid." Rookhaven laid his hand on Madeleine's sleeve. "I know this is hard."

The hound flipped the stone over. Its corrosive saliva damaged portions of the bas-relief. The stone was part of a fresco, a section perhaps four feet long depicting a scene of great triumph. A warrior strode across a field littered with the butchered bodies of the slain. A faithful hound trotted at her side. Her weapon was a scythe, her helmet the sun, broad rays streaming outward to touch the border of the carving. Behind her, the dead marched in rank after endless rank. In the distance, dragonflies flitted across the surface of a gibbous and rising moon.

All this detail was distraction. Madeleine's gaze kept returning to the warrior's face, and to her smile. She seemed to revel in the slaughter.

"Is this the past, or the future?" Madeleine said. She licked her lips.

"Yes," Madame Aubergine said.

"Time runs at different speeds on either side of a Gate," Rookhaven said. "The question makes no sense."

"Then we're on the other side of the Arduvulin Gate?"

"Tell me I'm not really this dense," the hound said. "Can't you feel it?"

"Make this nasty creature go away," Madeleine said. "Or I'm going home. I'll wake up."

"You just don't get it." The hound backed Madeleine up against the stone. "We're stuck here. All because we sent six! Six grimfoxes here!" The hound took a step back and shook its head side to side. "I thought we were better than this. You're a major disappointment."

The hound head-butted Madeleine in the stomach. Madeleine bent over and struggled to breath as the hound lurched under her and swept her off her feet. It trotted along at ever increasing speed. Madeleine clung on in desperation. The hound stopped suddenly and tossed Madeleine into the dust. "Look," it said. It held up a paw and pointed behind her.

Madeleine turned, and there it was. The shattered remnants of dragon bone wept in the monochrome dark. Once Madeleine imagined the Arduvulin Gate large enough to swallow the moon. This gate might have swallowed the sun. Even splintered and fallen, its remains dwarfed the living Arduvulin Gate.

"There's more than one Gate," Madeleine said. The door leaves of this one lay as broken toys on the bone-blasted basalt scoured clean beneath the Gate. That any portion of the Gate remained standing was a testament to the power of the enchanters who constructed it.

"There are four Gates," the hound said. It seemed to survey the ruins of the Gate. "There were four."

In the distance, Madeleine could just make out Madame Aubergine and Rookhaven crunching across the ruined soil.

The hound circled and sat at Madeleine's side. "Why do you hate me so?"

"I don't know," Madeleine said.

"But you do. Hate me."

"With all my heart," Madeleine said.

"You can't afford to," the hound said. "Not if we're going to stop them."

"Maybe we won't," Madeleine said. "Stop them."

"And leave our sister to her fate?" The hound stood and growled. "I won't."

"What are you talking about?"

"We're beyond the Dead Gate," the hound said. "There isn't any difference between past and future. There isn't any way to tell one from the other."

"What does this have to do with Emma?"

The hound huffed and gripped Madeleine's sleeve in its jaws. The cloth of her gown dissolved in its caustic bite. "Oh. That won't work. Climb on my back."

"Why should I?"

"Walk back to the stone if you want," the hound said. "And look again. Then tell me that isn't Emma Sunbury leading Grey Men and grimfoxes to war."

Madeleine dusted herself off and climbed onto the hound's disgusting back. "Don't you ever bathe?"

"I don't like getting wet." The hound began to trot in a ground-devouring gait. If Maddy closed her eyes, it wasn't so bad. The horrid beast stopped before the stone. Madeleine climbed off.

"Look."

Madeleine looked. It looked like Emma, all right. And she was smiling.

"Is that you?" Madeleine said. "At her side?"

"Not if we're together in this," the hound said. "It doesn't have to be."

"How do you know all this?" Madeleine said.

"All those nasty times with the crypto-naturalist pirates," the hound said, "when you ran away and hid. I stayed. And listened."

"I couldn't bear it," Madeleine said. She wiped her eyes.

"Don't cry," the hound said. "Grimfoxes can smell tears from a mile away. And right now we have the element of surprise."

"That's good," Madeleine said. She wiped her nose.

"Right," the hound said. It turned away and sniffed the air for danger. Madeleine could tell.

"We need to make a plan," Madeleine said.

"You're good at that," the hound said.

"Thank you," Madeleine said. "But I think I need all the details first."

"Rookhaven used to live here. Before the Oligarchs came," the hound said. "And Madame Aubergine knows how to work magic here. Without becoming a sorcerer."

"Really?" Madeleine said.

"Of course. Our brother's the best," the hound said. "And our friends are, too. This is so much better than being in a cage. Even if it isn't all that good."

"Maddy," Madame Aubergine said. "Come to me please."

"She means me," the hound said. "In Night, I'm Maddy. You're Madeleine."

"But I don't want to be Madeleine."

The hound shook its big, jowly head and peered at Maddy with its hellfire eyes. "Liar. You'd ditch Maddy in a heartbeat if you could." The hellhound trotted away, melting the ground beneath its feet with every stride.

That couldn't be good. Maddy's paw prints were every-where. And grimfoxes were pure, cunning evil. Madeleine didn't believe they had the element of surprise at all. Certainly not for long. Rookhaven, Madame Aubergine, and Maddy clustered around the baleful lantern. Madeleine rose and dusted off her nightgown when Madame Aubergine called for her to join them. Madeleine considered her options. There really weren't any. She didn't necessarily believe everything Maddy told her, but she couldn't afford to discount it, either. If there was the slightest possibility that Emma was in danger, Madeleine had to find out and stop it. Even if Emma was in danger from herself.

Madeleine's fingers hovered an inch above Maddy's shaggy head. Especially if Emma was in danger from herself. Madeleine gritted her teeth and scratched Maddy behind the ear.

"I like that," Maddy said.

"I know," Madeleine said. But that was enough. Maybe in time she could get used to this. But definitely not all at once.

"You need to fill me in," Madeleine said to Rookhaven. "And then we can figure out what to do."

"That may take all night." Rookhaven said.

"I have time," Madeleine said. She conjured a stone and dusted it off before she sat.

"Competently done," Madame Aubergine said. "Though your spell wastes strength, and draws attention."

"Will you show me how to do better?"

"I live for nothing more," Madame Aubergine said. "Though your father refuses to comprehend. Nonetheless, it is true. Aubergine was made for this."

"Come on," Maddy said. "We don't have all night." She circled about before stretching out at Madeleine's feet.

"Yes, we do," Rookhaven said. "But this won't take that long. Most tales of light and dark, of good and evil can be summed up in a sentence or two."

"Then do so," Madame Aubergine said. "Madeleine's spelling needs much work."

"This isn't such a tale," Rookhaven said. He leaned forward

into the light of the baleful lantern. "You'll have to decide what it is for yourself when I'm done."

"It's a tale of death piled upon death," Maddy said. She rested her muzzle on her paws.

"No spoilers," Rookhaven said.

"Are you certain you wish to hear this, Madeleine?"

"No. But I need to." Madeleine shifted her seat. "This stone is not comfortable, so just do it."

"Rookhaven's makers woke the Oligarchs," Madame Aubergine said. "The Oligarchs nearly destroyed them, but they fled from Night through the Gate we call the Dead Gate to Ghula, where they became the dark witches we call kylochs, destroying the gate behind them. Somehow, Madeleine, you opened a pinhole to Night and shoved an evil number of grimfoxes through. If the Oligarchs are still here, they can possess the grimfoxes and use them. If the pinhole works in one direction, it must work in the other. That we are brought here nightly proves that the pinhole still exists."

"You've spoiled the story," Rookhaven said.

"I have saved it," Madame Aubergine said. "Madeleine does not need a history lesson. She needs to learn to defend herself. So that she can defend the world."

"Kylochs are evil," Madeleine said.

Rookhaven studied his hands. "Well..."

"The Oligarchs are evil," Madame Aubergine said. "Kylochs are willful, and amoral by most standards."

"And terrifically loyal," Maddy said. She tapped Rookhaven's boot with her paw.

"Rookhaven is a kyloch?" Madeleine said. That didn't seem possible.

"An Emissary," Rookhaven said. "A kyloch's work in flesh."

"Though a poor work," Madame Aubergine said. "Not as good as desired, not as bad as expected."

"You are too kind," Rookhaven said. "At least I breathe."

"And snore," Madame Aubergine said.

"Lightly," Rookhaven said. "Melodiously."

"I need to think about this," Madeleine said.

"You will need to do it in Arduvulin," Madame Aubergine said. She pointed at the hideous lantern. It was fading.

"Sleep," Rookhaven said. And Madeleine did.

When Maddy woke, she was in Emma's bed. Emma was missing.

17

E mma was not at breakfast. She had not been at breakfast for more than ten days. Emma stumbled home at noon, slept for six hours, and then disappeared again after dinner. Nadine was fit to be tied. Emma didn't seem to care. She ignored everyone, even Maddy. There was no explaining her behavior. Or excusing it. Maddy didn't know what to do.

The morning paper remained thankfully thin, all of the nasty bits left out. Maddy read the sailing schedule, the financial news, and the obituaries. There was little else. Nothing that looked like a cage.

Quille moved slowly, still recovering from his fracas with Justice Goodfellow. He said little. Nadine said nothing, her mind fixed on the Department case files spread out on the dining table before her. Maddy imagined that kept Nadine's mind off Emma. She wasn't sure that was a good thing. She wasn't sure it was a bad thing, either. When Emma's obsession with the Folk and Nadine's dislike for them finally collided, sparks would fly.

Rookhaven tossed a cherry onto Maddy's plate and hopped

onto her shoulder. He pulled Maddy's earlobe thrice and croaked, "to work, to work."

Maddy excused herself and retrieved her writing materials from her bedroom.

"Let me see those," Quille said as Maddy passed.

He studied her pens and pads. "Very nice," he said. "Where did you find them?"

"Easom's," Maddy said. "Uncle Leo directed us."

Quille nodded. "I'm shy about two hundred ammunition spells for the Department. Do you think you might find time to ink them out?"

"Yes," Maddy said. If she did that, she'd recover all she spent on supplies. "I'm better at the work now, though," Maddy said. "I think I deserve a raise."

Quille blinked. "If you're better at it, then you can do them faster. There's your raise right there."

"But you won't have to rework as many," Maddy said. "Surely your time is worth something." She smiled.

"Surely," Quille said. "Did you have a figure in mind?"

She did, but only a fool named her price first. They taught crypto-naturalist pirates that in the cradle. "What do you think would be fair, Dad?" That 'Dad' was cheating, but Maddy had no idea how much money she would need for her investigations.

"I think you could do the work, and I could judge the quality, and then we could talk again."

"Do you need them soon?" Maddy said. She liked dickering with her dad. He knew what he was doing.

"As soon as you can get to them."

That was the same as saying yes. "It's Anne's Day. Time and a half is traditional."

"Not for piecework," Quille said.

Maddy knew she'd pushed it as far as she could. Even at the

usual rate, it would be fine. Quille didn't really need the spells. He was just being supportive.

"I'll get right on it," Maddy said. Even if Quille was only being kind, he'd expect her to do the job right away. "I'll be in the tower."

"Take your time," Quille said. "I'll be in and out."

"Right."

Nadine's gaze jerked up from her Department file and her hand dipped toward her sidearm. "Maddy—"

"I mean, 'Yes, father'." Maddy darted through the back garden and up the stairs. The enchanted lift was too slow.

MADDY FINISHED the work for Quille in less than two hours. That would have taken her a week when she had first started helping her dad, and it would have taken Quille at least two hours to correct all her mistakes back then. She didn't have time to really dig into Quille's library before lunch, but she did have a task that she desperately wanted time and privacy to complete.

Maybe Tan couldn't perceive Maddy directly, but that shouldn't stop him from reading a letter from her. She'd never written to anyone before, and from Quille's description of the spell on Tan, she doubted her handwriting could be recognized. Maddy thought about writing the letter with her right hand, but she decided that was going overboard, and she could try that later if writing the usual way didn't work.

Dear Tan, Maddy wrote, then she tore up that sheet and started again.

Dear Its Royal Tanist,

I'm sorry I missed you at the Spelling Bee trophy presentation but that was probably for the best. I made a hash of the whole event;

you would have laughed, but I was mortified, and so were my parents, and probably everyone else there as well.

I hope there will come a time when we can see each other soon. I think about you a lot, but it's not like you're all I think about. I have many interesting projects to work on and they would be more fun if we worked on them together. And who knows, maybe the world would be a better and safer place if we could see each other and talk and share, and you and Its Royal Highness wouldn't have to do everything alone, because you had friends you could trust and rely upon. I'd like to be that type of friend to you. I think I could be. I want to be.

Regardless of what you read in the newspaper or what anyone else says or thinks, I wanted you to know that.

Sincerely,

Madeleine Oortsgarten-Quille (Maddy Dune)

P.S. If you know or can find out anything about the history of the Spelling Bee trophy, I would like to learn of it in person or in writing. In person would be best.

Maddy read her letter a dozen times and it seemed stupider every time she read it. She almost tore it up, but she'd spent the last two days thinking about the wording, and either she sent it as is or she'd never send it. She borrowed an envelope and stamp from Quille since the letter was really personal business. Any enchanting business was all in the postscript.

After lunch, Maddy put the letter in the post and climbed back up Quille's tower to use the library. Quille sat at his desk, hunched over his correspondence. Every now and then he would mutter and his nostrils would flare. He wadded page after page and tossed them one by one into the fireplace. He had very good aim. The pages flared blue as they incinerated instantly to ash.

Now would not be a good time to interrupt, so Maddy flopped down on the divan and considered her options. She needed to decide which problem to investigate first.

There was the curse on Tan and Its Royal Highness, but that was probably too hard a problem to start with, since Quille said every enchanter in Arduvulin had been working on that one since the beginning of time.

Then there was the spell on Tan that made it impossible for Tan to sense Maddy. If her letter worked and they began to correspond, that was almost as good as seeing Tan. Tan needed someone, and so did Maddy. When she'd had time to think it through, though, the idea of seeing Tan again made Maddy uncomfortable. If she saw her soul reflected when she looked at Tan, then it wasn't Tan she saw at all. It was like falling in love with her own reflection. That idea made her skin crawl. Tan was witty, and smart, and talented, and really, it didn't matter what he looked like. She missed his voice, but he really could sound awfully smug. Sometimes. Maybe not seeing him was for the best, at least until Maddy learned enough about magic to lift the curse.

That left the Spelling Bee trophy, which was tied into another problem in a way: Maddy's journeys into Night and her spelling six grimfoxes into the arms of the Oligarchs, whoever they were. And Rookhaven's secret identity. And the possibility that Emma was really some sort of undead-mustering general from the future or the past, which in a way tied into Emma's secret work with the semi-illegal Night Court and the Folk. Not to mention The Fifteen, who might be related to the mysterious disappearance of Beatrice Cannon. And Maddy's dad getting shot in the face by Justice Goodfellow, which wasn't even the newspaperman's real name. It was all too hopelessly knotted and there was really no good place to begin. Maddy had to just pick one.

The Spelling Bee trophy, she decided. It was physical, it could be examined and experimented on, and the best enchanters for over a thousand years had all had it in their possession. There would be a wealth of knowledge about the trophy in Quille's library. Maybe that research would spark other ideas. Too many of the other questions led back to Emma, and Maddy didn't want to think about where Emma disappeared to, why Emma missed breakfast, and if Emma was in danger. Emma was fine, and Maddy could interrogate her later in person; because Emma was fine and would be home for dinner. There was nothing to worry about. Even if she worried there was nothing she could do. Emma didn't want Maddy's help. Emma didn't trust Maddy enough to want her help.

Maddy needed to get to work else she'd get angry. Her heart raced as she slid the key Quille had entrusted to her into the lock on the library doors. Maddy swung the doors wide and stepped forward. This was it. Quille's real library, not the schoolbooks he kept on a low bookshelf in the parlor for her. The very same books Eusebius Quille used to become the greatest enchanter in the world.

Maddy ran her finger down the spine of one volume after another. The text swam before Maddy's eyes. It wasn't long before her stomach churned. Maddy opened a volume at random and tried to read it. She tried another book and again she felt so violently ill that this time she had to race to the lavatory. By the time she got there, she didn't feel sick anymore.

Quille looked up from his desk as Maddy ran past, and again when she returned. "Problem?"

"There's something wrong with your library."

"It could stand to be larger," Quille said. "Though that's hardly the library's fault."

"You know what I mean," Maddy said. "I can't read a word without getting sick."

"You're in the wrong section," Quille said. "Those are books on permanent magic."

"I promised not to work any permanent magic," Maddy said. "You didn't have to—"

"Before you go accusing your old da," Quille said, "did it occur to you that there's more than one language of magic?"

"You said there's really only one type of magic, and—"

"I'm attempting to prove just that," Quille said. "And failing. But that has nothing to do with magic written in books. There are three languages in Ghula, more than a hundred I know of in the Archipelago, and your Uncle Leo claims that's just scratching the surface. There are four languages at use here in Arduvulin, if you count that spoken by Trammans and the various other classes of Folk. And that doesn't even include trade cant or sign language or the language of flowers, or—"

"I get the idea," Maddy said. "So you're saying those books are in one of these languages."

"I'm not," Quille said. "I'm saying that there's a lot of languages. Those books, they're ones your Uncle Leo brought back from the Southern Polar Expanse. They're old, and they're rare, and I doubt there's another set like them in the world."

"And you can read them without getting sick?"

"I can't," Quille said. "I'd say only their makers could do that."

"But you can read them."

"I can," Quille said. "They're what gave me the idea for the Unified Theory of Magic."

"Can I learn to read them?"

"I don't see why not," Quille said. "But I'll not teach you. You've no need for permanent magic yet, and no need to be corresponding with dragons."

"Those books were written by dragons?"

"Not hardly," Quille said. "They were translated by dragons."

"From what?"

"Word of mouth, I'd say. There are textual inconsistencies indicating oral transmission of the material."

"No, I meant from what language was it the dragons translated?"

"I'm not sure," Quille said. He rubbed his chin. "But I don't think you'll find the same material in any easier-to-read format, if that's what you're asking."

"Maybe what I need to know about the Spelling Bee trophy is in those books," Maddy said.

"It's not," Quille said. "Go to the far right-hand corner of the library and start there. If you find a book in Annish that seems promising, bring it here and I'll help you. Most in that section are in Ardu, High and Low, and I doubt you'll find a word you don't recognize."

"Are there a lot of books written by dragons?"

"Not that I'm aware of," Quille said. "And Maddy, you'd be doing me a favor if you don't mention those books to anyone."

"Are they banned?"

"If they were, I wouldn't say," Quille said. "Now go on and do your research, and if you need any help bring it to me."

"I will, Dad."

Maddy gazed at the dragon books long enough to get sick again, but not so long as to need the lavatory. Their ill-making effect didn't seem any less powerful after repeated exposure, but a girl never could tell. Maddy went to the section Quille suggested, and the first book she pulled off the shelf was all about the Spelling Bee. So was the second. And the third. It was going to be a long afternoon, but at least if Maddy was reading, she wouldn't be fretting about Emma.

18

M addy picked at her omelet. Today, again, the newspaper was silent, only reporting the regular goings-on in the most important commercial city in the world. Births and deaths, arrivals and departures, profits and losses. Maddy began to understand why Justice Goodfellow's nasty articles were so discussed, why Beatrice Cannon's illustrations were so popular. Even if they were lies, they at least were about the journey, the middle, the hours between arrival and departure, where all the work was done, all the struggle, regardless of success and failure. Those vile stories breathed life into the paper. Perhaps Maddy had been thinking about this all wrong. Quille's unseen enemies weren't trying to fit him for a cage. They were simply illuminating one that already existed, invisible to all but the most careful observer. Or perhaps Maddy had been studying the Spelling Bee trophy too long and it had warped her thinking.

Emma was absent from the table again this morning, and Nadine was visibly wrought. Emma had missed breakfast for two solid weeks. Quille pawed through the morning post. Maddy's heart skipped a beat when he handed Maddy a letter addressed to her. Maddy tore the envelope open and read.

Dear Mademoiselle Oortsgarten-Quille,

Thank you so much for your kind words. It is always a pleasure to receive a missive from a loyal subject. I regret that I cannot respond personally to every letter due to the volume of correspondence I receive. Rest assured your opinion matters and will be given all due consideration.

Thank you so much for writing,

Its Royal Tanist

Maddy stared at a spot on the wall over Nadine's shoulder until her pulse settled. She didn't know if she was angry or mortified. Angry that Tan would respond to her is such a cold way. Mortified that she had ever considered the idea that the prince of the realm would notice her at all. Tan was probably rescued from certain death several times a week. Maddy hadn't done anything special. That still didn't mean that she was just some faceless goon. He'd come to her room. He'd kissed her fingers. He'd seen past her skin and straight into her heart. Now she was nothing. Worse than nothing. A loyal subject. A cog.

"Quille," Nadine said. "Why is Sir Silas corresponding with our daughter?"

"What?" Quille looked up from the lengthy letter in his hands.

"Maddy has a letter from Sir Silas."

"It's from Its Royal Tanist," Maddy said. She'd managed to say that without crying. She must be getting over the shock.

"I doubt that," Nadine said. "I'd know Sir Silas's hand anywhere."

"Sir Silas is blind," Maddy said.

"Quille makes pens for him," Nadine said. "Sir Silas need only speak his mind and the pen does the rest."

"Dad," Maddy said. "Is that true?"

Quille studied the letter in his hands, flipping through the pages. "Eh? If your mother says it, then it's true." Quille clutched the letter in his fingers. "I need to get to work." He snatched up his ashplant and hobbled from the room. He hadn't touched his breakfast.

Nadine eyed Quille's plate with a look little short of amazement.

"How do you know this is Sir Silas's writing?"

"What?" Nadine's gaze drifted toward the entry hall, where Quille grumbled and cursed as he struggled into his street coat. "Oh. Each pen is distinctive. Sir Silas's *s*'s slant sillily. Sir Edgar's *e*'s ease eastward. That sort of thing. It wouldn't do to have several dozen anonymous pens in the world."

"Could someone borrow Sir Silas's pen?"

"Certainly," Nadine said. "But they could not use it. Unless they could mimic his voice perfectly. And grip the pen just as Sir Silas does." Nadine pushed her chair back and stood. "Clean up, will you, Madeleine? I need to watch after your father."

Maddy muttered the spell Quille had taught her. The breakfast plates and cutlery began their stately drift toward the kitchen stairwell. Rookhaven hopped on Maddy's shoulder and tugged her ear.

"Does Sir Silas read all of Tan's mail?" Maddy said.

"He may now." Nadine adjusted her holster and the Undeath Hood on her belt. "Two letter bombs in as many weeks." Nadine met Maddy's gaze. "It would not surprise me."

Maddy swallowed. "Two letter bombs?"

"Indeed," Nadine said. "The first aimed at Its Royal Highness. The second at Its Royal Tanist. It seems that the Folk have escalated from grumbling to gunpowder."

"It could be anyone," Maddy said. Its Royal Highness was not well loved by anyone, human or Folk.

"It could be," Nadine said. "But it is not."

The street door squealed on its hinges. Quille had promised to have it oiled months ago.

"We may be out all day," Nadine said. "If Emma reappears, send her to the Department immediately."

"Is Emma in some kind of trouble?"

"Without question." Nadine's jaw worked. "Trouble with me. Nothing official. Yet. I worry merely she is in some danger. Lock the street door after me. Open for no one save family."

"I'm going to the tower to study," Maddy said. "I won't hear the door."

"Better still," Nadine said. "Lock up now." Then she was gone, chasing after Quille.

Maddy couldn't think about Emma. She didn't dare. It was easier to think about Sir Silas answering Tan's mail. Tan hadn't even seen Maddy's letter. There had to be some way around that impediment. Sir Silas probably didn't even read the letters. Maybe Tan hadn't forgotten her.

The more Maddy learned about the Spelling Bee trophy, the more it worried her. She needed Tan's help. Nadine wouldn't understand, and Quille was too distracted, and Emma was missing. Rookhaven and Madame Aubergine were only interested in stuffing Maddy's head with boring history and language lessons and the sort of spells Maddy was certain Quille wouldn't approve of.

Maddy held her palm toward the hissing gaslight and splayed her fingers. Jets of flame rocketed from the lamp to her hand, five thick ropes of fire. Maddy knotted them together into a raging fireball and cut the strands. No, Quille wouldn't care for this at all. Maddy hefted the fireball in her palm. It was much more solid than the ones she made in Night. Now what was she going to do with it? In Night, Maddy sent the fireballs rocketing toward a target Madame Aubergine painted on a large stone. Maddy had quite a throwing arm now, but that wouldn't do here.

Rookhaven leapt up and down on Maddy's shoulder. "The forge, the forge."

"Of course," Maddy said. She juggled the fireball on her way to the back garden.

Maddy tossed the magical fireball into the fire pit of Quille's forge. She waited for the flames to subside. Mundane House was largely brick, but most of the outbuildings were wood. It never paid to be careless with fire. Maddy conjured a powerful stream of water from the quenching trough. After a hissing, steaming battle, the fire eventually died. Maddy felt like crying when the last spark winked out, but it wasn't safe to leave magical fire lying around untended, and she didn't have any choice. She still didn't like it. She decided it was best to practice offensive arts only in Night, when she wasn't surrounded by people and places she loved.

Once in the tower, Maddy didn't go straight to Quille's library, but to his files. Quille kept meticulous records, and Maddy eventually found the work order for two dozen pens. She cross-referenced that with the bill of materials, and used the reference number she found there to locate the design documents. Then it was just a matter of digging through Quille's working papers from that time period.

Maddy had everything she needed. It took half the day to create a temporary facsimile of Sir Silas's pen, modified to work with Maddy's voice and fingers. Maddy had promised not to work with permanent spells. Her version of Sir Silas's pen only wrote for a minute before it melted into slag. A minute was long enough.

Madeleine Oortsgarten-Quille is to be taken to see Its Royal Tanist immediately. Do not delay her in any way.

Maddy thought that would sound like Sir Silas when the Nonesuch Palace Guards ran their reading lenses across the letter. Maddy had wondered how Sir Silas could read Tan's correspondence until she'd discovered the sketches for the reading lens pinned to Quille's notes. By then Maddy had a pretty good working knowledge of magical pens. Making a reading lens didn't take very long at all. She shivered when she passed the lens over the letter. Sir Silas's commanding voice boomed in the silence of Quille's inner sanctum. Maddy felt bad about using Quille's supplies, but she was desperate. Maddy put everything back where it belonged. She tossed the remains of the pen into the forge and lobbed a fireball in after it. She waited for the fire to die naturally.

Quille probably wouldn't approve of Maddy's work, and Nadine definitely wouldn't approve of her using forged documents, but then, Sir Silas had started it. He should have passed Maddy's letter on to Tan. It was more important than ever to talk to Tan. Maddy had spotted one of the grimfoxes in Night. From a distance, it looked as though a tiny man was riding it.

Other than Quille, Tan was the only enchanter Maddy knew. Maddy slipped the letter into an envelope, and the envelope into her pocket.

There was still more research to do on the Spelling Bee trophy. Maddy didn't have to use the letter yet, but now she was prepared. She'd go to Tan when she had proof positive about the trophy. Together they'd figure out what to do. Maddy was also still worried about Emma. She'd promised not to tell anyone in her family that Emma was training to be a Deemster of the Night Court. She could tell Tan. That wouldn't be breaking her word.

It might be incredibly stupid, though. If Tan and Its Royal Highness were getting letter bombs from the Folk, then they'd been judged and sentenced by the Night Court. But that couldn't be, because if Emma was involved with the Night Court, they wouldn't send letter bombs. They'd send Emma.

Emma didn't remember who she was, or where she was from, or what she was made for, but she seemed to remember everything else. How to speak and read and write, how to deport herself in proper company, how to ride, and play the pianoforte, and even how to sew, though she would never admit that. None of those were Emma's principal talents, though.

Maddy didn't like to imagine Emma materializing out of the shadows, her cold gaze falling on Tan, the swift and fluid motion of her arm, the rock-steady set of her wrist, the barely perceptible squeeze of her trigger finger.

Emma Sunbury never missed. It was easy to imagine Emma as a conquering warrior. It was easy to imagine Emma leading legions of the undead out of Night. It wouldn't be out of character. Not if Emma thought she was doing right.

Nadine and Quille were focused on Emma. If Maddy tried to help, she would just get in the way. She had other problems —not bigger problems, but ones she could tackle.

The Spelling Bee trophy wasn't just a trophy, and it wasn't just a baleful lantern of rage. It was a magical device, and one that defied classification. It wasn't powered by enchantment, the distilled magic that enchanters bound into made things; or by true magic, the inherent magic of magical creatures; or even by common magic, that weak magic sometimes found in humans. There was only one other class of magic. Sorcery. A distilled magic like enchantment, but one that could only be practiced on flesh. Only undead humans and kylochs practiced sorcery.

The Spelling Bee trophy wasn't flesh, and, in any case, Maddy couldn't detect sorcery until after it was used. She'd have to be a sorcerer or a kyloch to perceive its latent power. That meant that whatever she saw in the Spelling Bee trophy was a fifth type of magic, something no one had ever heard of. There couldn't be any other explanation.

Maddy jotted this line of reasoning down in her working notebook. She scanned the long shelves of Quille's library. There was no telling how many of these books referred to the

Spelling Bee trophy, or to some arcane knowledge that might help her understand it better. It would take weeks just to browse the tables of contents.

Still, the trophy would be in her possession for nearly a year longer. If it truly was evil, as Maddy now suspected, it would be safe in her hands until she had to pass it on to next year's winner. Unless she won again next year. With all she learned in Night, that would probably be easy. Madame Aubergine was an excellent teacher. Maddy doubted the Spelling Bee would ask her to throw great bolts of lightning from her fingers, but the idea made her smile. Perhaps if she brought back the six grimfoxes she'd accidentally spelled into Night and whatever things rode them now. She could really send them to Hell this time. Maybe she'd win on flair points again. It was something to consider.

Maddy pulled down one of Quille's volumes of dragon magic and stared at it. She felt sick, just like she always did, but it was nearly a minute before she dropped the volume and sprinted for the lavatory. That was a good ten seconds longer than yesterday. She was building up a resistance to whatever it was about those books that make her stomach heave.

Maddy reshelved the book and went to work. When the daylight was nearly gone, Maddy stopped. She liked to work above the fog, where the sun ruled half the hours of the day. She didn't want to take the long staircase down to the endless half-light and her dark little room.

It was easy now to see why Quille was as he was. It was agony to close her book and rise. Tomorrow, Maddy promised. "I'll be back tomorrow." If she could wait that long. She ran her fingers down the spines of Quille's dragon books, one at a time.

There was an experiment she wanted to try with the baleful lantern, but she'd have to wait until everyone was asleep to do that. Maddy so hoped Emma wasn't in any danger. She missed her sister. Maddy hadn't realized just how much she missed

Emma until Emma wasn't around whenever Maddy needed her.

That was a selfish thought. That Emma existed just for Maddy's needs. Maddy wondered if Emma ever felt like she needed Maddy. Because if she did, Maddy wouldn't consider that a selfish thought at all, but a very great kindness. A vote of confidence. Of trust. It was strange, how something good could be bad if you did it yourself. If you needed or wanted someone. Yet, it was good, it felt so good to be wanted and needed. Emma had to be safe. Maddy didn't care if it was selfish to need her sister. She did, and she always would. Even if Maddy could never admit to Emma just how selfish she felt toward her. Even if Emma wouldn't believe her.

Nadine and Quille were home from work, and Maddy started to ask about Emma, but then she saw Emma. She was carrying a small valise. Her lips were set in a thin line, but her eyes held no anger whatsoever. Her eyes held no feeling whatsoever, a look that was so typically Emma. She marched past Quille and Nadine without a word. Maddy thought that Emma hadn't even noticed her standing there. Maddy tried to make herself small, projecting invisibility.

"I didn't tell," Maddy whispered.

Emma stopped abruptly and pivoted on the ball of her right foot. She faced Maddy with that same calm stare she wore when she met handsome young gentleman on the street or when she gunned down crypto-naturalist pirates on the deck of a burning slave ship.

Emma took Maddy's hand in hers. The knuckles of Emma's left hand were white against the handle of her valise. "I know, Sis. I'm moving out, getting my own place. Half-place, anyway."

"Oh," Maddy said. She wanted to ask if Emma had even considered that now Maddy was stuck at home, with no chaperone, and that she would never get out of Mundane House without her parents hovering over her until she was Emma's age. But that was selfish, and mean-spirited. She owed her sister love and nothing else. "You have a roommate?"

"Beatrice Cannon," Emma said. "I found her."

"Is she alive?"

Emma laughed. It was as if someone brushed a sunbeam across Maddy's heart.

"Very much so," Emma said. "I'll explain everything tomorrow, if you would like to visit."

"I can't," Maddy said. "Not tomorrow. I'm conducting an experiment on the baleful...the um, Spelling Bee trophy, and it won't be done until the next day."

"That sounds important," Emma said.

"I'm free the following day," Maddy said. "I'd like nothing better."

"I'll stop by at lunchtime," Emma said. "You won't believe what I've discovered." Emma glanced over her shoulder. Quille and Nadine stood side by side, mismatched statues of iron and ice. "I'm sorry," Emma said to her parents. "I don't wish to hurt you."

Quille and Nadine said nothing. If they'd been as close to Emma as Maddy, they would have seen the brief flash in Emma's eyes. Emma wasn't just sorry. She was ashamed. The street door of Mundane House closed with a grumble of finality.

"I don't feel much like dinner," Quille said.

Nadine said nothing. Quille wrapped his arm around her and wiped a tear from her eye.

"Rookhaven and I will forage," Maddy said. "Don't worry about us."

"You're a good girl, Maddy mine," Quille said. "It's been a long day for your mother. I'm going to tuck her in."

"See you in the morning," Maddy said. She wasn't one hundred percent certain of that, but Quille and Nadine had enough to worry about as it was.

19

Maddy consulted her notes. She'd distilled three weeks of painstaking research down to a handful of facts she was certain of.

Fact one, the Spelling Bee was far older than the Spelling Bee trophy. Most sources claimed that the Spelling Bee began as a contest of skill between enchanters. Quille's most ancient book, *An Cataloge of Bestes Wilde and Feie*, mentioned the Spelling Bee in passing, as a drinking game acted out fortnightly. The trophy was a bottomless tankard of mead possessing the power to conjure strange and wondrous visions. The more recent sources agreed that the original trophy was a tankard, now lost, and that the current trophy was found and brought into use (on order of the Department of Criminal Magic) one thousand fifteen years ago as reckoned by Its Royal Highness's standardized calendar.

Fact two, the current Spelling Bee trophy was found in a recess near the summit of Mount Gorim. Because of its unique nature, it was studied by the finest enchanters in all of Arduvulin, who concluded its resemblance to a beehive was the result of some natural process, just as stalactites and stalag-mites resembled dragon's teeth.

Fact three, the trophy was reputed to glow with an unex-plained "interior flaime" for several years. It lost this "self-projecting lustre" more than a thousand years ago (if it ever really had it).

Fact four, no one had ever commented on the trophy radi-ating baleful beams of rage, or having any magical properties whatsoever. Quite the opposite, in fact. It was routinely described as being an ugly lump. Many enchanters noted their displeasure at having their miraculous tankard replaced with the "nasty piece of buge-encrusted tree-sappe." Several times the trophy was reported lost only to be discovered buried in a pit of discarded fireplace ashes, or drowned in a waste pool beneath a garderobe, or smothered under a Dockside oyster-midden. It was only two hundred years ago that the Sisters of St. Anselm came into possession of the trophy, but by then the Spelling Bee had degen-erated into a competency test for children suspected of having common magic and thus the potential to become enchanters.

Maddy flipped to a new page. She had recently observed a number of facts that at first seemed to have no relationship to the trophy.

Observation one, that Maddy Dune liked working in Quille's chambers. The shot tower projected above the endless haze that gave the Fogbound Realm its name. Sunlight cheered her, and the feel of it on her skin was one of the few experi-ences she missed from her years of captivity amongst the crypto-naturalist pirates. This feeling of well-being persisted for hours, even days, but eventually faded if she did not visit Quille's tower.

Observation two, Maddy could see Mount Gorim from the balcony of Quille's chamber.

Observation three, the summit of Mount Gorim projected

above the fog. It was a barren place, but it was bathed in sunlight all day long.

Observation four, lenses used for reading magic penscript possessed other properties as well, one of which was focusing sunlight to a fine and painful point.

Observation five, that the Spelling Bee trophy only superficially resembled a beehive. Observed closely, its surface might as easily be described as a beehive-shaped array of amber lenses.

Observation six, enchanters knew very little about lenses a thousand years ago. Quille possessed knowledge of lenses; however, his physical inspection of the trophy was rather cursory, his attention being focused on the unsubstantiated and imprecise rantings of his childish youngest daughter at the time.

Maddy almost scratched out observation six, since part of it was really a fact she learned while reading Quille's books, and thus belonged in the fact category, but she could straighten that out when she scribed her notes permanently in the pearl pages of her philosopher's notebook. She was on a roll, and she wanted to note her theories before she forgot them.

Theory one, that the trophy was an array of lenses, amongst other things.

Theory two, that these lenses could collect and focus something, including, but not necessarily limited to, sunlight.

Theory three, that...

There really wasn't any theory three. Not yet. Maddy had an idea that the reason the trophy lost its internal light over time was that it didn't like the Fogbound Realm any more than Maddy did. That made little sense, since it wasn't alive. But Madame Aubergine wasn't alive. She was largely gears and cogs, but she thought and felt. Sorcerers weren't alive, and they thought. Quille said he imagined that they also felt, but that was as unproven as his Unified Theory of Magic. Maddy knew better than to stack theory on top of theory.

Now came the hard part. The null hypothesis.

Maddy scribed a line across the page. She wrote:

N. H. The Spelling Bee trophy cannot collect, distill, or store sunlight.

That was simple enough to disprove. Maddy jotted down her experimental procedure.

Step one, carefully observe the S. B. trophy in the Fogbound Realm and in N.

Once Maddy had carefully observed the Spelling Bee trophy in Night, she could mark step one of her experiment as completed.

Step two, expose the S. B. trophy to sunlight for one full day.

Step three, carefully observe the S. B. trophy in the Fogbound realm and in N.

Maddy scribed a double line. PROOF. If the trophy exhibited any behavior consistent with the descriptions "interior flaime" or "self-projecting lustre," then the N. H. is DISPROVED.

Maddy read through her notes and felt a little bit of interior flaime herself. This was her first real experiment as an enchanter, and it looked pretty good. Even if the experiment didn't work, she would learn something. But it would work, and then she could go to Quille with her findings, and he would help her develop new theories and experiments to discover more about the trophy. It was a wild hope that the trophy repined for sunlight, but it wasn't all that unfounded. Maddy certainly repined for sunlight on those days when Quille's work demanded solitude and he banished her from his tower. Of course, the trophy was just a thing, but things felt. Her notebooks were positively overjoyed to be of service.

I t was late. Mundane House creaked and groaned. Madame Aubergine lounged on Maddy's pillow. Rookhaven perched on the windowsill, head beneath his wing. Maddy unsheathed the Spelling Bee trophy. It roared in sickening waves of rage, but she could bear that for the moment. She lay down on top of the covers and crossed her arms over her chest. She stared at the ceiling.

The fog outside was the opposite of a lens, diffusing the spilled light from the streetlamps, coating the world in endless grey. Maddy watched the breeze stirring the cobwebs overhead, thin tendrils dancing in the half-light seeping through the window.

Quille's housekeeper really did rob him blind. Maddy had nothing against spiders. She just didn't like sharing a bedroom with them. Maddy wished Tan could be here. She thought of Tan, alone in the Nonesuch Palace. Not even a spider for company. She hoped he didn't think she'd forgotten him. She feared that he thought just that.

It was a long time before Maddy drifted off into Night.

21

The baleful lantern materialized in Night no faster when it was out of its lead sheathing than when it was in it. That observation was curious, but not informative.

"Madeleine," Madame Aubergine said. "We must practice your defensive spells."

"In a minute," Madeleine said. She studied the Spelling Bee trophy as closely as she had in her bedroom. There were many differences in its appearance, but none that were surprising. In Mundane House, the Spelling Bee trophy only felt like a baleful lantern. In Night, it looked like one, with sickly, pale green spears of light thrusting out in every direction. It seemed to be a much more efficient radiator of feelings in Night. The anger and rage slammed into Madeleine with a physical force as she leaned in close to study the device. The closer she drew to it, the worse she felt. That experience held for Arduvulin and Night, but in Night, the illness seemed to be one of body as well as soul. Madeleine's heart ached in both worlds, but here her skin crawled.

"I've thought of another anecdote from the Days of Migration," Rookhaven said. "It's the most interesting period in Ghulan history, and this story involves The Bishop."

"Give me a second," Madeleine said. She clapped her hands together and a little squeak sneaked past her lips. Each hideous, gut-wrenching ray projected from a single facet of the lantern. That didn't prove they were lenses, but it certainly was consistent with that assumption.

Madeleine closed her eyes. The light of the baleful lantern did not abate. In fact, the flesh of her eyelids seemed to focus the beams, to concentrate them. Madeleine peered deep into the structure of the lantern, seeking out the source of the light. The light wasn't coming from the dragonflies trapped forever in amber, but from deeper in, near the heart of the lantern. There was a moment when Maddy thought she saw the light move, writhe. She jerked her eyelids open. The lantern seemed less bright.

"Madeleine," Madame Aubergine said. "We are to begin your studies now. You are not yet able to defend yourself, and—"

"And truly, no understanding of the Oligarchy and the Ghulan exodus would be complete without revealing The Bishop's role." Rookhaven grasped his eyeglasses and adjusted them further down his nose. He peered over the rims at Madeleine. "Truly."

"I'm running an experiment here," Madeleine said. "Do you interrupt Quille while he is working?"

"Yes," Rookhaven said. "When he's in danger of losing himself."

"Such is true," Madame Aubergine said. "Or when he focuses on trivialities while important matters are at stake."

"I'm not in any danger, and this isn't a triviality," Madeleine said. "Now leave me be, and I will tell you when I am finished." Maddy closed her eyelids and the lantern grew in brightness.

"She has Quille's tongue," Rookhaven said.

"And his bullheadedness," Madame Aubergine said. "These are not endearing character traits."

"No," Rookhaven said. "They are not."

Madeleine leaned forward and looked. It felt as if her skin were bathed in rage, as if every wrong in the world collected, pooled, and spewed forth at her and through her. She didn't flinch. She looked, deeper, deeper; time seemed to slow, the air seemed to thicken, and she could see it, nearly. Something wriggled, worming deep in the amber, something that wasn't quite dead, but wasn't quite alive, either. Madeleine reached out, eyes closed, and touched the surface of the lantern. It was cool, and soft, and if she pushed against it, it yielded. The tip of her finger forced past the boundary between the world and whatever the lantern held. Then her first knuckle did as well.

This truly was unexpected. She might be able to pluck the source of light free, might be able to lodge it in her heart. But that wasn't what she wanted. But it was. And her fingers knew even if she didn't. And they were destined for this, they were penetrating, they would touch the heart of the lantern and make it hers, it would be so very good to be free, to shake off the cage, Madeleine understood the cage, Madeleine would—, and then she was tumbling, head over heels, rough grit in her mouth, pulverized stone sanding her skin raw.

"It's back," Maddy said. "And you were acting strange." The hellhound's sulfurous breath was overpowering.

"The lantern," Madeleine said. "It needs me."

"We need you," Maddy said. "The grimfox, the one we saw before. It's back. And it's different. You need to look."

"But the lantern," Madeleine said.

"This is important," Maddy said.

"Not as important as the lantern," Madeleine said. Nothing was as important as the lantern.

"Maybe not," Maddy said. "But this is urgent. Don't make me drag you."

Madeleine stood and dusted off her nightgown. Her bedclothes were beginning to look a little worse for wear: sweat-stained, acid-burned, and charcoal-marked. She'd have to think about getting a new outfit. The lantern would like that. Beneath its rage, she knew what it really felt. Madeleine followed Maddy up to the edge of the crater.

"Get down," Maddy said.

Madeleine did, stretched out beside the hellhound inches below the crater's rim.

"Keep your head down, and try not to move too fast," Maddy said.

Madeleine wanted to tell Maddy that she knew what to do, but Maddy already knew that. Maddy was just talking because she was afraid of the silence. Madeleine had learned many things about Maddy in the past few weeks, and not all of them bad. As spectral hounds went, Maddy was pretty decent. That didn't mean that Madeleine had to like her.

Maddy inched forward on her belly and peered over the crater's edge. Madeleine did the same.

At first, all Madeleine saw was the ruined city and the slashing burn of lava and the cracked and dried waste that had once been seabed, now bisected by a dully glowing rent in the world.

Then she saw it, moving through the half-light, a grimfox with something man-shaped astride it. It was hard to judge distance in the flat light of Night, but the creature loomed, seeming much too close for comfort. Still, it hadn't spotted them.

"It doesn't look all that different," Madeleine whispered. "We thought it had a rider last time we saw it."

"Watch," Maddy said.

The grimfox sniffed the ground, its rider motionless. It was far enough away, and the light so poor that Madeleine was barely able to pick out subtle movements; eyes searching the horizon, head pivoting back and forth to sweep the endless ruin for whatever it searched for. As if there could be any doubt as to what it sought. The grimfox disappeared into the shadows of a crumbling row house.

"See?" Maddy said.

Madeleine swallowed. "It's not as close to us as we thought it was."

"Right," Maddy said. "I don't like it. Grimfoxes aren't supposed to be as big as horses."

"Bigger," Madeleine said. "I'd say it's bigger than a horse." And that made whatever rode it a giant.

"It might not be one of ours," Maddy said.

"It is," Madeleine said. Rookhaven had made sure Madeleine understood Ghulan history. There was nothing but trees remaining in Night, nothing else, living or dead, until a fool named Maddy Dune sent it there. It made sense that grimfoxes could be different in Night. Madeleine was different. Shattered into pieces. Grimfoxes were shades of evil men. There was no telling what they might be capable of in Night.

Madeleine slid down the crater face until she could stand without being seen from afar. She trotted over to Madame Aubergine and Rookhaven.

"We need to get out of here and never come back," Madeleine said. "Before the grimfoxes find us."

"That's not an option," Rookhaven said.

"We can't run away," Maddy said. "We have to save Emma."

"We don't even know if that figure in the bas-relief is a depiction of Emma," Madeleine said.

Madame Aubergine hissed. Her fur stood on end. Steel claws gleamed in the half-light of Night. "It will be if we don't do our jobs."

Maddy growled and shoved past Madeleine. "Coward. She

saw a grimfox and it scared her. Scared her enough to abandon her family."

"You don't understand," Madeleine said. She glanced at the baleful lantern. It needed her. And it absolutely couldn't fall into the hands of anyone else. Not when it was too sick to defend itself.

"You're the one who doesn't understand," Rookhaven said. "Madeleine, you will continue to come here whenever you sleep. Until you've sealed the pinhole you made."

"I don't even know where the pinhole is," Madeleine said. "And there's no way a grimfox bigger than a horse would fit—"

"Pinhole is a metaphor," Rookhaven said. "Call it a breach, if you like. Relative to a Gate, it isn't very large. Yet. It will grow unless you repair it."

"The grimfoxes aren't hunting prey," Madame Aubergine said. "They're seeking a way out."

"To our world," Maddy said.

"It's just a matter of time," Rookhaven said. "That is why you must listen and pay attention and learn."

"Why aren't we searching for this breach ourselves?" Madeleine said. "We have to find it before I can fix it." If she could fix it.

"We don't have to find it," Madame Aubergine said. "We know where it is."

"Stupid and cowardly," Maddy said. "I am beginning to dislike you, Madeleine Oortsgarten-Quille."

"It takes time to come to terms with certain facts," Madame Aubergine said. "Were you able to defend yourself—"

"And understand the mistakes of the past, so that you don't repeat them," Rookhaven said. "The truth would be more—"

"Combatable," Madame Aubergine said.

"Bearable," Rookhaven said.

"Just tell me," Madeleine said. "Enough with the games and half-truths."

"You," Maddy said. She paced over to confront Madeleine, the fires of hell burning behind her eyes. "They're not hunting us. They're searching for you."

"It's pretty obvious they're after us," Madeleine said.

"No," Maddy said. "They're not. Rookhaven, Aubergine, and I are nothing to them. They're after you. Not to kill you, but to use you. Use you a very bad number of times."

"Madeleine," Rookhaven said. "You're the breach. The rift."

"And only you can mend yourself," Madame Aubergine said. "Time grows short, even in Night. We hoped you would realize this by now and ascertain how to accomplish it."

"No," Madeleine said.

"They need you," Rookhaven said. "They will not stop until they have you."

"I'm sorry, dear heart, but this is true." Madame Aubergine said. "The stakes will only grow higher if the grimfoxes stumble across the Oligarchs."

"No!"

"It's too much for her," Rookhaven said.

"We're better than this," Maddy said. She pressed her disgusting muzzle into Madeleine's palm. "We have to be."

"No!" Madeleine pulled away. "I can't!" She was not an animal. She would not become an animal. "No!"

"Sleep," Madame Aubergine said.

Maddy awoke screaming. "No!" Her lungs burned. Her ears rang with her own shouts. "No! No! No!"

It was a moment before Maddy realized someone was in her room. Something. It burned with a brilliant flame as it moved to her nightstand and slid a note beneath her bedside lamp.

A door slammed in the hallway outside Maddy's room, followed by the sound of running feet. The creature turned toward the door and hesitated before it crouched before the windowsill, peering down the four stories to Quille's littered back garden.

"I beg your pardon, Sir Bird," Tan said. "But I'm in need of your perch." It shoved Rookhaven aside and leapt.

By the time Nadine burst into Maddy's room, sidearm in her fist, Its Royal Tanist was a disappearing ember in the fogbound twilight. Maddy clutched Tan's note to her breast, careful to keep it hidden beneath her fingers.

"Mom," Maddy said. "It was just a bad dream."

Nadine studied Maddy's face before she turned to the window. "I blame this ugly monstrosity." Nadine waved her pistol toward the Spelling Bee trophy. "I will remove it."

"No!" Maddy couldn't allow that.

Nadine's eyebrows arrowed down as she peered at Maddy.

"I'm conducting an experiment," Maddy said. "In two days I'll be finished." She licked her lips. "All I need is two days."

"Where have I heard that before?" Nadine stared at Maddy for the longest time, her gaze never leaving Maddy's eyes. "In three days, I will come and remove the Spelling Bee trophy to the Department vaults. Were you not your father's daughter, I would remove it now."

"I need it," Maddy said. "For my experiment."

Nadine shook her head. "Enchanters. You are very needy people." Nadine paused at the door. "Maddy, if you were in trouble, would you come to me?"

"Of course, Mom."

Nadine nodded. "Would your sister?"

Maddy was still thinking about her answer when Nadine gently closed the door. Maddy slipped Tan's note beneath her pillow before she tiptoed across the floorboards and peeked into the hall. Nadine sat on the floor, knees hugged to her chest, her red-rimmed eyes aimed at nothing more than Emma's empty room. Maddy let her door swing shut with a click loud enough for Nadine to hear. Nadine's gaze fixed on Maddy.

"She will," Maddy said.

Nadine nodded. "You'd best wash up. I hear Quille clanking dishes downstairs."

22

Q uille and Nadine went out for the day. Maddy had Quille's workrooms to herself. She carried the Spelling Bee trophy up the shot tower and placed it in a sunny spot on the balcony. Maddy dashed into the library and pulled out one of the dragon books, staring at it for a full five minutes before her roiling stomach forced her to stop. She reshelved the book and took a seat. She pulled Tan's letter from her pocket and slit the envelope. The anticipation threatened to overwhelm her. Maddy wasn't certain if it was hope or fear that made her fingers tremble and her heart race.

Dearest Maddy,

My heart could once sense yours from a thousand leagues. Now some agency has come between us. I have searched for you time and time again, and yet you elude me. I have waited for word from you in vain. I can only conclude that you are captive to some dark coercion.

Meet me at the home of L. A. at noon tomorrow if at all possible. I long to see you, Maddy Dune.

Your eternal soulmate,

Tan

Maddy fanned herself and considered Tan's note. Of course it wasn't from Tan. Maddy only wished that it were. *Her eternal soulmate?* Tan would never write that. She wasn't even done making her soul yet. It certainly wasn't ready for mating. No, this was someone masquerading as Tan, trying to lure her into a trap. Though the flaming being that delivered the letter surely looked like Tan. Or rather, looked like the reflection of Maddy's soul-in-progress. If someone were masquerading as Tan, would they know how Maddy saw Tan? And that smug voice. That was Tan's.

The home of L. A. had to be Uncle Leo's boathouse. Where he kept *Lady Adamantine*, his pleasure sloop. Leo mentioned once that Its Royal Tanist borrowed the vessel now and then. On the open sea, Tan could escape his box and the crumbling solitude of the Nonesuch Palace. No one could see him as he sailed alone, far from shore. Particularly if he left before dawn and returned after dusk. Or if he sailed at night. Except Maddy might be able to see him at night. He blazed like a bonfire, after all.

It was best not to think about that.

Maddy practically had to pry this little information from Leo. Her uncle had let slip that he knew Its Royal Tanist. More than knew Tan, really. He liked Tan, and that was endorsement enough for Maddy. Uncle Leo said that Its Royal Tanist was a competent, if overconfident helmsman. That was high praise coming from Uncle Leo. Leo had never met another captain who wasn't a Johnny-once-a-month, sunblind dabbler or a ham-handed, slack-jawed abecedarian of the first order. At least not in Maddy's presence.

Maddy couldn't possibly go today. She was right in the middle of an experiment. She folded the letter carefully and slid it into the envelope. She checked on the Spelling Bee trophy basking in the sun. It didn't appear any different, though, in sunlight, it wasn't nearly as repulsive. Maddy thought that the baleful lantern might just feel a little less angry than it had yesterday. Comparing emotions across time was unreliable, though. Joys and horrors faded. Horrors, anyway. Maddy's joys were rare enough that she could hold them all in memory and contemplate them like a theatrical play. That Tan starred in the most memorable scene was no secret. Someone wishing to trick her could find no better lure.

An enchanter didn't abandon experiments once begun just because they felt like it. That was unprofessional.

Maddy slid Tan's letter into her pocket. The letter masquerading as Tan's.

Why would someone wish to lure her past the wards of Mundane House? That was the real question. Ten muffled clicks from the parlor repeater declared that it was early yet. Quille had silenced the irritating clock, insisting that he did not need his ever-dwindling hours punctuated with grim tolling.

Maddy had two hours until noon. It was half an hour's walk to the Docklands, and Maddy thought she might remember the way. Oortsgarten-Quilles did not traipse about Arduvulin City at night unescorted. Noon wasn't at night. Though that was a technicality. Maddy wasn't in any danger. It was Quille's reputation that would suffer. Quille said himself that he had little of that left. He wouldn't care, but Nadine would. Nadine's reputation would suffer if her youngest daughter were spied wandering the city unchaperoned. And that reputation was an additional ward around Mundane House. And Eusebius Quille.

Perhaps if Maddy went disguised, as the Hag of Barna had. Quille had books on glamours and enchanted disguise. And Maddy had time. If this... assignation was a trap, no one would expect Maddy to arrive in disguise. And if it were really Tan? Maddy raced to the library and began unshelving books. The

Spelling Bee trophy would be fine on the balcony. She'd hurry back from the meeting and continue her experiment. She didn't need to keep an eye on the trophy every hour of the day. Nothing would happen to it while she was gone.

23

Maddy was hopelessly turned around. And the clock was ticking. She wandered past elegant row houses with freshly scrubbed brickwork and lovely new-painted doors in bright, fog-battling colors, all fronting an expansive and flower-garlanded central green. Well-dressed ladies and gentlemen, all fully human, traipsed the sidewalks in clumps, heads together, chatting. Most did not notice Maddy from a distance. But all backed away as she drew near.

Her disguise worked against her in the finer neighborhoods of Arduvulin City. She'd modeled her outfit on Pango, Uncle Leo's second mate. That had been a flash of brilliance and desperation at once. It turned out to be impossible to disguise her eyes, at least without more time for research. Maddy wore a broad-brimmed deckhand's flat, the sort of headgear sailors and crypto-naturalist pirates wore in the windless and baking sun of the Deadrums. Her eyes were in shadow, but revealingly plain to see if one were to approach closely.

No one ever approached Pango closely. Maddy made a half dozen tries before she conjured the ideal reek of rancid fish oil, hot tar, and a year of man-sweat and salty grime. Her Pango-guise would blend in perfectly in the Docklands. In a fine, law-abiding residential neighborhood, it had the opposite effect. Maddy drew stares and pointed fingers. She couldn't even ask for directions. Pango was mute. All of Leo's sailors were. Maddy had carried her costume's verisimilitude a bit too far.

Maddy walked as if she knew where she was going. When she spotted a patrolman following her, gaining on her, she ran. He gave chase, but she was fast and desperate. Once she passed the first boarded-up tenement he lost interest. Maddy pressed her hand to her side, catching her breath. She watched the patrolman from a distance. He made a rude gesture at her. He began walking back toward the fine homes and solid citizens who paid his salary.

Maddy's pulse slowed. She was in one of the tattered neighborhoods clinging to the cliffs above the River Selby. Maddy followed the street as it wound in the general direction of the Docklands. As she continued, the neighborhood grew rougher and rougher. Once, she was accosted, but she opened her mouth and pointed at Pango's butchered tongue. This didn't seem to discourage the street courtesan. Unsheathing a facsimile of Pango's curved scimitar and shaking it did. Pango's weapon gleamed in the noonday sun, a bright crescent Maddy always found curiously at odds with Pango's filthy appearance.

Maddy was glad she didn't have to do more than shake the weapon and ululate as well as a tongueless man could. She wanted to run, but that was just the sort of behavior predators looked for. Maddy sheathed her scimitar when the woman retreated and did not return with reinforcements. Maddy kept her fingers on the scimitar's hilt as she walked along.

The fog thinned as Maddy approached the water. That was normal, and in the future she'd remember to use that thinning as a guide. Magic was much more difficult to do near water.

And the fog was magic in a way. Fuel for magic, Quille said. An accelerant.

Eventually Maddy recognized the streets, and better still, she could see the tall masts and spars jutting above the long wooden warehouse piers, and hear the shouts of draymen and the jangle of harness and the cobble-grinding roll of iron-shod wheels. Uncle Leo docked his two merchant vessels, the *Moorhen* and the *Moorcock* at various terminals depending upon the journey's cargo, but he kept his pride and joy, the trim sloop *Lady Adamantine*, in a covered boathouse on Grunion Quay.

Maddy darted across the street between a wagon hauling great hogsheads of ale and a lumber wagon, its drayman whipping two swaybacked nags to no effect. The horses were miserable. Maddy could feel it. The drayman was miserable as well, and sick, and destined to die within a week. The air reeked of a thousand warring scents; rotting fish and fine perfume, sweet wine and workman's sweat. Tar, and molasses, and whale oil. Not for the first time, Maddy wished that Mundane House were in the Docklands, where strange people and exotic products came and went without comment, where everywhere was frantic industry, and every man and woman judged solely on their skills and willingness to work hard. Where a half-human girl with an ugly past might just fit into the shadows and stay there. Unnoticed. Uncommented on. Unfeared.

Maddy made her way from shadow to shadow along Grunion Quay. She was already late. Still, she reconnoitered the boathouse before she dared try the door.

Lady Adamantine's home was whitewashed and gleaming, unlike the rotting and greying terminals surrounding it. Uncle Leo was a stickler when it came to anything concerning ships and maintenance. His finely painted boathouse blazed in the thinning fog, a beacon of prosperity in this rundown part of the Docklands. Leo kept *Lady Adamantine* farther up the Selby where rents were cheaper. Past the more profitable, and thus expensive, terminals closer to the mouth of Third Bay, but not so far upstream to require passing the falls of the Selby and Its Royal Highness's toll locks.

The door to *Lady Adamantine*'s boathouse was unlocked. Uncle Leo would never do such a thing. *Lady Adamantine*'s figurehead had fist-sized diamonds for eyes. *Lady Adamantine* was laced through and through with wards against any number of eventualities, including pilferage. Arduvulin City crawled with threadbare hedge-enchanters and common thieves. Few could undo Quille's invisible wards. Even fewer could pick one of Quille's permanently enchanted locks. That was how Leo and Quille had first met, arranging security for *Lady Adamantine*.

A heavily laden scow eased upriver under oar, the helmsman calling out and laughing. "'Ware the shore boys, it's *Pongo!* Bear upwind, lads, and put your backs into it!"

Maddy couldn't stand in front of the door all day woolgathering. Someone was inside Uncle Leo's boathouse, or had been inside, and she wasn't going to discover who it was without going inside herself. Maddy let a little fragment of hope creep into her heart. It really might be Tan. He had a key to Uncle Leo's boathouse.

Maddy hoped her Pango illusion held. It was temporary, after all. She touched the hilt of the scimitar. Best leave it sheathed. She might hurt someone with her unpracticed flailing. She might hurt Tan. Maddy glanced behind her before she ducked through the doorway.

It was dark in the boathouse, *Lady Adamantine* looming large and pale, her tall mast unstepped and lashed along her deck. The diamond eyes glistened in a placid and implacable face, a figurehead that always reminded Maddy of Emma. Fog-dimmed rays of light slashed through the darkness from pinholes overhead, illuminating drifting dust as sparkling jewels. Dust meant someone had been here recently. Might still be here. Maddy stopped and listened. The only sounds were the gentle lap of water, the soft creaking of lines, and the ragged rasp of her own breath.

Uncle Leo was extremely neat and organized, every line in its place, every box and bale lashed down just so. There was little other than *Lady Adamantine* in the boathouse, but Leo did have a small workroom where he could carry out routine repairs on working tackle and the like. The door to the workroom was closed. Though not completely. That was not like Uncle Leo at all. To leave any latch unlatched.

Maddy's heart hammered in her chest. It took her a moment to realize the sun-darkened and tattooed fingers gripping the door pull were her illusion-wrapped own. Maddy's legs shook. Was it better to creep the door open imperceptibly, or burst through with a wild push?

The boathouse smelled of salt air and dry rot, nothing out of the ordinary. The only sounds were Maddy's harsh breathing and the regular lap of waves against pilings. It was too dark to see into the workroom. Why, then, did it feel as if every hair on Maddy's body stood on end?

Maddy listened to the magic of the world. *Lady Adamantine* drowsed, not content, but resigned to her circumstances. Every nail and board, line and lashing seemed at peace. A rat chewed an unexpected treat, shivers of joy racing down its spine. Another rat's heart swelled with anticipation. And another. Rats were a fact of life around ships and cargo. But there was no cargo in Leo's boathouse. There shouldn't be anything to draw rats.

Maddy burst into the workroom with a wild push.

The flooring seethed with rats skittering amongst dying and scattered remnants of flesh and flame. Maddy shouted and stamped her feet. All but the boldest rats raced away. A being of flame had exploded in the workroom. Strange and unfamiliar organs lay framed by the shattered remnants of a ribcage, every bone bent and twisted as if from the inside out. As if inverted.

"NO!" Maddy kicked a rat and sent it scrambling for cover. "No no no no!" This couldn't be Tan. It couldn't be. Tan.

Maddy panted, panted in a way she never had before, not when she was captured, and recaptured by crypto-naturalist pirates, not when the man who stole her away from the Wild Hunt pointed a pistol at her point-blank and fired. Her brain did not want to work. Her eyes did not want to see. Her heart felt as if it had died. *Tan.* Not Tan.

It had to be Tan. Unless the curse Tan wore rode so deep that even the smallest remnant remained soaked with it, a curse so tightly bound to Tan that even Tan's hair and fingernails, if Tan even had hair and fingernails, were cursed. Then a changeling would be cursed, and would look just like Tan. Cursed. A being of flame. A changeling of flame. Maddy's stomach knotted again and again. When she swallowed, it felt as if acid burned her throat.

Maddy had to know for sure. She dropped to her knees amidst the hideous ruin and forced herself to look. Not to feel. To look.

How was she going to make certain this was Tan? It couldn't be anyone else. No one would have access to Tan in order to make a changeling. The ruin of the body, the internal organs, weren't even vaguely human. Bipedal. Humanoid. Maddy wondered what her own body looked like inside. Certainly more human than this. Probably, anyway. Maybe not. It didn't really matter. If this was a changeling of Tan's then it would look like Tan, inside and out. It just wouldn't be Tan.

How had Quille detected the difference between Beatrice Cannon and her changeling double? He hadn't said. Surely Maddy could figure it out. Maddy closed her eyes so that she could think. All she could see at first was the wreckage that had been Tan. Maddy forced herself to breathe, slowly, deliberately. To breathe in and think. To breathe out and think.

Oh. It was obvious. If this were Tan, then Maddy would still be able to feel Tan's essence. The remnants of his life-force. Even if he were dead. But what would a changeling's essence feel like? It might feel identical to Tan. But it wouldn't. Because it wasn't Tan. That was how Quille was able to tell.

Maddy forced her eyes open, forced her mind to bear the ruin that might have been Tan. She concentrated, listening for those whispers she usually struggled to ignore. Everything that once lived and everything that might live whispered to Maddy in life and in death. Trees, and rock, and stone. Folk, and humans, and beasts, magical and otherwise. They all whispered. They all spoke eternally in their own distinctive voices. If you knew how to listen. If you could bear to listen. Maddy rocked back on her heels and touched her fingertip to a dying flame.

There was nothing of Tan's joy, of Tan's pain, of Tan's singular spirit in the wreckage strewn about the workroom. There was nothing of life at all. This wasn't Tan.

It was a trap.

Maddy leapt to her feet and raced for the door. The haft of an oar buried itself in the pit of her stomach. She rebounded, sucking wind, trying to twist to the side, but the attacker was too fast. The oar lashed out again, a wide sweep aimed for her ear. Maddy ducked and kicked back; the oar splintered against the doorframe. Maddy sprinted past him, the man with the oar, he wouldn't catch her, she had to tell Nadine, he couldn't catch her. She glanced back. She had gained ground. She ducked through the boathouse door. A callused fist hammered her into Night.

24

Maddy woke soaking wet and strapped to a chair. It was no use trying to pretend unconsciousness. She'd sputtered and moaned when the bucketload of water struck her face. Her jaw hurt abominably. Maddy imagined that was how a broken jaw would feel. The bucket clattered across rough floorboards.

If she hadn't been killed already, her captors meant to keep her alive. She'd escaped and been recaptured by crypto-naturalist pirates dozens of times. She wasn't afraid after the first few times. She'd seen others captured as well. Hundreds of times. Magical creatures, even half-magical creatures like Maddy, were just too rare and valuable to kill outright. And too difficult and dangerous to kill as well. A lot of magical creatures had horrible powers at the moment of their death.

As long as she was alive, she had hope. It never paid to take these sorts of situations too seriously. Skin scabbed over and bones mended. Sometimes there wasn't even a scar to show for it. The butchered thing in Uncle Leo's boathouse hadn't been Tan. That alone made Maddy smile.

Maddy's heart skipped a beat. There was just one problem with her reasoning. She was in disguise. As a common sailor.

People killed common sailors every day. And didn't even think about it twice. She could be in a lot worse trouble than she had imagined.

"Look at him," a man said. "He thinks this is funny."

She was definitely in a lot worse trouble than she imagined. Maddy opened her eyes. She recognized the man, though she'd never heard him speak. Bushy-haired, with a thick, drooping mustache. He'd been at the Spelling Bee trophy presentation. He was the one who'd tried to speak with Nadine. Detective Nightingale.

Nightingale wore a dark suit under his street coat, both the suit and coat the latest in fashion. He was trim and muscular. His shirt cuffs were frayed and his shoes needed a shine. His balled fists were enormous. Emma wouldn't like him at all. Any girl with a brain in her head would cross the street to avoid him.

They were in a warehouse, one of the great freight terminals built atop the piers jutting into Third Harbor. There were no ships docked at this terminal. All the cargo handling doors were shut. The air was close and smelled of rotten straw. A floor-to-ceiling stack of moldy bales towered behind the second man.

Maddy knew the second man as well. Bolive Defarish, the man who had tried to kill her dad. Justice Goodfellow. That was what he called himself.

Maddy jerked her chin toward Goodfellow's bandaged and clearly infected hand. If Goodfellow had been to a surgeon, he should ask for his money back.

"You ought to have that looked after," Maddy said. What she heard, and thus Justice Goodfellow heard, and Nightingale as well, was a great deal of inarticulate tongueless mumbling. Maddy glanced at her hands. The backs of her fingers were hairy, but, despite that, they were tattooed in crimson and bronze and yellow ochre to resemble a dragon's scaled claws. Maddy was still in her reeking Pango guise. No wonder the men kept their distance.

"Look at its eyes," Goodfellow said. "They are just like Quille's beast-girl."

"Not at all," Nightingale said. "There's intelligence in these. I mean to extract that intelligence and get to the bottom of this."

Goodfellow shook his head. "But if it is like Quille's monster, it's apt to be dangerous."

Nightingale laughed. "All of Quille's so-called children are nothing more than specimens to him. He collects half-castes so that he can study their pitiful bastard magic. There's nothing dangerous about a single one of them, and nothing special either, to him or to anyone else. Though I wouldn't mind strapping that Emma Sunbury down and cross-examining her."

"It's getting agitated," Goodfellow said.

"I'll fix that." Nightingale stepped forward and drew back his fist.

"Detective Nightingale." Justice Goodfellow grasped the other man's arm.

"What?"

Maddy struggled against the ropes binding her to the chair. Everything Nightingale said was a filthy lie. Maddy shouted, "You lie!" but it only came out as a roaring, tongueless noise.

"Don't kill it. I know people who will pay good money for such a thing."

"I'm not about to kill it," Nightingale said. "It's the prime suspect in my investigation."

"But that wasn't even a human being back there."

"Its Royal Tanist isn't a human being," Nightingale said. "That's true. But this is the work of sorcery, and this thing is as close to a lead as I have. I'm not wasting it. So let the hell go of my arm unless you want a second useless paw."

Nightingale massaged his knuckles and grinned at Maddy. "It's a damned shame I can't pound that stink off of you."

Maddy saw the fist coming this time. It still knocked her so far into Night that she made a fresh crater.

25

T his was serious. There were a number of problems, and Madeleine needed to address them carefully, one by one.

Maddy paced at her side. "I'm going to go see where we landed."

"What?" Madeleine said. "Oh. Fine." She glanced quickly around. It was impossible to tell where they'd landed. The cloud cover above was just as blank and slate colored as ever, the endless lightning coursing from cloud to cloud just as random and meaningless. This crater wasn't very deep but every bit as monochrome and dead-feeling as the usual crater Madeleine cowered and practiced her spell casting in—and suffered through her history and language lessons in. Madeleine thought they'd landed a little closer to the ruined city, but that didn't matter for now. There were a couple of ugly possibilities she needed to sort out first.

Nightingale might conclude that his punch had killed her. If he decided to dispose of her body—by tipping it into the harbor, say—then she had serious worries. Maddy Dune couldn't swim even if she was alive.

Madeleine was certain that she died whenever she entered Night. Since Nightingale had knocked her into Night once before and revived her, he might try that again. Or he might look closer and see the truth. There was no way of knowing, and nothing to be done but worry.

Tan was missing, just like Beatrice Cannon was missing until Emma found her. Madeleine had no idea where Tan was, but Nightingale wouldn't believe that. If Maddy Dune's enchanted disguise failed, he'd discover who she was and every clue would lead back to Quille and, worse, to Nadine. Madeleine was terrified for Tan, but she could crumble over that later. Now was not the time to be a wilting flower, and even if that was a mixed metaphor, Madeleine simply did not have time to fret about it. Nightingale was frightening, and if he discovered who Madeleine really was, he would be able to hurt her with more than his knuckles.

Quille said Nightingale hated him because Quille had stolen Nadine away from Nightingale. Nadine said that was a lie, but a lie that Nightingale believed. Madeleine didn't have time to sort out all the possible ways the facts could be distorted to harm her family. Quille's half-caste monster was found in disguise, crouched over the remains of the missing heir's sorcerously butchered changeling twin.

The truth was that Nightingale's arguments—that Emma, and Rookhaven, and Maddy were Quille's specimens for study —were utterly true and false at the same time. Those were the sort of arguments that people believed, because there was a time when Maddy Dune believed that and hadn't had the sense to see that being a specimen could be true without being the end of the story. Madeleine believed that there was a time when even Quille might have agreed with Nightingale, that he adopted his children purely as an intellectual exercise. And to make Nadine happy. Less unhappy, anyway. At some point, though, that had changed, just as at some point Maddy Dune's enchanted disguise would fade and she would be revealed to be all the horrible things Nightingale and Goodfellow said and believed about her. But not merely that. She was Tan's friend, and she had been lured there, and she had done what she'd done for all the best reasons. But no one wanted to read about that in the newspaper.

Certainly the horrid details would make the most brilliant fodder for *The Times of Arduvulin.* That was if Goodfellow decided to publish the affair rather than cover it up and sell Maddy Dune to the people he knew. Not that there was any doubt as to who those people were. If Justice Goodfellow knew how to contact crypto-naturalist pirates, then he was not good. Not good at all. The sooner Maddy Dune exposed him, the better.

Madeleine needed to devise an escape plan that kept her parents strictly out of the picture.

Maddy streamed past Madeleine at full speed, her tongue lolling, acid dripping, paws leaving bloodred lava tracks with each ground-eating stride.

"Run!" Maddy shouted. She hurtled on like a bullet.

A deafening cry rent the air, the shriek of a baby being tortured. Madeleine's gaze jerked to the source of the sound. She took a step back. Her fingers weaved just as she had practiced. Channeling magic to gather lightning from the sky.

Grimfoxes larger than horses shouldn't exist. Nor should they be mounted by black robed, faceless manshapes. Armed and armored creatures whose legs melded into the grimfox's skeletal flanks. Whose cruel talons gripped broadswords twice as long and thrice as cruelly sharp as a sailor's puny scimitar. The grimfox cried again.

Madeleine ran.

Maddy passed Madeleine, running the other way at top speed. She stopped ten feet from Madeleine, ten feet closer to the grimfox. Two more grimfoxes crested the brow of the crater.

"Where there's three, there's six," Madeleine said. She continued to gather lightning in her fingers. She knitted the crackling bolts into a tight, tight ball of blue fire.

"I know," Maddy said.

The grimfoxes advanced slowly.

"I'll hold them off," Maddy said. "They can't get to our family through me."

"I'm not deserting you," Madeleine said.

"If they get to you, they can get to Arduvulin," Maddy said. "You can't let them catch you. Run, before they get behind us."

"Maddy," Madeleine said. "Come here."

"No, I have to stop them. I have to save you so that you can save Emma."

"We have to stop them, Maddy." Madeleine could see that now. Grimfoxes simply could not be defeated alone. None of the most horrid foes could. "Hurry here, and I'll get us out of this."

The spectral hound growled at the advancing grimfoxes and trotted over. The grimfoxes took their time. Madeleine didn't think that the grimfoxes were used to thinking of themselves as large, powerful creatures. They couldn't see past what they'd been to what they'd become.

Madeleine continued to weave her ball of lighting. She crouched next to the animal part of her. She'd hated that part of herself all her life. It wasn't merely hate. Madeleine feared the monster that now stood between her and certain death, teeth bared and defiant. She didn't want to be part girl, part beast. She didn't want to be harnessed to a demon.

"I think I can kill them all with a gaze," Maddy said. "But it will take three days for them to die."

"They're already dead," Madeleine said. "And there's no such thing as a day here. But it wouldn't hurt to try."

Madeleine squeezed the ball of lighting tight, until it was

small enough to grip in one hand. She looped her free arm around Maddy's neck.

"They're getting ready to charge," Maddy said. "I gazed at three of them, but the other three aren't looking my way."

"Maddy," Madeleine said. She pressed her cheek against the hellhound's own. She inhaled the spectral hound's sulfurous breath, an odor straight out of the fumaroles of hell.

"What, Madeleine?"

"You're a good friend," Madeleine said. "Better than I deserve." Madeleine could barely see the outline of her fingers, of her hand, of her arm. It was growing increasingly difficult to remember where Madeleine ended and Maddy began.

"You're the best," Maddy said. "Don't be afraid. I won't let anyone hurt you."

"I'm not afraid," Madeleine said. The dust of Night danced as six grimbeasts paced around Maddy and Madeleine, circling in for the kill. They were horrid, wicked creatures and they were going to win.

That was not acceptable. It didn't matter what it cost to stop them.

"Maddy?"

"What, Madeleine?"

Madeleine rose up on her hind legs and gripped the ball of lighting in her hand. There was no telling Madeleine from Maddy. Not anymore. "Sleep," Madeleine whispered.

26

A third bucketful of water struck Maddy in the face. Maddy was still more than halfway in Night. She'd thought she'd managed to gaze at all six grimfoxes, but she wasn't sure. She shook her head and droplets of filthy water scattered.

"Damn it," Nightingale said. He wiped his face with one hand while he drew back his other in a fist.

"Don't," Goodfellow said. "I think it's hiding something."

"That's not exactly breaking news," Nightingale said. "It can't speak. I wonder if it can write? Just drawing pictures might be enough."

"Hey," Nightingale said. He shook Maddy, chair and all. "Stop resisting. I need you to cooperate."

Maddy nodded.

"Nightingale," Goodfellow said. "I think it's hiding something in its hand."

"Really?" Nightingale grabbed Maddy's fingers and pried. She was stronger than she looked, but no one ever believed her. She decided that just for today, Nightingale was marginally stronger than Pango, though that wasn't really fair to Pango since there really weren't any jobs in Arduvulin City that demanded the sort of strength and endurance sailors developed, and Pango was both wiry and incredibly centered.

"Check the other one," Goodfellow said.

"I will," Nightingale said. He gripped Maddy's left hand and squeezed with both hands. Almost all magical creatures were left-handed. A strange but true fact, and one that might be useful if Maddy ever needed to unmask an enchantedly disguised magical creature. Or half-magical creature. Unless that half-magical creature had the sense to pretend otherwise. Maddy let the fingers of her left hand yield.

The cargo door on Maddy's right slid open with a squeal just as Nightingale managed to pry Maddy's fingers open. The lightning-ball rolled across the decking toward the dry-rotted bales of straw. It began to expand.

"Nightingale," Nadine said. "I understand a suspect was apprehended."

"Bloody Nora," Uncle Leo said. "It's Pango!"

Nightingale said nothing. His eyes were fixed on the lightning ball. Maddy had planned this all out. Fire wasn't as powerful in Night as it was in Arduvulin, so it stood to reason that lightning wasn't, either. Maddy intended to bring back just enough lightning to ignite the bales of straw and cause a distraction. But apparently lightning brought from Night was at least as powerful as lightning from Arduvulin. Bolts began to break free, spearing off on unpredictable vectors.

That was just a side effect. Lightning packed densely expanded for a while. Then it exploded. If that were a ball of Arduvulin lightning, it would have enough force to rip the guts out of the entire warehouse. Night lightning looked to be about twice as powerful as Arduvulin lightning. At least twice as powerful.

Uncle Leo drew his work blade and began to saw through Maddy's bonds. "Hang on, Pango, you filthy odiferous little indispensible fool. Mercy man, I think it's time for your annual swim."

Goodfellow screamed when an arrant bolt of blue fire speared the column next to him, tearing away great splinters. He stared dumbly at the six-inch shard of oak driven through his left hand.

"Leo, stop," Nadine said. "He is Nightingale's prisoner."

"He's my man," Leo said. "And he's been tied to a chair and beaten."

"I doubt that," Nadine said. "It's against regulations. Nightingale!"

Nightingale drew his weapon and aimed it at the lightning ball. Goodfellow sprinted toward the far end of the terminal.

Maddy shrugged the last of the restraints off. She turned to Uncle Leo. His pupils dilated when her gaze met his.

Nightingale cocked his weapon.

"Run!" Maddy shouted, and tongue or no tongue, Leo had no problem understanding her. He dashed for the doorway. He tackled Nadine on the fly. Maddy didn't wait to hear the splash. She slammed into Nightingale's back, her hands still weaving the spell Madame Aubergine taught her. Together they tumbled across the filthy wood of the warehouse deck.

Defense against lightning was a tricky spell. It was impossible to tell if it would work until it had to. The spell drew all its power from the lightning itself. Either Maddy got it right or both she and Detective Nightingale were dead.

The stacked bales of straw exploded in a ball of blue fire.

Maddy couldn't hear her heartbeat or feel her pulse. She draped over Nightingale, a boneshaken cape of weeping, half-human flesh and blood.

Nightingale began to struggle. Maddy kicked away. The

warehouse decking shifted under her feet. Nightingale struggled upright. He reached for Maddy's collar. She squirmed away from his grasp.

The lightning had ripped gaping holes in the warehouse's deck. The entire building sagged on its pilings and groaned. Fire spread across the nearest end of the warehouse.

Nightingale lunged for Maddy again. Maddy leapt to a thin supporting beam. Jagged splinters and rusty nails studded the beam. One nail ripped its way through Maddy's left shoe. She yipped in tongueless pain.

Nightingale stretched across the gap, gripping Maddy by the collar. Maddy kicked his shin and felt bone snap. They both plunged into the debris-strewn waves below.

Maddy jerked to the surface, sputtering foul water. She couldn't swim. She flailed her arms but only managed to attract Nightingale's attention.

Nightingale began stroking weakly toward her.

Maddy spit out a mouthful of brackish water. She didn't know any magic to keep her afloat. Magic didn't work well around water, and it didn't work at all in water. She was going to drown. All her struggle had accomplished was to move her away from Nightingale and into the central current, where the muddy water of the River Selby ran undiluted through the salty water of Third Bay.

Nightingale closed the gap to forty feet. His arms and legs churned away, bringing him closer. Gaining on Maddy.

Maddy spotted a shattered strip of decking caught in the Selby's current. She tried to invent a body motion to move her toward the timber while keeping her head above water. She could do one or the other. Not both.

The timber drifted toward the faster, central current. Nightingale gained on her with each stroke.

Maddy closed her eyes and plunged beneath the surface.

She kicked as hard as she could in the direction of the decking. Her head broke the surface. She sucked in a great breath of air along with a mouthful of water. She looked behind her.

Nightingale flagged. She'd gained ground. The timber floated within arm's reach.

Massive fingers clamped onto Maddy's legs and yanked her beneath the surface. Enormous limbs gripped and tugged her along.

Maddy struggled, but the sea creature was too strong. They raced along faster than the current. Then she was rising, her chin breaking the surface. Maddy gasped for air, managed two short breaths.

The creature pulled her under again. Maddy lost count of the number of times she nearly drowned before she was hoisted by the collar and tugged onto the course gravel of a narrow and driftwood-strewn strand.

Uncle Leo flopped down next to her with a sodden squish and a groan. "You don't swim any better than Pango, Maddy Dune."

Maddy pitched onto her stomach and coughed up a bellyful of estuary water. She coughed for a good five minutes, every cough punctuated with a sob.

"Nadine," she managed to spit out at last. "Is she—"

"Your mother swims like a merrow," Leo said. "She paddled away clean, and that disgusting little newsman as well. Though he was on fire for a short time, or so it seemed when he plunged into the bay."

"He said he would sell me to crypto-naturalist pirates."

"He bluffs," Leo said.

"No," Maddy said. "When he thought Detective Nightingale might kill me—"

"That won't happen," Leo said. "Imagine a man. Striking a woman. I won't stand for it, Maddy. No decent person would."

Maddy rolled over and propped herself up on shaking arms

and elbows. Her foot ached abominably. The flesh around her right eye felt puffy. It burned with salt. "He thought I was a man."

"A man strapped to a chair," Leo said.

"I wasn't cooperating," Maddy said.

"Who would, strapped to a chair?"

"I imagine a lot of people would," Maddy said. "Nightingale seemed to know what he was doing."

"Wait until your mother hears about this."

Maddy's stomach roiled. "You can't tell her anything."

"They'll say that Pango killed Its Royal Tanist," Leo said. "I believe I can tell anyone anything I like to save my man."

"Oh no!" Maddy said. "I didn't mean to—"

"I was born bored with that phrase," Leo said. "Spare me, if you will. There is no need for you to fret about our Pango. He, and Mango, and Sarajule are wise in the ways of the world. They will have heard and will have hoisted anchor. So long as the truth comes out in time, all will be well."

Leo stood and held his hand out for Maddy. "You've a more pleasant odor about you, Maddy Dune." Uncle Leo's jaw worked as if chewing some invisible bit of gristle. He glared at the surf. "We'll look after that eye as soon as possible."

Maddy glanced at her hands. Her enchanted disguise had abated. It was good to have a functioning tongue again.

"Your wardrobe is a tad worse for wear," Leo said. "We'll stroll around this headland and get you out of the wind to dry. When the longboat from the *Moorhen* arrives, we'll see you properly outfitted for the journey home."

"I thought the *Moorhen* was outbound," Maddy said.

"We've a system arranged for this sort of eventuality," Uncle Leo said. "It's important to know how to slip out of any port silently. Sarajule knows where to look for our fire. And how to navigate a longboat through the shallows."

"So you have a plan," Maddy said. She tried to keep up with Uncle Leo but her foot felt as if it were roasting.

"Always," Leo said. He scooped Maddy up in his arms. He carried her as if she were weightless.

"Me, too," Maddy said. "Usually."

"Let us hope my plans are a little less interesting," Leo said.

27

M addy watched the little cutter as it picked its way through the shallows. Sarajule waved and Uncle Leo waved back. He glanced over at Maddy.

"Here is where our desert island adventure ends, Maddy." Leo's big smile disappeared. "Once we have you settled on board, you will tell me everything you've been up to."

Maddy nodded.

"Everything, Maddy Dune. No matter how trivial you might think it is."

Maddy shivered in the rising breeze. "And then what?"

"And then I'll think on it," Leo said. "And together we will devise exactly what to tell Detective Inspector Nadine Oortsgarten and Professor of Enchantment Eusebius Quille. And exactly how to tell it."

"I already have some ideas," Maddy said.

"I'm sure you do," Leo said. "But I am deadly serious, Maddy. There is only one captain on this vessel, and you are looking at him. I will decide. The more I know, the better equipped I'll be for the job. You won't help your cause by glossing over the ugly parts. Or by omitting the embarrassing ones."

"I understand," Maddy said.

"Make certain you do," Uncle Leo said. "I love you as much as anyone in the world. But if I find you've lied to me, or omitted a single fact? I'm done with you. I don't tolerate dishonesty in a seaman, and I won't abide it in my own kin."

"We're not really kin," Maddy said.

"That sort of thinking is for fools, young lady." Uncle Leo spread his arms wide, as if claiming the world as his own. "Look around, Maddy. We share all of this, you and I. How can we be anything less than kin?"

"I'm afraid you won't want me as kin once you know the truth." Maddy swallowed. "All the truth."

When Leo spoke, his voice was quiet and serious. "Leonides Farrago has no right to judge another. Remember that, Maddy Dune."

The bow of the longboat crunched against the gravel of the beach. Pango leapt out, painter in hand. He held the bow while Maddy clambered aboard and Leo doused the fire. Leo stepped aboard without getting his boots wet.

"Can't be too careful with fire," Leo said. He grinned at Maddy and waggled his fingers back and forth to Sarajule and Pango. Pango shoved off and Sarajule poled until they were clear of the shallows, then stepped the mast and set the sail. The fog was thinning toward Grunion Quay. Black smoke rose in the distance.

"Sarajule says it was just Tanner's old warehouse, and no one was seriously injured," Uncle Leo said.

Sarajule signed something else, and Uncle Leo signed back. "Sarajule says that your parents know you're safe, and not to worry."

That was easy for Sarajule to say. Maddy felt the blood drain from her face. "Are they on board the *Moorhen*?"

Uncle Leo laughed. "After our last adventure, Quilley swore to never set foot on one of my vessels again. And your mother gets seasick."

"That's not an answer," Maddy said.

"Now you're as big a stickler as Emma Sunbury," Leo said. "No, Maddy, they're not on board. We'll be ready when the time comes for you to face them."

Maddy nodded and watched the bow wave dance along the hull. Maddy had to decide if she could tell Leo the truth.

Uncle Leo, I die every night. Then I go to a borough of Hell and practice frightening magic under the tutelage of my father's clockwork cat. In the morning, I kiss my sorcerer-hunting mother. And smile as if I hadn't a care in the world.

Being dead and practicing magic. According to Its Royal Highness's law, that made Maddy a sorcerer. Everyone knew the penalty for being a sorcerer. And the penalty for knowingly harboring a sorcerer. If she told Uncle Leo the truth, Maddy's problems would become his problems.

28

"Is that all?" Uncle Leo said.

Maddy had told Leo everything. He had listened silently with a bland look on his face.

"I'm a sorcerer," Maddy said.

"Of course you aren't," Leo said. "Your breath would fog a mirror, would it not?"

"Now," Maddy said. "But not when I'm in Night."

"Its Royal Highness doesn't rule in Night."

"But my body remains here," Maddy said. "When I'm in Night, it remains in Arduvulin, and it is dead."

"The Folk of Penfold Vale make a potion," Leo said. "That potent drink will lay a man out stiff for three days and nights. Jackson, the *Moorcock*'s surgeon at the time, proceeded to have the legs of my trousers shortened. Can you imagine? He also had my captain's frock altered to suit his narrow backstabbing shoulders. He was a fast worker, was our Jackson." Uncle Leo shook his head. "No, Maddy, trust me when I tell you. Appearances can be deceiving." Leo scratched his beard and frowned. "That fine coat was ruined and fit for nothing but a betrayer's shroud."

"But—"

"No buts," Leo said. "It's late, and I need to consider all you've said. If you'll permit it, I'll watch over you as you sleep, and ascertain if there's any truth to your fears."

"And if there is?"

"The usual. We'll invent an explanation that seems perfectly normal." Uncle Leo patted Maddy's hand. "Perfectly normal and legal. No task is too hard for the flexible mind. Only dogma possesses the power to ruin the world, Maddy. Remember that."

"Leo—"

Leo turned down the wick on the gimbaled deck lamp swinging over the tiny desk in his cabin. "I apologize in advance for the hardness of that bunk, niece. If you like, I can have Pango bring a hammock, and we'll let the *Moorhen* rock you to sleep in the sailor's cradle."

"The bunk will be fine," Maddy said. "I'm used to sleeping on a deck."

"I thought by now you'd be accustomed to the feathery-soft mattresses and pillows of Mundane House."

"Me, too," Maddy said. "But they never go anywhere interesting."

Maddy stretched out on the tiny bunk. It was truly hard, but other than that there wasn't a thing to complain about. Maddy felt so much lighter now that she'd shared her burden. It was still terrifying, the idea of facing Quille and Nadine. But it wasn't nearly as terrifying as having to face them alone. Maddy closed her eyes and waited to die again.

29

M addy stood before the great street doors of Mundane House. She felt like a stranger. Uncle Leo had loaned her a dark, hooded cloak and a bull's-eye lantern. He'd escorted her through the fogbound streets, the pale moons of gas lamps punctuating the early morning dark as they paced along, their footfalls echoing off brick walls and iron-shod doors. Leo had left Maddy there to face her parents alone. He had offered to stay, but Maddy didn't want him to witness what was to come. His demeanor toward her had changed noticeably since her confession of last night, and there was no way to undo that damage. She didn't want to pile ruin on ruin. She had slept, really slept, and for the first time since the Spelling Bee she hadn't been torn from her bed and thrust into Night. Maddy felt Uncle Leo was to thank for that. Perhaps she couldn't die while he watched over her.

Maddy's fingers hesitated. Once she brought the massive, verdigris-tinted knocker against its anvil, Mundane House would come alive. Maddy would be thrust between the worried and angry flaying of her mother's tongue and the soul-crushing weight of her father's disappointed gaze. She could run away, like Emma, but no one would have her, not even Uncle Leo, because he wouldn't tolerate dishonesty in a sailor. Running away from her mistakes was the worst kind of dishonesty. If she started lying to herself, she'd lose sight of the truth, and her soul-in-process would turn dark, and then even if Tan could see her, she wouldn't be able to bear the sight of Tan. Tan needed Maddy to find him, and to do that Maddy needed to be strong. Maddy hefted the knocker and let it fall. She did that three times before Quille answered the door.

"Now they're aiming at the noggin and the heart." His expression was indecipherable.

"May I come in?" Maddy said.

"Do you want to?" Quille tilted his head to the side and considered Maddy.

"More than anything in the world," Maddy said. She wouldn't cry. She wouldn't let herself cry.

"You've hurt your mother. That changes things between you and me."

"I know," Maddy said. "I've hurt you, too."

"Only at arm's length," Quille said. "But Nadine. I've sworn on my honor to protect her at any price. I renew that oath every night. I love your mother more than life. I wonder if you can understand that. I am not a forgiving man."

"I understand." Maddy unshuttered the bull's-eye lantern. The beam burned a narrow track through the fog. Maddy could aim the beam in any direction and follow it. It wouldn't matter. She turned away so that her father wouldn't see her shatter. She would walk away, and keep walking, once she managed to get her feet to move.

"Madeleine Quille." Quille struck his ashplant against the flagstones. Maddy's lantern blinked out. "I've sworn five oaths, Maddy. In all my years. One I failed through weakness. Now these remaining four, I'd no idea they might pull me in cross directions."

Rookhaven landed on Maddy's shoulder and tugged her earlobe thrice. "Come home, come home."

"Sons are so much easier than daughters." Quille wrapped his arm around Maddy's shoulder and turned her toward the open doorway of Mundane House. "Don't force me to choose sides. And don't expect me to forgive you."

"I won't, Dad." Maddy wiped her cheek.

Quille wrapped his arms around Maddy. "I love you more than life, Madeleine Quille."

"Madeleine Oortsgarten-Quille." Maddy leaned her cheek against Quille's shoulder.

"That's an unruly moniker." Quille kissed the crown of Maddy's head. "Let's go see you mother. Surely we can untangle this rat's nest before it strangles all joy."

30

Nadine watched in silence as Maddy crossed the broad carpet of the public drawing room. She sat in her stiff-backed chair by the fire, her hands folded in her lap. The silence was uncanny, and not at all like Nadine. Maddy wished her mother would just rage at her and get it over with. Except this time there might not be any getting over it. The gas lamp overhead hissed and hissed.

The strong scent of old magic wafted across the drawing room. Nadine's gaze drifted away from Maddy, to Maddy's right. Two young gentlemen lounged on the sofa, one on either side of Emma. Old magic ponged off them.

"Maddy," Emma said. "You had us so worried."

The two young gentlemen rose and bowed to Maddy. One was thin and dark, the other tall and curly-whiskered. Both were mind-numbingly beautiful.

"Mr. Nayheightly, Mr. Whindarrow," Emma said. "My sister, Mademoiselle Madeleine Oortsgarten-Quille. These gentlemen volunteered to search for you. They are quite strong swimmers."

"Your sister is too kind." Mr. Nayheightly smiled and

brushed his hair back. His ears were pointed, as were Mr. Whindarrow's. They were both glashtins, shape-shifting Folk that some people mistook for water horses. And they were in Nadine's home. Because of Maddy.

"I imagine you are unparalleled swimmers," Maddy said. "I didn't realize the Folk were concerned about my well-being."

"The Folk are concerned about the well-being of all citizens of the Aos Sí," Mr. Whindarrow said.

"I am particularly concerned about the pretty citizens," Mr. Nayheightly said. "And their pretty sisters." He smiled at Maddy, a look of unbearable attractive force.

Maddy's knees nearly buckled. "Right. Um—"

Nadine's gaze snapped to her right for an instant. She frowned at Maddy. "Emma and her friends were just leaving."

"Now that we know Maddy is safe." Emma clasped Maddy's sleeve. She pulled Maddy close before she whispered. "You missed our lunch. It is essential that we speak."

"I don't know what's going to happen to me," Maddy said. "I can't—"

"I understand," Emma said. "I'll call each day at noontime. Sooner or later Nadine will relent."

"I'm not so sure."

Emma patted Maddy's sleeve, "I am. Take care, Sis."

"Emma," Maddy whispered. "Glashtins are terrible rakes." The crew of the *Polyphemus* had captured one. They'd had to bridle and chain it to keep it from seducing every one of the female deckhands.

Mr. Nayheightly plucked Emma's hand from Maddy's sleeve and stage-whispered. "We are excellent rakes, and our hearing is excellent as well."

"The great Eusebius Quille has just muttered that we've overstayed our welcome," Mr. Whindarrow said. "Now he's muttering to his cane in the Annish tongue."

Emma raised her voice. "We're going, Dad!" Mr.

Nayheightly and Mr. Whindarrow bowed to Nadine. Mr. Whindarrow attempted to kiss Nadine's hand.

Quille said, "Enough," and shuffled the pair toward the street door.

"You can stay," Quille said to Emma.

"No, I can't," Emma said. "I have work to do."

"Your sister might benefit from your support."

"My sister is steel and my mother flint," Emma said. "Sparks will fly and there's nothing I can do to stop it. We both know who will end up sharpened by the encounter. And who will remain unchanged."

Quille blinked. "And what does that make me?"

"Superfluous to this engagement," Emma said. "I can send my valiant stallions on if you have time for a chat. In the dining room."

Quille nodded, backing out of the drawing room and closing the doors behind him.

"THEY SEEM NICE," Maddy said.

"Come here," Nadine said. She didn't move from her seat.

Maddy placed her lantern on the sideboard and hugged her cloak tight. Those few steps toward her mother were harder than swimming the Selby.

"Let me look at you," Nadine said.

Maddy folded the hood back. Her gaze kept dropping to Nadine's ankles. On the third try, she found the strength to look her mother in the eye.

Nadine sucked in her breath. Maddy took a step back.

"Oh, my baby." Nadine held her hand out toward Maddy.

Maddy ran to her mother.

Nadine touched the tender skin around Maddy's eye. "Who did this to you?" She hugged Maddy tight.

"I did," Maddy said. "It was all my fault."

"I doubt that," Nadine said. "I will have a full accounting."

"I understand."

"I was so worried, Maddy. I never want to be that worried again."

"I know, Mom." Maddy hugged her mother tight. Nadine needed that. It wasn't because Maddy needed it. Not just because Maddy needed it.

Maddy swallowed. "Uncle Leo said that you like to get statements as soon after the crime as possible."

"Did he?" Nadine blotted at her eyes. "Your uncle is correct."

"I'm ready whenever you are."

"In a moment," Nadine said. "Go get your father, and I will meet you both in the dining room."

"Ri—I mean, yes, ma'am."

31

Maddy went through nearly every detail, just as she'd discussed with Uncle Leo.

Quille ran a reading lens over Maddy's note. Sir Silas's voice rattled the stemware.

Madeleine Oortsgarten-Quille is to be taken to see Its Royal Tanist immediately. Do not delay her in any way.

"You made this yourself?" Quille examined the lens.

"I used your notes."

"That's a terrible transgression," Quille said. "But you did this without help?"

"Where would I get help?"

"I see." Quille pocketed the lens.

Nadine examined Tan's note with a magnifying glass. "This appears to be Its Royal Tanist's handwriting. Though if Maddy can make magical pens—"

"No," Quille said. "It's not that simple."

"It can't be that hard," Nadine said. "Given the plans, and—"

"Trust me on this, Nadine." Quille examined the note.

"Making magical pens and lenses is not simple. And this note is no magical forgery."

"Why would you not bring this to me, Madeleine?" Nadine sniffed the envelope. "Why would you steal away and risk yourself so?"

Maddy shifted in her seat.

"Maddy?" Quille peered at her over his pince-nez.

"Both of you work for Its Royal Highness."

Nadine shrugged. "So?"

"It doesn't want me to see Tan, and if I told you, you'd tell It, and then I'd never get to see Tan."

"Why would Its Royal Highness not want you to see Its Royal Tanist?" Nadine said.

"Because I'm distracting," Maddy said. "And Its Royal Tanist has to remain focused on protecting the Arduvulin Gate."

"Keeping you apart only makes you more distracting," Nadine said. "Does Its Royal Highness know nothing of youth and love?"

"That's what I said, but Dad said that Its Royal Highness was adamant, and that's why Its Royal Highness enchanted Tan so that he literally couldn't see me."

"Its Royal Highness is no enchanter," Nadine said. "And your father would never do something so foolish. Even if Its Royal Highness commanded it."

"I wouldn't go so far as to call such an enchantment foolish," Quille said. "Ill-advised in retrospect, perhaps, but—"

"I knew It wasn't an enchanter," Maddy said. "The Nonesuch Palace is filled with such unhappiness."

"Much like our bedchamber tonight." Nadine glared at Quille. "Quille, you have contributed to Its Royal Tanist's disappearance. Else Its Royal Tanist would not have strayed into Arduvulin City unescorted to deliver this note."

"It's my fault," Maddy sad. "Tan was abducted while delivering a letter to me."

"We don't know that," Quille said. "Its Royal Tanist might have made it safely back to the Nonesuch Palace. And been abducted there." Quille consulted his pocket watch. He fiddled with the buttons of his waistcoat. "Don't be blaming our daughter, Nadine."

"This is not the time for levity, Eusebius."

"It is exactly the time, my dear." Quille turned to Maddy. "It is prelude to that long, uncomfortable silence, when all know the conversation will turn grim. And none wish to begin."

Nadine stared at Quille. Maddy figured it was best to keep silent. Nadine sucked in her breath and peered out the window into the fog.

"Now, Maddy mine, let's talk about how you found Its Royal Tanist's changeling, and how you knew it to be a changeling. Start at the beginning."

"This might take a while," Maddy said.

"The sooner we start—"

"All right," Maddy said. "After I got the note from Tan, I knew I needed a disguise, so I read a couple of books on enchanted disguises and figured out how to work the spells."

"Hold up," Quille said. He went to the sideboard and poured a glass of whiskey. "Which books were these?"

"Flannery and Ixatlryn."

"Ixatlryn is written in Lanish," Quille said.

"Prelanish," Maddy said. "Rookhaven says that there is no subjunctive mood in Lanish."

"Rookhaven can't form a complete sentence."

"He can in Night."

Quille rubbed his chin. "Where's that?"

"A borough of Hell." Maddy took a deep breath. "At least I think it is."

"And you and Rookhaven have been there?"

"And Madame Aubergine. She wears white gumboots in Night."

Quille smiled at Nadine. "Does she? Why's that?"

"So she won't get electrocuted when we play catch with balls of lightning."

"I see." Quille laughed.

"I fail to see the humor in this," Nadine said.

"It's absurd," Quille said. "Most enchanters occasionally lose sight of—"

"Madeleine, what was that blue object that exploded in Tanner's warehouse?" Nadine stared at Quille.

"A ball of lightning," Maddy said. "When Detective Nightingale punched me in the face, he knocked me into Night. I brought the lightning back to use as a distraction, but I think the fog makes it a lot more powerful here. It got out of hand."

"Did it now?" Quille said. The smile had disappeared from his lips.

"Did it ever," Maddy said. "I'm sorry about Mr. Tanner's warehouse."

"It's insured." Quille retrieved the whiskey decanter from the sideboard. He dropped into his chair and massaged his eyebrows.

Nadine's jaw muscles knotted. Her nostrils flared. "Detective Nightingale punched you?"

"He didn't know it was me," Maddy said. "He thought I was Pango."

Nadine's ice-cold gaze drilled into Maddy. "Tell me you were not restrained at the time."

"He thought I was Pango." Maddy didn't like Detective Nightingale. But she didn't want her mom to murder him. Everything had been her fault.

"Nadine, sit down," Quille said.

"He struck my child."

"We can deal with that later." Quille squeezed the bridge of his nose and inhaled slowly. "Let's start over. Ixatlryn's written in Prelanish?"

Maddy nodded. "Definitely."

"How long did it take you to learn Prelanish?"

"Not long, once I learned Lanish. It's just like Lanish with the addition of the subjunctive mood."

"I see. How long did it take you to learn Lanish?"

"That sort of question doesn't make sense," Maddy said. "Time works differently on the other side of a Gate.

Nadine lurched to her feet. "We're going to the Nonesuch Palace. Right now."

"Hold on," Quille said.

"If the Arduvulin Gate is involved—"

"It isn't," Quille said. "What sort of Gate are we talking about here?"

"A broken one," Maddy said. "Rookhaven and Madame Aubergine call it the Dead Gate."

"Quille—"

"Nadine, sit down." Quille rubbed his hands through his hair and leaned back in his seat.

"This is a big Gate, is it?"

"Enormous," Maddy said. "Far larger than the Arduvulin Gate."

"And it's in a place called Night."

"Yes. I thought for sure you knew about it. We went there on our way to the Nonesuch Palace. You know, the detour."

"That wasn't any place called Night," Quille said. "I don't think we'll be calling Its Royal Highness until we get to the bottom of this." Quille stared at Nadine until she nodded.

"If it wasn't in Night, where was it then?"

Quille sipped his whiskey. "It's called the Cauldron of the Damned."

"Where's that?" Maddy leaned forward in her seat.

Nadine retrieved a glass from the sideboard. Quille poured until she said, "Stop."

"Ghula," Nadine said. She took a swallow of her drink and glanced at Quille. "It is not a place for young ladies."

"It's not a place for any decent person," Quille said. "Why don't you just tell us the whole story, Maddy, and we won't interrupt. We'll hold our questions until the end. Start from the moment you received Its Royal Tanist's note."

"I can do that." Maddy started slowly, but eventually the words just began to flow. It felt good having her parents' undivided attention for once.

32

The mattress shifted beneath Maddy as Nadine sat down.

Nadine brushed a lock of hair from Maddy's forehead. "Quille and I agree. Your sleep seems normal, and you fog a mirror."

"That's because my sleep is normal now." Maddy yawned and stretched. "Something has changed."

"I will continue to monitor you," Nadine said.

Maddy sat up in bed. "When will you sleep?"

"Don't worry about me," Nadine said. "Worrying is a mother's principal job. I cannot abide competition." She patted Maddy's hand and rose. She turned at the doorway. "Those horrible newspaper articles are back. All purely fictitious innuendo and ill-spirited illustrations. I see no point in it, but your father would like your opinion of today's issue."

Maddy clambered out of bed. "I'll be down in a moment."

It was amazing how her life had settled into routine once Maddy returned to Mundane House. There was something fundamentally wrong about that. Maddy needed to investigate to discover the source of her parents' blithe acceptance of her story. Once Maddy had been debriefed, it was as if the events of the previous few weeks had never happened. Quille withdrew into his ruminations on his unified theory of magic. Nadine wore herself thinner chasing after The Fifteen and searching for Its Royal Tanist.

Once safely settled in Mundane House, Maddy allowed herself to feel the full effects of Nightingale's beating. She had also picked up an unlucky half-dozen ailments from the filthy bay water she'd swallowed. She'd been bedridden for the better part of a week, and that was too long. Tan needed her. Needed her upright and searching for him.

Maddy felt better now, but not fully herself. Uncle Leo had visited and it went about as to be expected. She was still his favorite niece, but she had changed. Maddy wasn't a little girl anymore. No one who died nightly and fell into a borough of Hell was. Uncle Leo wasn't comfortable around young women who were no longer girls but not yet experienced women. Experienced women like Nadine. And Emma.

Emma refused to enter Mundane House, though she called daily at noon as promised, inviting Maddy to lunch. Perhaps Maddy would feel well enough to go today. If Nadine would let her. She didn't feel much like having breakfast, but she had to eat something, and she needed to get started trying to locate Tan.

In addition, there was her experiment with the baleful lantern to complete. It needed her, too. The Spelling Bee trophy had been exposed to the sun for many days. There were still parts of her experiment that could be performed in Arduvulin, even if Maddy was somehow barred from Night for the time being. She didn't dare breath a word to Nadine. Her mother had sworn to lock the trophy in the vaults of the Department of Criminal Magic ages ago. Nadine seemed to have forgotten. Maddy did not wish to remind her.

MADDY PERUSED the paper for anything that looked like a cage. The exciting events of a week ago were ancient history. There was an illustrated Justice Goodfellow article, though. The first in weeks.

The illustration depicted the back of Mundane House as seen from within its garden walls. Heaps of strange scrap towered beside puddled wagon tracks, oily water reflecting dim sunlight as the rutted tracks swerved to avoid oddly threatening stains; stains that were not so much splashed about the muddy yard as revealed in blotchy scabs where no lawn would grow. Dozens of bright, eager rats' eyes peered from the darkness of the foundry shed. A mysterious twist of smoke rose from the banked glow of a recently abandoned forge.

In an upstairs window of Mundane House, a window set in the most protected and secretive corner of the house, gossamer curtains drew back. Pale and slender fingers gripped the decaying windowsill. The haunted eyes of a young woman peered from between shaggy tresses, her nightgown thin and scandalously revealing, her body slim and budding. Her blazing hellgaze focused on the unsuspecting reader, her eyes horridly angry and pleading at the same time. "Damn you all for not rescuing me," they seemed to say.

The illustration painted an uncomfortably accurate picture of the private aspects of Mundane House but for the girl. Emma was much taller. And more fair. And Beatrice Cannon had given her Maddy's eyes. Maddy wondered if the wards of Mundane House had failed. No one but family should be able to enter the back garden.

The associated story was pure fiction. It insinuated that the misunderstood and mistreated beast-girl was held prisoner against her will, just as the Folk were forced to live beneath the earth at Its Royal Highness's high-handed whim.

The poor, helpless child was at once nothing more than a specimen for the vile experiments Quille conducted at Its Royal Highness's command, and simultaneously a succulent, nubile tidbit Quille lusted after on those nights when Nadine Oortsgarten and Leonides Farrago locked Quille out of his own bedchamber.

Fortunately for the half-magical and wholly captivating beauty, Quille's medical dysfunctions (the very same dysfunctions Its Royal Highness suffered) prevented Quille from ravishing the helpless waif with anything more potent than his poisonous gaze.

The Times of Arduvulin had at last penetrated to the core of Mundane House, where dark magic and even darker secrets lurked. A smaller inset illustration depicted a paddle-footed Leonides Farrago chasing a rosy-cheeked and definitely out-of-uniform Nadine around a billiard table. Above the mantle, a buck's head with Quille's face watched on in malicious silence.

Part one of a ten-part exposé, the article concluded.

"Justice Goodfellow's prose has improved," Maddy said. "He writes as well as Emma now."

Quille sipped his tea. "Goodfellow has a canny understanding of what sells newspapers." Quille placed his cup gently down. "It's one thing to tell despicable lies about your old da, to cruelly attack your mother's virtue, and to portray poor Leonides as a ludicrous buffoon. It's quite another to rail against Its Royal Highness. One is tasteless, the other treason."

"Which one will sell newspapers?" Maddy said.

"Both," Quille said. "Though to different classes of readers."

"Its Royal Highness has no sense of humor," Nadine said.

"And you do," Quille said.

"I am not offended for myself," Nadine said. "There is not one shred of truth in this article, and even a child would perceive it is farce. However, the illustration of Maddy is scandalous."

"I don't mind," Maddy said. "That girl doesn't look like me, anyway."

"That girl looks exactly like you, daughter." Quille cleaned his pince-nez. "I'm not so sure about your mother's picture, though." Quille turned his attention to Nadine. "Can women really race like that in court heels, my dear?"

"I don't wear court heels," Nadine said.

"And we don't have a billiard table to race around," Maddy said.

"Jape if you will," Nadine said. "I find none of this amusing. It is childish, and ludicrous, and worst of all, dangerous. As if I didn't have enough to worry about already."

"You're right," Quille said. "Something must be done. I'm off to the library. I could use some company, Maddy mine."

"I was headed up the tower anyway," Maddy said. She needed to check on the Spelling Bee trophy.

"And I have a lead to chase down," Nadine said.

Maddy's breath caught in her throat. "A lead about Tan?"

"Only if Its Royal Tanist is captive of The Fifteen," Nadine said. "I will lock up when I leave."

QUILLE HEADED STRAIGHT for his library. Maddy padded across the carpet to the glass-paneled balcony doors. The sun was bright in the sky. Maddy stood for a moment, letting the sunlight warm her face. Rookhaven hopped on her shoulder and tugged her earlobe thrice.

"Gone, gone."

"What?" Maddy peered through the doorway. She opened the balcony doors and peered down toward the weed-choked yard far below. The fog was unusually heavy today. Maddy saw little more than dim shapes and shadows of shapes. She scanned the balcony again. The Spelling Bee trophy was gone.

Maddy rushed to the library. Quille had just settled into his seat, the dragon books fanned out on the table before him.

"Where is it?"

"Where is what?"

"The Spelling Bee trophy. I left it on the balcony."

"Then it should be there." Quille levered himself out of his chair and sighed. His ashplant tapped in annoyance as he followed Maddy to the balcony.

"See, it's gone." It couldn't be gone. It needed her.

Quille studied the balustrade.

"Nadine wasn't supposed to take it until I was done with it." That wasn't strictly the truth, but Quille wouldn't care to sit through the long version.

Quille ran his fingers across a pair of fresh scratches in the granite of the balustrade rail. He leaned perilously far out over the rail and peered down. "Your mother wouldn't scale the tower with rope and grapple," Quille said. "I don't think she's to blame."

Maddy had to find the trophy. She was responsible for it for a year and a day. It needed her. Maddy leaned over the rail and peered into the gloom. It needed her.

"Can you find it?"

"Possibly," Quille said. "Though that may be the least of our worries." Quille examined the blankness of space between the doors. He frowned and turned toward his desk. "Let's see what else is missing."

"We have to find the trophy first."

"Help your old da. The sooner we start—"

"And then you'll help me find the trophy?"

Quille waved his hand, already pawing through his files. "I'll try."

"I'll start in the library," Maddy said. "I've practically memorized the titles."

"I'll begin in my personal files."

"Dad?" Maddy caught Quille's sleeve. "Who would want to steal the Spelling Bee trophy?"

"No one who'd seen it up close," Quille said. "Though I'm beginning to believe that ugly lump is more than the Spelling Bee trophy."

"I'm sure of it," Maddy said. It was almost alive. And definitely in trouble. "I'll make a list of any missing books."

AFTER TWO HOURS, Maddy was certain. There wasn't a single book missing. Maddy inventoried all of Quille's tinctures, reagents, and small goods against the logbook he produced from a hidden drawer in his desk. The only things missing were the materials for a magic pen and an enchanted reading lens. Maddy noted the discrepancies. She vowed to replace the consumables she'd pilfered as soon as possible.

"Nothing unexpected," Maddy said.

Quille massaged his forehead, elbow on his desk. His nostrils flared.

"What's wrong?" Maddy raced to her father's side.

"The contents of a file are missing," Quille said. The empty folio lay on Quille's desk.

Maddy flipped the folio so that she could read the label. *A Sensory Filter Based Upon the Principal of Negation Through Sinister Dualism.*

"It's just one file," Maddy said. "And it's just your notes."

"In my handwriting," Quille said.

"So?"

"So the principal of negation through sinister dualism is a bunch of blather I made up."

"Why?"

"Because I didn't want to write, 'A sensory filter based on the principal of sorcerous inversion.'"

Maddy laughed.

Quille's forehead gleamed with sweat.

It felt as if a phynodderree had head-butted Maddy in the gut. "You're serious."

"That's the procedure I invented for Its Royal Highness. To make you invisible to Its Royal Tanist. Technically, it's not sorcery. It's not worked on living flesh. Living flesh is dipped in it. But you'd have to know a fair bit about sorcery to perceive the difference."

"So what's the problem?" Maddy said. "It's not sorcery."

"Well, to begin with, knowing a fair bit about sorcery might just make your fellow enchanters vilify you as a sorcerer, don't you think? So, no upstanding enchanter will admit to such a thing, and the ones who would admit to any knowledge are fools and ignorant of what they're talking about. They'd declare enchanting a bit of hairbrush leavings as sorcery through sheer unmitigated stupidity.

"But in the case of the great Eusebius Quille, not a bit of fact need enter into account. Worrying about the truth and falsity of a charge would get in the way of payback and decades of accumulated envy and spite."

"But you can't be a sorcerer," Maddy said. "You're not dead."

"I would be by the time a court convened." Quille knitted his fingers together. "I'm not widely held in esteem, and some have been waiting a lifetime for just such an opportunity. I don't need to tell you what can go on in a prison cell."

"Hang on," Maddy said. "Do you have other files around here that people could use to accuse you of sorcery?"

"Just about every new invention for the past ten years."

"Then why would anyone steal only this one?"

"Oh." Quille scratched his eyebrow. "This might not be about me at all."

"It might not be," Maddy said. "You said hair and fingernails. Could you use this spell to make a changeling?"

"It doesn't have to be hair and fingernails for my spell," Quille said. "Those items are simply easiest to acquire. Any dead tissue from the subject could be used to create the filter. You have to increase the quantity of material for the filter, since of course a little hair doesn't go a long way, but it's not analogous to growing something living. It's just the replication of the media itself and those sensory esthers that are associated with the media. The most difficult part is inverting the handedness of the esthers to their sinister complements."

Maddy tapped her foot. "And that means?"

"Oh." Quille scratched his chin. "I doubt you could grow a changeling through enchantment or sorcery."

"But you're not certain?"

"Certainty is for fools," Quille said. "I was once certain I'd never have children. Can you imagine?"

"You're not worried anymore?"

"Oh, I'm worried all right." Quille began reboxing his files. "I'm not scared of being called a sorcerer, Maddy. But I'm terrified of being hauled out of bed, and stripped of my defenses, and being made into one."

"Whoever stole this file and the Spelling Bee trophy doesn't intend to do that."

"I think you're right about that. Though I don't think we have the evidence yet to conclude it's the same criminal in both cases."

"What are we going to do?"

"Well, you're going to think about these disappearances and I'm going back to my reading," Quille said. "If my son is an emissary of the kylochs, I ought to have some idea as to what that implies."

Quille marched toward the library, Maddy following behind.

"But isn't this more important?"

"I don't know," Quille said. "But worrying about it isn't going to help, in any case. I'll get to it when I get to it."

"So you're not going to worry," Maddy said. Maddy couldn't stop worrying about the missing Spelling Bee trophy.

"Of course I am," Quille stamped his ashplant. "Now are you through cross-examining me?" He plopped into a chair. He picked up the first dragon book.

Maddy had never seen her father so upset. Regardless of what he said. "Are the dragon books about emissaries and kylochs?"

Quille seemed to relax now that Maddy had changed the subject. "Half about kylochs. They're books about a magical war between the kylochs and... Oh. Never mind."

"What were you going to say?"

"More than a young lady enchanter needs know," Quille said. "I sometimes forget myself."

"I don't mind."

"Well, I do. And your mother does. So back to your ruminations on our pilfered possessions. I'm counting on you to outsmart whoever thinks they can take advantage of the Quilles."

"When are you going to help me look for the trophy?"

"After your mother comes home and we know for certain it isn't in Department hands. And after you've done your best to find it on your own. As a young enchanter who takes her responsibilities seriously should."

"I take my responsibilities seriously." Quille wasn't listening. His nose was already buried in the dragon book. Nothing in the world could tear him away.

33

Maddy searched the grounds below the tower for any trace of the Spelling Bee trophy. She didn't find the trophy or any evidence of the trophy. She found nothing out of the ordinary at all. She listened with all her senses. Only a quarter-cask of rusting nails complained that it was out of place. Maddy shifted the barrel of nails into the dark comfort of the foundry shed.

This wasn't the first time someone scaled or descended the walls of Mundane House. Tan must have alighted in the yard after leaping from her window. It was four stories from her bedroom to the ground. Maddy wasn't inclined to try the leap herself, but many fully magical creatures could have made that leap without injury. Maddy couldn't recall a single class of creature, human or magical, that could make the climb up to her bedroom unaided. They'd need wings. Or tools, enchanted or otherwise. Maybe a dragon could climb up. A full-grown buggane wouldn't need to climb. They were taller than a house. But both bugganes and dragons would leave footprints in the mud of the back garden. And there weren't any footprints but rat-sized and human-sized ones.

Maddy had simply assumed Tan had entered Mundane House from the street. Now that she considered it though, that seemed unlikely. Mundane House was strongly warded. Tan couldn't have entered at all without one of the family as escort.

Maddy didn't have any clues about the sneaking thieves who stole her trophy and Quille's papers. But she did have facts about Tan's visit. If Maddy could figure out how Tan got past Quille's magical wards, then she might discover how the sneak thieves did as well, and then she would be one step closer to catching them.

Maddy felt a flush of warmth race through her. This was how Nadine felt when she was chasing down The Fifteen. It was like figuring out an enchantment and reverse engineering it, like solving a puzzle with most of the pieces hidden. If Maddy weren't so worried about Quille and the Spelling Bee trophy, she could grow to like detecting. Except she had an idea of what she would discover, and she definitely didn't like that.

Maddy took the stairs two at a time as she rushed to her bedroom. She inspected her window. Those wards she could detect seemed intact. Tan had headed for the door before he darted for the window. Perhaps another window or door had been tampered with.

The only unused rooms on the third floor were a pair of guest rooms and Emma's recently vacated bedroom. Maddy checked the guest rooms first. Uncle Leo stayed in one when he visited overnight. Its wards were intact. The other room was spider-infested and cold. Quille didn't have many friends and fewer guests. Its wards were intact as well. That only left Emma's room.

Maddy's stomach sank as she ran her fingers over the deep gouges in Emma's windowsill. The wards about Emma's room were tattered and breached, the invisible edges of the breach polished smooth from repeated passage. A thin young woman could worm her way through that breach. A man of Uncle Leo's size would find it impossible. It would even be a tight squeeze for Nadine, and she didn't have an ounce of fat on her. Maddy had imagined Tan's true form to equal Uncle Leo's in stature and bearing. It seemed likely Tan had entered through this breach. She would have to reevaluate her impressions when she found Tan. And she would find Tan.

Maddy clambered through the breach. She clung to the narrow window ledge and peered down. The fog flattened all distances. Falling, though, would be a bad idea. A very bad idea.

The wind swirled about her, whipping her hair into her face. She puffed, blowing the strand clinging to her lips free. It came back with company as another strong gust slammed into the corner where the two wings of Mundane House met. The wind rebounded unpredictably, setting Maddy's street coat fluttering.

Maddy dangled, four stories up, and inspected every inch for evidence of any kind. She pressed her fingers against the intact portions of the invisible wards. They felt strong as steel. Maddy wormed her way back through the tiny breach. She lost a shoe in the process and had to rush down the stairs to retrieve it. She found it impaled on a discarded heap of rusting pikes and broadswords. Maddy plucked it loose, her heart hammering. She glanced up. The wind had swept the shoe into the corner, away from Emma's window. And under Maddy's. Maybe all of Quille's wards weren't purely magical. It would be impossible to stand directly beneath Maddy's window without clambering over a heaping mound of jagged steel. If crypto-naturalist pirates and their sorcerers somehow made it into the garden, they wouldn't be able to simply toss a line up to Maddy's window. But they wouldn't need to. Not with the wards breached in Emma's room.

After she inspected all the remaining doors and windows, Maddy was certain that Tan had entered through Emma's window. She had also gained a much better understanding of house wards. The ones Maddy could detect—and that would be the simplest ones—would not pass liquids or solids from out to in. They did let the breeze in, though strong gusts outside never made it inside. The wards seemed to impede nothing from in to out. Maddy concluded that this was to allow rapid egress in case of fire. Or in case one was cornered by enemies. There was a great deal of practical knowledge she did not possess, not only about spells and their working, but of their proper application as well. Maddy knew that Quille had installed wards to prevent his escape if he died and became a sorcerer. She just couldn't detect them. Maybe only Quille could, or maybe you needed to know a lot more about sorcery than Maddy did to see them.

Maddy vowed to pay attention in the future and look at the world with an eye to detail. For example, if one were to transform oneself into a gas, as enchanters could not do, but kylochs and sorcerers were reputed to be able to, one could pass through these simple wards. That meant that Quille had further wards for this eventuality, and further wards and more, all invisible, and all layered one on the other, and all permanent magic. No wonder Quille refused to move from Mundane House. Emma insisted he could afford better. Maddy wasn't sure. A great deal of Quille's life was invested in the protection woven into every brick and stone of Mundane House.

Someone with more power than skill had torn through the wards protecting Emma's room. That rend would let anyone small enough access to the house. It was difficult to believe that Emma didn't know her room was being used. Not only was Emma courting danger herself, but the breach destroyed the protections of everyone in the house. That was just selfish.

Emma didn't possess a scrap of magic. She'd need help. She was out and about at all hours. Anyone or anything could use this route when Emma wasn't in her room. Emma might not even know the wards were breached.

Right. And kittens could fly by flapping their whiskers and wishing really hard.

Still, Emma hadn't been in her room the night Tan left his note. Nadine had slumped down in the hall in grief. Maybe Emma didn't know. Tan was probably powerful enough to breach the wards. He'd seemed plenty strong at the Spelling Bee. Maybe it was wrong to doubt her sister. Maddy searched Emma's room and found nothing incriminating. She dashed downstairs and out the doors to the back garden.

Maddy found the rope and grappling hook stuffed into the hollow of a mossy urn, the urn itself a discarded remnant of the once graceful gardens Nadine spoke so longingly of. The grappling hook had three barbs. The rope was knotted every three feet. A longer rope, also knotted, was spliced on; a sailor's splice, and a nice piece of work. Maddy had been forced to work line while a captive of the crypto-naturalist pirates. It was a tedious and never-ending chore for the deckhands, and the sort of thing a caged beast-girl's nimble fingers could do.

Whoever had done that splice was a sailor, almost certainly, though there might be other occupations that required such handy line work. Unlikely, though. Maddy carried the whole affair to Emma's window. She latched the grapple onto the windowsill and dropping the line down through the breach. The fog was thicker than usual. She had to run downstairs and then back up.

Her hypothesis was correct. The original rope was long enough to reach the ground from Emma's window.

Maddy dressed the rope into a tidy coil and raced across the back garden and up Quille's tower. She settled the grapple and dropped the line over the edge of the balcony. Down the tower she went, only to discover that the tag end of the line dangled ten feet above the ground. Emma couldn't have used the rope. Not unless she could leap like a springhorn. Or unless she stood on something.

It was easy to see how that could be done. There'd been a quarter-cask of nails out of place, after all. When Maddy apologized and brought the nails out to where she'd found them, she could almost reach the rope if she stretched. She was not nearly so tall as stately Emma. Maddy leapt and caught the tag end of the line. She pulled herself up, hand over hand. The going got easier once she could bring her legs to bear. It was a long way up the rope. Clambering over the rail was the hardest part, but that would have presented no challenge to someone as skilled as Emma.

The balcony doors wouldn't open. All of the door wards Maddy could perceive were intact. Maddy hammered on the glass for what felt like hours. Eventually Quille came to let her in. He glanced at the grapple and grumbled.

"Is the balcony door usually locked and warded?" Maddy said.

"Both." Quille frowned. "The wards have been breached by a tyro with more power than control. I can only think of one such."

"Tan," Maddy said.

"Madeleine Quille."

"Oortsgarten-Quille. And I have a key," Maddy said. "I wouldn't need to break in. Who teaches Tan enchantment?"

"Not I," Quille said. "I have no idea of Its Royal Tanist's powers, if that is what you're driving at. The rend was simple to repair. Such damage is possibly within Its Royal Tanist's powers. But there's only one way this could have happened without my knowledge. It was done by one of the family."

"Emma doesn't have a lick of magical talent," Maddy said. "And neither does Nadine. And I didn't do it."

"That leaves only one possible culprit," Quille said.

Rookhaven landed on Maddy's shoulder. "Innocent, innocent."

"No," Maddy said. "It leaves three. Besides Rookhaven there is Uncle Leo and Madame Aubergine."

"Leonides Farrago couldn't have done this," Quille said. "He can detect true magic and some forms of enchantment. Wielding magic is beyond his powers. And Madame Aubergine can only assist with magic. She lacks the intellectual power to initiate spells. By design."

Madame Aubergine cracked an eyelid at Quille. She sighed and settled deeper into her cat basket.

"That's not true in Night," Maddy said.

"It is true in Arduvulin."

Arguing with Quille was pointless. "There's another rend, in Emma's bedroom window."

While Quille hurried away to deal with that, Maddy stole into Quille's library and pulled down one of the dragon books. The text wormed and writhed before her eyes. She was able to stomach the reading for seven minutes.

Maddy reshelved the book. She picked up Quille's stuffed dragonlet and climbed back down the rope to prove her latest hypothesis. It would be difficult to descend encumbered with the Spelling Bee trophy. But it could be done. Maddy returned the dragonlet to its place. She even dusted it in thanks.

By the time she had returned to the back garden, the sky had opened up in earnest; enormous raindrops splattered the already muddy puddles. Maddy shivered and raced for Mundane House.

Maddy took the stairs two at a time and dashed into her room. She cleaned up. It was nearly noon. She'd decided that she would have lunch with Emma today.

Of course, once she decided to go, it began to pour. She would just have to bear it. There were too many unanswered questions piling up and Emma was central to most of them. Emma liked to talk about other people's business, not her own. Today Maddy was going to dig and keep on digging. Until she got answers.

34

E mma called at noon on the dot, Beatrice Cannon at her side. Beatrice Cannon had no sooner dropped the door hammer than Maddy was out the street door. Despite the weather, she plunged through the overly deep fog, struggling to keep up. The sky poured buckets. Maddy didn't own an umbrella and apparently neither did Beatrice Cannon. Or she'd forgotten it.

Maddy pulled the collar of her street coat up and gripped the neck tightly closed. She hustled to keep pace. Her foot hadn't fully healed from her mishap in Tanner's warehouse.

Beatrice and Emma made no effort to make the trip an easy stroll. Quite the contrary. They seemed in a hurry, Emma in particular. Maddy had the distinct impression that Emma was purposely keeping her distance. She hadn't so much as greeted Maddy. Emma outpaced even Beatrice by a half dozen strides. Emma didn't mind rain. Not like Maddy. Plus she had an umbrella. She wasn't hurrying because of the filthy weather.

Maddy gritted her teeth and practically ran to catch up with Beatrice Cannon. Her feet sloshed with each cold step.

"Where are we going?" The wind seemed to blow Maddy's words away. She shouted again to be heard.

"We have little time," Beatrice said. Far from attempting to catch up with Emma, she slowed. Emma disappeared into the dense fog and sideways rain ahead of them. They wound through the sensibly empty streets of Arduvulin City, Beatrice Cannon mouthing the most evasive and unenlightening answers to Maddy's questions, Maddy growing more and more uncomfortable with every stride. It wasn't just that she was soaked to the skin, her hair dripping ropes clinging to her scalp, weeping water down her neck. There was something very wrong with this whole outing.

Eventually they paused before a boarded and padlocked tenement house. Emma proceeded down the water-slick stairs leading into the basement. She furled her umbrella and shoved through the tradesmen's and servant's entrance. Emma Sunbury would never enter a house in such a way. Not willingly.

Maddy paused at the stair head. She didn't like this at all. The basement windows were boarded, leaking no light whatsoever. Not a streetlight burned on the entire block. That was not accidental. Its Royal Highness decreed that the streetlights be never extinguished. There was an entire class of public servants tasked with nothing but ensuring that Its command was obeyed. The wind picked up, the rain lashing sideways. Maddy shivered in her coat.

Maddy turned to Beatrice Cannon and shouted, "This is where you and Emma live?"

Beatrice Cannon grasped Maddy's wrist and tugged.

Maddy jerked her arm free. She glanced down the stairwell. The weather-beaten dealwood of the door panels grumbled beneath cracked and peeling paint. The entire building grumbled, broken and uninviting.

Beatrice Cannon drew a pistol from her sodden handbag.

She fumbled with the weapon with both hands, trying to cock it. Maddy slapped the weapon away. It tumbled into the rain-soaked gutter. Maddy chased after it, but it disappeared down a storm drain.

"Listen, whelp!" Beatrice Cannon shouted. She gripped Maddy's wrist again. "If you value your sister's life, you will come with me. Now."

"Why?" Maddy knew why. This all had an ugly familiarity. She just wanted to know if Beatrice Cannon knew.

"To save Emma!" Beatrice Cannon tugged on Maddy's arm. "You have to come!"

Maddy let herself be pulled along. She scanned the entry for anything that looked like a weapon. For anything that could be turned into a weapon. This was not about Emma. Maddy was certain that she was being abducted. She had little choice but to go along with it. For now. Beatrice shoved the door open on well-oiled hinges. Beatrice and Maddy plunged into darkness.

"I brought her," Beatrice said. "Now release Emma Sunbury from your thrall!"

A man chuckled in the darkness. "That wasn't our deal."

Maddy didn't recognize the man's voice. She dripped in silence and waited. It never paid to be in a hurry. Not when being abducted. Now was the time for clear thinking. Maddy wasn't like the other magical creatures crypto-naturalist pirates preyed upon. She was never like them. Not entirely. Now she was so unlike them as to be unrecognizable. She barely recognized her own thoughts. Maddy was not going to be taken alive. Not again.

Beatrice Cannon flicked a fairy light to life. A Reynardine's fairy light. It illuminated a dim and sickly circle around her and Maddy. Beatrice still held Maddy by the wrist. Maddy didn't resist. It was best to appear compliant. Until Maddy knew what she faced, she wouldn't know how to fight.

"You said you'd give Emma to me," Beatrice said.

"Did I?" The man stepped into the light. Maddy recognized him. The man with the shaved head and eyebrows from the Spelling Bee presentation. Esmond something or other.

He held Emma by the neck. Emma didn't struggle. Her face was expressionless, her eyes closed, passive and seemingly lifeless. That was so unlike Emma as to be impossible.

"Give me the beast-girl and I will give this one to you," the man said. He glared at Maddy. "You are nearly more trouble than you are worth. Still, cargo bought and paid for must be delivered. Reputations are at stake. And livelihoods."

"Do it," Maddy said. She dipped her free hand into her pocket. Her fingers found a matchstick. She hoped it was dry. "Beatrice. Give me to him and go."

Crypto-naturalist pirates never gave up. And they never, ever kept their word.

"Give me Emma first," Beatrice said. "That was the deal."

The man made a subtle gesture with his left hand, the sort of hand-sign Leo used with his mute sailors.

A snake of oily blackness rose from the shadows to wind around Emma's waist.

A second snake crept across the floor toward Beatrice Cannon and Maddy.

"You promised to give me Emma," Beatrice said. Her grip on Maddy eased.

"No, he didn't," Maddy said. "He promised to give that one to you." Maddy pointed at the thing pretending to be Emma.

Crypto-naturalist pirates were forever playing word games. It was just one form of torture they delighted in.

The man laughed. His fingers twitched in sign.

The black snake of darkness struck. It pierced Emma below the rib cage. The second snake licked out and would have caught Beatrice if Maddy hadn't kicked Beatrice's legs out from under her.

The fairy light skittered free and bounced across the rough oak floor. It struck Emma's foot just as the black snake tore up the length of Emma's torso and exited through her neck. Emma's entire body inverted and toppled over in a squishing heap, internal organs and shattered rib bones moist and glistening in the dim fairy light.

Maddy jerked her gaze away. She flicked the matchstick onto the floor. She hoped that she knew how to use it.

Beatrice Cannon shrieked. "Emma! You promised!"

The man chuckled. The black snake writhed toward Maddy.

"Get behind me," Maddy said. She concentrated all her attention on Quille's enchanted matchstick. Quille had used that matchstick to create a golem of spinning and deadly oak. Maddy understood the basics, but she didn't have a hope of accomplishing the same.

She concentrated on what she could do. The oak of the flooring began to vibrate and pull free, splintering and squealing against the rusted nails that held it captive.

The black snake leapt toward her.

Maddy batted it away with a spinning shaft of shattered timber. The wood danced and swirled.

The crypto-naturalist pirate took a step back. Then another step as the wood gathered and grouped into the pacing shape of a great and powerful hound. A hound the size of a donkey.

Maddy's oak golem ignored the man and leapt into the shadows. The black snake wormed away.

Maddy's wooden hellhound chased off into the darkness. There was a sorcerer hiding in the shadows. So long as Maddy's golem harried it, she was free.

It wouldn't take long for the sorcerer to master the golem, though. Enchantment was no match for sorcery. Especially Maddy's weak enchantment. She wished Quille were here. Or Nadine. But they weren't.

She was on her own.

"Come on," Maddy said.

Beatrice Cannon ignored her, her eyes fixed on the inverted ruin of the changeling. It looked so much like Emma that it had fooled even Maddy at first.

The man stepped into the light. He raised a pistol at Maddy.

Maddy tied off the spell animating her hellhound and met his gaze. He smiled and cocked the hammer back.

Maddy smiled, too, a great toothy grin, and held his gaze. "Where is my sister?" Maddy said.

The man's face paled. "Where you'll never find her." The man took a step back. "I'll take you to her if you come along quietly."

"Why don't you just tell me," Maddy said.

There was a great clattering of wood in the darkness. The man seemed to gain confidence at the sound.

Maddy's gaze never left the man's eyes.

The man took a step forward. "I think you're out of options." A dark snake wormed out of the darkness toward Maddy. "I need you alive."

"I know," Maddy said.

The sorcerer's snake of blackness began to work toward Beatrice Cannon.

Larque. Esmond Larque. That was his name. If Maddy was going to kill someone, she ought to at least know his name.

The man's pistol arm swung toward Beatrice Cannon. "If you come peacefully, I won't kill your friend."

"No," Maddy said. "Your sorcerer will kill her."

She continued to peer into the man's eyes. The raging fires that forever burned inside her made it to her eyes. "And she's not my friend."

Maddy growled.

The man's smile faded. He swallowed. "October," he said, calling his sorcerer to his side.

A hellhound's gaze would kill a man in three days.

Maddy was half hellhound. It might take a little longer, but not that much longer. Certainly less than a week.

The sorcerer shambled out of the darkness. He was long dead and it showed, only the spark of obsession lighting his sunken eye sockets.

Maddy wasn't sure that the sorcerer could see a hellhound's curse, but it seemed as if he could. He took one look at the man and stepped aside. His coils of oily blackness retreated.

"I don't know what he promised you, Mr. October," Maddy said. "But if I were you, I'd get whatever it was out of him before the cock crows thrice."

"Kill the woman," the man said. "And bind the girl."

"Or you could bring my sister Emma Sunbury to me, Mr. October," Maddy said, "and tell her what it is you've been promised. If it's in our power, we'll see you have it."

Snakes of oily blackness entangled Esmond Larque's arm.

He tried to jerk free. When that failed, he fired a ball into the forehead of the sorcerer. An oily fluid wept out of the entry wound, a blackness darker than night.

The sorcerer laughed. He wound his spells about the man's arm until bone shattered. The sorcerer entwined the man's legs in blackness until the man's legs were pulpy, bloody ruins.

The crypto-naturalist pirate screamed and screamed.

One thing about sorcerers, they made their minds up quickly. They were obsession incarnate, only interested in their own wants and needs, and coldly calculating in achieving them. Anyone who spent time in their company knew that.

Maddy had been prisoner of crypto-naturalists for many years. She came to know three sorcerers in that time, and they were more to be pitied than feared, unless you stood between them and their goal. Then they were to be feared above all else.

What she'd promised was against Its Royal Highness's laws. That was why sorcerers had to truck about with crypto-naturalist pirates and other such low creatures. No one decent would help them achieve their insane aims.

The sorcerer wasted no time killing a dead man. It shambled off into the dark, leaving the man, disarmed and unable to stand.

Maddy scooped up the pistol and shoved it into Beatrice Cannon's handbag.

"Mundane House," Maddy called out. "Bring Emma Sunbury to Mundane House!"

Maddy plucked the fairy light from the weeping ruins of Emma's changeling. She yanked on Beatrice Cannon's arm. "Let's go."

Beatrice Cannon jerked away. "Emma—"

"We'll get her back," Maddy said. "Now come on!"

Maddy growled.

Beatrice Cannon took a step back, than another, her eyes wild.

She bolted for the stairwell.

Maddy let her go.

She crouched down next to the man. "If you tell me who you're working with, I might be able to save you."

He spit at her feet. "Or you might not." His unshattered arm wormed toward the dirk in his waistband.

"Only the Folk can make changelings," Maddy said. "And they hate crypto-naturalist pirates."

"When did hate ever stop anyone?" The man groaned. "You hate us, and yet here you are, ready to dicker with me." He coughed and twisted in pain. "You are so young. So innocent. I envy your ignorance."

"Tell me!"

Maddy plucked the blade free. She knelt beside him, closely, watched his muscles clench and release in spasm after spasm.

That was a hellhound's curse at work. That was what he deserved.

That was what they all deserved.

Maddy fingered the blade, watching it catch the fairy light. "I could kill you now, and save you three days of torturous pain."

"Look at you," he said. "Not so innocent after all. No one gets away clean." His laugh died in a wet cough and a trickle of blood.

It came to her then, where she'd learned that motion of blade against light.

She tossed the knife into the darkness as if it were poisoned.

Maddy's stomach churned. Crypto-naturalist pirates had raised her. That didn't mean she could act like one.

The man coughed again and dragged himself toward the blade. "You've grown. We underestimated you." He panted for a moment before he spoke. "That won't happen again."

"If I kill you now, it might," Maddy said. "No one knows what happened here."

"He does." The man jerked his head toward a dark-shrouded corner.

Maddy waved the fairy light toward the darkness. A man bolted. She caught a glimpse of two hands bandaged and a burned and ruined face.

Justice Goodfellow, the newspaperman.

Maddy didn't bother to chase him as he raced up the stairs.

"You would have been wise to come with me," the man said. "When The Fifteen catch you, they won't be so kind."

"Crypto-naturalist pirates aren't kind," Maddy said.

"You have no frame of reference," the man said.

He groaned and balled on the splintered flooring before he screamed and screamed. He panted for the longest time before his voice called out, hoarse and raw. "Help me find the damned knife."

He screamed again before he lay there panting forever.

"I won't ask you to wield it." Sobs wracked his body. "Just help me find it."

He hauled himself through the gore that had once been a thing grown from Emma's cast-off flesh.

"Please."

Maddy ran, up the stairs, into the fog and rain, ran as far and as fast as her legs would carry her.

She pitched up against the dripping iron gates of St. Michan's Field, her sides heaving.

Dark shapes moved through the blanketing greyness, untouched by the weeping rain, silently passing her to enter the ancient graveyard, countless shadows of Folk. Not a word was spoken, and Maddy wasn't sure if they were living Folk or shades, shades forced to pace the fog forever for the evil they'd done in life.

Or for the good they'd left undone.

Maddy shook her sodden head and caught her breath.

She began retracing her steps through the punishing rain. She was turned around, and it took forever, but eventually she spied the tumbledown tenement.

She'd killed a man. The least she could do was help him die.

Maddy worked her way through the darkness. A halo of fairy light illuminated the basement gloom.

Maddy picked up the dim lamp, her gaze sliding across the ruin of the thing made from Emma's hair and fingernails.

The light glinted off the hobnails of a boot.

She was too late.

He'd found the knife.

Maddy Dune closed the man's eyes. She had no idea who he really was.

Who he'd been.

Maddy sat on the cold floor and clutched her knees to her chest.

She was still sitting there, rocking, when Detective Nightingale found her.

35

The ruined basement of the tenement was brightly lit, revealing every macabre detail of the scene. Detective Nightingale consulted with Detective Inspector Nadine Oortsgarten. He scowled at Professor of Enchantment Eusebius Quille.

Quille bent over the dead man and examined the evidence. He motioned for Maddy to approach.

Maddy froze to her spot. Quille motioned again, and Maddy's limbs responded with some hidden power she'd forgotten she possessed.

"What do you make of this?" Quille glanced at his daughter.

Maddy hugged her arms tight about her chest. Water dripped on the splattered floor. The dead man had scrawled out a message in blood.

Farrago.

"I don't know," Maddy said. She didn't want to know.

Quille stood. "You recognize the man, though."

"He was at the Spelling Bee trophy presentation."

"Esmond Larque," Quille said. "A competitor of your Uncle Leo's. A fellow alchemist."

"No," Maddy said. "No." Not an alchemist. Alchemists dealt in magical objects. Crypto-naturalist pirates dealt in magical beings. There was a difference.

"Maddy, do you know something you're not saying?" Quille bent and picked up a matchstick. He studied it silently before slipping it into his pocket.

Maddy glanced at Nightingale, who stood staring at Quille with eyebrows narrowed.

"No." Uncle Leo and this man had nothing in common. Quille was mistaken.

"That's good," Quille said. "This is ugly. The man does... um... did, a great deal of work for the Enclave of St. Anne. Powerful enemies. He is... esteemed. Above reproach. It's fortuitous that you followed Emma's changeling to this location, by mistake, and came upon this... tableau. Long after whatever heinous scenario had already played out."

"Dad—"

"It's strange," Quille said. "Strange that Larque has pulled up a great number of the floorboards and piled them in a haphazard heap near the interior stairwell."

"I—"

"Strange, but not inexplicable," Quille said. "One could conclude the man was searching for something."

"But—"

"No buts," Quille said. "Perhaps he found what he was searching for. Let that be a lesson, Maddy."

"What?"

"On searching," Quille said. "Searching itself is not so dangerous."

"Dad—"

Quille held up his hand, silencing her. "Finding, Maddy. Therein lies the danger. Excuse me, daughter. I believe my considerable finding skills are in demand by the esteemed

Detective Nightingale. Another man above approach, Maddy. Well favored by Its Royal Highness. Remember that."

Quille paced across the room, ashplant tapping angrily. He and Nightingale conversed. Nadine picked her way through the debris to Maddy. Her face was quite pale. Her gaze shied away from the ruined changeling.

Maddy knew it wasn't Emma. Nadine didn't possess a single shred of magic. She couldn't feel the difference. Nadine's senses were lying to her. Her body acted as if it couldn't believe what Quille and Maddy assured her was true.

"Nightingale will want a statement," Nadine said. "This is his crime scene."

"I understand," Maddy said.

"You and Beatrice Cannon and Emma were going to lunch," Nadine said. "Emma paced ahead, is that not so?"

"I couldn't understand what the hurry was," Maddy said. "Not at first, and then—"

"You couldn't understand Emma's hurry," Nadine said. "And you became separated in the fog and lashing rain. You thought you saw Emma entering this building."

"I did see, except—"

"You did see, and it was frightening," Nadine said. "Eventually you worked up the courage to investigate, though. Being your mother's daughter."

"Mom—"

"Maddy, we will speak at home, in private," Nadine said. "But first Nightingale needs a statement." Nadine turned her back to Maddy. "When you investigated, you found the scene just as Nightingale did, but the horror of it overwhelmed your young lady's sensibilities.

"It is perfectly normal, *perfectly normal*, for a sensitive girl of tender years to be dumbstruck by such a sight. Anything less would be... remarkable. Nightingale is above reproach, and held in great regard by the Department. His word will be believed."

Nightingale motioned for Nadine and Maddy.

"I'll need a statement," Nightingale said.

Maddy nodded. She couldn't look him in the eye. Her gaze kept dropping to his fists. His left leg was in a cast. He leaned heavily on a cane.

"Alone," Nightingale said. He glared at Quille.

"Eusebius," Nadine said. She and Quille walked out of earshot.

"Tell me what happened," Nightingale said. "Don't be afraid. The truth never hurt anyone. I swear you're safe with me."

Maddy lied. She said exactly and only what her mother and father had coached her to say.

Every word was true. The lie was all in what she didn't say.

It was still a lie.

"I'm sorry about your sister," Nightingale said. He leaned in close and whispered. "You have a black eye, and you're limping."

"I—"

"Does he beat you?" Nightingale whispered. He wasn't looking at Maddy, but at Quille.

"No!" Maddy said. "Never!"

"You're safe," Nightingale said. "All you have to do is tell me the truth and I'll take it from there. If you're under any coercion—"

"No," Maddy said. "Quille wouldn't hurt a fly."

Nightingale patted Maddy's arm. "You and Nadine aren't flies.

"If you ever feel in danger you must come to me. You'd have the support of the Department. If you are suffering—"

"I'm not," Maddy said. "Neither is Detective Inspector Oortsgarten. Who also has the support of the Department."

Nightingale straightened. He sucked in a great breath. "I don't understand women." He shook his head. "I see it all the time. Cowed wives, battered children, and worse. There's no shame. No one should have to bear up under a monster."

Maddy jerked away. "No. Nothing like you say has ever happened in our home. You are mistaken."

"Where there's smoke, there's fire," Nightingale said. "I read the papers."

"Don't believe everything you read."

"I don't," Nightingale said. "And I only believe half of what I hear. It's what I don't hear that I worry about."

"Don't," Maddy said. "Don't worry about me. Or my mom."

"You should." Nightingale studied Maddy's eyes.

Maddy didn't flinch. "Are we done here?"

"For now." Nightingale motioned for Nadine and Quille. "But remember what I said. Find me when you change your mind." Nightingale handed Maddy a calling card. She nearly chucked it away.

"I won't," Maddy said. "Change my mind." She tucked the card into her pocket and tried to pretend it didn't feel like poison against her fingers.

Quille hailed a cab in the pouring rain. How he'd found one in this part of town was magic in itself. He escorted a dripping and silent Maddy home to Mundane House while Nadine stayed to assist Nightingale in his investigation.

Maddy didn't care to talk. Neither, apparently, did Quille. He squeezed Maddy's hand. She leaned her head on his shoulder and closed her eyes.

That was a mistake. Esmond Larque's dead eyes stared back at her.

She opened her eyes and stared blankly at the back of the driver's head. The horse's hoof-falls clopped against the cobbles and echoed off the boarded and barred row houses. The wind had fallen, and the rain simply poured down in endless soaking torrents. The horse's flanks steamed, adding to the fog. Maddy wondered if the cab was real, or if Quille had conjured it whole cloth from the fog.

She decided it was real when Quille thanked the driver and paid him three scillingí for a one-scilling trip.

Emma was waiting in the drawing room. Her gown was

filthy. There were leaves and sticks in her hair, her fingers dirt-stained, her nails caked with mud.

When she met Maddy's gaze, her eyes were as calm as if she had been out for a stroll.

"Buried," Emma said in response to Quille's questioning gaze. "I'd nearly dug my way out when I was levitated from my temporary grave, soil and all."

"Who did this?" Quille's face bent into a terrifying scowl. His knuckles blanched white against the handle of his ashplant.

"Mr. October," Maddy said.

"That's right," Emma said. "Thanks, Sis. There were a score of men waiting for me should I excavate my way to freedom. It seems they were wagering on my progress."

Maddy explained to her dad and Emma about what really happened in the tenement, and how she'd recruited the sorcerer October to her cause. "He would have killed Beatrice Cannon," Maddy said. "I don't like her much, but I couldn't let her die when I could stop it."

Emma's voice quaked. "Beatrice is safe?"

"She was when she ran away and abandoned me."

"But she was safe?"

"Yes." Maddy turned away from her sister.

"Employing a sorcerer is punishable by death," Quille said.

"I'd rather die than be captured by crypto-naturalist pirates again." Maddy twisted her fingers together. "I promised to pay Mr. October."

"Already done," Emma said. "It seems that prior to his expiration, Mr. October was none other than Gilead McAlpine."

"The fog-engine man," Quille said. "I'd heard he'd nearly finished his prototype." Quille slumped into a chair.

"He had finished it," Emma said. "I saw it run in his ramshackle lair. It's a wheel-driven carriage powered by an engine that runs on compressed fog. Gilead October is obsessed with producing a full-scale version."

"He'll never do it," Quille said. "Not in Arduvulin."

"Well, he has a ton of scrap steel dumped down the coal-chute of his grubby little laboratory in any case," Emma said. "And there isn't any magical fog anywhere but in Arduvulin."

"How did you arrange to pay for all that steel?" Maddy said.

"As I said, those sailors guarding me were wagering on my fate. They had no need for their losses once Mr. October concluded his business with them."

"They weren't sailors," Maddy said. "They were crypto-naturalist pirates."

"They looked like sailors to me," Emma said. "They bled like sailors."

"How did they capture you?" Quille said.

"They must have drugged our meal."

"Our meal?" Quille leaned forward in his chair.

"Beatrice's and mine."

"But Beatrice wasn't drugged," Maddy said.

"No one could drug your meals if you came home," Quille said.

"Nadine wouldn't like that," Emma said.

"She would like nothing better."

"Me, too," Maddy said.

Emma stood. "I only stopped by because Mr. October insisted. Forcefully." She gathered her rather grubby parasol. "I would still like to have lunch, Maddy. Tomorrow, I believe you have an appointment for a fitting with the modiste. I'll call at noon."

Quille tapped his ashplant against the flooring. "Emma—"

Emma kissed Quille on the cheek. "What you don't know can't hurt you."

"That is the most idiotic—"

"Try this, then," Emma said. "Your knowing could hurt

Nadine." Emma squeezed Quille's arm. "And that would defi-nitely hurt you." Emma marched into the entry hall.

Quille and Maddy followed. "Are you in danger?"

"I believe I am," Emma said. "I believe we all are."

Quille gripped his ashplant more tightly. His gaze searched every shadow. "Spell it out, daughter. To be ignorant is to be unarmed."

"It's my fault," Maddy said. "The crypto-naturalist pirates used you to—"

"No, Maddy," Emma said. "I'm responsible for my own safety."

Emma turned to Quille. "Ignorance is a blessing in this case, Dad. You and Maddy are in no more danger than the rest of us."

"The rest of who?"

"The rightful citizens of the Aos Sí." Emma opened the street door and vanished into the fog.

Quille stared at the open doorway. The rain whipped in, wetting the flagstones. Maddy closed the door. She led her dad back to his chair. He sat with the unconscious motion of a somnambulist.

"What is the Aos Sí?" Maddy said.

"It's what the Night Court calls the world."

"Why would Emma think the world was in danger?"

"Because she's misguided," Quille said. "That rightful citizen blather, it's something the Folk cooked up to make their selfishness seem reasonable."

"Why?"

"So that when they rise up against Its Royal Highness, they'll feel righteous doing it." Quille slumped in his seat. "Your sister is in over her head. Someone needs to talk sense to her. Someone she'll listen to."

"But she won't listen to Nadine," Maddy said.

"She'll listen to you," Quille said. "And to her brother."

Maddy laughed. "That's crazy."

Rookhaven called from the dining room behind her, "It's not, it's not."

"It is, too," Maddy said. "Emma never listens to me."

Cold fingers tugged Maddy's earlobe thrice. "Not just to you."

Rookhaven bowed. He pushed his murky glasses up his hooked nose. He stroked the feathers of his burnsides and smiled. "To us."

Rookhaven couldn't take man-shape in Arduvulin. He said he'd tried hundreds of times. "How—"

"It was quite elementary," Quille said. "Once I knew what to look for."

"I was restricted to a single form," Rookhaven said. He shapeshifted painfully into a raven and then back into the form of a feathered young man Maddy knew from Night. Rookhaven panted for the longest time. Eventually he caught his breath. "A curse extending the length and breadth of the Aos Sí. Our father has lifted the curse."

"Counteracted it," Quille said. "Temporarily. Only those who set it can lift it."

"In any event," Rookhaven said, "Emma will listen to us."

"Why?"

"Because it was Queen Aevil who cursed me," Rookhaven said. "And it is Queen Aevil who wishes Maddy Dune gone from Arduvulin. At any cost."

"Oh." Maddy didn't even know Queen Aevil. Except from the Spelling Bee presentation. Where Maddy had made enemies.

"Queen Aevil is Chief Deemster of the Night Court." Rookhaven pushed his glasses up his nose. "Me, Emma will believe. You, she loves. She will see the error of her ways and terminate this foolish association."

"I'm not so sure," Maddy said.

"I'm confident," Quille said.

"I am certain," Rookhaven said.

The hinges of the street door squealed. Nadine pushed her way in out of the lashing rain. She paused with one arm still in her street coat, dripping.

Rookhaven smiled and waved. "Welcome home, Mom. We were just discussing—"

Nadine slid back into her coat and exited. When she entered again, Rookhaven had shifted back into his bird form. "Welcome home, welcome home," he cawed.

Nadine stumbled flatfooted into the dining room. Maddy, Quille, and Rookhaven followed. Nadine crossed to the sideboard and poured a massive drink. She slumped into a mud-stained dining chair without looking.

"Come here, all of you." Nadine sighed. "Begin at the beginning, and leave nothing out."

A crack appeared in the surface of the dining table, then two more, at right angles to it. A portion of the tabletop hinged back. Madame Aubergine peered out, her long whiskers twitching about her almost-human face. "I hope to make the entrance grand. I perceive my timing is somewhat premature." Madame Aubergine placed her steel-clawed fingers on either side of the opening and pushed forward.

"I've been very busy, my love," Quille said. "Very busy."

"I see," Nadine said.

"What did I tell you, Mom?" Maddy said. "Madame Aubergine wears white gumboots."

"I suggest she keep them off the dining furniture in the future," Nadine said.

"This is but the simplest to do," Madame Aubergine said. She shape-shifted smoothly into her cat form and stretched out on the table. She batted at Nadine's fingers with her paw.

Maddy picked Madame Aubergine up and put her on the floor. "Show off," she whispered. Madame Aubergine licked her shoulder and hopped onto a dining chair, purring. She began to bathe.

Nadine sipped her whiskey in silence. Quille poured a tall glass. He took the seat next to her. "I can explain."

"Please do," Nadine said. "And—"

"Begin at the beginning and leave nothing out," Maddy said. "We know."

Quille and Maddy began at the beginning, but they both left out the parts about Mr. October. Nadine had suffered enough shocks for one day. If she learned a new sorcerer was loose in Arduvulin City, she would have to rush out and kill it. Besides, Mr. October wasn't really loose. He was working on his fog-engine for now.

Maddy was starving, and her dad had that look in his eyes that said he was, too. Nadine was knackered. The last thing she needed right now was to go traipsing across the city hunting the undead.

"What's for dinner?" Maddy asked. Maybe settling back into routine would keep Maddy from seeing Esmond Larque's dead eyes every time she blinked.

37

Maddy lay in bed and stared at the spider webs decorating her bedroom ceiling. Closing her eyes did no good. No good at all. She couldn't sleep. It would almost be preferable to drop into Night than live with her memories. She had never killed anyone before. She'd never done anything irreversible. Anything permanent.

She tried to tell herself that she acted in self-defense. She could not have survived another day in a cage. On a filthy ship full of murderers. That was absolutely true. But now she was a murderer. Perhaps now she deserved that fate.

Maddy knew what killing looked like. What it sounded like. What it smelled like.

Murder was an everyday affair on board the *Polyphemus*. Death had been a natural part of her life before she was captured and caged as well. She had just never killed anyone herself. She hadn't known what it felt like.

Now she did. It felt like being in a cage of her own making, and never, ever being able to escape. She couldn't undo what she'd done. Ever. Esmond Larque probably had a huge family. A pretty wife who loved him. Dozens of helpless children. Who depended upon him. Who were blameless in his evil. Who would suffer for what Maddy did. Would grow up to hate. To be evil.

Because of what Maddy had done.

It wasn't just killing someone. Crypto-naturalist pirates were evil. They needed to die. But cursing someone. That wasn't something decent people did. That was one of the reasons the Folk were so detested. For most of the Folk, their principal magical power was the ability to lay curses and blessings. All the shape changing, and disappearing into thin air, and conjuring illusory horrors and marvels meant little. It was the curses people feared. That, and the rather random-seeming and trivial ways one could offend the Folk.

Maybe Maddy should have killed Esmond Larque some other way. Maybe she could live with that. But she didn't know any other way except sorcery. Killing people with enchantment was sorcery. By definition. Killing them with old magic wasn't.

It was worse. Even if it wasn't against Its Royal Highness's law.

Killing grimfoxes didn't count. They were already dead and were meant to stay that way. Maddy didn't know if she'd killed the grimfoxes in Night for certain. She hadn't had time to loiter about to see. And now she couldn't get back to Night. So she had to lie here and see Esmond Larque's dead eyes every time she closed her own.

That wasn't the worst part. Old magic, what Quille called true magic, wasn't predictable except in one way. When Maddy cursed Esmond Larque, she had simultaneously blessed someone else. She had no idea who. It usually ended up being someone the curser regretted.

Maddy might have blessed Detective Nightingale, or Its Royal Highness, or any number of people she hadn't met; people who didn't wish her well at all.

Old magic was a zero-sum game. Otherwise, the Folk would

be practicing it all the time. As it was, Maddy's curse was pretty typical of the sort of curses that were cast. She'd been cold, and wet, and miserable. She was already angry with Beatrice Cannon for her stupid, evasive answers. She was overwrought about Emma. Especially once she realized that Emma's changeling had to have been made by someone close to Emma.

Worst of all, Maddy was terrified of what she would become if crypto-naturalist pirates captured her again. She didn't think she had the strength to keep fighting them. And she wasn't a child anymore. She was just the sort of fresh young meat kylochs and sorcerers paid a fortune for. With the *Polyphemus* sunk, Maddy's crypto-naturalists' rainy day was upon them. Maddy would be sold.

And used.

She wasn't thinking straight when she faced Esmond Larque. That was why she had overreacted. Curses were the sort of mistakes a spellcaster never lived down. Fully human girls couldn't work curses. Not even enchanters. That was one of the reasons why Maddy wished she were fully human. It was why Madeleine feared Maddy in Night. She knew what Maddy Dune was capable of.

And she hated it.

Maddy had always believed that she was better than her birth mother. And now she'd proved that she wasn't. Once and forever.

It would have been better if she'd died. Except then Beatrice Cannon would have died. And Emma cared for Beatrice, even if Maddy didn't. So Maddy didn't really have any choice. That didn't make it any better. She'd probably blessed Beatrice Cannon. Or Justice Goodfellow. That would be just perfect.

Maddy stared at the ceiling until she heard dishes clinking downstairs. She filled the bath with water. She eyed the water with disgust. She would never get used to this. But maybe something of yesterday's horror would wash off.

38

Maddy tossed her towel in the bin. She eyed herself in the mirror. The horror hadn't washed off. It had seeped in and settled. Forever. Maddy pulled her gaze away and began to dress for breakfast.

39

M addy flipped past the Justice Goodfellow article in the morning's paper without glancing at it. It had been nearly three days. Esmond Larque wasn't listed in the obituaries. She flipped to the sailing schedule.

Maddy glanced at her father. "What is the name of Esmond Larque's vessel?" Larque had pretended to be an alchemist like Uncle Leo. A supplier of goods to enchanters. Quille would know.

"He had three," Quille said. He eyeballed Maddy. "*The Hand of Mercy*, *Herself*, and *Annabel's Wish*."

When Maddy could speak again she barely recognized her own voice. It was hard as Emma's. "*The Hand* is outbound on the morning's tide. Esmond Larque, Master and Captain."

"It's not as if the newspaper listings are unqualified fact," Quille said.

Maddy flipped to the postings page. "*Annabel's Wish* is advertising for crew. Twenty able seamen, references desired but not required. It sails on the morrow."

"A score, eh?" Quille blinked. "I'd say Larque had a fair estimation of your sister's worth."

"I can't believe you're so...blithe about this."

"How would you like me to be?" Quille said. "What's done is done. The Department won't investigate further. Not with Larque's association with the Enclave. They'll hand it off to the Sisters. Who will do nothing. Put it behind you."

"I can't," Maddy said. "I keep seeing him."

"That goes away," Quille said.

"When?"

Nadine leaned across her breakfast plate. "When you come to terms with the consequences of inaction."

"I could have—"

Nadine snorted. "Esmond Larque could have stayed a decent man. Evil men get what they deserve. Sooner better than later. Nothing you could do would change that."

"That's cold," Maddy said.

"That's life, dear heart." Nadine buttered her toast.

"You only wish it was, my dear." Quille crossed his silverware on his plate. "Life is somewhat less just than you admit."

"We will fix that," Nadine said. "Together."

"Look at our daughter and tell me again about justice," Quille said. "She hasn't slept a wink. All because she was forced to stand up to evil."

"She wasn't forced," Nadine said. "She chose to."

"I was furious," Maddy said. "I wasn't thinking clearly."

Quille smiled. "Now the truth is revealed. If you'd been thinking clearly, you would have done differently. You would have let Beatrice Cannon die."

"I—"

"She would be dead." Quille pushed back from the table. "And Emma. Dead."

"You don't know that."

"You remember how I warned you that certainty was for fools?"

"Yes."

"Do you think your old da a fool?"

"No."

"Then you'll trust his judgment when he tells you, Maddy." Quille tapped his ashplant against the floor. The breakfast plates began drifting toward the kitchen stairwell. "They were dead but for you. That is fact. Not speculation."

"And you saved them, dear heart." Nadine folded her napkin. "You'll just have to live with that." Nadine pushed back her chair and stood. She munched her toast on the way to the entry hall. "Now we have work to do."

Quille grinned. "And you, Maddy, have to get your brother off the dessert tray. Before he plunges down the stairwell."

"One more," Rookhaven cawed. "One more." He swallowed a cherry and hopped to the next dessert on the tray. He swooped away at the last moment and winged toward the ceiling, dive-bombing Maddy.

The cherry landed in Maddy's palm. Maddy considered it dispassionately. She hoped she did, at least. That was her new watchword. *Dispassionately*. She wasn't going to let herself be trapped into acting rashly and regretting her actions. She was going to be thoughtful. And deliberate. And dispassionate. From now on.

Maddy tasted the cherry. It was good. Not as brilliant as yesterday's, before she'd done something terrible that she could never undo. But good enough. Passable.

Maddy had the rest of her life to decide if she could live with that.

40

Maddy sat at the dining table long after her parents were gone. She had a lot to think about.

Tan was still missing. The Spelling Bee trophy was still missing. Crypto-naturalist pirates were in Arduvulin City, hunting her and endangering her family. Emma was mixed up with the Night Court, and that horrid Cannon woman, and who knows what else. And Maddy had killed one man and blessed someone else. Someone unknown and not her friend.

Detective Nightingale believed Quille brutalized Nadine and did horrible things to Maddy. And Justice Goodfellow had witnessed what really happened with Esmond Larque. Maddy couldn't remember if he had witnessed her negotiating with Mr. October or not. Trading with a sorcerer. Punishable by death. She was surely forgetting something else dreadful, but that was enough to think about for now. Maddy had to decide which problem to tackle first.

At least she wasn't dying every night anymore. That was an improvement.

Oh, right. Now she remembered. Someone was creating

changelings. And sorcerously inverting them. And it was probably The Fifteen. Maddy didn't have to worry about The
Fifteen. That was Department business and Nadine was on the
case.

Except Esmond Larque said The Fifteen were after Maddy.
Which had to be a lie. Because The Fifteen only wanted young
men and women truly in love and truly loved in return. And
Maddy wasn't truly in love with anyone. She had only thought
she loved Tan. And that Tan loved her.

Eternal soul mates. Quille said Tan had really written that. If
Quille believed that, then The Fifteen might as well.

But Tan wasn't even half-human. And she'd met Tan only
once. And then she'd been looking at the reflection of her own
soul. She couldn't love Tan. She barely knew Tan. And The
Fifteen couldn't touch Tan, anyway. Because Tan was clever,
and Its Royal Highness's progeny, and a powerful enchanter.
Tan could look after Tan.

Just like Emma could look after Emma—before she'd been
drugged, captured, and buried alive. And would have died if
not for Mr. October.

Maddy's mouth was very dry. She wished she'd had the
sense to hold onto a water glass when Quille cleared the table.
Maddy tried to ignore the sick feeling churning in her stomach.

There was no question. The Spelling Bee trophy had to
wait. Tan needed Maddy to find him. Maddy needed to find
him, just to make sure he was safe. He might simply be hiding.
Maddy would certainly run away and hide if she had to live in
the Nonesuch Palace. With Its Royal Highness. Alone.

Maddy would start searching for Tan. That was top priority.
Right after lunch with Emma. Everything else could wait.

Maddy glanced up at the clock. It was nearly noon. And she
hadn't even dressed yet. She peered out the window. It wasn't
raining.

Things could be worse. Maybe her luck was changing.

41

"**D**o something Emma-like," Maddy said.

Maddy and Emma stood on the broad stoop before Mundane House. Emma had called at noon just as promised.

"Whatever for?" Emma stared blandly at Maddy, her expression perfectly emotionless.

"Good enough," Maddy said. This was really Emma.

Rookhaven tugged Maddy's earlobe and cawed.

"Let's go," Maddy said. "Rookhaven is starving."

"You remember we're to stop at the modiste's first," Emma said. "For your measurements."

Maddy hadn't remembered. "Has it been a month already?"

"It is hard to believe, Maddy," Emma said. "A month ago, I was miserable. Now—"

"Now you're making the rest of us miserable." Maddy paced along at Emma's side.

"Tell me what you really think, Sis." Emma tapped her parasol against the pavement. The gesture reminded Maddy of Quille. On a bad day.

"I think we should get this measuring over with, and then we should go to Adrigole's for lunch, and you should tell me the truth," Maddy said. "All of it. No matter how embarrassing. No matter how ugly."

"I wish I could," Emma said. "I will tell you what I can."

"And I will still love you as much as I can," Maddy said.

Emma stopped. She looked Maddy in the eye. "You've changed."

"Are you certain it's me who has changed?" Maddy watched Emma's impassive face.

"Yes," Emma said. "I am. You would never expect me to—"

"Share?" Maddy said. "Trust?"

"Maddy—"

"Emma," Maddy said. "I know how you are. I accept that. It's just that I—"

"You what?" Emma seemed truly interested.

"I want more," Maddy said.

"What if I don't have more?"

"You do," Maddy said. Emma was the best sister a girl could want. When she let herself be. "We're going to be late for my measurements."

Maddy stuffed her hands into the pockets of her street coat and trudged onward. She was beginning to understand the street plan of Arduvulin City. It wasn't so difficult to figure out if she kept her eyes open and tried to think like a human being.

THE MODISTE'S shop was empty of customers when Emma and Maddy arrived. "Adrigole's, Adrigole's," Rookhaven cawed as he launched himself from Maddy's shoulder. The shop bell jangled once, and Madame Peria appeared from the back room. She was dressed in a simple black gown, as if she were in mourning. Her dark hair was swept back and dressed into a queue down her back. Madame Peria might be beautiful if she didn't seem so... hard.

Madame Peria frowned as she studied Maddy. "You have changed."

"Not you, too," Maddy said.

"You have changed," Madame Peria said. "But not enough." Madame Peria slapped Maddy's right shoulder. She frowned. "Go into the changing room and get undressed."

Maddy glanced at Emma. "Is this customary?"

"Normally, no," Emma said. "It is not customary to disrobe in public."

"Peria's is not public," Madame Peria said. "Peria's is as private as any place in the world. Now do as I say, or no gown for you."

"I paid you," Maddy said.

"A deposit only," Madame Peria said. "Nonrefundable."

"I'll come with you, Maddy." Emma stared blandly at Madame Peria.

"You will not," Madame Peria said. "This gown, it is for the wearer only."

Maddy shuffled her feet. "I don't like—"

"People inspecting you," Madame Peria said. "As if you are some sort of animal."

Maddy swallowed and nodded. "Right."

"Get used to it," Madame Peria said. "It will not change for a young woman with your features."

"That's rude," Maddy said.

"She means it as a compliment," Emma said. "You are very lovely, Maddy and—"

"She is not lovely," Madame Peria said. "She is challenging. Defiant. Even dressed in rags."

"I'm not," Maddy said. "I don't mean to be."

"Nevertheless," Madame Peria said. "You are. Let us say few notice your eyes. First."

"I like that," Maddy said.

"It grows tiresome," Emma said. "Trust me."

"Peria will change this."

"I don't want to change that," Maddy said.

"You do," Madame Peria said. "You will. Men will seek you. Not to love you. But to break you. Many men are not good men."

"She's not even sixteen," Emma said.

"And how old are you, Emma Sunbury?" Madame Peria quirked an eyebrow at Emma.

"Old enough." Emma held Madame Peria's gaze. "What sort of gown is this that you are making for Maddy?"

"The sort the world has never seen." Madame Peria clapped her hands. "Now. To the changing room."

MADAME PERIA SLAPPED Maddy's left shoulder again. Her hand was warm against Maddy's bare skin. She slapped Maddy's right shoulder and frowned. "You are unbalanced."

Madame Peria had Maddy stand on a box, one about eight inches tall. Its surface was so small that she had to stand on tiptoes to stay upright.

"You cannot be lovely," Madame Peria said. "Do not even try."

"I don't try," Maddy said. "Much."

"This is nice," Madame Peria said. "Your left arm is sculpted. Elegantly muscled. Your right arm. It is a flaccid bag of bones."

"It isn't."

"Give it time. It will sag like vulture skin."

"I thought you were fitting me for a gown."

"I am. Turn around. Let me see the back."

Maddy tiptoed around on top of the tiny box.

"Much better," Madame Peria said. "Though not good. You must run stairs."

"I don't run," Maddy said. "Emma says it isn't ladylike. I walk fast." Which wasn't very ladylike, either. According to Emma.

"Your walk," Madame Peria said. "It is fast as some who run?"

"No," Maddy said. "Not quite."

"Show me the feet," Madame Peria said.

Maddy turned around again on tiptoes.

Madame Peria bent nearly in half as she peered closely at Maddy's toes. She glanced up at Maddy. "You are hurting in the foot?"

"No," Maddy said. "I—"

Madame Peria slammed her fist down on Maddy's damaged foot. Maddy howled and hopped. Madame Peria jabbed her open palm against the center of Maddy's chest. Maddy tumbled off the platform. Madame Peria brushed Maddy's legs out from under her with a simple sweep of her own leg.

Madame Peria held out her hand to help Maddy rise. "You are unbalanced. See?"

Maddy shook her head, too stunned to be angry.

A pistol cocked behind Madame Peria.

Madame Peria ducked and pivoted. She hammered into Emma, chest to chest. Emma's pistol barrel wrinkled the flesh of Madame Peria's forehead.

Madame Peria's dagger pricked the skin of Emma's neck.

"This is a private fitting," Madame Peria said. Her eyes were every bit as emotionless as Emma's. And every bit as terrifying.

"I'm fine," Maddy said.

"Young ladies don't howl and moan when they are fine," Emma said.

"Some do," Madame Peria said. "You are not as experienced as you believe, Emma Sunbury. This is a private fitting. If you would like to schedule an appointment, I will be happy to accommodate you." Madame Peria smiled a long, slow smile.

"Really," Maddy said. "I'm fine. Emma, you should browse. I don't think this will take much longer. Will it, Madame Peria?"

"We are nearly done."

Emma turned her back. She stalked away without a word.

Madame Peria let out a long slow breath. She watched Emma retreat. "Now *she* is balanced."

"No, she isn't," Maddy said. "Not on the inside."

"Peria does not concern herself with the inside." Madame Peria clapped her hands. "Stand with your feet flat on the floor and your arms extended to the side. Relax, and breathe naturally."

Madame Peria circled Maddy. She chewed her fingernail. She mumbled and sighed.

"Smile," Madame Peria said.

Maddy smiled.

"That is not a smile," Madame Peria said. "It is a snarl. Try again. And don't bare so much tooth."

Maddy tried again.

Madame Peria shook her head. "I fear six months will not be enough time."

"To make a gown?" Maddy said.

"To make a woman worthy of this gown," Madame Peria said. "Get dressed."

Maddy found Madame Peria seated at a desk. Peria inked out a page in an archaic script. High Ardu, the language of scholars in Arduvulin. Madame Peria blotted the page. She handed it to Maddy. "Take this to Quille. He will read it to you."

"I can read it," Maddy said.

"Can you?" Madame Peria drummed her fingers on her desk. "That is unexpected." Madame Peria's brows narrowed. She searched Maddy's face. "Can you read other languages?"

Maddy nodded. "Low Ardu." And all the languages of Ghula, ancient and modern. And Annish, the enchanter's script. But Madame Peria didn't need to know that. In fact, she didn't even need to know that Maddy could read at all. Beast-girls raised by crypto-naturalist pirates weren't expected to read. Maddy didn't know Madame Peria very well. She shouldn't have said anything at all.

"It is an offer of employment," Madame Peria said.

"For Quille?"

Madame Peria watched Maddy's eyes. "For you."

Maddy sucked in her breath. "As what?"

"Girl of all tasks," Madame Peria said. "Shifter of bolts of cloth, maker of deliveries, perhaps even helper with clients. Once you learn how to smile."

"I'm training to be an enchanter," Maddy said.

"Enchantress," Madame Peria said. "I believe that is the correct word. But not for you. And this is part time work."

"I—"

"Would be gainfully employed. An excuse to leave Mundane House. And learn the ins and outs of Arduvulin City. An independent income, one that could be used to further your enchanting studies. A foolishly generous wage."

"Would I be expected to sew?"

"Absolutely not. Nor reap. Peria does not take apprentices."

"That's good," Maddy said. "Because I don't think I'd be very good at it."

"You might surprise yourself," Madame Peria said. "If Quille agrees, and you agree, bring the signed contract to me."

"How long do I have to decide?" Maddy said.

"Two weeks." Peria leaned forward in her chair. "Make certain you read the terms before you sign."

"Why are you doing this?" Madame Peria didn't even like Maddy.

"I cherish a challenge," Madame Peria said. "Now go, before Emma Sunbury draws down on me again. And I am forced to kill her."

42

E mma and Maddy strolled through the fog toward Adrigole's.

"That was disturbing," Emma said. "What is that in your hand?"

Maddy detected actual interest in Emma's voice. Maybe she had been approaching her sister all wrong. "Papers to deliver."

A cab jangled by, the driver pretending to whip the horse, the passenger, a red-faced man, shouting for more speed. The horse cocked an ear back, unconcerned. The driver was in good health, and so was the horse. The passenger would be dead in a fortnight. Maddy didn't care enough to puzzle out the cause of death. She switched her attention back to Emma. Her sister eyeballed the papers in Maddy's hand.

"Deliver to who?"

"Whom," Maddy said.

"You are toying with me, Maddy," Emma said. "Why won't you tell me?"

"I will tell you, Emma." Maddy glanced over at her sister. "But first you have to tell me about Madame Peria."

"Her given name is Karlijn Peria. She is a modiste. And some sort of lunatic. Now, who are the papers for?"

"What sort of lunatic?"

"You know as much as I do," Emma said. "We've both witnessed her lunacy."

"She is fast with a dagger," Maddy said.

"I wasn't concerned." Emma stepped around a puddle.

"Neither was she," Maddy said.

"And thus, a lunatic," Emma said. "Now who are those papers for?"

"A man," Maddy said.

Emma huffed. "Maddy—"

"You can't stand it, can you? Not knowing."

"I—"

"That is all you know about Madame Peria? I find that hard to believe."

Emma pulled Maddy into the door alcove of a chemist's shop. She whispered. "All right. Her accent marks her as from the Archipelago. From deep within the Archipelago. A refugee. Her reputation is one of back-room dealings. And her friends are not beloved by the Enclave of St. Anne."

"In addition to being the finest modiste in Arduvulin City."

"On Greanling Street," Emma said.

"That's the same thing."

"Her prices are outrageous," Emma said "And she haggles like a penniless whoremonger."

"You didn't have any problem with her prices when you were spending Quille's money."

"How did this become about me?"

"I haggle like a penniless whoremonger."

"But that's because you were raised by..." Emma bit her lip and looked skyward for a moment. She squeezed Maddy's hand. "That was rude. I'm sorry."

"For what? Nearly stating a fact?"

"It's not your fault."

"I know that," Maddy said. "Do you think I'm challenging and defiant?"

"I didn't," Emma said. "But that was before you..."

"What?" Maddy forced her sister to look her in the eye. "Before I killed a man?"

"Before you got comfortable in your own skin," Emma said. "Now you act like you look. Not like a sullen child anymore."

"I've never been sullen," Maddy said.

"You've never been sunny."

"There's something in between."

Emma sighed. "Maddy—"

"Quille."

"What about Quille?"

"That's who the papers are for." Maddy stepped out of the doorway. She couldn't see Adrigole's sign through the fog. But she knew it was there. On the next block. Maybe she was getting comfortable in the Fogbound Realm. She started across the street.

Emma took her hand. "For old time's sake, Maddy."

Maddy nodded, her throat tight. She fished in her pocket for a handkerchief.

"What do the papers say, Sis?"

"I'll tell you over lunch," Maddy said. After she'd haggled like a whoremonger with Emma for every scrap of information Emma didn't want to share.

Captain Adrigole held the door for Maddy. He tipped his bicorn hat and smiled. "Mademoiselle." He smiled at Emma, too. Adrigole was a retired sailing Captain, not exactly the sort to run a tearoom, or so Maddy once thought. Uncle Leo put her straight.

When Captain Adrigole's eyesight failed, he needed work. There was nothing in the Docklands for a man missing an arm, a leg, and most of the fingers of his remaining hand. Sea captains, particularly those like Captain Adrigole and Uncle Leo, who mastered their own vessels, had to be adept at accounts. Adrigole was too honest to work in the Docklands for long.

When Madame Temple's tearoom advertised for a book-keeper, the Captain applied. Madame Temple, long-widowed, accepted the Captain instantly. She was Madame Adrigole in a fortnight, and The Temple of Tea renamed to Adrigole's in less than a year. Adrigole's did a ripping business, particularly since Captain Adrigole literally turned a blind eye to any strange goings-on. That Madame Adrigole made the best tea and small foods in all of Arduvulin City didn't hurt either. So said Uncle Leo when he brought Maddy there for her first store-bought meal.

"Master Rookhaven awaits in the Posey Room," Captain Adrigole said. "I hope the young ladies Quille find this acceptable."

"Very much so," Emma said. "Though we are expected to answer to Oortsgarten-Quille, sir."

"That's an unruly moniker," Captain Adrigole said. "My dentures won't bear it, I fear. And half my customers would evacuate the premises if I so much as breathed the fearless Detective Inspector's name."

"Only half?" Emma said.

"Slightly more, perhaps," Adrigole said. "Do you recall the way?"

"We do, Captain." Maddy squeezed Adrigole's hook. Quille had made the hook, and while it was still a hook, it could feel. It was warm as flesh.

"The Maddy Dune herself," Adrigole said. "Your touch feels different, child. More centered."

"That's good, I guess," Maddy said.

"Brilliant, I'd say." Adrigole leaned in close. "How is Leonides?"

"Well, I expect," Maddy said.

"It's said the Enclave seeks him. The militant arm."

"Have they some other sort of arm?" Emma said.

Maddy jerked her fingers away. "Seeks him for what?"

"Not that I've ever heard of, and nothing good," Adrigole said. "They found their Captain Larque butchered. Farrago's name scrawled in blood. Can you imagine?"

Maddy didn't need to imagine. Her stomach churned. "Farrago isn't just a name. It's a word."

"It's a curse on Larque's lips," Adrigole said. "It was. Oily man. No sense of joy. To think your Uncle Leo and Larque were once business partners."

"Uncle Leo and Esmond Larque?"

"For cert, Maddy. Ancient history, but still. A bad match, Farrago and Larque. Dirty man, Larque, if you ask me. But no one asks a blind man a damned thing. Even if he has fifty years plying the seas of the world and storing its wonders in his noggin."

"Most people are fools," Emma said.

"Aye," Captain Adrigole said. "And most Folk as well. Still, most young ladies have to find that out for themselves. Even if the young lady herself isn't a natural-born fool."

"Is that so?" Emma's eyes took on that dark look Maddy knew spelled trouble.

"It's a fact," Captain Adrigole said.

Maddy grabbed Emma's wrist. "Rookhaven is waiting. We'll see you on the way out, Captain."

"I expect you will," Adrigole said. "There's only the one door."

Maddy laughed. "I'll make sure to tell Nadine."

"Like I said, Maddy Dune." Adrigole swept his bicorn in a

long arc, bowing at the waist. "You're feeling very centered to me. I'm glad to know you're settling in."

Maddy nearly had to drag Emma up the stairs.

Emma grumbled, "That man—"

"Is Uncle Leo's second-best friend in the world," Maddy said. "And very wise. Don't you dare harm him."

"Being ancient doesn't make you wise," Emma said.

"It doesn't make you a fool, either," Maddy said.

"It must disconnect your mouth from your brain," Emma said.

"Maybe," Maddy said. She put her hand on the Posey Room's door latch. "Don't you dare hurt him."

"I won't, Maddy." Emma sighed. "I promise."

A promise from Emma was as good as gold. Maddy stood on her tiptoes and kissed her sister's cheek. She pushed the door open.

Rookhaven shoved back from the table and jerked to his feet. He brushed his fingers through his feathery burnsides nervously. "Emma Sunbury. Sister."

Emma's eyes rolled back. Maddy barely had time to catch her sister before Emma's skull struck the floor.

43

Rookhaven propped Emma in a chair while Maddy fanned her. Emma's eyes blinked.

"Give her air," Rookhaven said. "And take her handgun."

"Where does she keep it?"

"I don't know," Rookhaven said. "It just seems to materialize in her hand."

"I'll grab her hands," Maddy said.

"Good idea."

Emma blinked again. And again. Her eyes focused. They weren't black pools of ambivalence as usual. They practically blazed. "You!"

"Emma—"

"You are the creature that haunts me? My own brother?"

"We were bound together in a sorcerer's recording device," Rookhaven said. "Such bindings inevitably produce side effects."

"I thought you were imaginary. A pedantic, inescapable, incredibly boring nightmare turning my sleeping hours into a hellish infinity of droning, miserable, sobbing punishment."

"Is that why you go out all night?" Maddy said.

"Wouldn't you?" Emma said. "Do you know him in this guise?"

"Somewhat," Maddy said.

"Has he tortured you with his tales of The Bishop?"

"I was busy," Maddy said. "Though I seem to recall The Bishop being mentioned." She glanced at Rookhaven and shrugged.

"Come now—"

"Rookhaven!" Emma jerked upright in her chair. "The Little Professor is Rookhaven?"

Maddy laughed. It was wrong to laugh. But Rookhaven was somewhat obsessive with his history lessons. "He is quite good with languages. Did he—"

"If I wanted to learn to jabber like kylochs, I would go to Ghula. Do you see me booking passage?"

"Calm down," Rookhaven said.

Emma sucked in great lungfuls of air. Her chest rose. She let her breath out slowly.

"You cohabitated my personage," Emma said. Her eyes still blazed.

"It was no picnic for me," Rookhaven said. "I assure you."

"I don't under—"

"He was inside me!" Emma jerked out of her chair. She nearly ripped her hands free of Maddy's. Maddy clung on. "It's one thing to be forced to share your body with a rook. That is only hideously unbearable. But a bird... MAN!"

"You make it sound so sordid," Rookhaven said. "And as if I had some say in the matter. I assure you, Emma Sunbury, that your discomfort does not even touch on the depths of mine. And I am not a bird-man." Rookhaven pushed his shoulders back. "I am an Emissary." He peered down his nose at Emma and shuddered. "In any event, we weren't brother and sister at the time."

"No," Emma said. "I was a sorcerer's plaything."

"And what does that make me?" Rookhaven hammered his fist on the table. "*Me!* The Rookhaven! The Bishop's acolyte in all things. A civilized being. A scholar. Bound by oaths. Oaths of penitence, of mortification and spiritual retreat for which you have no comprehension. No mere human can—"

"Oh?" Emma glared at Rookhaven. "Can't I?"

Rookhaven took a step back. "Perhaps you can. Having cohabitated *my* personage." Rookhaven's face colored.

"I don't recall an instant of it," Emma said.

"Nor do I," Rookhaven said, "recall an instant of our time together. Only the moment when I woke from Ilse January's thrall."

"And began to haunt my dreams," Emma said.

"That was not by design," Rookhaven said. He shoved his glasses up his nose. "You are a miserable pupil. Willful. Argumentative. Overly emotional."

"Emma?" Maddy said. "Overly emotional?"

"Seething," Rookhaven said.

"I do not seethe." Emma smoothed her skirts.

"If you say so." Rookhaven stared at Emma.

"It is quite a proven fact that you are a liar. In addition to being dreadfully boring, *Doctor of Philosophy Sir Hugh Munninson.*"

"I thought using a human name in your dreams would put you at ease."

"Name and titles."

"I have never lied to you, Emma Sunbury." Rookhaven jerked his chin up.

"Maddy, release my hands."

Maddy held on. "Are you going to—"

"Kill him? No."

Maddy released Emma. She took a seat where she could

reach Emma in an emergency. An emergency seemed imminent.

Emma and Rookhaven glared at each other for the longest time.

"Madame Adrigole's small foods are getting cold," Maddy said.

Emma glanced at the table. Her body shook. She forced herself to sit. "It would be a crime to waste them."

"The desserts in particular," Rookhaven said. He touched the bridge of his glasses. "None of that was my doing, Emma. With Ilse January."

"I know it," Emma said. "But you are boring." A fragment of a smile flashed across her face.

"I suppose I can be," Rookhaven said. "It isn't by design."

"You really are good at languages," Maddy said. "And very patient." She passed a lemon tart to Rookhaven.

"I suppose I must be good at something." He picked at his dessert.

"You're the best," Maddy said. "I never had a brother before, but I know."

"And I never expected to have a sister," Rookhaven said. "Sisters." He glanced over the rims of his glasses at Emma.

"You two are up to something," Emma said.

"Us?" Maddy said.

Emma didn't seem to hear. She dug into Madame Adrigole's cooking like she hadn't eaten for a month.

EMMA EVENTUALLY CAME up for air. She was back to her old self. Self-contained, closed-lipped, willingly revealing nothing.

Maddy tried to draw Emma out, thinking that seeing Rookhaven in his natural form would have somehow touched Emma. That the shock might have made her realize she wasn't alone. That she was hurting her family by locking them out. By leaving them.

Emma was infuriating. She didn't seem to care about anyone but herself. Eventually Maddy had enough. Emma couldn't be bargained with. Stronger measures were demanded.

"You wanted to talk," Maddy said. "So talk."

Emma's eyes revealed nothing. "You really have changed," she said. "You seem hardened toward me."

"You're the one who deserted me," Maddy said. "You're the one who won't share."

Emma considered her tea. "You wouldn't understand."

"I understand that I had to face a sorcerer and a crypto-naturalist pirate alone, and I had to stumble upon the ruins of Its Royal Tanist's changeling alone, and I was beaten by the authorities alone, and I had to escape. Almost alone. I'd like to run away from home, and leave our parents to suffer alone, but I'm not a coward, nor an ingrate, and I don't have so much of a high and mighty opinion of myself that I think I could stand aloof and witness decent people being tortured in the press, separate and unconcerned. I understand perfectly well."

"Maddy—"

"Don't 'Maddy' me. I'm not a child, and I'm not a fool, and I can see that you've made your choice in life, and it's to have nothing to do with Maddy, or Nadine, or Quille, or Rookhaven, or Madame Aubergine, and it's to cause pain and suffering on your true friends and family that would stand by you if you'd only let them. But you won't because you need to know who you are. The Emma we know is nothing. The Emma we care for is nothing."

Emma swirled her teacup. "Or, perhaps I care too much for you." She watched Maddy with her indecipherable eyes. "If I were a magnet for danger, I might not wish to draw it home with me. Perhaps I would spare those I loved that danger."

"I hadn't thought of that," Maddy said.

"Of course not," Emma said. "You are hunted and hounded for an aspect of yourself that the rest of us are spared. We aren't the half-human prey of crypto-naturalist pirates. Your danger can't touch the rest of the family. Mine can."

Emma was so wrong. Maddy's danger had already touched her family. "Quille is hunted," Maddy said.

"Hardly." Emma absently speared a bit of fish. "Our father is hated. That isn't the same thing at all, and you know it. No one goes out of their way to harm him."

"Someone stole his papers."

"I did," Emma said. "Aren't you going to eat anything? The salmon isn't half bad."

"Emma!" Maddy lurched out of her seat.

Rookhaven picked at the fish. He wasn't supporting Maddy in any way.

"Don't sound so shocked," Emma said. "You do know our father is studying sorcery. Now sit down."

"Studying, maybe," Maddy said. "Not working sorcery."

"Of course," Emma said. "Others wish to study sorcery as well. Particularly as it relates to changelings. And inversions."

"Quille had nothing to do with—"

"You and I know that," Emma said, "and now the Night Court does as well." Emma speared another bit of salmon. "We're done with the file. Quille is cleared. You can return it to our dear old da. I have the documents in my handbag."

"What about my baleful lantern? Do you have that in your handbag as well?"

"Your what?"

"My Spelling Bee trophy."

"That thing?" Emma chewed slowly. She swallowed. "You really should try this."

"What did you do with it?"

"Me?" Emma scooped up a spoonful of capers. "Not a thing. Though Geoff took a shine to it right away."

"Who is Geoff?"

Rookhaven cleared his throat. "He is—"

"I don't know what he's done with it," Emma said. "But you didn't like it, and he did, and he's promised to give it back when you need to return it to the Sisters of St. Anselm's."

"No," Maddy said. "It needs me. Now tell me. Who is—"

"The boy from the ironmonger's," Emma said. "Helped us home with your anvil. Surely you remember."

Rookhaven leaned across the table. "Emma—"

"Though he's not really a boy, and he's not only from the ironmonger's. That's what I wanted to tell you so urgently. I suppose it doesn't matter now."

"I think it matters," Rookhaven said. "Geoff is—"

"You're not making any sense," Maddy said. "Where is my—"

"It's technically not yours," Emma said. "It belongs to the Sisters of—"

Maddy loomed over her sister. "Emma, I won't ask again."

"Sit down," Emma said. "You're getting worked up."

"Getting?"

"Geoff has disappeared," Emma said. "I expect he's gone home to the Nonesuch Palace. I don't know where your trophy is."

"He wouldn't go to the Nonesuch Palace," Rookhaven said. "He would go to—"

Maddy pounded her fist on the table. "Emma—"

Emma's voice cracked like a whip. "Sit down!"

Maddy sat. She crossed her arms. Emma wasn't making any sense. "Why would the ironmonger's boy steal my trophy?"

"Oh," Emma said. "He wouldn't. I don't think it was the ironmonger's boy who stole your trophy."

"You just said it was," Maddy said.

"I also said that Geoff isn't just the ironmonger's boy. He's an enchanter. That's how I was able to breach the wards of Mundane House, with Geoff's help. But he's also something else as well. It's important to keep the personas separate."

"Geoff isn't an enchanter," Rookhaven said. "He is a—"

"I need to find that trophy. You have no idea—"

"I have some idea," Emma said. "It glows like the sun now, did you know that? I think that's why Geoff liked it so."

"It glows?"

"Irritatingly so," Emma said. "Do you know how hard it is to scale Quille's tower? And then to climb over the rail, and that thing there, lighting up the night sky like a..."

"Lighthouse," Maddy said.

"Yes," Emma said. "Exactly. Beams of light, jetting out in all directions. We could be seen breaking and entering, plain as day, if anyone were to choose to look. Thankfully, no one did. The fog has been unusually thick lately, don't you think?"

Maddy was going to be sick. "We need to find it."

"Geoff will return it when he's done with it," Emma said.

"Maddy." Rookhaven tapped Maddy's sleeve. "Listen."

"How can you be so certain?"

"Because he loves you," Emma said.

"The ironmonger's boy loves me?"

"That's what I wanted to tell you."

"But now it doesn't matter?"

"Correct."

Maddy glanced at Rookhaven. "Does any of this make sense to you?"

"Yes," Rookhaven said. "He intends to—" Rookhaven's eyes widened. He rocked back in his seat. "Kill them all."

"Oh, Maddy," Emma said. "I thought you were over that."

Rookhaven lurched forward and gripped his water glass. He drained it. He cleared his throat and pointed his finger at

Emma. His voice cracked. "Kill them all." Rookhaven grabbed Maddy's arm.

"Its Royal Tanist will be so disappointed," Emma said. "I thought for certain you two were soul mates."

Maddy shook Rookhaven's hand off. "I don't know if we are or not," Maddy said. "What has that got to do with anything?"

"Geoff will be crushed when he finds out," Emma said. "We did all of this for you."

"All of what?"

"All the enchantment. Reverse-engineering Quille's spell. Devising a new spell, one that would overlay any other spell with its power."

"You can't do any of that," Maddy said.

"Its Royal Tanist can."

"And Tan helped you?"

"Let's say I helped Tan," Emma said. "And Tan helped me."

"I thought you said Geoff helped you." Maddy glanced at Rookhaven. His eyes bugged out. He grasped his throat.

"Rookhaven?" Maddy's brother was acting strange. Maybe the fish didn't agree with him. He usually ate only desserts.

"Geoff is Its Royal Tanist," Emma said.

"What?" Maddy's heart leapt, her breath rushing from her lungs. "He is *not*."

"He is," Emma said. "He knew exactly what had been done to him to make you invisible to him, exactly what to look for in Quille's files, exactly how to breach the wards of Mundane House. He knew everything. Once we worked the spell, you were to meet, I was to bring you to lunch, and you would be reunited with your soul mate, and—"

"Geoff has disappeared."

"Correct."

Rookhaven pounded his fist on the table.

"Hang on," Maddy said. "How long has Its Royal Tanist been masquerading as a hardware boy?"

"Oh, forever," Emma said. "Tan likes to get out and experience the world, and with the curse and all, Tan can't really do it in his natural form, so Tan worked an enchantment to mask the curse and—"

"Spent his free time shifting anvils and hammers."

"Put that way, it seems rather absurd, but Beatrice assured me that—"

"What does Beatrice Cannon have to do with this?"

"She introduced us."

"Did it not occur to you that she might be mistaken? Or lying?"

"Beatrice would never do such a thing." Emma smiled. "She is not at all what she seems. Talented, of course, that's true, but Maddy, if you really knew her—"

"I know quite enough of her," Maddy said.

"I thought you of all people would understand," Emma said.

"Understand what?"

"That I love her, and she loves me," Emma said. "That we're soul mates."

"Kill them all," Rookhaven cried. "Kill them all." He hammered his fist on the table again and again.

"Hang on," Maddy said. Rookhaven's eyes watered. He grabbed at Maddy again. She shook him off. This was important. "Emma, the hardware boy smiled at me."

"Why wouldn't he?"

"Because if he were Its Royal Tanist, he wouldn't have been able to see me," Maddy said.

"But the overlay spell—"

"When did...ugh...Geoff devise this antidote?"

"Several weeks ago," Emma said.

"But after I bought the anvil."

"Well... Yes."

"What on earth has muddled your brain?"

"Cannon!" Rookhaven hammered his fist on the table. "Cannon!"

"Beatrice would never lie to me," Emma said. "We love each other."

"And you are so experienced in love," Maddy said.

"That's cruel," Emma said. She studied her plate. She glanced over at Rookhaven. "Is he always so twitchy in human form?"

"I'm not trying to be cruel," Maddy said. "But I am experienced with liars and lying. Crypto-naturalist pirates do it just for the fun, and—"

"No," Emma said. "Not Beatrice. We're soul mates and—"

"And she loves you for who you are," Maddy said. "Because she alone truly knows you."

"Yes."

"Because she can see that hidden part of you that doesn't fit, that isn't like everyone else, that is the core that sets you apart, that drives you like some strange engine that even you don't understand."

Emma glanced at Maddy with her impenetrable gaze. "Yes."

"Oh, Emma." Crypto-naturalist pirates had tried every one of those lies on Maddy. More than once. Maddy rose and opened the window. The fog swirled outside, a grey and endless emptiness that threatened to swallow everything decent in the world. Maddy turned to Rookhaven. "Get Quille."

Rookhaven's entire body twitched. He pitched forward onto the table, his nose hammering into the nearly empty plate of smoked salmon. He slid beneath the table.

"Rookhaven!" Maddy hoisted the tablecloth and wormed beneath it.

Rookhaven shifted into his raven form. The transformation looked as disturbingly painful as ever. Rookhaven grabbed Maddy's earlobe in his beak. He pinched down so hard Maddy yipped. When she pulled her hand away, it was slick with blood. She shoved out from under the table when Rookhaven leapt to the windowsill. "Hey!" Maddy shouted.

The door shattered as Detective Nightingale rammed his bulk through. His pistol barked. Rookhaven cawed in pain before he disappeared into the fog.

Nightingale pulled a second pistol from his belt and pointed it at Emma. Beatrice Cannon and Justice Goodfellow shoved their way into the room. Goodfellow was bandaged and half-roasted. He wobbled like he was on his last legs.

"In her bag," Beatrice said. "All the evidence you need. In Quille's own hand."

"I get the beast-girl," Goodfellow said. "That's our deal."

"I didn't say that," Nightingale said. "Step over here, ladies."

Emma's face shifted through a thousand expressions, all of them grim.

"Emma," Maddy said. "Detective Nightingale wishes to protect us."

"That's right," Nightingale said.

"He'll deliver us from evil," Maddy said. "Emma, step away from your handbag. Get over here with me."

"I said I get the beast-girl." The left side of Goodfellow's face was a scarred and weeping ruin, his bandaged hands soiled with corruption. He hadn't been to a surgeon, and he didn't seem overly concerned with the state of his health at all.

"Shut up," Beatrice said. "The bag, Detective Nightingale. All you need to prove Quille is a sorcerer."

Emma seemed frozen in place. Her eyes were fixed on Beatrice Cannon. Maddy grabbed her sister by the collar and pulled her away from the table. Emma was a dead weight, her eyes midnight pools of emptiness. She came along without a struggle.

Maddy gripped her sister's wrists. "Don't, Emma. She isn't worth it."

"Good," Nightingale said. "Don't move." He advanced into

the room, his gaze fixed on Emma's bag. He didn't see the black bulk of Mr. October step through the doorway behind him.

Goodfellow did. He smirked and signed to the sorcerer.

A dark tendril of oily blackness snaked out.

"Detective!" Maddy shouted.

Blackness wrapped Nightingale's throat and squeezed. Nightingale's eyes bulged. He turned on the sorcerer. He snapped off a shot. October rocked for an instant. Night-black fluid wept from a gaping hole in his neck. The tendril faltered. A laugh gurgled from October's lips as he tightened the black grip on Nightingale's throat.

Nightingale dropped to his knees. His hands never slowed. He began to reload.

"I get the beast-girl," Goodfellow said.

"Emma," Maddy said, "don't. I can get us out of this."

"What?" Emma blinked. "Oh. I've been such a fool."

"Stop it, Bolive," Beatrice said. "We need him alive."

"I need the beast-girl," Goodfellow said.

"Then take her," Beatrice said. "Take the other one as well. Or kill her. But leave me Nightingale. Quille will—"

The booming report of a pistol tore through the bedlam. Beatrice Cannon dropped like a stone. Maddy snatched the Undeath hood from Nightingale's belt. She'd never used the device before, but she'd helped Quille make them. She knew how it worked.

Emma tore the Hood from Maddy's grasp. "Get Adrigole." Emma raced toward Mr. October.

There was no time to get the captain. Maddy reached her hand out, palm up, fingers splayed, and sucked the life from the gas lamp. Five thick strands of crimson fire wove together and spun, compressing to form a flaming ball balanced on her fingertips.

Emma jammed the hood over the sorcerer's head. She depressed the plunger. The hood collapsed and collapsed.

The black tendril around Nightingale's throat withered and shrank.

Maddy hurled her fireball. Nightingale snapped off a shot as Goodfellow ducked out the door. The doorframe splintered. Emma's handbag erupted in flames. As did the carpet and most of the furnishings. The spreading fire began to eat away at the floorboards. Magical fire was more powerful in Arduvulin than in Night as well. Maddy had misjudged again.

A whirlwind erupted in the room, fanning the flames, tearing at the rafters, scattering the remains of lunch to the four corners. Quille leaned on the shoulder of a feather-haired man whose dark glasses reflected the firelight and seemed to dance in the flames. Quille muttered a word and every flame leapt to the swinging gas lamp, igniting a blazing ball, singeing Maddy's hair, forcing her to cover her eyes. When she dared look again, Nightingale leaned against the doorframe, his arms wrapped about Emma, protecting her. Emma shrugged him off and began to reload her pistol.

Beatrice Cannon lay on the charred and smoldering floor, her face a mask of surprise, a single bullet wound weeping red above her heart. As Maddy watched, the blackened floor joists cracked. Cannon's body tumbled into the parlor below in a cloud of fiery sparks and dark cinders. The clatter of shattered crockery and a chorus of angry shouts rose above the crackling and popping of dying embers.

Quille slammed his ashplant down and the entire building shuddered. His face twisted into a demon's dark mask. "Explain this!"

Nightingale stammered, "I—"

"Not you, fool!" Quille's lip quivered. "Emma Quille—"

"Let's go home, Dad," Maddy said. "Rookhaven is hurt."

"A flesh wound," Rookhaven said. "Not as bad as it looks."

"I'll be the judge of that," Quille said. "Let me see that, boy."

Rookhaven let Quille inspect his shoulder. "I'm older than you."

"You're my son until I say different."

"I'm not arguing." Rookhaven sucked in a great breath as Quille probed his wound.

"He's one of The Fifteen," Maddy said.

Quille turned, his ashplant pointing like a flaming dagger. "Nightingale?"

"No," Maddy said. "Goodfellow."

"He wasn't when he shot me," Quille said.

"He is now," Maddy said. "And I think Beatrice Cannon was as well."

It all made sense. Goodfellow didn't care what happened to this body. He could just steal another when he needed it. And this Beatrice Cannon didn't act right. Emma wasn't that easily fooled. This Beatrice Cannon hadn't tried to save Emma by selling Maddy to crypto-naturalist pirates.

"Emma, come over here," Maddy said. "Detective Nightingale can take it from here. Can't you, Detective?"

"What?" Nightingale peered into the parlor below. He massaged the purpling flesh of his neck. "Oh. I'll need statements."

Quille pulled out his pocket watch. "You know where to get them." He grabbed Emma by the wrist.

Rookhaven glared at Maddy when they linked hands. "You should listen to me here. Not just in Night."

"But I didn't mean to—"

Rookhaven peered at Maddy over his glasses.

Maddy swallowed. "I mean, you're right. I will next time."

Quille began his countdown. Nightingale seemed a man lost at sea. Maddy could almost pity him.

Almost.

Rookhaven linked his fingers in Maddy's. "If there's a next time. You know that Geoff isn't Its Royal Tanist."

"I know that." Maddy touched her dad's sleeve. "Shouldn't we leave by the doorway like regular people? This never works when I'm—"

"He's a kyloch," Rookhaven said. "A spy. I've had my eye on him. And now—"

The world dissolved as Quille's spell took hold. Emma's soft sobs dropped to a whimper, a whisper, a memory of a whisper, then they grew, grew quickly to a scream, and Maddy was expanding, growing, towering over the bleak and blasted land-scape, then shrinking and growing again in a dozen dissipating oscillations around her natural size. Maddy was going to be sick. She just knew it.

44

"Not again!" Quille slammed his ashplant down. Acres of dust rose in the air.

They'd materialized in the Cauldron of the Damned, that place in Ghula that looked so much like Night, with its crater shape and sprawling, smoldering deadfalls.

"We have company," Rookhaven said. He pointed toward the heart of the crater.

A man-shaped creature in dark robes bent over a pillar topped with a crystal orb. Flanking him were beasts, what once might have been women, creeping forward on all fours, their limbs human and animal at once, naked-skinned, heavily muscled, and terminating in massive paws bristling with gleaming claws. Here and there, patches of fur erupted from their bare flanks. A great lion's muzzle thrust forward where a woman's nose and mouth should be, black lips curling back in a growl. Dagger-sharp teeth gnashed as they snarled and paced toward Maddy and her family.

They were mostly human. At least their shapes were. They advanced silently and cautiously. That they had ceased being human in all but the most animal aspects became clear as they paced closer. Their eyes were golden, like Leo's, and their hands more than two parts claw for every part human flesh. The wind was still, but their scent carried, a musky, moist odor of lathered flesh, animal and human at once. One roared, and then the other.

The man looked up from his crystal. Swaddled entirely in a hooded robe, blood-dark and patterned with golden skulls and silver jawbones, he unbent and stretched. Only his spider-fingered hands were visible. They seemed less human than Rookhaven's talons. He pushed the hood back and began to stride forward. He walked with an odd, bobbing gate, as if an unseen rider spurred him forward. He halted not ten feet from Quille. His face was blank; no eyes, no nose or mouth, just unlined grey flesh like the flanks of a narwhal. Lank hair dripped from the crown of his head in grease-slick hanks, seaweed glistening and brownish-green, with dark, pustule-shaped blobs woven in here and there.

"Get behind me," Quille said. "All of you."

Rookhaven's gaze never left the two woman-beasts. "What about the Levelers?"

"Ignore them," Quille said. "Now do as I ask." Quille smashed his ashplant against the earth and dust flew in ever-widening rings, ripples on a sea of pulverized stone. Quille shouted. "Iptaxlryn!"

The robed man bent down and scooped up a sharp bit of stone. He began carving on the smooth blankness of his face, great bleeding rents, for eyes, for nostrils, for a bloody slash of a mouth. Blood wept from every wound, rivulets of crimson pouring down his neck, soaking his robes. He gripped his seaweed hair at the top of his head and tugged backward. The skin on his face tightened, distending about the eye slits. A pair of violet irises peered out between swollen rips of flesh. He grasped the flesh above his nostrils and tugged, fished his talons inside the mouth slit, jaw working, until sharp and jagged teeth appeared, not so much fangs, but teeth like those of a shark.

He blinked.

"Quille," the man-thing said. His voice sounded as if it came from a great distance. He spoke in Lanish, his accent thick and guttural. "You were warned to stay clear of here."

"Just passing through," Quille said.

"No," Iptaxlryn said. "That is unlikely. What did you bring me to trade this time?"

"I'm not here to trade. As I said. Just passing through."

The man thing pointed a hook-nailed talon at Maddy. "I will give you a dozen books for the chimera. Though I have already paid for this one." It pointed at Emma. "And five books for the one from beyond the Yellow Gate." It turned to Rookhaven.

"And what would the foul usurper offer for me?" Rookhaven spat into the dust. "Master."

"You I will take." Iptaxlryn pointed his bony talon at Rookhaven and muttered in Prelanish. "May you be a bird and silent as the grave."

Rookhaven's hand felt for Maddy's as he twisted and writhed, shrinking into his rook's form in abrupt, painful jerks.

He fluttered noisily, struggling to rise.

Iptaxlryn gestured for his women-beasts. Levelers, Rookhaven had called them. He bellowed at the beasts. "May you feast on these human fool's bones, and may you save the chimera and the Rookhaven for me."

"I don't know what sort of spell he's incanting," Quille said. "But it doesn't sound good. Now Maddy, get Rookhaven, and both of you girls link hands."

The Levelers crouched and growled, preparing to leap.

"He's just giving orders," Maddy said. "In Prelanish."

"There's no such thing as Prelanish," Quille said. "And this isn't the time to argue."

The Levelers leapt.

Maddy closed her eyes and stepped in front of Quille. She shouted in Prelanish. "May you disregard Iptaxlryn's commands now and forevermore!"

A Leveler smashed into Maddy, pinning her to the gritty earth of the Cauldron of the Damned. Its fetid breath burned hot on her face. Its tongue licked Maddy's brow. When it spoke, its voice was that of a young woman. "We obey."

The second Leveler trotted over. Maddy didn't dare open her eyes. "We obey," it said. "Command us."

"May you never harm my family or me."

"Huh," the first Leveler said. Its breath smelled of rancid meat.

"Huh," the second Leveler said.

The first removed its paws from Maddy's chest. Maddy scrabbled backwards on her palms.

Rookhaven tugged on her earlobe.

Maddy touched her brother's beak. "May you always be yourself, in whatever guise you choose, and may you always speak your mind if you wish to."

Rookhaven began to twist and grow.

The earth beneath Maddy erupted. She was gripped in enormous fingers of air and lifted. Maddy's breath was torn from her in a scream. A crushing weight bore down on her chest. She dangled in Iptaxlryn's invisible grip, a hundred feet or more above the crater floor. In the distance, the ruins of the Dead Gate caught the sunlight, and, further in the distance, a walled black city of towers and spires clung to the poisonous slopes of a rocky range of jagged mountain peaks. The obsidian city dwarfed Arduvulin City a dozen times over. An army of winged beasts poured forth from within its walls, a black cloud rising from the nearest tower-girdled gate.

Far below Maddy, the Levelers paced, circling. Iptaxlryn pointed his bony talon at Maddy as Quille, and Rookhaven, and Emma watched, clustered together near the crystal-topped tripod in the center of the crater.

Iptaxlryn's invisible grip tightened on Maddy. She tried to shout, but the breath was squeezed out of her. Her chest felt as if a thousand pounds of iron bore down on it. She couldn't breathe.

Beneath her, Emma drew her pistol.

Quille pointed his ashplant at Maddy and the pressure on her increased before it began to abate.

Iptaxlryn thrust his other palm toward Quille. Quille dropped to his knees, and Iptaxlryn's crushing grip redoubled. Maddy tried to wriggle free. That only tightened the invisible fingers crushing her.

Emma pointed her pistol at Iptaxlryn. It was utterly hopeless. Like Quille, Iptaxlryn was certain to keep his body sheathed in wards. He couldn't be killed by something as simple as a bullet.

Maddy tried to imagine a spell that might save her. Bright spots swam before her eyes. Her ribs ached as she struggled for one more breath.

This was all so wrong, so hopelessly wrong. Maddy would not give up. She howled and squirmed. Her family needed her. Iptaxlryn's grip tightened.

Emma fired. A puff of smoke enveloped her handgun's barrel for an instant before the tip of Iptaxlryn's outstretched talon exploded in a cloud of blood and bone.

Maddy heard the pistol's report a instant later, and then she was plunging toward the earth, the air roaring past her ears, her street coat whipping, fluttering louder than pennants in a gale. Maddy sucked in great lungs full of air.

She plummeted like a stone. Maddy didn't know any spells to save her from a crushing fall. Madame Aubergine had only trained Maddy in defense against magic.

Quille aimed his ashplant at Maddy, and a pillow of air

struck her, slowing her. He brought her gently to the ground, muttering in Annish.

Iptaxlryn sprinted toward the crater rim.

The Levelers trotted, circling Maddy. "Command us."

Maddy bent over, hands on her knees. She was going to be sick. Her breath rasped in and out.

She shoed the beasts away. "I don't want to command you or anyone else."

The Levelers backed a step and stared at her with their strange inhuman eyes. Uncle Leo had golden eyes like that. They weren't all that inhuman. Not if she looked closely.

Maddy couldn't help them. She couldn't even help herself. She spoke in Prelanish. "May you do as you wish from this moment forward."

"We wish to be commanded," The first Leveler said.

"By our master," the second one said.

Maddy didn't have time for this. Her ribs ached and her foot had never fully healed. She had a miserable headache. If that was all the damage she had to show from confronting a kyloch, she'd consider herself lucky. And she wasn't lucky. She limped toward her family. "There are others coming!" Maddy called out. "Fast. On winged beasts."

"We'll go in a moment," Quille said. He stared at Iptaxlryn's crystal device. Maddy had imagined it a crystal orb at first. From a dozen feet away, it appeared to be a crystal skull. From a foot away, it made her want to run screaming. It was a woman's head, its flesh transparent. Blood still pulsed through its veins. It seemed melded to the tripod it sat upon, a black-cloth-draped affair. Maddy wondered what could be so hideous hidden beneath that cloth that a kyloch couldn't bear to gaze upon it.

"A Farseer," Rookhaven said. "A scrying device." Rookhaven's gaze followed Iptaxlryn's retreat. "We had best hurry."

"But it's human," Emma said. She took a step back.

"Kylochs work in flesh," Rookhaven said. "It's no different than Quille's pocket watch, or—"

"Oh, it's different, boyo," Quille said. "What was Iptaxlryn viewing?"

Emma grasped Quille's arm. "You don't intend to use that thing."

"It's already been used," Quille said. "I intend to study it."

Emma stamped her foot down. "We're not taking that abomination with us."

Quille peered at Emma. "I don't recall you being overly concerned about such things in the past."

"You've never been *used*," Emma said. "And the subject hadn't arisen." Her gaze followed the Levelers. Emma's whole body shivered.

That was why she was always afraid. Emma imagined a sorcerer might use her again. A sorcerer or a kyloch.

"Let's get out of here, Dad," Maddy said. It was her fault they were here in the first place.

"In a moment." Quille tapped the Farseer on the forehead with the iron grip of his ashplant. Its eyes popped open. It licked its lips and moaned. Quille fished in his coat pocket. "Where are my optics?" He patted his chest pocket.

"Step back," Maddy said. "What do I do?"

"Gaze into its eyes," Quille said. "Tell me what you see."

Maddy had to lean down, her face inches from the hideous thing. It swallowed, and the veins beneath the transparent skin of its neck pulsed.

Maddy fought down the bile rising in her throat and gazed into its pale eyes. She jerked her gaze away.

"We need to get home. Now." Iptaxlryn's Farseer had shown Maddy Arduvulin.

"What did you see?"

"Emma, you have to look."

"No."

"Please."

"Maddy—"

"Please."

Emma crossed her arms and shivered. She bent over the Farseer, her lips close enough to it to kiss.

"Does that look like Geoff to you?" Maddy said.

"The ironmonger's boy?" Quille said.

"You know him?"

"Of course, he delivers all my supplies. Ah." Quille fished his pince-nez out of his trouser pocket. "He also delivers supplies to the Nonesuch Palace. And to every reputable enchanter in the city. Very dependable."

"That's Geoff," Emma said. She stepped away from the Farseer, her face pale. "And he has the Spelling Bee trophy with him."

"Does he?" Quille said. "Why would he?"

"It's a long story," Maddy said. "Let's go." Geoff had the Spelling Bee trophy, and it glowed like a lighthouse. He was out of the fog, on a rocky talus, and climbing.

Climbing Mount Gorim.

"Using a Farseer is an awful chore," Quille said. "Just to watch a boy. When we return home, I'll help you find the trophy, Maddy. It must be more important than—"

"Look." Rookhaven pointed. A dozen flying beasts topped the crater wall, hooded figures mounted on them.

"That will be Iptaxlryn," Quille said. "And his cohort. Best we go." Quille pulled out his pocket watch.

"I thought we just defeated Iptaxlryn," Maddy said.

"We fought Iptaxlryn's meat-golem to a standstill," Quille said. "There's no way in the world we could defeat Iptaxlryn in person. Not in Ghula, and not out in the open like this. Link hands, all of you."

"Command us." A Leveler shoved her disgusting muzzle

against Maddy's palm. The second one bumped against the first.

"I don't want to co…" Maddy sighed. "Never mind. Do you have names?"

"Iostan," the first said.

"Tsolde," the second said.

The flying beasts landed on the crater's rim. One roared, a sky-rending scream. And then the others chimed in, long necks extended, dagger beaks spearing the sky. They flapped their featherless wings thrice before folding them as they began pacing down the steeply sloping crater wall. Maddy was running out of time.

"May Iostan be Tsolde's master," Maddy said. "May Tsolde be Iostan's master."

The Levelers stared at each other.

"May this be true so long as you both agree."

Quille began his countdown. "In five, four…"

"Your Prelanish is flawless, Maddy." Rookhaven took his sister's hand. "One would take you for a powerful kyloch from your diction."

Maddy wanted to say that she couldn't imagine anything worse than being taken for a kyloch, unless it was being taken by one, but then the world began to dissolve and flow like a river of molten lead.

45

W hen Maddy congealed into solid form again, she found herself staring at a river of dense fog streaming through the Arduvulin Gate. She shook her head, and her mind seemed to catch up with her body.

"Disgusting," Iostan said.

"Very, very pretty," Tsolde said. She blinked once and proceeded to sniff the fog.

Maddy swallowed. "Oh no."

Quille sputtered. "Of all the—"

A droll voice called out from behind a massive stalagmite. "A brace of Ghulan Levelers. How unusual."

Maddy's heart soared. "Tan!" She ran toward Tan's voice.

"And a Ghulan Emissary. Of course, none outshine the beauty of Mademoiselle Emma Sunbury."

Maddy rounded the corner. She backpedaled. Tan wasn't a giant heaping mound of ashes and smoldering embers. He wasn't five times the size of a normal human. He wasn't—

"Maddy Dune," Its Royal Highness said. "Do I blaze in glory for you, I wonder?"

Maddy swallowed and took a step back.

"I take it I do not. Avert your eyes, all of you." Its Royal Highness stood and paced behind a draping fall of accreted limestone.

"It's ugly," Iostan said. "Like a toad."

"It's pretty," Tsolde said. "Like a bonfire."

"Quille. I'd never imagined you'd bring me admirers," Its Royal Highness said. "Sweet as this is, I'd much prefer results."

Quille eyed the Arduvulin Gate. "There's an imbalance in the Gate."

"Leave that to me," Its Royal Highness said. "Concern yourself with Department matters. What of The Fifteen?"

"Possibly the Fourteen as of today."

"And Its Royal Tanist?"

"Still missing."

"And these attacks against my person?"

"Investigating."

"Is he, Associate Deemster Sunbury?" Its Royal Highness's voice boomed. "Is the Great Eusebius Quille investigating his eldest daughter's comrades?"

"I have no reason to doubt my father's word."

"That makes one of us. What of these changelings littering my streets?"

"I suppose—"

"Do not answer me, girl. Unless you possess facts."

"I command you, Tsolde, to approach the toad," Iostan said.

"I command you, Iostan, to accompany me to the bonfire."

"Who is master of these creatures? Would that be you, Emissary?"

"Rookhaven. And no, it would not be."

"A Rookhaven?"

"The Rookhaven, Your Majesty."

"Quille's boy. I liked you better as a bird. You're not nearly as amusing as an enigma."

"They command each other," Maddy said.

"Whose fool idea was that?"

Maddy's face burned. "Mine."

"Come here." Its Royal Highness's voice rumbled the cavern.

Maddy tried to catch her father's eye. Quille was busy studying the Gate.

"Would you come any faster if Its Royal Tanist commanded you?"

"I—"

"Hold your tongue as well. I've heard enough treason for one day. Now the rabble goes so far as to print their venom in the paper."

"Perhaps if the Folk weren't oppressed, you might hear nothing from them," Emma said.

"Perhaps. Or perhaps if I ruled as reason advises, I would rid Arduvulin of the Folk. Just as the Folk rid the Archipelago of humans."

"The Folk were here first," Emma said.

"Girl, I climb these stairs nightly. I do not see the bones of the Folk slide past in stone."

"Touch the toad, Tsolde," Iostan said. "I command you."

"I command Iostan to touch the bonfire first," Tsolde said.

Its Royal Highness shifted its bulk. It spoke in Prelanish. "May Iostan and Tsolde lie down and sleep."

"Who are you to command us? The Pretty Mistress gave us to each other. Tsolde is my slave."

"Iostan is my slave."

When Its Royal Highness laughed, it shook the very stone of the cavern. "I would buy Iostan from Tsolde, and I would buy Tsolde from Iostan."

"Tsolde is not for sale. She is mine."

"What do you offer for Iostan?" Tsolde said.

"This is unbearable," Maddy said. "You can't just—"

"Silence! Bite your tongue and learn. I would restore Tsolde to human form. That is what I would pay."

Tsolde paced back and forth.

"You must do it, Tsolde." Iostan paced back and forth. "I long to own a human once more. You must agree."

"They're halfwits," Maddy said. "It's not fair—"

"Fairness is not my concern," Its Royal Highness said. "Now be quiet."

"No," Tsolde said. "That is not enough."

"Name your price then," Its Royal Highness said.

"You must make Iostan human," Tsolde said.

Iostan shrieked. "No! Never!"

"I can't make Iostan human," Its Royal Highness said. "Here is my final offer. I will restore both Iostan and Tsolde to their natural state."

"No," Tsolde said.

"I agree to these terms. And I command Tsolde to agree to these terms," Iostan said.

"I command Iostan to set me free," Tsolde said.

"So be it." Its Royal Highness stamped its foot and the cavern rumbled. It stamped its foot again and the cavern shook. It stamped its foot a third time and the floor beneath Tsolde and Iostan collapsed.

"No!" Maddy rushed to the edge of the pit. Choking dust blocked Maddy's view. "You've killed them!"

"That would be fair," Its Royal Highness said. "Fair and just."

A hand gripped the edge of the pit. Maddy gripped it and pulled. "Emma, help me."

Maddy and Emma pulled the coughing women onto the water-slick cavern floor.

"Thank you," Tsolde said.

"You bitch." Iostan slapped at Tsolde.

Maddy rocked back on her heels when the women rolled

over. One of the women was human, a plain looking, lank-haired rail, the other alabaster-skinned, with red flowing hair and flashing green eyes. Her naked body seemed lush and perfect in every way.

"Oh," Maddy said. Iostan was a merrow, one of the Folk.

"Oh, indeed," Its Majesty said.

Iostan spit. She pointed at Tsolde. "Get me away from that creature."

"Thank you, My Lord." Tsolde said. "Iostan—"

"Get it away from me," Iostan said.

"The kittens, Iostan." Tsolde pointed at the pit. A pair of pitiful mewing voices sounded from below. "We can't abandon them."

"Then climb down and rescue them, you ignorant, sentimental—"

"I'll do it," Maddy said.

"No," Tsolde said. "They're our responsibility. Iostan and I—"

"Leave me out of this," Iostan said.

"Fine." Tsolde descended into the pit. She returned with a pair of lion cubs.

"I take it this demonstration was for my benefit," Emma said.

Its Royal Highness sighed, a sound like hissing steam. "It certainly wasn't for mine, Emma Sunbury."

"How did you transform them?" Maddy said. "You're not an enchanter, and you can't be a sorcerer, and you don't feel like a magical creature, and—"

"It's an Oligarch, you imbecilic child," Iostan said. "It—" Iostan gripped her own throat as Its Royal Highness muttered something unintelligible. Her fingers tightened until all that came out was wordless air.

Maddy took a step back from Its Royal Highness. She took another step back.

Quille touched the Gate one final time before he strode to Maddy's side. "Merrows lie, Maddy."

"Then all the Folk lie," Emma said. "They say—"

"If they claim Its Royal Highness is an Oligarch, they lie," Rookhaven said. He smoothed the feathers of his burnsides.

"And how would you know?" Emma said.

"Stop choking her," Maddy said. "Please."

Iostan crabbed across the floor and pressed her back against a stalagmite. She massaged her throat and glared at Rookhaven.

"He knows because he lives," Its Royal Highness said. "Because you all live. Even the most deluded fools live."

"Then what are you?" Maddy said. "Are you a dragon?"

"I am Its Royal Highness. You would do well to remember that."

"But—"

"Quille," Its Royal Highness said, "this has all been very amusing, but you must take your menagerie home and *get to work*. You are of no use to me gallivanting all over the world."

"The Gate—"

"Is my problem," Its Royal Highness said. "You have your own tasks. Wipe your progenies' memories once you are on the street. Kill the woman and merrow. Dispose of the animals as you wish."

"No," Maddy said.

"I'm not in the habit of arguing with children," Its Royal Highness said.

"You can't wipe my memory, or Emma's or Rookhaven's. And you can't harm innocents."

"I am Its Royal Highness. I can do anything I wish."

"But what's the point? If you were trying to teach us a lesson, we won't remember it. We won't have learned a thing."

Its Royal Highness sighed. "And have you learned a thing?"

"That depends," Maddy said.

Its Royal Highness shifted its weight. "On what?"

Maddy forced herself to look at Its Royal Highness. It slumped like a giant, man-shaped heap of coals. That was what her soul looked like now. When she saw Tan again, if she ever saw Tan again, he would look the same. Not a being of flame, but of dying embers and ash. That wasn't good enough. "You said you can do anything you wish."

"I can."

"I guess I'll learn what sort of man you are. By what you do next."

Its Royal Highness stamped its foot and the cavern rumbled. "I am not a man."

"And I'm not human," Maddy said. "But I haven't given up trying to be."

Its Royal Highness leaned forward. Maddy felt the heat pouring off of It. It could blister the skin from her bones, but she wasn't about to back down. She didn't want to be the thing she saw when she looked at It. She would rather die now than die a little one day at a time. She'd had to kill Esmond Larque. She didn't have to stand by while Its Royal Highness slaughtered innocent people just to hide Its secrets. Even if one of the people was a merrow.

Its Royal Highness's breath was hot as steam on Maddy's face. "You play with fire, child."

"I've never been a child," Maddy said. "And I'm done with playing. And being played."

Its Royal Highness loomed over Maddy, staring at her for the longest time. Its eyes blazed like a forge. "Quille, can you alter the Levelers' memories, make it seem as if we had this conversation elsewhere?"

"Um, well...that would be sorcery."

"I take it that means that you can't. Or won't." Its Royal Highness stamped its foot. The cavern rumbled. It stamped its foot again. The cavern shook. It stamped its foot a third time.

46

Maddy blinked and stared up at the great doors of Mundane House.

"That was strange," Emma said. "We were transported from Ghula to Its Royal Highness's throne room. How did we get here?"

"There is a woman and a merrow listening to us," Rookhaven said. "Oh, the merrow is sloping off."

"You there," Emma said. "What are you doing here?"

"I—"

Its Royal Highness might have found better clothing for Tsolde. She looked more a haggard charwoman than a fit housekeeper for Mundane House.

"Her name is Madame Tsolde," Maddy said. "She's our new housekeeper."

"Is she?" Quille stared at Maddy.

"I have a good memory for names," Maddy said. "And for places." She met her father's gaze.

"I'd say you have friends in high places," Quille said.

"I don't know about that," Maddy said. Its Royal Highness seemed more like a nasty schoolmaster than a friend.

Rookhaven was a much better teacher. So was Madame Aubergine.

"I'm a housekeeper?" Tsolde said. She balanced a squirming lion cub on either hip.

Quille peered at the woman. "How do you feel about spiders?"

"I don't care for them at all," Tsolde said.

"But you can wrangle them?"

"I can kill them," Tsolde said. "If they're not much bigger than a pony."

"Then I'd say you're a housekeeper," Quille said. "Who is going to tell Mrs. Cadogan that she's redundant?"

"I will," Maddy said. "If I ever see her."

"Telling her would be redundant," Emma said. "Mrs. Cadogan expired the week we returned with Maddy."

"Really?" Rookhaven said. "Then who is that in the rocking chair by the kitchen fire?"

"Mrs. Cadogan," Emma said.

"Oh," Quille said. "You mean she wound down at last. Mrs. Cadogan was one of my first creations. Long before Madame Aubergine."

"Can you wind her back up?" Rookhaven said.

"I don't see the point," Quille said. "Maddy has already engaged a new housekeeper."

"You'll need to let Mundane House know that Tsolde is safe," Maddy said.

"I will," Quille said. "Once I know that she is." Quille unlocked the enormous street doors of Mundane House. "Maddy will show you to your quarters, Madame Tsolde."

"And I'll show her what needs doing," Maddy said.

"Not too much uproar, now," Quille said. "You know how your mother hates uproar."

"Oh," Tsolde said. She peered into the entry hall. "Your manservant is bleeding onto your fine flagstones."

"That's just Detective Nightingale," Quille said. "Step in and around, one and all."

"Hold on," Nightingale said.

"I imagine you're here for statements," Quille said.

"I was, but that's all changed," Nightingale said. "Detective Inspector Oortsgarten is missing."

All the blood drained from Quille's face.

"Dad—"

"Wait." Quille twisted his puzzle ring, the one that allowed Nadine to summon him, and enabled him to find her wherever she was. "She's very near."

"Who is?" Nadine sloughed off her street coat. She was slightly out of breath.

Nightingale peered deeper into Mundane House. "You left me here an hour ago. I searched for you after half an hour, but—"

"You wandered around in my house?" Quille leaned on his ashplant.

Nightingale stiffened. "If you have nothing to hide—"

"Of course we don't." Nadine glared at Quille. "I'm certain of it now."

"Now?" Nightingale said.

"Statements," Nadine said. "You'll want to get them soonest."

"They can wait." Nightingale said. "I'll call in the morning. I need to see a surgeon. And consult with the Director." The street doors of Mundane House slammed with authority.

"I NEED HELP WITH A BODY," Nadine said. "I've wheeled it to the foundry shed, but—" Nadine's lips clamped shut, her gaze fixed on the strange woman standing in her entry hall.

"That's Madame Tsolde," Maddy said. "Our new house-keeper. It Royal Highness has judged her fit."

"Pleased to meet you, ma'am," Tsolde said. "I'll help you with the body. Is it living or dead?"

"I'm not sure," Nadine said.

"Those are the worst." Tsolde said. "Just lead me to it, mistress, and point out where you'd like it dumped."

Nadine spoke to Quille. "It's Beatrice Cannon in the foundry. Her eyes popped open while transporting her to the morgue. I had her propped up in the dining room when Nightingale called."

"That betrayer." Emma looked as if she might cry.

"How did you spirit her away from the morgue?" Quille asked.

"Does it matter?"

"I suppose not," Quille said. "I just wondered."

"We're wasting time," Nadine said.

"VERY CLEVER," Quille said. His fingers worked Beatrice Cannon's jaw. "Brilliant work."

Nadine tapped her foot. "Quille—"

"A remotely operated automaton," Quille said. "Wish I'd thought of it."

"I've been sleeping next to a machine?" Emma said.

"I did not need to know that," Nadine said. "Emma—"

"Please, Mother," Emma said. "Spare me. It's not like you're surprised, and—"

"And now I am 'Mother'?" Nadine glared at Emma.

Emma stared blandly back at Nadine. "Yes."

"Then we will talk," Nadine said. "Later."

"We've already had that talk," Emma said. "I—"

"We have discussed love," Nadine said. "We have not

discussed betrayal."

"Oh, I like that," Beatrice said. "A little lower."

"Ick," Maddy said. "Turn it off."

"It's masterful," Quille said. "I doubt I could do better."

"Oh, Emma," Beatrice Cannon said. "Do that again."

Emma stormed out into the night.

"Wait a minute," Maddy said. "If it's a machine, how could anyone make a changeling of it?"

"The same way that flesh and hair was grown over the clockwork mechanism," Quille said. "There's likely a real Beatrice Cannon out there. Or there was."

Quille muttered something in Annish, and Beatrice Cannon's head turned. Her eyes blinked, and she smiled at Nadine. "You're looking very lovely tonight, Madame Quille."

Nadine took a step back.

Quille clapped his hands together like a child. "It's brilliant! I can see through its eyes and spell it to do my bidding!"

Beatrice Cannon lurched to her feet before toppling over with a thud.

"Emma's gunshot damaged the ambulatory mechanism," Quille said. "I believe it can be repaired."

Nadine's face blanched. "Quille—"

"There's one more thing I'd like to try. Help me prop it up, Maddy."

"No," Maddy said. "That's sick. I won't."

"I will," Madame Tsolde said. She hoisted Beatrice Cannon onto the chair like a sack of grain.

"Sit tight," Quille said. He stepped outside.

Beatrice Cannon's arm jerked. She held her hand palm up. Her lips muttered in Annish. A flame ignited on her palm before it winked out.

Quille trotted back in. "Did you see a flame?"

"Aye," Madame Tsolde said. "Ghost flame."

"Uncanny," Quille said. "I can spell through it at a distance. It's a triumph of the enchanting art. Utterly brilliant."

Nadine lurched onto a chair. "Quille—"

"So there's a changeling Beatrice Cannon, and a real Beatrice Cannon, and this thing," Maddy said.

"Oh, there could be any number of these," Quille said. "The hard work of enchantment is all in the invention."

"But it's permanent magic," Maddy said.

"Definitely," Quille said.

"How many years of life would it strip away to make one of these?" Maddy said.

"Decades," Quille said. "But you wouldn't need to make more than one yourself. You could hire machinists to duplicate the mechanism, you could enlist other enchanters in the drudge work of replicating the flesh and hair. Animating it? A month of life, maybe less."

"Or you could just have the Folk grow the skin and hair," Maddy said. "They can make changelings."

"The Folk aren't trustworthy," Quille said. "And they charge too much."

"What about raw materials?"

"I don't know, Quille said. "Help me drag it to the tower and we'll dissemble it."

"It's alive." Maddy wasn't about to touch it.

"It's a machine."

"Madame Aubergine is alive," Maddy said. "This is sick."

"She only seems alive," Quille said. "She isn't really."

"I can't tell the difference," Maddy said. "She's alive to me."

Nadine coughed. "How do we tell one of these mechanical monsters from a real person?"

"I'm not sure," Quille said.

"Find out."

"First I need to—"

"No. First you must identify some method of hunting these

vile things down."

"But—"

Nadine's voice was hard as iron. "You will, Eusebius. This is not a toy!"

"No," Quille said. "It's a masterpiece."

"Could one of these walk in our front door, Dad?"

Quille's brow wrinkled. "I imagine it could."

"Could it walk into The Nonesuch Palace?"

"Oh."

"I'll bet it's strong," Maddy said. "Strong enough to carry a changeling."

"Probably," Quille said. "If I'd made it, certainly."

Maddy didn't like where her thoughts were taking her. But she had to press her dad. He wasn't thinking straight. "If you'd made it, you wouldn't be able to spell an inversion through it. Because you're not a sorcerer."

Quille glanced at Madame Tsolde.

"He could," Madame Tsolde said. "He just doesn't want to say so in front of the help."

"I wouldn't," Quille said.

"So whoever made this is probably a really powerful enchanter," Maddy said.

"Undoubtedly."

"And that sort of enchanter could work an inversion."

Quille said nothing.

"So we're looking for a really powerful enchanter," Maddy said.

"Or a sorcerer," Nadine said. "Employed by such an enchanter."

"Or a kyloch," Tsolde said.

"But that's too complicated," Maddy said. "Too many suspects for someone like Detective Nightingale. If there are more of these out there, and he finds one, he'll know there's only one person who could have made it."

Quille swallowed. "I sign my work."

"I bet this one is signed," Maddy said. "By you."

"I didn't make it, Maddy."

"I know that. Someone who hates you did."

Madame Tsolde slung Beatrice Cannon over her shoulder. "Where do you want her, sir?"

"Dad—"

"What, Maddy?" Quille's face was sweaty and pale.

"I'll help if you really need me."

Quille nodded. "I'll come get you when it no longer looks like someone you knew."

"This thing is bloody heavy," Madame Tsolde said. "No offense, sir, but if you're to stand here jabbering—"

"So it will leave deep footprints," Nadine said. "And it won't float." Nadine jerked from her chair. "Maddy, go get Emma and bring her to the tower. Tell her to come in her bathing attire. And you come, too, in yours. I'll be back in an hour."

"Where are you going?" Quille leaned on his ashplant.

"Leonides is moving in with us," Nadine said. "Do nothing irreversible until I return."

EVERYONE FLOATED. Maddy bobbed in the cooling pool at the base of the shot tower. The water was horribly cold and wet. Leonides leered at Nadine. Quille was so lost in thought that he didn't notice.

Leo stretched his arms out on the rim of the pool. "You're a trim woman, Madame Tsolde."

"Thank you, sir."

"Call me Leo." Uncle Leo turned on his brightest smile.

"Yes sir," Tsolde said.

"All right," Nadine said. "Until Quille can devise proper wards for this house, we will all return here after every outing.

For a dunking trial. Two witnesses, and one of them either Quille or me."

Maddy gripped the rim of the pool. "Can I get out now?"

"Yes, dear heart, you may," Nadine said. "To bed, one and all."

Quille shook his head. "I need to deanimate the device tonight."

"Madame Tsolde, chuck Beatrice Cannon into the pool," Nadine said. "Quille will freeze the pool solid before coming to bed. He will resume his work with a refreshed mind."

"Yes ma'am," Tsolde said.

Quille waved his hand. "No, no, that might damage—"

"Then you can fix it in the morning," Nadine said. "Do not argue with me when I am right."

"Say," Uncle Leo said, "do any of you ladies fancy a bit of late night ice-skating?"

"Don't, Leo," Emma said. She lurched out of the pool. "Just don't."

Uncle Leo watched Emma stalk away. "I believe that's the first time she's called me by my given name."

"She's upset," Maddy said.

"Who wouldn't be," Leo said. "To be betrayed by a lover is the cruelest pain."

"As if you'd ever truly loved anyone," Nadine said.

Maddy jerked out of the pool and shook herself.

"Use a towel, sweetheart," Nadine said.

Uncle Leo levered out of the pool and toweled off.

"He loves me," Maddy said. "Don't you Uncle Leo?"

"Yes. Yes, of course." Leo retrieved his cutlass and peered toward Mundane House. The light in Emma's window winked on. "Excuse me." He nearly tripped over Quille's ashplant. "Excuse me."

"Wait for me," Maddy said, but Leo must not have heard. He disappeared into the dark.

47

Maddy shook Emma's shoulder. It was after midnight and Mundane House was silent but for the sound of a pistol being cocked and the sudden inrush of Maddy's breath.

"It's me," Maddy said.

Emma lowered the hammer of her weapon gently before the pistol disappeared beneath her pillow. Emma lit a fairy light. Maddy could see in the dark a lot better than most people, Emma included. "You might have knocked."

"If I wanted to wake Mom, I would have." Maddy needed help and Emma was the key. "Do you suppose your friends Mr. Nayheightly and Mr. Whindarrow would help me?"

"I suppose they'd help anyone for a price," Emma said. "What do you need?"

"Transportation to the headwaters of the Selby," Maddy said. "From there, a ride to the top of Mount Gorim."

"They are excellent swimmers," Emma said. "You'd need someone else to take you to the summit."

"Who?"

"Garrulous Dan," Emma said. "He's a roc."

Rocs weren't friendly. The crew of the *Polyphemus* had captured one. The giant bird had splintered the mainmast trying to escape. They'd had to beach and refit, and all the while they kept the roc pinioned on deck. It had nearly starved to death by the time they set sail again, and it barely brought enough at auction to pay for the repairs. Still, rocs were big, and strong, and they could fly anywhere, even carrying someone Maddy's size. Healthy ones could.

"Rocs are animals," Maddy said.

"I know," Emma said. "You should see the disgusting hovel he lives in."

"No, I mean they're not magical creatures. Don't you know any griffins, or hippogriffs, or sphinxes? Someone who can speak? I need to be able to bargain."

"Garrulous Dan can talk your ear off," Emma said.

"Rocs can't talk," Maddy said. She'd talked to the roc chained on deck for hours. All it did was stare at her with its predator's eyes.

"This one can."

"Let's go, then," Maddy said. "Take me to Garrulous Dan."

"Now?" Emma shifted beneath the covers. "Nadine would skin me alive."

"When have I ever asked you for anything?" Maddy said.

Emma stared at Maddy for the longest time. "Never." She flung the covers back and pulled her pistol from beneath her pillow. "Get dressed and I'll meet you in the entry hall."

"Thanks," Maddy said.

"Save it, Sis. You can thank me when we get home without being found out."

⊹╫⊹

Maddy paced along at Emma's side. She was utterly turned around. There was no way she could retrace their steps. It seemed as if Emma didn't know where she was going, either.

"We'll have to get a guide," Emma said. "We'll go to the Night Court and recruit someone there."

"You can't find the roc's home?"

"It's not that easy," Emma said. "The Folk like their privacy."

"But a roc isn't Folk," Maddy said. "It's mythic, not magic."

"There are all sorts of Folk," Emma said. She turned down a narrow alley. "Silly and serious, trouping and solitary, shape shifting and fixed form. I have a little notebook to keep all the different classes straight."

"But they're all untrustworthy," Maddy said. "I don't see why you like them."

"I like you and Rookhaven," Emma said. "You're trustworthy."

"We're not Folk," Maddy said. "Rookhaven is from Night, and my mother is from Hell. The Folk are from someplace else."

"They're from here," Emma said. "Before humans and Its Royal Highness drove them underground. And there's no such place as Hell," Emma said. "That's made up to scare little children."

"I think you're wrong," Maddy said. "And Rookhaven and I aren't Folk."

"The Folk think you are." Emma paused before a graveyard gate. "Here we are."

The gate creaked open on rusty hinges. Emma led Maddy to a crumbling mausoleum. She ducked inside and Maddy followed. Emma shoved the lid of a lichen-encrusted sarcophagus open and climbed inside. "Let me do the talking."

Maddy followed Emma down a long stairway to a barred oaken door. Emma hammered on the door until it opened and a phynodderree waved them in. It was the standard kind, man from the waist up, goat from the waist down. Phynodderrees were easy to catch, but they ate so much that they rarely brought enough at market to justify their upkeep. They were strong as bugannes, though. They usually smelled of earth and sunlight and open fields, but this one had a scent like rancid tallow and wet stone.

"The Silly Court," Emma said.

"S'truth," the phynodderree said. He handed Maddy and Emma each a playing card.

"Stare at it," Emma said.

Maddy glanced at Emma's card, then at hers. "Are they supposed to be different?" Maddy's card was the picture of a black tower, and beneath it, in Vulinish script, the words "The Unseelie Court."

Emma stared at her card. It showed the picture of a pretty white castle. Maddy shook Emma, but she didn't respond.

The phynodderree grumbled. "Be ye suppose da stare da carid." He placed a moldy burlap sack over Emma's head.

Maddy gripped his massive bicep. "No."

"The sack be surety," the phynodderree said. "Case she waken up on the way. Leggo me arem."

"On the way to where?"

"The Sealy Cart," the phynodderree said. "Now stare da carid. And leggo me arem."

"My card's different."

A female spoke behind Maddy. "Let me see that."

Maddy turned and held out the card. It wasn't a woman behind her, but a keener. Maddy took a step back. Keeners weren't at all nice. They moaned all night long when someone died. The crew of the *Polyphemus* said that hearing their singing was the cause of death. Maddy thought that was pretty stupid circular reasoning, but either way, all the keeners she'd met had terrible dispositions.

"Look," Maddy said. "My card says, 'The Unseelie Court'."

The keener wasn't looking at Maddy. She was gazing over Maddy's shoulder.

The keener nodded. The phynodderree looped his iron-hard forearm around Maddy's neck and tugged. Maddy jerked forward, but all she did was pull herself off balance. The phynodderree's cosh struck Maddy squarely on the temple. Maddy dropped to her knees. She scuttled between the phynodderree's legs, tripping him as she passed. He hit the floor with a thud. The keener bellowed. Maddy slammed her hands over her ears to block out the horrid wailing.

She wasn't fast enough. She howled as the keener increased the volume of her song.

The phynodderree scowled as he swung his cosh with all his might.

Maddy sputtered when the bucketful of water struck her face. She was tied to a chair. Again.

She needed to learn a spell to get out of these situations. Madame Aubergine taught Maddy an arsenal of spells for fighting magic, but all someone had to do was conk Maddy on the head and all that learning was useless. It was so incredibly frustrating. They'd blindfolded her this time, and the sodden eye-rag wept onto her cheeks and down her neck.

"She's smiling," a man said.

"Who wouldn't smile," a female said. "She nearly bested Honest Peter."

"She's nimble'n quick," the phynodderree said. "I taught she was only youman strong."

"She's the spawn of the Moddey Doo," the first man said. "Give a look at her yourself."

"Not too close, Saoirse," the phynodderree said. "She's a grip on 'er."

"She's bound to a chair," the woman said. Maddy felt hot breath on her ear. Fingers gripped Maddy's cheeks. Maddy jerked her head but the fingers just dug in. "My, what big teeth you have."

"Day're very nice," the phynodderree said. "Emma Sunbury be taking her to Eavil's Court. I seen dose teet and ice and give 'er your carid instead."

"Nicely done," the woman said. "Now take yourself back to the door, and when Emma Sunbury leaves, come and tell me."

"Yes ma'am."

"Both of you," the woman said.

"This one's trouble," the first man said. "You'll want a strong arm, and—"

"Emma won't leave me," Maddy said. "She'll find me."

"That would be very unfortunate," the woman said. "For Emma Sunbury. Go, Josef, or I'll make you go."

"You're not my boss," the first man said.

"But I can make you go."

"I don't have time to argue," the first man said. "Don't come looking for me on your day of need."

The woman chuckled. "I won't."

The woman released her grip on Maddy. There was the sound of a chair being dragged across stone, followed by the rustling of skirts.

"I have a little problem, Maddy Dune."

Maddy lips had a mind of their own. "That's a shame."

"It's more than that," the woman said. "I've lost something, and I need it back."

Maddy didn't say anything. Interrupting the woman would only drag out the inevitable. Maddy couldn't reach any of the knots on the ropes binding her to the chair, and blindfolded, it would take her forever to run through all the potential spells for summoning elementals to her command. There wasn't likely to be lightning or wind in the room, but perhaps there was a fire, or a gas lamp. She'd try that first, and then stone, and then water, and then—

"If I remove the blindfold, do you promise not to try to murder me?"

"That depends," Maddy said. Being able to see would be a plus, and better than that, maybe she wasn't as bad off as she imagined. Not if the woman wanted to dicker. Maddy didn't want to kill anyone. Ever again.

"Would you hear me out," the woman said, "before you decided to try?"

"How long would that take?"

"Not long."

"That's not very specific."

"Well, if I went on too long, you could just tell me to wrap it up, and that you were going to try to murder me in another minute or so."

"If you remove the blindfold and untie me," Maddy said.

"I couldn't do that," the woman said. "I'd need two minutes' warning in that case. Before you began your death-gazing."

"A minute and a half."

"Two minutes or nothing."

"Three minutes, and you promise that no harm comes to Emma."

"I couldn't do that," the woman said. "Three minutes, no blindfold, untied, no harm to Emma Sunbury from me or mine without a day's warning."

"Three days' warning."

"Two."

"How would you send the warning?" Maddy said.

"I'd have Honest Peter deliver it to Mundane House. In writing. What languages can you read?"

"Vulinish," Maddy said. There was no way she was telling some unknown person what languages she could read, and she'd already revealed that she could read Vulinish when she'd read the card.

"Surely that's not all," the woman said.

"I prefer to get my threatening letters in Vulinish," Maddy said. "Or not at all."

The woman laughed. "Most girls would be terrified in your position."

"I'm not most girls," Maddy said. That didn't mean she wasn't terrified.

"No," the woman said. "I've checked around. You're the only magical girl ever captured by the *Polyphemus* that wasn't sold off in less than a year."

Maddy licked her lips. "They were saving me."

"For what, I wonder?"

"A rainy day, they said. Nothing good, in any case."

"That's a given," the woman said. "I imagine you're still in demand."

Maddy's forehead began to sweat. "I—"

"Now that terrifies you," the woman said.

"You..." Maddy licked her lips. "You don't know that."

"I know what I know," the woman said. "Now hold still, and I'll untie you. You remove the blindfold yourself, and no trying to murder me."

"We don't have a deal," Maddy said.

"Yes, we do, girl," the woman said. "There's some who said you'd turned and were helping the crew of the *Polyphemus*."

"That's a disgusting lie!" Maddy struggled against her bonds. "Who said that?" Maddy jerked again and again. "Tell me!"

"Quit your jiggling," the woman said. "Fools, that's who. Now quieten down."

Maddy felt the ropes fall away. She pulled the odious weeping rag from over her eyes and blinked.

Maddy was in a large stone room, candlelit and bare except

for her chair, an empty bucket, and the chair of the grey-haired woman in a dark blue gown who stared intently at Maddy with ruby eyes. She seemed almost human until she smiled. The woman's fangs gleamed in the dim candlelight.

"I'm in a bit of a pickle," the woman said.

"Who are you?" Maddy said.

"You can call me Saoirse," the woman said.

"What are you?"

"I think we both know that," Saoirse said. "I'm known locally as the Hag of Barna. Right now I'm also the Chief Deemster of the Unseelie Court in Arduvulin. What savages call the Serious Court."

"You're not a hag." She was actually quite pretty in a mature way. "You have nice skin."

"And I aim to keep it," Saoirse said. "There's a towel on the floor next to you if you want to wipe off. There's little worse for the complexion than water."

Maddy dried her face. "Where's the rest of the Court?"

"You're looking at it," Saoirse said. "Our kind, we don't exactly get on, unlike our ludicrous neighbors, all thronging, and dancing, and capering about. We take turns on the Court, those of us with the wits for judgment. You won't find a buganne in this chair, but all the competent Unseelie have the duty, and no one looking over our shoulders for the seven lucky years we agree to serve. There's not many of us left in Arduvulin, but it's still been more than a thousand years since I've had to sit and pass judgment."

"You're well preserved," Maddy said. "You don't look a day over..."

"Go on," Saoirse said.

Maddy swallowed. It was better not to lie. "Forty." Quille was almost forty, though he moved like he was decades older in the morning.

"Forty if I was still an enchanter, and spinning permanent

spells till my elbows creaked," Saoirse said. "I spend most of my days beyond the Yellow Gate. I only return to Arduvulin when it's my turn to serve. The fog doesn't agree with me."

"Oh."

"Oh is right," Saoirse said. "Pleasant as this chat is, I expect Emma Sunbury to be hunting you soon, and it's best we get down to business. As I said, I've lost something, and I need you to find it."

Maddy leaned forward in her seat. "What is it?"

"A prison," Saoirse said. "Though you might not know it to look at it."

"I don't see how I can help," Maddy said. "Can't any of the Folk—"

"No. You can't find this prison with eyes or ears, with nose or lips. I can't locate your mother else I'd ask her. It has to be one of us."

"You can't find Nadine Oortsgarten? In Arduvulin City?"

"No, it's your real mother I'm talking about."

"You know my birth mother?"

"Her and that bloody Hunt. It's all she ever thinks about. I don't need to tell you."

"No." Maddy's birth mother hadn't even bothered to search for her when the crypto-naturalist pirates stole her away.

"I'd do it myself, but I'm past the age of adventure," Saoirse said. "This is very important. Imagine a prison for creatures that Hell couldn't hold, and you get the idea."

"Emma says there isn't any Hell."

"Emma Sunbury has never spent a night in a cage. You tell her that when she starts spouting ignorance."

"I don't think I will," Maddy said.

"Suit yourself. Now this prison. You'll know it when you feel it. It could be the size of a mountain or as small as a pin, but you'll know it." Saoirse leaned forward in her seat and gripped Maddy's wrist. She whispered in Maddy's ear. "It rages." She leaned back and grinned. "I admit it's very nice work, even if I made it myself."

Maddy's stomach churned. "Um." She swallowed. "Could it look like a beehive?"

"No."

Maddy let out a long slow breath. "That's good."

"It's transparent. Like glass, but not really. Mostly it's tramman blood and a dozen slowtime spells layered one on the other. I wanted the prisoners to be able to see out and watch the world rolling on without them."

Maddy felt as if she were falling. "Where was it...um...when you lost it?"

"I stuck it on top of Green Mountain so that the filthy creatures could see a long way. Some fool humans have been up there prospecting, digging hell out of the place. It's gone, and I need it back soon."

"Why?"

"Maintenance," Saoirse said. "The slowtime spells aren't permanent. Just very long-lived. Bring it to me and I'll show you how to work the spells."

"You could just show me now," Maddy said. "In case I find it, I can freshen it up."

"No," Saoirse said. "I want to look it over. It's been so long since I worked those spells that I need to see them again. This fog plays hell on the memory. I hate it with a passion."

"I'll do it," Maddy said.

"I knew you would," Saoirse said. "Don't go mucking with the prison. Just bring it to me."

"How will I find you?"

"Same way you did today. Only without the beating."

"Can I go now?"

"If you think we're done."

"I think so."

"I'm surprised."

"Why?"

"Well, you didn't ask me how you were going to bring the prison to me if it was big as a mountain." Saoirse leaned forward in her seat. "And you didn't ask me what it was a prison for. And you didn't dicker with me over what I'd pay you to do my bidding."

Maddy licked her lips. "Oh."

"Oh is right." Saoirse chuckled, and it wasn't a pleasant sound. "You've felt it."

"I think so," Maddy said.

"And it looks like a beehive."

"Of amber. Full of dragonflies and..."

"A sunwyrm."

"Something."

"Those aren't dragonflies," Saoirse said. "They're war machines. The most fantastically complicated clockwork creatures you're ever likely to see. It was a nightmare catching them. But they were nothing compared to the sunwyrm."

"You saw it," Maddy said. "The baleful lantern. At the Spelling Bee trophy presentation."

"The what?"

"At the Nonesuch Palace."

"I never go near that foul place," Saoirse said. "I send Honest Peter. In my slightly-more-beautiful-than-Aevil glamour." Saoirse grinned. Her smile faded. "Is the prison there? In that miserable hovel?"

"I've never heard of a sunwyrm," Maddy said. She felt like bolting from the room.

"That's odd." Saoirse's forehead wrinkled. "It's like a dragon, and then not."

"Like Its Royal Highness?"

"No," Saoirse said. "Its Vile Travesty is a dragon, or It was once upon a time. Terrible creatures, dragons. Willful and brimming with true magic. You can't kill a dragon. Everything but curses bounces off. That's why sunwyrms are so nasty. They can't be cursed."

"But they can be killed?" Maddy said.

"Hardly," Saoirse said. "They're like dragons, only dead. And they're not just brimming with true magic, but they're enchanters of incredible skill. You can't curse them, and you can't kill them. You can only imprison them." Saoirse shook her head slowly. "The Aos Sí lost a perfectly good Gate keeping the sunwyrms out. All but one of the sunwyrms, anyway. Now it's not just humans but kylochs mucking up the place."

Maddy wiped the sweat from her forehead. "Oligarchs."

"That sounds right," Saoirse said. "I seem to recall that the kylochs call them that."

Maddy nodded and swallowed.

Saoirse stared in silence at Maddy. Maddy glanced toward the door. It wouldn't be wise to run, even if her legs wanted nothing better. Maddy felt as if her whole body dripped sweat.

"What are your terms?" Saoirse said after the longest time.

"Oh."

"Oh is right."

Maddy didn't have any choice. She took a deep breath and let it out slowly. Maybe she could use this encounter to her advantage.

Maddy had no idea how far it was to Mount Gorim. Only that it was upriver. And if she had to go upriver she wanted to do it fast. She only knew one roc and he was slow as molasses. Flying there wasn't an option. Once she was there, though, she needed lifting power. That a roc could do. "I want the assistance of a pair of glashtins named Mr. Whindarrow and Mr. Nayheightly, and of a speaking roc named—"

"Garrulous Dan." Saoirse chuckled.

"Right," Maddy said. "And I'll need you to find out who made changelings of Beatrice Cannon, and Emma, and Its Royal Tanist. You can send me a note at Mundane House."

"Written in Vulinish."

"No. Prelanish. Make certain no one who reads Lanish can decipher it."

"You know that anything written in Prelanish is a spell."

"In Ghula," Maddy said.

"Anywhere," Saoirse said. "Though admittedly, those spells only work on Ghulan vassals."

"That figures."

"You've been a busy girl."

"Oh," Maddy said. "That reminds me. Do you know a modiste named—"

"Madame Peria."

"Right. Well, she's making a gown for me. I'd like you to pay the balance owed."

"How much is it?"

"Six months pay for an enchanter's copyist."

"A thousand scillingí?"

"No, ten scillingí."

Saoirse laughed. "I think I can afford that. Anything else?"

"No," Maddy said. "Unless you can find Its Royal Tanist. And remove the enchantment that keeps him from seeing me."

"I can't promise miracles," Saoirse said. "Rather the opposite, in fact."

"I didn't think so. I'd better go look for Emma."

"I'll send for Honest Peter, and he'll bring her to you."

"Thanks."

"Thank you, Maddy Dune," Saoirse said. "And one word of advice."

"What?"

Saoirse grinned, and it was still a disturbing sight. No wonder people backed up when Maddy smiled.

"You might want to research the going rate for enchanter's copyists."

EMMA GRABBED Maddy by the elbow and hustled her out into the street. "Where were you? We need to get home now."

"Right." Maddy nearly had to run to keep up with Emma's long strides.

"I couldn't find the glashtins," Emma said. "And no one would take us to Garrulous Dan's."

"I think it's taken care of," Maddy said.

"Really?"

"Really," Maddy said. "You're hurting my arm."

"Sorry, Sis," Emma said. "I think we should run."

"I've felt that way for weeks." Maddy began to jog. "Come on."

48

Rookhaven tossed Maddy a cherry. He was in human form, and seemed to have slept well.

Emma yawned and studied her breakfast plate. "Where's Quille?"

"Where do you think?" Rookhaven said.

"The tower," Maddy said. "Where's Mom?"

"She and Leonides Farrago left for the Docklands an hour ago."

"For a sailing captain, Leo spends a lot of time in port," Emma said.

"That's not unusual," Maddy said. "Voyages can last for more than a year, and then there's the selling, and getting the best price takes time."

"A year?" Emma said.

"Longer, if he's going to the Southern Polar Expanse."

"Is it nice?" Emma said. "The sailing?"

"It depends on where they put your cage," Maddy said. "If it's in the bow, it's not very nice at all. The mid-deck is nicest. Unless you're in the hold."

"Maddy, I'm sorry," Emma said. "I didn't mean—"

"I know," Maddy said. "But it can be nice. At night, when it's just you and the stars. I miss the stars."

"This damned fog," Emma said.

"Emma," Maddy said. "Don't let Nadine hear you curse."

"She's not here."

"That doesn't mean she can't hear us," Maddy said. "Quille might have rigged up some sort of magical megaphone." She winked at Rookhaven.

"Possibly," Rookhaven said. "Or perhaps she just has very acute hearing." He picked at the dessert tray.

"You can see the stars from Quille's tower." Maddy speared a sausage. "Madame Tsolde is an excellent cook."

"Did she cook this?" Emma picked at her breakfast.

"She must have." Maddy said. "Dad burns everything."

"Not the desserts," Rookhaven said.

A pounding began at the street door. Maddy was out of her chair, but Madame Tsolde was already in the entrance hall with the door cracked. Madame Aubergine barreled by, a pair of lion cubs fast on her heels.

"A phynodderree," Madame Tsolde said.

The phynodderree that Saoirse called Honest Peter was in human guise, his threadbare suit a size too small. "Ledder for da Maddy Dune," he said. "What give me away?"

"Your stench," Madame Tsolde said.

"Ach, you're no fresh breath yourself," Honest Peter said. "Smell like cats."

"I'll take that," Maddy said. "Thank you, Madame Tsolde."

"Don't trust that lot." Madame Tsolde stalked away.

"Any other word, Mister..."

"Honest Peter," the phynodderree said. "Heal fast, d'ya. Feared I mighta brained yourself."

"No," Maddy said. "Any additional message?"

"Ach, I smell, d'ya tink?"

"Madame Tsolde is very sensitive," Maddy said. "Did Saoirse ask you to tell me anything?"

"Didn't," Honest Peter said. "Jest give da ledder t'ya an say dare's a pair of glashtin call at ten. The morning, mind ya."

"Thank you," Maddy said.

"'Tis my job," Honest Peter said.

"Nevertheless, thank you."

Honest Peter shrugged. "Best get back." He staggered off into the fog.

MR. WHINDARROW and Mr. Nayheightly arrived promptly at ten. They were dressed in their finest, and Mr. Whindarrow carried a picnic basket.

"Two glashtins to see you, Miss," Madame Tsolde said.

"Let them in, Madame Tsolde."

"They prey on young women," Madame Tsolde said. "Carry them off and drown them."

"That is a myth," Mr. Whindarrow said.

"We only drown men," Mr. Nayheightly said.

"Generally men who deserve it," Mr. Whindarrow said. "You're looking very lovely today, Mademoiselle Dune."

"Glashtins are shameless flatterers," Madame Tsolde said.

"Your doorman has lovely eyes," Mr. Nayheightly said.

"And exquisite posture," Mr. Whindarrow said. His smile bounced off Madame Tsolde.

"Could we perhaps come inside and flatter you in private?" Mr. Nayheightly said. "We believe we are expected."

Maddy eventually convinced Madame Tsolde to stand down. She settled the pair of glashtins in the public drawing room before she returned with Emma. Maddy was nearly bowled over by Madame Aubergine and the pair of lion cubs as they darted out from under the settee and into the hallway.

The glashtins might never have stopped flattering Emma and Maddy had Rookhaven not sauntered into the room and taken a seat next to Maddy.

"Our brother, Rookhaven," Maddy said. "Misters Nayheightly and Whindarrow."

"Mr. Rookhaven."

"The Rookhaven." Rookhaven peered over the rims of his glasses. "It appears you're planning a picnic."

"We're going to the headwaters of the Selby," Mr. Nayheightly said. "It's quite a long journey. We might not return until late."

"Or in the morning," Mr. Whindarrow said. "It's really terribly far, but we've had the foresight to pack a meal."

"And wine," Mr. Nayheightly said. "An excellent vintage."

"I can fly to the headwaters in an hour," Rookhaven said. "It's not that far."

"You must be a powerfully fast flier," Mr. Whindarrow said.

"Really?" Maddy said. "In an hour?"

Mr. Nayheightly glared at Rookhaven. "Perhaps as the crow flies, it is near, but—"

"I am no crow. And I follow the river," Rookhaven said. "It is but an hour skimming the surface."

"Have we ever drowned a crow, Whinny?" Mr. Nayheightly said.

"They generally don't stick their beaks in where they doesn't belong," Mr. Whindarrow said. "I suppose we could, though."

"Maddy is in a hurry," Emma said. "The sooner she completes her business, the better. A picnic would be very nice, though, wouldn't it, Maddy? If you weren't distracted by work."

"That's true," Maddy said. "I am very distracted. I couldn't possibly enjoy a fine meal and pleasant company until after I've recovered the trophy."

Mr. Nayheightly glanced at Mr. Whindarrow. "I suppose if we expended ourselves, we might be able to carry our fine lady friends to the headwaters in an hour."

Rookhaven adjusted his glasses. "I doubt that."

Mr. Nayheightly stared at Rookhaven coldly. "We are excellent swimmers."

"And divers," Mr. Whindarrow said. "There's the problem of Garrulous Dan, though."

"Saoirse said that she'd get the roc to help us," Maddy said.

"He will help," Mr. Whindarrow said. "He's waiting at the headwaters for us."

"We told him it would take all night and most of the morning to arrive," Mr. Nayheightly said. "He'll think we're liars."

"We'll tell him you are very modest," Maddy said. "That you don't like to brag about your incredible speed, and that given my great need, you plumbed new depths of your already significant powers."

Rookhaven snorted.

"That works," Mr. Whindarrow said.

"It's not even a lie," Mr. Nayheightly said. "We are very modest."

"I'd say," Mr. Whindarrow said.

"If we leave immediately," Maddy said, "we may have time for that picnic today."

"Or tonight," Mr. Nayheightly said. "We've brought blankets." He leapt from his seat. "Come on, Whinny. The sooner we're off, the sooner we'll—"

Rookhaven coughed. "I'll fly ahead and alert this roc to your imminent arrival."

Mr. Whindarrow chuckled. "You do that."

"He won't beat us there," Mr. Nayheightly said.

"If he does, he'll have Garrulous Dan for company," Mr. Whindarrow said.

"He will, won't he?" Mr. Nayheightly smiled. "But he won't beat us there."

49

Once on the street, the glashtins assumed their horse forms. Mr. Whindarrow was a very tall grey and Mr. Nayheightly a coal black with a white blaze on his forehead.

"It's faster this way," Mr. Whindarrow said.

"I don't know how to ride," Maddy said.

"I'll boost you up," Emma said. "Then hang on as best you can."

"I've never lost a lady," Mr. Nayheightly said.

"You've never lost a pretty lady," Mr. Whindarrow said.

"Is there some other sort, Whinny?"

"I've heard rumors," Mr. Whindarrow said.

Emma helped Maddy mount, then leapt to Mr. Whindarrow's back. The two glashtins took off like the wind for the River Selby. They whipped along narrow streets and alleyways, the fog blurring shop windows and doorways, hooves pounding the pavement, odors wafting by half detected. As they drew nearer the river, their speed became a blessing. Gone were the scents of baking bread and fresh cakes, replaced by the stench of street-emptied chamber pots and the general odor of poverty and decay. The River Selby loomed large ahead, the sluggish brown water churning through the lighter water of Third Bay. The glashtins never slowed as they hammered down a rickety pier. Workmen leapt aside, the railing at the end of the pier glistened with condensation, they were surely going to stop at the end of the pier, but Mr. Nayheightly gathered speed, bunched his great flanks, and leapt, sending Maddy airborne and howling. They soared over the rail, Mr. Whindarrow and Emma a half-length behind. The surface of the river hurtled toward them. Maddy closed her eyes and gripped Mr. Nayheightly's mane tightly.

There was no sensation of striking the water. Rather, it was as if Maddy became the water, and when she glanced at Mr. Nayheightly, he seemed to be a cresting stallion of foam. When she glanced at her hands, she seemed to be a rider of foam. Maddy whooped and tightened her grip. She didn't feel wet at all. It was just like Quille's teleportation device, except they were suspended in a state between solid and gas. The glashtins manipulated that state, pushing upriver faster than a sloop on a broad reach.

Maddy glanced over at Emma. Her sister waved back, then they were leaping the first falls, ignoring the locks entirely. They pitched into the roaring, rock-strewn waters of the Selby and began the steady climb toward the Mountains of Flann and the tallest of them all, Mount Gorim. The fog was thinnest near the river, but it was still thick enough that it was difficult to judge landmarks. Up the river they leapt, three falls, and then the winding, tumbling stream seemed to propel them upriver in direct proportion to the rate at which the churning water plummeted toward the sea. Rookhaven must outrace the wind if he had any chance of beating the glashtins to the headwaters. Maddy settled in for the ride.

The glashtins leapt from the river, and paced, stretching

their long legs. Maddy and Emma dismounted in a small grassy field bordered with thorn trees, not a one of them decorated with the offering tatters so common in the civilized region around Arduvulin City. The glashtins shifted shape into their human forms. Mr. Whindarrow spread a blanket in the grass. Mr. Nayheightly opened a bottle of wine.

It seemed that less than an hour had passed. Rookhaven appeared through the fog just as the glashtins began to pull fresh apples and ripe cheeses from their picnic basket. A great white roc hopped at Rookhaven's side, taller than most house-tops in Arduvulin City.

"Maddy Dune," Garrulous Dan said, "I've never been able to repay you for saving me. Until now."

Maddy recognized the roc. It was the silent one from the deck of the *Polyphemus*.

"Had you not fed me, I would have starved."

"Speaking of starving," Mr. Whindarrow said. "We've brought—"

"You nearly did," Maddy said. She had hoped never to see that roc again.

"Nearly is good enough," Garrulous Dan said.

"This wine is certainly good enough," Mr. Nayheightly said. "Considerably better than good enough. Here, Emma, let me—"

"In a moment," Emma said.

"I didn't know you could talk," Maddy said.

"I couldn't then," the roc said. "But I can now. It's a long story."

"Then perhaps you might go over yonder, and write it in a book," Mr. Whindarrow said. "While we entertain the ladies with short stories and long—"

"Best tell it on the way," Rookhaven said. He glared at Mr. Whindarrow and Mr. Nayheightly. "We'll wait here."

"Right," Garrulous Dan said. "Hop on, Maddy Dune, while

I give you the background. See, I was born on Mount Joy, in the Archipelago, and I always wanted to go adventuring, so..."

50

Garrulous Dan rambled on and on while Maddy, mounted on his broad back, gripped his neck feathers and tried not to look down. Her pockets were jammed with supplies. Her coat hammered against her in the perilous breeze. Maddy gripped tightly with her left hand and used her right to gather her coat about her. She buttoned it to the neck and tucked the tailing hem beneath her. If she were to ride a roc again, she would know to make a better wardrobe selection. Her street coat was not meant for airborne travel, for cert.

Beneath her, the rocky scree of Mount Gorim dropped away. They soared high above the foaming waters of the River Selby.

It was rude to interrupt, but Maddy needed to know where they were going. "Garrulous Dan—"

"Just Dan," Garrulous Dan said. "The Garrulous part is a nickname, you see. It's useful in certain circumstances. I fear we're past those for a while."

"Right," Maddy said. The wind whipped around them as Dan soared over the river valley far below. This far inland, the fog was thin over the river, showing the tops of trees only, not a sign of cultivation or any other scrap of civilization in sight. "We're supposed to be going to the top of Mount Gorim."

"We are, Maddy Dune," Dan said. "First we have to find a thermal."

"What's that?" Maddy said.

"A column of rising air," Dan said. "An invisible magical lift."

"If it's invisible, how do you find it?"

"Skill and experience," Dan said. "The same way you find most valuable things. A good thermal is hard to beat, Maddy Dune."

"No one ever calls me that anymore," Maddy said. Only the Folk and crypto-naturalist pirates. "Now I'm supposed to be Madeleine Oortsgarten-Quille."

"Do you miss it?" Garrulous Dan dove. Maddy gripped on tight. The fog rushed toward her. Her stomach jerked out from under her as they gained fifty feet in elevation in an instant. Garrulous Dan held his wings out straight, and slowly the sweeping flanks of Mount Gorim began to grow nearer while the River Selby retreated beneath them. The air was very cold and very crisp. Garrulous Dan had an outdoorsy scent that wasn't at all like Rookhaven's dusty smell.

"Well, do you?" Dan said. "Miss being Maddy Dune?"

"I'm still her," Maddy said. "I'm just expected to be something more now."

"By whom?"

As they circled up and up. the wind seemed to stop. They were moving with the wind, they were like the wind, and Maddy didn't want to speak, she just wanted to listen to the silence, to feel the sun, to imagine what it must be like to be so at home soaring that you were part of the sky. Not how hard it would be to be chained and pinioned on the pitching deck of a sailing ship.

"By my family," Maddy said. "But mostly by me."

"You'll always be Maddy Dune to me," Garrulous Dan said. "The girl who saved me."

"I didn't do anything," Maddy said. "I couldn't." She was locked in a cage.

"You could have killed them all," Dan said. "I was so very angry at you. I couldn't do anything. And you wouldn't. But you fed me when they weren't looking. And you talked to me."

"I couldn't have killed them all," Maddy said. "I could have killed some of them. Then they would have blinded me or blindfolded me. Anyway, if I'd killed them all I'd still be in a cage, and no one to pilot the vessel."

"And I would have still been chained," Dan said. "I finally figured that out."

"I was glad when they sold you," Maddy said. "Even if that meant you would die."

"I admit to being poor company then," Dan said. "But I know what you mean. There are worse things than dying. Having no hope is first amongst them."

"Can we just watch the sky go by?" Maddy said. She didn't like thinking about her days with the crypto-naturalist pirates. In all her free life, she had never met another prisoner. She just assumed they were all dead, or used in some sort of experiment by sorcerers or kylochs.

"Sure," Garrulous Dan said, and he said no more until they were high, high above the top of all of the mountains but Mount Gorim. They were even with the top of Mount Gorim and still they rose.

"Where are we going?" Maddy said at last.

"It's best to have some velocity when facing trouble," Garrulous Dan said. "We'll swoop down and have a look-see, and then circle around once we find a safish place to land."

They plunged out of the thermal and began a racing headlong dive toward the top of Mount Gorim. The wind whistled past. Maddy's coat flapped wildly. "There's a cave," Maddy said. Her eyes watered in the buffeting headwind.

"I see it," Dan said. He flared his wings and they slowed. With two strong thrusts, they hung motionless before the rocky outcrop that crumbled away in a long fall of jagged stone. A single black portal punctured the sheer cliff-face. It looked as if it had been bored by some enormous worm, or drilled by a vast machine. Dan pointed his beak earthward. They plunged toward the valley far below, gaining speed. They struck the thermal and jerked skyward. Dan flared his wings and began the slow, circling, effortless rise again.

"Did you bring a rope?" Dan said.

"No," Maddy said, "but I'm good at climbing."

"With your hands full?"

"I brought a spider-string sack," Maddy said.

"Good thinking," Dan said. He adjusted his wings minutely and their ascent slowed. "I'll land on the ledge above and watch. When you're ready to go, just catch my eye. I'll swoop down and you can jump on as I pass."

"I don't think so," Maddy said.

"What do you suggest?"

"I'll think of something."

"Well, we'll stick with my plan as backup. In case of emergency."

Maddy swallowed. "Right. In case of emergency."

"That's the spirit," Dan said, and then they were plunging again. His wings flared at the last instant. They landed with barely a bump, sharp talons gripping stone.

Maddy hopped off and surveyed the narrow ledge. She checked her pockets for her emergency supplies. "I think I can climb down from here."

"You could wait here, and I could bring backup," Dan said. "That Emma Sunbury looks to be handy in a tight spot."

"She is," Maddy said. "But I have to do this myself."

Garrulous Dan shifted his grip on the cliff-edge. "Why?"

Because Emma had an itchy trigger finger. Maddy didn't want to hurt anyone unless she had to. Geoff the ironmonger's boy might just be what he seemed to be. There might be some normal explanation for what he was doing, climbing Mount Gorim, and stealing the baleful lantern, and being studied from afar by kylochs. Rookhaven could be wrong about Geoff being a spy.

"I just do," Maddy said.

Besides, she didn't need any witnesses if she had to use some of the magic Madame Aubergine taught her in Night. It wasn't exactly sorcery, but it might look that way if you didn't know what went into the spells. It was very cold on the stony precipice, and Maddy wasn't going to get any warmer until she was done with this.

"Suit yourself," Garrulous Dan said. "Remember our backup plan. Just catch my eye."

"Right," Maddy said.

The cliff face was fractured with plenty of narrow shelves and finger-sized fissures. About halfway to the cave, Maddy's descent crossed a path of purposeful handholds chipped into the cliff face. She pressed her cheek against the stone and rested for a moment. She used the man-made handholds for the remainder of the climb to the foot-wide ledge before the cave. The edge of the shelf crumbled beneath her feet. Her heart hammered as one foot hung in space. It was a long, sheer fall, a hundred feet or more to a sloping talus of rocky scree that descended to the tree line.

Maddy clung to the cliff-face with both hands and peered into the cavern. It wasn't a natural cave, but a tunnel or bore, as if some giant creature had ripped the rock of Mount Gorim open and forced its way in. The cave made Maddy think of the Nonesuch Palace, a mountain that had been hollowed out and forced into a shape it was never intended to take. She listened to the sound of rock and stone, but detected nothing but a faint grumbling, as if the mountain slept.

She peered into the blackness of the cliff opening and contemplated using a fairy light. Her eyesight was a lot better than regular human eyesight in the dark. Lighting a lamp would just give her away sooner. Assuming Geoff was inside. Or something worse was. Anything could be in there. Anything. There was only one way to find out.

A few steps in, Maddy rested in the blackness of the cave and let her eyes adjust to the darkness and her pulse settle. The cave plunged featureless and straight into the heart of the mountain. She slipped her shoes off and jammed them into her street coat's already bulging pockets. Maddy kept close to one arcing wall and crept into the dark.

51

The cave floor rose gently toward the summit of Mount Gorim. Maddy stopped from time to time to listen. Other than her own breath, her own rapidly beating heart, there was nothing. No sound. The cave was pitch black for the longest time and still Maddy didn't dare light a fairy torch. She kept her fingers against the wall and crept along. Her eyes began to play tricks. She thought she saw a light ahead, but when she closed her eyes, it was still there. The cave curved gently as it ascended, mercifully free from branching and more like a tunnel than a cave. Maddy didn't know anything about mining, but she imagined this was a mine. A mine drilled with magic. This deep into the tunnel, magic still clung to the cave walls, unmaking magic that burned her fingertips so that she had to stop running her touch along the wall.

There was a light ahead. A thin shadow of a figure moved in its glow. Maddy fished in her pocket and withdrew the vial she'd borrowed from Quille. "Stolen" would probably be what Nadine would say, but Quille would understand if Maddy needed to use it. Probably. Maddy held her breath and crept forward.

A BOY STOOD in the brilliant light pouring forth from the Spelling Bee trophy. It really did glow with an inner flame long after it was exposed to sunlight. Maddy's experiment had worked. The boy knelt facing a stubby, black-swaddled tripod. A Farseer. He began to speak. Maddy couldn't make out his words. She crept closer still. The rusting husk of an ancient, enchanted drilling machine loomed in the distance behind him, unmaking magic ponging off it.

"—and it appears to be softening," he said.

Maddy recognized the voice. It was Geoff, and he was speaking in Lanish, the everyday language of kylochs.

"No," Geoff said. "The charges are in place." He shuffled into the darkness. He returned with a device trailing a great tangled mass of wires. He placed it before the tripod.

Maddy couldn't see if he was speaking to the Farseer or if there was someone with him. She needed to get closer.

Geoff nodded. "Yes. I understand." He stood and marched down the tunnel toward Maddy. "You can come out of hiding. Iptaxlryn saw you coming."

Maddy's breath caught in her throat. The kyloch Iptaxlryn? She didn't move a muscle.

"I know you're out there," Geoff said. "A bird brought you. You climbed down the cliff face. You entered the bore. Iptaxlryn sees all."

Maddy held her breath.

"I'm supposed to tell you: the prophecy will never come to pass. You're too late to free the Oligarch. Run, if you value your life."

Maddy took a step forward. This had to count as the stupidest thing she'd ever done. She fished in her pocket and pulled a fairy light free. She shook it to life. She felt naked in its warm glow. "I have no intention of freeing the sunwyrm. The Oligarch."

"That's not what Iptaxlryn says." Geoff gestured toward the tripod. "It was foretold. You brought it into the light. You left it to soak up power. You made it able to touch the world."

"I didn't," Maddy said.

"I found it in the sun," Geoff said.

"No," Maddy said, "I mean the last part." She took a few more steps toward Geoff. "I didn't make it able to do anything. And I don't know anything about a prophecy."

"You did," Geoff said. "Iptaxlryn does not lie. The Oligarch extends its will. I've seen its handiwork."

"What handiwork?"

"Machines with the faces of my friends. Decent people twisted to its will. Enchanters bending knee before it. You did this."

"I didn't," Maddy said. "What enchanters?"

"Pierre Reynard," Geoff said. "And his vassals."

"I don't know him," Maddy said. The name sounded vaguely familiar, though.

"You do. The Spelling Bee," Geoff said. "Now go. Before Iptaxlryn recognizes you and I am forced to break my word."

"I don't understand."

"That is very clear."

"I'm supposed to take the trophy...the baleful...the prison. To Saoirse."

Geoff shook his head. "No."

"The Hag of Barna," Maddy said. "She made—"

"You won't take it anywhere," Geoff said. "Now run, before it's too late." He turned and walked toward the tripod.

Maddy closed the distance quickly. Geoff knelt before the tripod. The Farseer's transparent flesh pulsed with deathless life. Its lips parted. It moaned.

Geoff leapt to his feet. He faced Maddy from less than ten

feet away. His gaze drifted toward the wired device. Maddy followed the wires into the darkness. She could only imagine where they led. Geoff said the charges were in place. Explosives. Maddy gazed up. The ceiling of the bore was laced with wires. Wires that vanished into drilled holes.

"You're going to collapse the ceiling," Maddy said.

"I'm going to bury the abomination," Geoff said. "Before it's too late."

"My friend is on the mountaintop," Maddy said. "Garrulous Dan. You'll kill him." She crept closer to the tripod. And the Spelling Bee trophy. And Geoff. She clutched the vial in her hand tightly. She couldn't work the stopper free and hold the fairy light.

Geoff's face wept sweat. "I'm sorry. You shouldn't have interfered. I can do this. I have to. Now go!"

A tinny voice came out of the Farseer's crystal lips. "Gyeftyrx. May you do your duty without delay. And may you slay the Maddy Dune."

"Wait," Maddy said. "Let me speak to Iptaxlryn." She took two quick steps forward, to within an arm's length of the tripod.

"You should have gone when you had a chance." Geoff turned toward the wired device. The trigger for the explosives.

Maddy swept her leg out, kicking the tripod from under the Farseer. It screamed and struck the floor with a sickening splat. If Geoff was being controlled remotely, that should break the link. The tripod legs twitched, and jerked, and scuttled off into the dark, hissing and moaning, trailing strands of viscous, clinging slime behind it.

Geoff shook his head once and scooped up the trigger. "I don't need her anymore."

"You don't have to do this. You're free."

"I'm a kyloch," Geoff said. "Of course I am free. And I intend to die that way."

"But what if that won't hold the Oligarch?"

"Iptaxlryn says it will."

"He could be wrong. I know another way. A better way."

"There is no time. I have my orders."

Maddy dropped the fairy light. Geoff's gaze dropped, following the light.

Maddy worked the vial's stopper free.

"May you stop and stand still," Maddy said.

"What do you take me for? Some sort of puppet? Maybe you really are evil. Maybe my friend was wrong and Iptaxlryn right all along."

"I'm not evil. And you don't have to die. We don't have to die."

"It's not every day I get to be a hero." Geoff looked up. "And evil is as evil—"

Maddy tossed the contents of the vial into Geoff's face. His hands jerked upward, dropping the trigger. Maddy sprinted for the Spelling Bee trophy. She gripped it. She lifted it free. Her hands sank into its surface. She scooped it up and ran.

Geoff sprinted after her. Maddy ran as fast as she could, Geoff's footfalls ringing in her ears. He had no choice but to chase her. She'd drenched him with the remains of Quille's enchanted elixir, the hateful magic that made her invisible to Tan. And to anyone else soaked in it. Even a kyloch had to be able to see someone to work magic on them. Maddy was no match for a kyloch. Except in a footrace. Maybe.

Maddy sprinted for all she was worth. She ducked into the shadows and peered behind her. Geoff adjusted course, heading straight for her.

He could see the Spelling Bee trophy in her hands. Anyone could see it now, even with their eyes closed. Maddy leapt from cover and ran as fast as she had ever run.

Geoff couldn't keep up. She outpaced him by twenty feet. By thirty. He stopped suddenly and reversed course. He sprinted back toward the end of the bore. Toward the detonator.

Maddy glanced up. The ceiling the length of the bore was covered in great snakes of wire. Geoff was going to trigger the explosives. The end of the tunnel was a tiny circle of light in the distance. Maddy would never make it.

She turned and ran toward Geoff. He had the trigger in his hands. Maddy bowled into him, shoulder first. He crashed to his knees. The trigger remained in his grip. Maddy landed on her side and the Spelling Bee trophy rolled free. Sickening green rays of light lanced from it, slashing the darkness to tatters. Maddy shouldered past Geoff. She gripped the trophy, her fingers sinking in, the magic twinning around her fingers, around her palm, around her wrist.

Maddy looked at the spell gripping her hand. And understood it. She tightened her grasp and pulled. Geoff's free hand jerked toward the plunger, his fingers reaching.

Maddy unfurled the slowtime spell and hurled it toward him. His fingers froze, touching the plunger, his lips curled in an endless victory grin. His eyes gazed at her unblinkingly, disturbingly bright amethysts, blazing clean and pure, overpowering the baleful lantern's sickening glow.

Maddy couldn't just leave him to die. He thought he was doing right. But she had to get away. The sunwyrm needed her to save it. Maddy shook her head. That wasn't her own thought. That was the sunwyrm. Trying to control her. Maddy needed to get the trophy to Saoirse soonest. The prison was failing. And the sunwyrm was growing stronger.

Maddy raced to the mining machine. She gathered strands of unmaking magic in her fingers. They slashed into her skin, scorching her fingertips like acid. Everywhere they touched, her fingers, her wrists, her arms, they caught and they clung and they burned.

One by one she laced the strands about the wires leading to the detonator. The strands of unmaking magic began to bite into the insulation. Acrid smoke rose in wispy, curling tendrils.

When the slowtime spell failed, Geoff might still trigger the detonator, but nothing would happen. And Maddy would be long gone by then.

Maddy scooped up the trophy and ran. It glowed brighter, and she could feel it, not just the rage, but the sickening physical pain she felt in Night. When she glanced at the trophy, the creatures within seemed to move. She had ripped away one of the tattered spells that bound the sunwyrm and its machines in an eternal prison, bringing the time of the prison's failure closer by some unknown amount. The trophy felt even softer in her hands, more plastic and definitely more horrid. Maddy sprinted, breath rasping in her throat.

She stood on the narrow ledge and glanced up at Garrulous Dan. His gaze met hers the instant the summit of Mount Gorim exploded and Maddy pinwheeled into the sky.

52

Cold talons dug into Maddy's shoulders, jerking her skyward. Maddy clutched the baleful lantern close with all her might. It bulged against her chest.

"It's faster going down," Garrulous Dan said. "Hang on."

"No," Maddy said. The slowtime spells must be weaker than she imagined. And her miscalculations had cost Geoff his life. The sunwyrm's prison might fail at any instant. If it did, she'd just killed someone for nothing. Even if it was an accident, it was still her fault. "Not the river. Take me to Arduvulin City. To Mundane House. Hurry!"

"Can't," Garrulous Dan said. "Not unless you want your friends to die. Look behind us."

Maddy twisted her neck to see, first one way and then the other. "Oh no."

An avalanche of stone poured down the slope of Mount Gorim, great boulders bowling down towering larches and pines, gathering speed, plunging towards the valley of the River Selby and Emma. Maddy's stupid failure hadn't only killed a kyloch boy. It had doomed her sister.

"I figure those glashtins can ride out any wave," Dan said.

"With you and Emma Sunbury on them, you'll be safe. Rookhaven and I can fly out of here."

"Then get to Saoirse," Maddy said. "Tell her to meet me at Mundane House. Tell her to be there and ready."

"That's the Hag of Barna we're talking about," Dan said. "I can't tell her anything. I can only suggest strongly."

"Dan," Maddy said, "pick her up in your beak and carry her there if you have to."

"But she could turn me into—"

"Please."

Garrulous Dan turned his head so that one bold black eye stared at Maddy. They rushed earthward, wind whipping around them. His talons dug deep into Maddy's flesh. It was all she could do to keep from crying out, to not let go of the hateful, evil thing Its Royal Highness had foisted on her.

"It will be done, Maddy Dune," Garrulous Dan said. "No matter the cost. I give you my solemn word."

"Thank you," Maddy said. "Can you go any faster?"

The ground raced toward them. "Hang on," Dan said. He folded his wings.

They plummeted like a stone.

53

G arrulous Dan backed air with his wings. He settled Maddy down gently before he flapped off toward Arduvulin City, gathering speed with every great wing stroke.

Maddy's flesh screamed in protest when Emma touched her wounds; deep, weeping wounds where Garrulous Dan's talons had dug in, and seeping, crusting burns on her hands and arms from the unmaking magic.

"Mount up," Mr. Whindarrow said. "We want to be well away minutes ago."

Emma helped Maddy to her feet. She mounted just as the great wall of tumbling boulders burst through the timberline and raced across the valley floor. Rookhaven took flight as the pair of glashtins, Emma, and Maddy disappeared into the foaming waters of the Selby.

Maddy gripped the baleful lantern with all her might. It wormed under her grip, her fingers sinking in, and magic, powerful magic, pulsed and coursed only a hand's breath away. Maddy loosened her grip, afraid that she might have the power to crush the sunwyrm's prison, that the very act of holding it tightly might cause the most horrible doom to break free in Arduvulin.

The sunwyrm whispered in her mind, begging for release from its prison. Maddy knew the cage. Maddy would do what was right. They could be together. In sunlight. Forever.

"Hurry," she called to Mr. Whindarrow.

"We are hurrying," Mr. Whindarrow said.

"To Mundane House," Maddy said. "Directly. No arguing."

"Very well," Mr. Whindarrow said. "But you will owe us two picnics. And a sleepover."

"Two picnics," Maddy said.

"And a sleepover," Mr. Whindarrow said.

"Fine," Maddy said. "If you get me to Mundane House before the world ends."

"You aren't much of a negotiator," Mr. Whindarrow said. "I like that in a lady."

"Can't you go any faster?" Maddy said. "Mr. Nayheightly is outpacing you."

"He is not."

"He is."

"We'll see about that," Mr. Whindarrow said. Maddy clung on, one handed, and felt the world slipping away.

MADDY HAMMERED on the doors of Mundane House. It was dark, well past dark, and Nadine would be furious. Maddy gripped the baleful lantern, kept it shielded beneath her street coat. Hateful shafts of sickly green light punched forth through buttonholes and those tattered rends that hadn't been there this morning. The sunwyrm never once relented in it pleading. When pleading failed, it turned to threats. Now it offered riches and physical delights if Maddy would only set it free.

Madame Tsolde answered the door.

Maddy nearly bowled her over as she shoved into the entrance hall.

"Where is Saoirse?" Maddy called out.

"That filthy hag?" Madame Tsolde said. "I turned her away."

"You what?" Maddy's blood boiled. She turned on Madame Tsolde. The sunwyrm painted pictures in Maddy's mind. Of her and Tan together. Of Tan's lips upon her fingers, upon her wrists, his kisses burning like fire. Tan's lips brushing hers, Tan's limbs entwining hers, Tan's breath the air she breathed.

Black shadows slashed across the cold stone of Mundane House's entry hall. One of the shadows shifted. It rose. It folded in on itself, and folded again, congealing, a grey-shrouded form, glowing red eyes, gleaming fangs of ivory. "I am not so easily dismissed." Saoirse glared at Madame Tsolde. "I'd curse your slattern here, but it would only improve her lot." She turned her attention to Maddy. "Have you the prison?"

Nadine shoved into the hall. "What is this?" Her pistol gleamed in her fist.

"A demon straight from Hell," Madame Tsolde said. "I sent her away once, but she skulked around outside like a common vagrant."

Maddy's pulse hammered. "Mom—"

"Not now, Maddy." Nadine pointed her pistol at Saoirse. "Explain yourself."

Quille shuffled into the hall at the heels of the mechanized Beatrice Cannon. "Can you hold it down? I'm right in the middle of a delicate adjustment. Oh. Most extraordinary."

Emma jerked her chin toward Saoirse. "She looks like Maddy."

"Thank you," Saoirse said. "It's my girlish figure."

"It's your pointy chompers," Mr. Whindarrow said. "They are very lovely, your eminence."

"And your entrancing ruby eyes," Mr. Nayheightly said. "They speak of love, your grace."

"Of lust," Emma said. "Maddy's eyes don't—"

"Of course," Mr. Nayheightly said. "Magnificent. Truly magnificent. Long might one gaze into that flame, and longer still—"

"Shut up, all of you," Maddy said. The sunwyrm's images flickered just behind her eyesight. It whispered a riddle, taunting her, coaxing her: it knew where Tan was, it would tell her the answer to the riddle, she would never guess, but it would say, if only Maddy would help it. It was sick, it was caged, it needed help, Maddy. It was alone. Maddy. Please.

Nadine clicked the pistol's hammer back. "Maddy—"

"Mom—"

Quille scratched his chin. "I take it you're the Hag of Barna."

"And you're the Sorcerer Cuckold of Arduvulin City," Saoirse said.

"Quille is no cuckold," Nadine said.

"Then you admit he's a sorcerer," Saoirse said.

"I admit nothing, you—"

Maddy stretched her fingers out, sucking all the light from the gas lamp, congealing it into a burning fireball in her fist. She smashed the fireball against the flagstones. It flared in a blazing sheet before it streamed back into the lamp. "Mom!"

Nadine blinked. "Maddy?"

"I have a sunwyrm and a bunch of mechanized war machines in a failing prison under my coat. Saoirse is here to help me bind them back into their own personal hell. Can we just hold the small talk? Because it feels like they're going to get loose any minute."

"A sunwyrm?" Quille said.

"An Oligarch, Dad."

"Oh," Quille said. "Oh. Best bring it to the tower."

"There isn't time," Maddy said. "The sunwyrm is trying to control me." A tear ran down Maddy's cheek. "And it's winning."

"Then bring it to the dining room," Quille said.

54

M addy plopped the baleful lantern onto the table and stood back. Quille and Saoirse bent over it.

"Not too close," Saoirse said. "It might want you."

"It does want me," Quille said. His forehead wrinkled. "Most unusual."

"It's modified the prison from within," Saoirse said. "Note how it has devolved the surface into a series of—"

"Lenses," Quille said. "To concentrate some external force."

"Sunlight," Maddy said. "I put it in the sun. As an experiment."

"And a successful experiment it was," Quille said. "It's quickened them."

"It's ripped an entire layer of slowtime off the prison," Saoirse said.

"I did that," Maddy said. "When I killed the ironmonger's boy."

"You killed the ironmonger's boy?" Nadine said.

"Yes," Maddy said. "He was going to collapse Mount Gorim onto the baleful lantern."

"What is the baleful lantern?" Nadine said.

"This is," Quille said. "A most appropriate moniker, given its—"

"So you killed him?" Nadine said. "This boy?"

"I didn't save him," Maddy said. "Iptaxlryn and he were—"

"The kyloch?" Quille peered over his pince-nez at Maddy.

"They were determined to bury the baleful lantern under a mountain of rubble and—"

"That would never work," Saoirse said. "A sunwyrm could—"

"And I broke the Farseer, but by then he was convinced he was a hero, and a martyr, and—"

Nadine's pistol quavered toward Maddy. "You killed him?"

"I draped a slowtime spell over him. So I could escape. It's a long story."

"Iptaxlryn and a Farseer are in the Fogbound Realm?"

"On Mount Gorim," Maddy said. "Only not Iptaxlryn. The Farseer. Above the fog line."

"Not in the Realm, then," Quille said. "How did he manage to—"

"I don't quite recall the incantation," Saoirse said. "It's been ages since I've worked a slowtime spell. This damnable fog does nothing for the memory." She glanced at Quille. "Care to try your hand? We have about five minutes before a sunwyrm bursts free of its prison."

"It doesn't look very big," Uncle Leo said. "I doubt it will be much trouble, eh, Quilley?"

Nadine turned her weapon on Uncle Leo. "Where did you come from?"

Leo's gaze dropped to the weapon. "The door was open. And I live here, for the duration, in any event. Unless I'm unwelcome. In that case, I'll pack my bathing attire and slope off. Though I really was looking forward to—"

"Dinner is ready to be served," Madame Tsolde said. "I've cooked enough for—"

Nadine eased the hammer down.

Quille rubbed his chin. "I'm not so sure size figures into the equation, Leonides. It's rather densely—"

Maddy hammered her fist on the table. "Everyone shut up!" She turned to her dad. "Do something. Quick." If someone didn't stop the sunwyrm, Maddy was going to do something dreadful. The sunwyrm needed her, and she didn't have the strength to fight it anymore. It had finally found something she wanted. Tan. It knew where Tan was. It would take her to Tan if she would only free it.

Maddy and Tan could be together. Forever.

Quille blinked. "I'll try." He licked his lips and ran his fingers over the surface of the trophy.

Maddy turned to Saoirse. "Can't you help him? If you'd made the prison permanent, none of this would be happening."

"And I'd be long dead," Saoirse said. "You know the price of permanent spells. Stand back, girl, and I'll see what I can do."

"Kill them all," Rookhaven said. "Kill them all."

Maddy felt the muscles of her jaw clench. The sunwyrm tightened its grip on her mind. It didn't need her to free it anymore. Its prison was failing. Now it wanted her to touch it. To reach inside and simply feel it. If she touched it, she would become part of it. She would know all that it knew. Be all that it was. She would find Tan. They would find Tan. And then, the things they would do. A warm fire began to burn deep inside Maddy. Began to flare. Began to rage.

Maddy could see the baleful lantern softening. Bulging. When it shattered, the sunwyrm would possess her. And she would kill them all. Quille, Leo, Emma, Nadine. All the people she loved. She wasn't strong enough to stop it. Not once she started. Not once she let go. No one was paying attention to her. No one was doing anything.

Maddy began to weave a spell. One that she had witnessed only once before. At the Spelling Bee. When a young girl worked sorcery and raised the dead.

Quille peered at the baleful lantern.

Saoirse peered at Quille.

Nadine needed something to point her pistol at.

Something evil.

"Mom," Maddy said.

Nadine's eyebrows arrowed together. "What?"

Maddy scooped up the baleful lantern and clutched it to her breast. Maddy released the spell. A pit of blackness opened at her feet. "I'm sorry."

Her mother's pistol swung toward her.

Maddy pulled the portal in after her, collapsing it. She plunged forever into endless, soul-crushing darkness.

55

The Spelling Bee trophy exploded in her hands. Madeleine flew backward. The back of her skull slammed against solid adamantine.

She shook her head, seeing stars. When she closed her eyes and moaned, the stars were still there. The air crackled with residual magic. Madeleine managed to rise to her knees.

She'd landed in the ruins of the Dead Gate. Beneath her, skeletal forms crept toward the gate, fossils locked in stone, but moving, just as they had at the Arduvulin Gate. To her left and right, shattered arcs of dragon bone thrust into the monochrome sky. Lightning coursed from cloud to cloud. Above her, dragonflies whirled and grew.

They were the size of ravens.

Of rocs.

Of dragons.

The sunwyrm writhed and screamed. Freed from the prison, the sunwyrm grew as well. It called out in wordless images of rage, scouring Madeleine's soul, twisting her stomach into acid-burning knots.

In the distance, grimfoxes answered with the hideous death-screams of tortured children. Six grimfoxes. An unlucky number. Maddy's gaze hadn't killed a single grimfox. The odds of getting out of Night alive had just gone from astronomical to unimaginable.

"Now what?" Maddy said. The spectral hound paced about, a shaggy, fuming beast the size of a pony. "That glowing flying thing is trying to control me. I don't want to do what it wants, but—"

"I need to think," Madeleine said. Her family was safe for the moment. But they wouldn't stay that way. Madeleine herself was a portal back to Arduvulin. As long as she was alive, her family would never be safe.

"Hey," Maddy said. Her sulfurous breath puffed out in great clouds. "I am about out of self-control."

"Give me a minute," Madeleine said.

"You need to come up with some sort of plan," Maddy said. "Fast. I'm this close to ripping your throat out," Maddy growled. The fur on her back stood up. "You really should run."

Madeleine watched the sunwyrm grow in size. It called to her and beat its tattered, bloodless wings. Its rotting flesh rippled in coruscating bands of sun-bright gold and weeping, oily black.

It was a dragon. Once upon a time. Now it was very, very dead. Curved razor fangs studded its jaws, a gaping, smoldering cavern laced with a thousand diamond scimitars. They glistened with viscous night-black secretions, spittle-flecked and dripping with rage incarnate. A dragon sorcerer. The worst nightmare imaginable.

"I'm the sunwyrm's only path to Arduvulin," Madeleine said. "And to our family. Without me, it's imprisoned in Night." She looked at Maddy. "You have to kill me." There was no other choice.

Maddy growled. She paced closer to Madeleine.

"Do it quick," Madeleine said. She closed her eyes and

bared her neck. The sunwyrm burned in her mind. Its baleful glow was everything.

Maddy took another step toward Madeleine. "You're not listening, Madeleine. It wants me to kill you!"

Madeleine opened her eyes. Above her, clockwork dragonflies the size of dragons plied the skies. Before her, the sunwyrm—a creature that so ravaged the kylochs of Night that they abandoned their homeland, destroyed the only way back to their world—wheeled and burned in the endless dark of Night, bright as the sun in a world where the Moon was meant to rule alone. Nothing could stand before it. No one could defeat it. To try was madness.

Maddy bared her fangs and crept forward. "It's scared of you."

"What?" Madeleine's face was inches from Maddy's.

Maddy's eyes blazed with the fires of hell. "It wants you dead."

"Oh." Madeleine shook her head. "Oh." The sunwyrm was trying to control her as well. It wanted her to lie down and die. To give up. Madeleine twined her fingers in the shaggy fur of Maddy's coat. She pulled herself upright. The sunwyrm glowed brighter. It drew nearer.

Maddy growled. Acid dripped from her jaws. "I can't hold it—"

Madeleine vaulted to Maddy's back. She dug her heels in.

Maddy leapt like a springhorn.

Madeleine scrambled to stay on board. "Run!"

Maddy tore away at breakneck speed. She headed for the crater where Madeleine had learned her spells and history. Where Maddy felt as safe as anywhere in Night.

"Head for the city," Madeleine said.

"That's where the grimfoxes are!"

"Maybe some of the buildings still have roofs," Madeleine

said. "Out in the open, we're easy prey from above. We've beaten grimfoxes before."

"Not ones bigger than horses, with armed and armored man-things on their backs."

"We're stronger now, too."

"Right," Maddy said, and then she was looping without slowing and Madeleine needed all her concentration just to hold on.

The city grew larger. A grimfox's cry tore through the sky. It lurked, somewhere off to the left. An answering cry sounded from far off to the right. Madeleine glanced behind. The clouds parted for an instant and they were there, following. Six dragonflies shadowed across the moon. She saw no sign of the sunwyrm.

Of the Oligarch. Sunwyrm was too pretty a name for the thing that stalked them. But Oligarch was scarier. It implied that there was more than one of them. That even now it could be trying to find—to wake—its comrades. Sorcerers were dangerous enough. They never banded together. They were too obsessed with their private, insane goals to combine forces. Madeleine didn't want to think about sorcerers working together. Or what sorts of sorcery dragons were capable of. Once they were dead. And hunting in packs.

Maddy trotted past a crumbling stone wall. Her paws left weeping tracks of bright lava on the shattered pavement of a deserted square. A bone-dry fountain centered the square, frescoed plaster sloughed off and mounded about its base. Decaying buildings surrounded the square on all sides. Narrow alleyways ran between the buildings. Maddy panted, her tongue lolling. "That was hard."

Madeleine dismounted. "In there," she said, pointing. One of the buildings was in better repair than the others. It looked like it might provide protection from above.

"We could get trapped inside," Maddy said.

"Do you have a better idea?" Madeleine wasn't being a smartmouth. Maddy saw things differently than her. It paid to get a second opinion.

"Let me take a look first," Maddy said. "If there's a back door—"

Lightning leapt from cloud to cloud overhead. Madeleine held her palm out and called the lightning down. She balanced the blue ball on her palm. "I can make a back door," Madeleine said. "If we need one."

"Right," Maddy said. "Good thinking."

A grimfox shrieked, much closer this time.

"I'm pretty sure we'll need one," Maddy said.

"Let's go," Madeleine said. She was pretty sure they'd need one, too. But standing out here where anything overhead could see them wasn't an option.

56

Madeleine crouched in a corner near the building's front door. Where she could keep an eye on the square. Maddy explored the building, searching for a back door. Madeleine racked her brain for some sort of plan, any idea that might keep them alive. If the sunwyrm wanted her dead, then she absolutely did not want that to happen. Madeleine didn't think she was enough of an enchanter yet to be a very dangerous sorcerer once she was dead. But she might still be a portal to Arduvulin. And a lot easier to control. So dying wasn't an option. Not if she wanted to keep her family safe. She would have to beat the sunwyrm. The Oligarch. Except Saoirse said they couldn't be cursed or killed. Which made perfect sense, now that she knew that they were undead. They could only be imprisoned.

Saoirse had used tramman blood and slowtime spells to make a prison. There weren't any trammans that Madeleine knew of in Night. Madeleine understood now how slowtime spells worked, but she'd never tried to make one herself. Plus you had to be a sorcerer or kyloch to work magic with fresh blood.

She needed something else, something she knew how to do. Or something Maddy knew how to do. Curse-gazing was out. It wouldn't work. Magic fireballs, balls of lightning, they wouldn't do any good.

A dark shape moved in the shadows across the square. Two dark shapes, pacing, searching. They moved silently. Pausing often, scenting the air. Grimfoxes. Madeleine didn't dare move.

Maddy huffed in Madeleine's ear. "Found a back door."

One of the grimfox riders looked up at the sound. It pointed a jaggedly barbed trident right at Madeleine.

"Let's go," Maddy said.

"No, wait," Madeleine whispered. There was motion overhead, the whirring sound of rapidly beating wings, stirring up great clouds of dust and tainting the air with the smell of machine oil. The first grimfox darted for the shadows. A beam of light lashed out after it. The façade of the building across the square exploded, spewing huge chunks of masonry and tiny shards skyward. A massive cornerstone shattered the courtyard fountain. A grimfox screamed in pain. A rusty trickle of water ran across the dusty courtyard.

"Look." Madeleine pointed. "There's water in Night."

"So what," Maddy said. "Come on."

"It thought the grimfoxes were us," Madeleine said. "The dragonflies can't see very well."

"They see motion," Maddy said. "Most bugs do, anyway. And not just with their eyes. So keep your head down and follow me. Quietly."

Maddy lead them to a door deep inside the building. Stone stairs led down.

"I thought you said this was a back door."

"There's a tunnel," Maddy said. "In the cellar."

"Where does it go?"

"I don't know," Maddy said. "I only went far enough to see light at the far end. I was worried about you, so I came back."

"You saw light?"

"I saw less dark, Madeleine." Maddy started down the stairs. "You're as bad as Emma. You knew what I meant."

A grimfox hammered through the front door of the building just as Madeleine took her first step down. There was a flash of light, a silent rush of air out of Madeleine's lungs, and she was hurtling down the stairs.

Maddy's prone body broke her fall. "Ouch!"

Debris cascaded down the stairwell after Madeleine. "Maddy, get clear!" Madeleine tried to scramble to her feet. Maddy bumped her as something harder than stone hammered her from behind and sent her sprawling.

"Ick." Madeleine shook her head. Stars danced. She'd fallen in a puddle of rotten slime. The stench was overpowering, musky and corrupt at the same time. She flipped dripping strands from her fingers. "Are you hurt, Maddy?"

Maddy growled.

Maddy spun about as the grimfox's scream shook the walls of the tunnel behind her. It rose on three legs. The rider on its back hung slack against its flanks.

That didn't matter. Rider or not, grimfoxes were deadly.

Its massive body filled the tunnel, blocking the tumbling wreckage of the stairwell. There was no way to go but further down the tunnel. The grimfox's one good eye beamed hate at Maddy. It gnashed its dagger-teeth in its horse-sized jaws. It advanced, dragging one hind leg.

"Maddy, come here." Madeleine began to work her spell.

"It's hurt," Maddy said. "I can take it."

The grimfox lunged at Maddy. She danced back. It was fast, blindingly fast.

Maddy was faster. This time.

Madeleine bent and picked up a stone. She tossed it at the grimfox.

"You can throw harder than that," Maddy said.

"Maddy, do as I say." The ground began to rumble. "Come here. Right now."

Maddy growled and began to back toward Madeleine. The earth began to shake.

Madeleine swung onto Maddy's back. "Run!"

Like finds like. The oldest spell of all. True magic. Every loose piece of stone within range of Madeleine's spell was headed for the grimfox. Madeleine hoped that Maddy was right about the way out. There was no way anything was getting back up those stairs. Or down them.

Madeleine kept her head down as pebbles hammered into her. Maddy did a good job of avoiding the larger fragments hurtling down the tunnel.

The grimfox screamed. It kept screaming as it fell further behind. Stones hammered into it so hard that it sounded like a drum. A sickening squish cut off its bellowing in mid-cry.

Maddy slowed to a walk. When she stopped, Madeleine dismounted.

"That was pretty clever," Maddy said.

"That was just plain luck," Madeleine said. She peered down the tunnel. "I don't see any light."

"That's because the tunnel curves," Maddy said. "Right after the book room."

Madeleine walked at Maddy's side. "You mean a library?"

"I mean a room full of books," Maddy said. "Crates of them."

"Maybe there's a book in there that will tell us how to defeat an Oligarch." Madeleine picked up the pace. She could barely see where she was going, and she had excellent night vision.

"Maybe."

The tunnel did curve, immediately past a doorway cut in the left-hand wall. And there was light at the end of the tunnel, a dim red light that didn't look like a sunwyrm's glow, but didn't look like moonlight, either.

Madeleine didn't like it. When she glanced into the book room, she forgot all about everything else.

There was a rack of fairy lights just inside the door. Very fine, very permanent fairly lights. As good as Quille could make. Maybe better. Maddy found a verdigris-tinted candelabra in the corner.

The room was ten times as large as Quille's library. It didn't have shelves at all, simply crate after crate stuffed to over-flowing with books, books tossed in as if in great haste. There was barely room to crawl between the crates.

"Help me search," Madeleine said.

"I can't read," Maddy said.

"Oh." Madeleine hadn't thought of that. Maddy could do lots of other useful things, though. "Do you want to keep guard?"

"Not really," Maddy said. "The tunnel is blocked behind us. And none of the flying things can fit in. I can help you search if you tell me what to look for."

"I don't know what to look for." Madeleine picked up a book and read its spine. It was in Prelanish or Lanish. One could rarely tell which from the title. *Flora and Fauna of the Alogical Highlands*, by Ectyl Abaryptalx.

"You could start with these ones that smell like that glowy creature," Maddy said. "The one trying to mind control us earli-er." Maddy scratched her side against a crate. "There's another crate that smells like the flying bug machines further back."

MADELEINE SCRATCHED Maddy behind the ears absently and read. She'd been at it for hours. The books about the Oligarchs were all in dragon script. Like the ones in Quille's library.

All but the last book she'd found. It was a dragon-script-to-Prelanish dictionary.

Madeleine had found a sick bucket and used it often at first. Now she really just got the dry heaves every now and then as the text gnawed at her guts. She'd long since emptied her stomach.

Reading was slow, using the dictionary for every word, but she was getting faster. Time ran differently in Night. There was no telling how long Madeleine could stay here studying. Maybe forever. That wouldn't be bad. Maybe for every second she hid here and read, her family lived a year. Though it had seemed just the opposite when she, and Madame Aubergine, and Rookhaven, and Maddy had practiced magic and history in the crater. She could study for hundreds of hours in Night and only a few hours passed in Arduvulin.

"Aren't you hungry?" Maddy said.

"No," Madeleine said. She was too interested in what she was learning to be hungry. And she'd just puke up anything she ate anyway.

"Me neither," Maddy said. She laid her head back down on her paws and leaned into Madeleine's scratching. "It's weird. I like to be hungry."

"You know you say that every time we come to Night."

"It's still weird."

"I'm reading."

"We're never going home, are we? Not this time."

Madeleine flipped her book face down. "I have an idea. Saoirse said that Oligarchs can't be killed or cursed. She didn't say—"

A grimfox screamed. It sounded like it was just outside.

Maddy jumped to her feet. She puffed brimstone from her nostrils. "I'll go look."

Madeleine stood. She clutched her dictionary. "We'll go

together." The book wouldn't fit in her pocket. And she might need both hands free.

The grimfox screamed again.

Madeleine reluctantly abandoned the dictionary for the moment. She could come back and get it when—

The sharp barb of a trident speared through Maddy's left paw. Maddy's growl turned into a howl as she was yanked through the doorway and into the corridor outside.

Madeleine ran into the corridor, her hands weaving the first bits of those elemental spells she knew, and those she didn't.

Calling on fire and lightning were much the same. Calling on stone, and wind, and water had to be similar. Madame Aubergine just hadn't had time to teach Madeleine those. She would have to improvise.

Maddy yanked her paw free with a scream and a growl. She sidled up next to the tunnel wall, backing slowly, limping on three legs.

When the grimfox spied Madeleine, it yipped.

Maddy growled and stopped backing up. She began to move in front of Madeleine. It was the bravest thing Madeleine had ever seen. And the most foolish.

Madeleine would try to call on lightning first. They were close enough to the end of the tunnel that it might work. "Maddy, move back."

"No," Maddy snarled. "Not this time. I'm done moving back."

"Please. I can spell it—"

Maddy bunched her hindquarters and leapt.

The grimfox's rider slashed out with its trident.

Maddy was too quick. Her jaws latched onto the grimfox's throat. She dangled, neck muscles working, growling as the grimfox writhed and slammed against the walls and ceiling.

Madeleine had to back up quickly to avoid the falling shards of ceiling. She tripped and fell.

The grimfox continued on toward her, a mindless, flailing beast larger than a horse. The rider's trident threw sparks as it speared into the rock inches from Madeleine's cheek. Stone chips peppered her face as the massive weapon tore free.

Madeleine crabbed backwards, barely avoiding one bone-crushing paw after another.

The grimfox slammed against the tunnel ceiling again and again.

Maddy was thrown free.

Slick, black fluid pumped from the tattered slashes in the grimfox's throat. Its limbs jerked and jerked as it bled out whatever vile fluid animated it. The rider was dead, too. Its flesh melded into the flesh of the grimfox, like they were one creature. It only looked like it was riding.

Maddy spit out a chunk of grimfox flesh. She tried to stand. She made it on the third try, wobbly and unsteady, her good legs wide-splayed and shaking. "I can kill them all, Madeleine. You don't have to be afraid."

"I'm not afraid, you idiot." Madeleine struggled to her knees. She ran her hands over Maddy. She wasn't afraid. Not with Maddy at her side. Her fingers shook as she searched Maddy for damage. "Don't ever do that again."

"I can't die, Madeleine." Maddy's rump hit the ground with a thump. Her tongue lolled out. "I'm like our mom."

"Nadine can die."

"No," Maddy said. "Our real mom."

"Our birth mother."

"Whatever." Maddy panted. "You have to be alive before you can die."

"You're alive." Madeleine slumped on the floor next to Maddy. She scratched Maddy behind the ears.

"No, I'm not," Maddy said. "Not here. I'm not alive, and I'm not dead. When we're together, in Arduvulin, then I'm alive."

"We're together now." Madeleine rubbed the fur between Maddy's eyes.

"Not really," Maddy said. "When that glowing thing tried to get me to kill you. And you wanted me to kill you. That's when I knew. I would be trapped here. Forever."

"Maddy—"

"I would be in a cage again, Madeleine. Only this time, I'd be in it alone."

"Can you walk?"

"Sort of."

"Let's go see what's at the end of this tunnel."

"I don't think it's daylight."

"Maybe it's something better."

Maddy scrabbled to her feet. "Stay behind me, Madeleine." Maddy crept forward on three paws.

It was a lot of nasty, smelly work to squeeze past the dead grimfox blocking the tunnel. Maddy walked very slowly, limping painfully. Madeleine walked next to her, fingers brushing the stiff fur of her neck.

"What did you learn in the books?" Maddy said.

"More than I wanted to. They were books about how to destroy a Gate. And what might happen if you did."

"I guess we know that already," Maddy said. "Is it getting hot in here?"

"I'd say so." The end of the tunnel glowed cherry red.

"Good." Maddy paced on. "I don't like being cold."

"I don't like it either. Hold up for a minute."

Maddy stopped.

Madeleine crouched down. "Maddy, what if we'd gotten it backwards?" She studied the floor of the tunnel. "What if I got everything backwards?"

"I don't know what you're talking about."

"In those books," Madeleine said, "it says that you can destroy a Gate by tearing a hole between our world and another world. A world that is always inches away. A nasty world. Full of things like the Oligarchs and their machines."

"So?"

"Well," Madeleine said, "all of Rookhaven's stories talk about how the Ghulans escaped into our world and destroyed the Gate behind them. To trap the Oligarchs in Night."

"To keep them out of the Aos Sí," Maddy said. "That's what the crypto-naturalist pirates said, too."

"I didn't listen to them," Madeleine said.

"I know." Maddy head-butted Madeleine. "Good thing you have me."

"That's what I mean," Madeleine said. "Maybe I don't have you."

"Did you get conked on the head back there?" Maddy puffed out a muzzle full of sulfurous steam. "You're not making any sense."

"Look," Madeleine said, "those books talked about how you can tear open the world to destroy a Gate. There were lots of formulae our dad would understand. But they were all equations. They added up to the same sums on both sides of the equal sign."

"Madeleine," Maddy said, "I'm not as smart as you. You need to just tell me what all this means."

"I think it means that not only can you tear open the world to destroy a Gate, but that destroying a Gate can tear open the world."

"So what?"

"So it's a different way of looking at things. Like Saoirse and the sunwyrm. The Oligarch. She said it couldn't be killed and it couldn't be cursed."

"Fascinating." Maddy scrambled to her feet. "Thanks for the philosophy lesson, but can we go see what's at the end of the tunnel now?"

"I know what's at the end of the tunnel."

"Then you can stay here and I'll go see." Maddy began limping toward the exit.

Madeleine shouted. She'd already admitted the truth to herself. It didn't matter who else heard. "I don't have you, Maddy!"

Maddy stopped, one paw in the air. She turned.

Madeleine stared at the tunnel floor. Her words were almost a whisper. Maddy would hear, though. She had uncanny hearing. "You have me."

Madeleine had been looking at everything backwards. All the good things that Madeleine believed about herself. That she was brave. That she was loyal. That she never gave up. They weren't part of her. She wasn't those things. Maddy was the strong one. Maddy never backed down. Maddy never deserted a friend.

Maddy was who Madeleine longed to be. Even if that meant she could never be fully human. Ever.

"Maybe we have each other," Maddy said. "That wouldn't be the worst thing in the world."

Madeleine nodded. "I have a plan."

"That's one of the things I love about you," Maddy said. "But you'd better tell me about it this time. Then we can both have a plan."

"I can do that."

"Can you do it while we walk?" Maddy said. "I'm tired of this place. We need to go home."

Madeleine's plan was elegant in its simplicity. The sunwyrm couldn't be killed. And it couldn't be cursed. So she would resurrect it. And bless it. If it wasn't dead anymore, it would only be a dragon. If she did the blessing right, it would be a good dragon. If there was such a thing.

"That's sorcery," Maddy said. "And evil. I won't be a part of that. You'd end up cursing someone we love by blessing the sunwyrm. And we promised Quille. No permanent magic."

"You won't be a part of it," Madeleine said. "I'll send you back to Arduvulin, and after you're gone, I'll do it." With Maddy safely home, the curse would have to fall on Madeleine herself. There wouldn't be anyone else in all of Night to curse.

"Right," Maddy said. "And I'll arrive home a halfwit. Or worse, an animal. That's a stupid plan."

"Then you come up with a better one."

The end of the tunnel was only a few feet away. It was roasting hot, the rocks themselves glowing red. The air smelled worse than a hellhound's breath.

"I'm thinking," Maddy said.

Madeleine peered out the end of the tunnel. "Think fast." She crept out onto a narrow ledge. Far below her, the fires of hell burned.

Maddy followed her out.

The tunnel ended at the great rend in the world, a mile or more above the boiling lava below. It was half a mile to the other side, and the ledge they stood on was only two feet wide and twenty feet long.

"Some backdoor," Madeleine said. She gazed up at the cliff top, a hundred feet above them. "We could climb, I guess."

"I don't think so," Maddy said. A grimfox peeked its head over the ledge. Then three more did. They all screamed.

"Four is luckier than six," Madeleine said.

"Barely." Maddy glanced down. "We could jump and swim for it."

"Maybe you could," Madeleine said.

"There's no maybe about it," Maddy said. "It feels pretty good to be warm for once."

"We'll stick with my plan, then." Madeleine began contemplating the spells she would need.

The sunwyrm rose above the tear in the world. Six clockwork dragonflies the size of dragons followed it. They hadn't spotted Maddy and Madeleine yet.

Maddy looked down. "Do you think this is where the Oligarchs came from?"

"I don't know." Madeleine began to weave her spells. The sunwyrm and its machines wheeled and drifted closer. "Come close. I'll send you home first."

"The Hag of Barna imprisoned them." Maddy kicked a stone over the ledge. It fell forever.

"We don't have tramman blood," Madeleine said. "And I don't think I can work a slowtime spell. I couldn't work magic with fresh tramman blood even if we had some. I'm not dead yet. Or a kyloch. "

"Half hellhound," Maddy said. "And half kyloch."

Madeleine's head jerked around. "What?"

"Come on," Maddy said. "You had to know. Rookhaven teaching you all the languages of Ghula. Madame Aubergine teaching you spells no enchanter knows. The Dead Gate sucking us toward it whenever Quille worked his travel spells. Even that boy, Geoff. He recognized us, Madeleine. No one is this thick."

"I'm human. We're half-human."

"Kylochs are human."

"They aren't."

The sunwyrm was nearly level with them.

"They seem human to me," Maddy said.

"Not to me." Madeleine was not a kyloch. She was *not*.

"I have a plan," Maddy said.

The sunwyrm filled the sky. It flapped its tattered, undead wings and screamed.

"It's trying to control me again. It still wants me to kill you." Maddy bumped her forehead against Madeleine's. "Do you trust me, Madeleine? Don't take all night to decide."

"I don't have to decide," Madeleine said. It didn't matter what else was true or what was a lie. She didn't just trust Maddy. She loved her. Madeleine nodded. "I do."

"I trust you too," Maddy said. "Don't let me down."

Maddy rose up on her hind legs and shoved Madeleine off the ledge.

57

Maddy jumped after her.

Madeleine screamed and kept on screaming.

The sunwyrm plunged toward them, its dragonflies in pursuit. The wind whipped around them, twisting Madeleine's hair in knots, pulling at the corners of Maddy's lips.

"We have to time this just right," Maddy said. "You'll need hands right up until the last minute."

"For what?" Madeleine felt the air sucked out of her lungs.

"If you can throw fireballs, we should be able to throw up a great ball of lava," Maddy said.

"I can't." Madeleine had never done such a thing. It was impossible.

"We can," Maddy said. "Together."

"No."

"Don't be afraid," Maddy said. "We're a hellhound. And a kyloch. We were made for this stuff."

"I'm not a kyloch," Madeleine said.

"Fine. Then we'll both die."

"You can't die," Madeleine said. "You said so."

"I'll want to die," Maddy said. "Without you. It's the same thing. Only worse."

"It can't catch us," Madeleine said. The sunwyrm and its comrades weren't gaining on Maddy and Madeleine. Maybe there was a chance. Just because Madeleine could throw balls of lava didn't mean she was a kyloch. If she could. Throw balls of lava. It didn't make her a kyloch. Even if she failed, Maddy might still live.

Madeleine began to work her spells, calling lava to her fingers.

"Just before we hit," Maddy said. "You have to send me home. I'll grab you and hold on."

"I could send you home now."

"Don't you dare."

"Shut up, then." Madeleine's fingers worked. "I need to concentrate."

The first ball of lava struck the lead dragonfly. It hammered into the cliff face and exploded in a blazing ball of light.

"Good shot!" Maddy shouted.

"I was aiming for the sunwyrm!"

"Lucky shot!" Maddy's words were whipped away. They plummeted toward the lava with increasing speed. The remaining dragonflies began to take evasive maneuvers. It was hopeless. Madeleine couldn't do this. It would be easier just to die.

"It's trying to control me again!" Maddy shouted.

Madeleine hurled another lava ball. Her hands burned. It missed by a mile. A dragonfly lashed a beam of sickly green light toward then. The cliff face below exploded and peppered them with stones as they fell past.

The sunwyrm needed her. She shouldn't fight it. She should just let herself go. Dying wasn't that bad.

Maddy's jaws clamped onto Madeleine's earlobe. She yanked.

Madeleine screamed. And hurled another lava-ball. It glanced off the cliff face and splattered a dragonfly. The dragonfly stopped flying and fell.

"You're getting better," Maddy said. "But we're about out of time."

"Hang on!" Madeleine shouted. She had an idea.

"Right!" Maddy draped a paw across Madeleine's chest. It was oddly comforting.

Just because Madeleine could work a slowtime spell didn't mean she was a kyloch. She'd reverse-engineered it using enchanter's skills. She wiped drying blood off her tattered earlobe. She worked it between her fingers. She flicked it into the air. The wind noise disappeared.

"What did you do!" Maddy's voice was deafening in the silence.

The sunwyrm gained on them. Madeleine didn't have time to explain. She began to call lava to her in great, heaping gobs. Maddy and Madeleine drifted down at half their normal speed. Still Madeleine gathered lava in her hands, compressing it tighter and tighter. Her palms burned like blazes. The sunwyrm gained on them, four dragon-sized mechanical dragonflies in its wake.

There was one more thing Madeleine could do. If she had time. She'd scribbled out Quille's spell for sorcerer-penetrating bullets so many times she'd memorized it. It worked on bullets. Maybe it would work on lava.

Madeleine muttered in Annish over her hands.

"It wants me!" Maddy growled. "I can't—"

The sunwyrm was close enough to touch. Madeleine neared the end of the spell.

The sunwyrm hovered, a great oily eye considering

Madeleine, its hideous, scything fangs filling the sky above her. It screamed in triumph. A rotting wind issued from between its gaping jaws.

Madeleine hurled the lava-ball. It moved at a crawl inside the slowtime bubble before exploding in sheets to slather the sunwyrm's hideous face. It dripped and spread, coating the sunwyrm's wings as the undead monster tried to rise. Boiling lava began seeping in, soaking in, penetrating and searing through decaying flesh and crumbling bone.

The sunwyrm plunged past tail first, cocooned in molten rock, before it began to tumble toward the boiling, heaving surface of the lava pooling below.

Without their master to control them, the dragonflies veered off wildly, hammering great slabs of stone loose from the cliffs.

Trapped in their slowtime bubble, Madeleine and Maddy could only watch in horror as a massive boulder plummeted toward them.

"That's not good," Maddy said.

"Shut up," Madeleine said. The boulder was the least of her worries.

Madeleine kissed Maddy on the forehead and wrapped her arms about her. "Sleep," Madeleine whispered. She felt Maddy pass through her the instant she struck the lava. Nothing else mattered.

Maddy was safe. Safe and free.

MADDY JERKED AND GASPED. "MADELEINE!"

Uncle Leo stood over her, his fist raised.

Quille released Maddy's wrist and grabbed Leo's arm. "Stop! She has a pulse!"

Maddy felt as if every bone in her body was broken. She was stretched out on the dining room table, her ridiculous family peering down at her.

Nadine's fingers hovered over Maddy's brow. "Madeleine."

Maddy didn't know. Didn't know if she'd held on to Madeleine with enough might to pull her back from Night.

To pull all of her back.

"Get me a book," Maddy said. She waved her family away and rolled over. The patterns in the carpet swam before her eyes.

"Get her a book, damn it all." Quille slammed his ashplant down and the walls of Mundane House shuddered.

Leo fished a softback book out of his coat pocket. "Here."

Maddy sat up. She flipped the book open, selecting a page at random. Her lips moved. "November fifteenth. I saw Emma Sunbury today. She looked very unhappy. I wish there was some way I could help her, to save her from whatever haunts her so. She reminds me of Adamantine in her darkest hours, when she believed she was alone, and had no one to turn to. I would change this if I could. I cannot bear the thought of Emma's suffering. It burns me to the core."

Maddy looked up. Quille's face hovered over hers. She handed the book to her father. "What language is this?"

Quille glanced at the page. "I'd say that is the language of love, Maddy mine."

"Low Ardu," Uncle Leo said. "I wouldn't have given it to you if I'd thought you might read it aloud."

Maddy could still read. Low Ardu, at least. Some part of Madeleine had lived on. Maddy wasn't alone. Not entirely.

"I need to find Tan," Maddy said.

"The Department is working on it," Nadine said. "You need to rest. We've called Dr. Palantire."

"No. You're not listening. I need to find Tan. Not the Department. Me." The surgeon could wait. It was absurd that she'd been distracted this long by a stupid, baleful hunk of rubbish.

Tan needed her. The sunwyrm had tempted Maddy with images of Tan. With whispered promises and lies. But it had let something slip. When it thought it had won. Maddy needed to find Tan.

"The Spelling Bee trophy was evil." Maddy pressed her palms against the table. "For the record." Her hands hurt like blazes.

Saoirse cleared her throat. "I wouldn't say it was evil."

Maddy's words leapt from her throat. "You could have made the spells permanent! But you didn't. For what? Vanity?"

"Maddy—" Emma grasped Maddy's arm to steady her.

Maddy growled and jerked away. "I don't need help." When she tried to stand, her left leg didn't work. She pitched forward onto the wine-stained carpet.

Nadine bent to help her rise.

"Get away!" Maddy roared. "Get away, all of you!"

"You're hurt," Nadine said.

"You have no idea," Maddy said. "Now leave me alone. Go away until the surgeon arrives."

SAOIRSE KNELT NEXT TO MADDY. "Let me see those hands."

"Get away."

"Do as I say, girl. Save your strength for a fight that matters. Do you want to find Its Royal Tanist?"

"Yes."

"Then let me see those hands."

Maddy screamed when Saoirse touched her hands. She kept on screaming as she began to burn.

She was a spark, an ember, a coal, a flame, a bonfire, a raging inferno, a glowing bit of ash, coasting on the wind. It rained then, cooling her, soaking her. She was soot, clay, stone, a shadow that writhed in stone, squirming toward the Arduvulin Gate.

Maddy opened her eyes. She was in the room where she had met Saoirse. The bare courtroom of the Unseelie Court. A headsman's bogle sat slack-jawed, his whetstone still against the blade of his ugly axe.

"Josef," Saoirse said. "Go get Honest Peter. Have him bring my bag." She turned to Maddy. "Sit down, girl."

"She's trouble," Josef said. "I told you—"

"Go get Honest Peter before I turn you back to stone," Saoirse said. "Be quick about it."

Maddy flopped into a chair.

"You listen to me now," Saoirse said. "It's one thing for us to fight in private. It's another to do it in public."

"I'm not fighting."

"Vanity, is it?" Saoirse gripped Maddy's chin and forced her to meet her eyes. "You're entitled to your opinion. But you're not all-knowing. Say anything you like about what I do. Don't you dare express an opinion about why I do it."

Maddy jerked her head free. She glared at Saoirse. "Or what?"

"Or you'll wish you hadn't."

"Because you'll hurt me?" Maddy's hands were killing her.

"I won't have to," Saoirse said. "You'll hurt yourself. Just like you did today."

"I'll heal," Maddy said. She always healed.

"I'm not concerned with your outsides," Saoirse said. "Maybe my concern is vanity, but not in the way you meant it. Did it touch you?"

"Did what touch me?"

"The sunwyrm."

"No, only the grimfox."

"Did you touch the sunwyrm?"

"No."

"How close was it to you?"

"Inches."

"And it didn't touch you."

"It was slathered in lava at the time."

Saoirse looked at Maddy's hands.

"That's good thinking. What sort of lava?"

"I don't know. How many different sorts are there?"

"Dozens. Some easier to handle than others." Saoirse blinked. "Your mother should have taught you all this."

"Nadine's my mother. I don't think she knows much about being a hellhound."

"It wouldn't surprise me if that one did," Saoirse said. "But you're right. I meant your birth mother. It isn't often a woman gets a do-over. I'm not one to let opportunity slip by."

"I don't understand," Maddy said.

"That's all my fault," Saoirse said. "If I'd paid more attention to raising your mother, none of this would have happened. I'll try to do better this time."

"I still don't—"

Honest Peter hustled in with a large black bag. "Afternoon, Maddy Dune. Dis da riyet bag, Saoirse?"

"It is," Saoirse said.

"Hava nasty sun-burren Maddy," Honest Peter said. "Grimfox do dat to your arem?"

"Yes sir," Maddy said.

"Saoirse fixer up den," Honest Peter said. "Jes like old tiyems."

"Right."

"When we're done here, I'll take you home," Saoirse said. "Now hold still, because this is going to hurt." Saoirse rubbed salve on Maddy's burns.

"That doesn't hurt." It actually felt pretty good. Maddy's

gaze met Saoirse's. The woman's eyes blazed with a hell-forge flame.

"Like I said." Saoirse gripped Maddy's chin again. "I'm not all that concerned about your outsides." She touched her forehead to Maddy's. A cyclone of swirling flame exploded behind Maddy's brow.

58

Maddy roasted in a burning gyre as she plunged into Night. She relived every horrible second, felt the moment that her grip on Madeleine slipped again, when she'd been certain the better part of her lay stranded and alone in Night.

When it was over, Maddy jerked free. She shivered as the last swirl of flame coursed through her limbs.

"I told you it would hurt."

"You didn't warn me that you would—"

"These sunwyrms are tricky. And you weren't exactly well composed when you came home. You weren't acting yourself."

"So you made me live it again?"

"I wish," Saoirse said. "I made us both live it." Her face was beaded with sweat. "And not again. You were too distracted the first time to comprehend the details. This time we saw it all. Felt it all. In excruciatingly fine focus."

"So you felt me lose hold of Madeleine."

"If you'd lost hold of her, I'd be laying on the floor twitching. I was riding in Madeleine. You saved her, Maddy. Every bit of her."

"You're lying to make me feel good."

"What did I tell you about ascribing motives to my actions?"

"Then you're lying for whatever reason."

"Time will tell," Saoirse said. "And you'll apologize to me."

"Maybe."

"Definitely. You're a very confused young woman." Saoirse massaged her temples. "But I'd say you're a very fine young enchanter."

"Kyloch," Maddy said. "I'm not even half-human."

Saoirse laughed. "Now that's unlikely, and more's the pity. Your kylochs get worse press than they deserve."

"It explains everything," Maddy said. "Geoff smiled at me."

"Who?"

"The boy who took the trophy. The kyloch."

"Ach." Saoirse looked like she wanted to spit. "That boy, he smiled at you because he wasn't a bigot like these Arduvulin people, and because you're a very pretty young woman.

"Pity you had to bury him alive, but we do what we must. And as far as your unconventional magic, well you get that from me, through your mother. We're refugees on a distant shore, Maddy Dune, and nothing you've done is strange or out of the ordinary where we hail from."

"Wait a minute—"

"Now it is true that you're likely to pull Quille and company toward the Dead Gate when traveling magically. Just as Quille would pull you to the Arduvulin Gate if he were stronger. We skimmed mighty close to the Cauldron of the Damned on our way here. I image you could feel it. You're a willful young woman, and likely to grow more so with time and training.

"If you live that long. Clinging on to a ripe old age runs in our kind, though. I don't fear for anything but misadventure. Now that I've seen you in action."

"You're saying we're related."

"Like it or not," Saoirse said. "There's a blood connection.

Your mother is my daughter. And if you don't believe me, I'll conjure up her and her filthy friends of the Hunt. Would you like that?"

"No."

"I wouldn't either," Saoirse said. "She's murder to locate, and a lot more bother than she's worth. A disappointment, and that's the truth.

"I blame her father. How are your hands?"

Maddy looked. "They're not much better."

"Then we best get you back," Saoirse said. "I imagine that surgeon is there by now."

Saoirse's fingers began to weave.

Maddy caught them in her salve-smothered grip. "Can we walk like regular people?"

"We can, but what's the point?"

"I need time to think."

Saoirse studied Maddy's face. "You must get that from your human father. Your birth mother never was much of a thinker."

"Or a mother."

"I'm confident the two skills are related," Saoirse said. "We'll walk. But I'm wearing my slightly-prettier-than-Aevil glamour. If you don't mind."

"You don't have a slightly-prettier-than-Emma glamour handy, do you?"

"I could whip one up," Saoirse said. "But you don't need it."

"Because you only worry about my insides."

"Because I have eyes in my head, girl." Saoirse fished in her bag. "This won't take but a minute."

59

Nadine's pistol barrel puckered the forehead of Saoirse's glamour. Her lips barely moved but her chest heaved with each breath. "You will never. Lay hands. On my daughter. Again."

"I'll ask first," Saoirse said. "Next time." She let her glamour drop. Nadine was aiming about a foot over Saoirse's head.

"I'd do it in writing, were I you," Uncle Leo said. "And use the post. Maddy, are you—"

"You're not me," Saoirse said. "Though I understand the sentiment."

"I'm fine," Maddy said. "I was shaken up and Saoirse knew it. She helped straighten me out inside. I wasn't in any danger. Not from her."

"And I am to know this how?" Nadine holstered her pistol slowly. She glared at Saoirse.

"Fair enough," Saoirse said. "The fault is mine. I'm not used to the idea of explaining myself."

"Don't bother getting used to it," Nadine said. "You can go now."

"I can go anytime I like," Saoirse said. "I don't need anyone's permission for that."

"I think Nadine would like you to go," Uncle Leo said.

"Then she ought to be woman enough to say so," Saoirse said.

Nadine pointed her finger like a gun. She leaned forward on her tiptoes. She towered over Saoirse without effort. "You—"

"Hag," Saoirse said. "I think that's the word you're looking for." She gazed up at Nadine and smiled. Her eyes flared with the fires of hell. Her fangs gleamed like ivory.

Quille chuckled.

Nadine turned on him. "You think this is funny? This woman steals our daughter in a puff of steam and—"

"Brimstone," Saoirse said. "Enchanters disappear in puffs of steam."

"My hands still hurt," Maddy said. "Can you yell at each other once the doctor is gone?"

"Dr. Palantire has undoubtedly experienced worse sickbed scenes," Emma said. "Haven't you, doctor?"

The surgeon cleared his throat. "Undoubtedly." He screwed an uncomfortable grin onto his face. "Perhaps if I treated the young lady in the parlor—"

"Come on," Maddy said. Dr. Palantire had treated her for grimfox bites once before. And for various maladies after the unfortunate Pango fiasco. He was very thorough, and liked to know about every injury, no matter how small. "I was stuck by a trident this time, Dr. Palantire. In the paw." Maddy held out her hands. "And as you can see, the lava balls were nasty. My hands hurt like blazes, but Saoirse says that was the very best class of lava to entomb a sunwyrm in."

Dr. Palantire nodded. "I see."

"And I bit myself on the ear."

"Did you?"

"Yes," Maddy said. "And my foot hasn't recovered from the

day I blew up Mr. Tanner's warehouse. Can you look at that again, too?" Maddy followed Dr. Palantire into the parlor.

"Of course." He fished out a pen and pad. "Is that all?"

"All the majors. Except the gouges from the roc's talons. From when I was blasted off the top of Mount Gorim."

Dr. Palantire moistened his thumb and flipped to a new page in his notepad. "Very well. List your ailments again, more slowly this time."

Dr. Palantire massaged his temples before he glanced over his shoulder at the shouting in the dining room, where Nadine argued loudly with Saoirse. "Let's start with the lava burns, shall we?"

"That would be great," Maddy said. "Do you think I'll have to wear gloves?"

"Someone will." Dr. Palantire muttered. "Boxing gloves, from the sound of things."

Maddy held out her hands.

Dr. Palantire bent close and went to work.

60

Maddy gripped Madame Aubergine's gumboot by its toe and moved it off the dining chair. "You know how Nadine feels about feet on the furniture." Her fingers still ached, though not unbearably.

Madame Aubergine blinked. "The thinking, it I do best when comfortable."

"You were napping." Rookhaven picked at his dessert. "Its Royal Tanist may not even be in Arduvulin. Perhaps Royal Its have their own version of Night. Or their own version of magical transport."

"Maybe." The Spelling Bee trophy had muddled Maddy's brain for too long. There was no time to waste. Tan needed her. "But we're still going to find Tan. The sunwyrm told me where to look."

Rookhaven peered over the rims of his glasses. "It told you a riddle about where to look."

"I shall cogitate upon this riddle." Madame Aubergine propped her feet up again. "While napping, my mind, she works doubly hard. "

"Maddy," Rookhaven said, "what is two times zero?"

Rookhaven was teaching Maddy mathematics now. Madame Aubergine said Maddy couldn't begin to understand alchemical calculus until she had basic math skills. And Madame Aubergine didn't teach the ignorant.

Quille was in his study, writing a response to Sir Hugh Munninson's latest correspondence. Rookhaven said Quille would never listen to him and Madame Aubergine if Maddy told him that Rookhaven was Sir Hugh and Madame Aubergine his consultant on all things geometro-alchemical.

Quille might have a better chance understanding Sir Hugh's prose now that Maddy was transcribing Rookhaven's academic nonsense into words normal people could understand.

Nadine was out on Department business, chasing The Fifteen and hunting for Tan. No one was better than Maddy's mother when it came to rooting out evil. Maddy couldn't just sit around, though, waiting for Nadine to find Tan. She just couldn't.

Emma was who knows where. She had been acting very strange since Maddy returned from Night. Uncle Leo had been acting strange, too. Saoirse was banned from Mundane House, but Maddy had missed the whole banning incident while Dr. Palantire had been seeing to her wounds.

All in all, Mundane House was back to normal, or as normal as it ever was. Maddy gazed out the dining room windows into the endless fog blanketing Arduvulin City and the Fogbound Realm.

The Fifteen roamed the fog, evil, powerful men and their sorcerers who hunted Maddy for some unknown aim.

The crypto-natural pirates hadn't given up, either. They would stop at nothing to recapture her. Maddy knew exactly what unspeakable end they had in mind.

Someone was building incredibly lifelike clockwork golems that could breach every magical ward and masquerade as anyone. And someone else, or maybe it was the same someone, was assembling changelings and working sorcery on them for some reason.

Not to mention that Detective Nightingale was trying to use Maddy to fit her dad for a coffin. And Its Royal Highness had a lot of explaining to do. Maddy almost sympathized with the Folk trying to violently overthrow the Royal It.

Almost, but not quite. She knew what the Folk were like. They were no improvement, but Emma was going to have to find that out for herself. There was no reasoning with her sister.

Maddy sipped her tea and consulted the map of Arduvulin City she'd borrowed from Uncle Leo. It was ridiculous that she hadn't thought of using a map until now.

"The printing date on your map, Madeleine." Madame Aubergine tapped the paper. "It is a hundred years gone."

"The city looks nothing like that from the air, Maddy." Rookhaven pushed his reading glasses up his hooked nose. "Not anymore."

"So, it's not perfect," Maddy said.

Somewhere out there, Tan was alive. And Tan needed her. Needed Maddy Dune.

Things weren't nearly as horrible as they might have been.

Maddy tapped her finger on the map. "There." She glanced up. "We'll start searching there."

Rookhaven's adjusted his eyeglasses and muttered. "Maddy—"

Madame Aubergine bared her fangs and hissed. "Madeleine—"

Maddy waved the breakfast dishes toward the kitchen stairwell. Rookhaven snatched a cherry from the passing dessert tray and flipped it to Maddy. She caught it in her mouth while her bandaged fingers continued to fold the map. "Get your things and meet me in the entry hall."

"We don't have any things," Rookhaven said.

"And Madame Tsolde is in the entry hall," Madame Aubergine said. "With her over-energized pets."

"Then meet me in the back garden," Maddy said. "I need to tell Quille something, then I'll be down. And don't worry."

Maddy smiled a toothy grin at her raven-feathered brother and her father's clockwork familiar. Her comrades in arms. Her accomplices. Her family. "I have a plan."

ABOUT THE AUTHOR

Patrick O'Sullivan is a writer living and working in the United States and Ireland. Patrick's fantasy and science fiction works have won awards in the Writers of the Future Contest as well as the James Patrick Baen Memorial Writing Contest sponsored by Baen Books and the National Space Society.

patrickosullivan.com

www.ingramcontent.com/pod-product-compliance
Lightning Source LLC
Chambersburg PA
CBHW020542120726
47903CB00001B/84